Sterling Nixon

NICKLE BRICKLE'BEE
IN THE FLOATING ISLES OF
BALINBAR

STERLING NIXON

Nickle Brickle'Bee: In the Floating Isles of Balinbar

© 2022 by Sterling Nixon

All rights reserved. No part of this book may be reproduced, stored in a retrieval system or transmitted in any form or by any means without the prior written permission of the publishers, except by a reviewer who may quote brief passages in a review to be printed in a newspaper, magazine or journal.

The final approval for this literary material is granted by the author.
First printing

All characters appearing in this work are fictitious. Any resemblance to real persons, living or dead, is purely coincidental.

ISBN: 978-1-951780-20-3 (Trade paperback)
978-1-951780-23-4 (Hardback)
978-1-951780-21-0 (eBook)

Printed in the United States of America

Sterling Nixon

Dedicated to Benjamin, Caleb, Emily, Hannah, Jaylen, Lincoln, and Spencer

Nickle Brickle'Bee: In the Floating Isles of Balinbar

NICKLE BRICKLE'BEE IN THE FLOATING ISLES OF BALINBAR

Prologue An Act of War
Chapter 1 The Isles of Balinbar
Chapter 2 Among Piddlers
Chapter 3 The Docker Quarter
Chapter 4 The Island of the Valkyrie
Chapter 5 The City of Valenburg
Chapter 6 Base of Operations
Chapter 7 A Visit from an Old Friend
Chapter 8 The King and Queen of the Valkyrie
Chapter 9 Lady Fiurda
Chapter 10 Shemway's One Stop Alchemy
Chapter 11 Meeting of the Minds
Chapter 12 The Plain of the Mind
Chapter 13 The BlueStar
Chapter 14 Just Jump
Chapter 15 The Order of BlackCreed
Chapter 16 The Land of Ash
Chapter 17 Race to the Big Leagues
Chapter 18 Summer Solstice
Chapter 19 The Eagle's Nest
Chapter 20 A New Alliance
Chapter 21 Hitilanda the Horrible
Chapter 22 A Bright Future
Chapter 23 An Old Friend
Chapter 24 The Island of Patmose
Chapter 25 The Ulanova
Chapter 26 An Old Acquaintance
Chapter 27 The City of North
Chapter 28 The Capital Building
Chapter 29 A Chilling Dinner Party
Chapter 30 Training Grounds
Chapter 31 Tidings of War
Chapter 32 Rule Number One
Chapter 33 Glorious Combat
Chapter 34 Among the Atlanteans
Chapter 35 In the Throne Room
Chapter 36 The Face of a Demon
Epilogue An Old Acquaintance

Nickle Brickle'Bee: In the Floating Isles of Balinbar

Prologue

An Act of War

The red-clad Raider sailed through the air, a vial in each of his hands. He never felt so alive as when he was only inches away from death. He threw the vials hard against the ground, releasing a gust of wind that slowed his fall. Technically, an Assassin only needed one potion to slow their landing, but he still relied on two. He was not an Assassin of the Midnight, at least not yet. He still considered himself a novice, despite years of study, and since his life was on the line, he always erred on the side of caution. But now he was headed for the Valkyrie Vault—one of the most protected rooms in all of Balinbar.

His clothing was loose in some parts, slowing his fall, but tight around his wrists and shins, as was the style of the Assassins of the Midnight. His heart thundered with euphoria, sending adrenaline through his chest and body. He was so close to succeeding that he could taste it on the frosty wind that whipped past him as he fell.

A Valkyrie suddenly appeared in the distance, her long white wings carrying her to a roost high above. The warrior was as deadly as she was beautiful. Her body was protected by a layer of silver armor highlighted in gold. In her hands, she held a spear, a bow on her back, a quiver full of arrows at her side. The Valkyrie were known as the deadliest warriors on the Isles of Balinbar, so the red-clad Raider pulled back, becoming part of the shadows behind him. If it came to a straight fight, there was little doubt that the Valkyrie would win. But, of course, the red-clad Raider had no intention of fighting fair.

The Raider was now staring at the base of a massive vault that was shaped like a smooth pyramid—crowned with a perch for the Valkyrie at the very top. Lines of protective magic zipped up and down the structure, briefly highlighting the dark room. It was frigid, as he expected, and even though the Raider had prepared for the cold, it was more than he anticipated. The cold itself was powered by the Lightning that was within the Vault.

As he held still, the cold filled him, spilling down the splits from his sleeves and open shirt. The clothing of an Assassin was designed with stealth in mind, not warmth. He had not anticipated being in this room for more than a minute, but with the Valkyrie present, he had no other option but to wait.

Ten minutes went by and then twenty, his body shivering more and more as each second passed. By the time thirty minutes passed, his body was trembling so badly, he looked like a palm tree during a typhoon.

He closed his eyes, shifting his focus from his discomfort to what he could possibly achieve this day. His actions might very well change the world forever—it could very well save his people as well as all the fools in EarthWorks. After forty-five minutes, however, his mind could not concentrate on the task at hand. Desperation set in as he pulled out a small vial no bigger than a pinkie. He poured a few drops on the ground behind him, leaving splotches of yellow behind. The Faerie Fire responded to the mixture of air and sent a wave of warmth out in an inconsistent pattern. The heat was so tantalizing that it was tempting to pour out the entire vial. But likely, the Faerie Fire would explode into flames, setting him on fire in the process, which, as cold as he was now, he would readily welcome, at least for a few seconds. He had already taken a significant risk in uncapping the mixture, and fortunately, it did not explode. He was careful to position his body so it blocked the splashes of burning liquid from the Valkyrie high above.

The small drops that the Raider poured out kept him warm enough to keep his mind alert. He occupied his time by thinking through all the information he knew about the legendary Vault of the Valkyrie. Few knew about the Vault, fewer still knew how to access the inside or even where it was located. It took months of research, even longer of stealthy surveillance. Even members of the royal family knew little about the Vault. That secret was left to the Queen and the Valkyrie Elite, whose legendary loyalty and fierceness were beyond comparison.

The Vault had been situated in a secret cavern hundreds of feet below the Palace. It was in a massive space surrounded by walls as sheer as a cliff and as smooth as glass. At the cliff's top was a small ledge and door that allowed access to the cavernous room. There were other ways to access the Lightning Vault, but these were secured by long hallways, a series of Lifters, and guarded by the Valkyrie Elite.

The large room was absent any stairs since the Valkyrie with their large wings did not need them, so getting in—although tricky in its own right—was much easier than getting out. Now that he was here, with little chance of escape, he realized that this mission could very well cost him his life—but that was a small price to pay for the chance to save the world.

Then the Valkyrie began to stir, like a winged bird preparing for flight. If she changed her perch, he would have only seconds to react. But his luck gave way to misfortune as two more winged females took perches next to the first. The other two were armed like their companion, except one held her bow in hand while her spear was strapped to her back. With six eyes scanning the Vault, it seemed impossible to complete the mission. The Valkyrie had legendary vision, far superior to any other creature alive. He was just relieved that they had not spotted him already in the pitch-black room, and that was only because he had barely moved.

The plan, such as it was, had gone to crap. The Valkyrie had apparently tripled the guard for no reason. He was so cold now that he doubted his limbs would work properly when he finally did move, and in any case, he still had a hundred-yard sprint before reaching the base of the pyramid. Not to mention, he still had to set the explosives by mixing three different chemicals in their proper order.

The Raider closed his eyes, focusing on the task ahead. "This is mine to do. Tonight, I save the world."

His hand slowly drifted to his side, pulling free a vial of Green Till. He had to move slowly, or the Valkyrie's eyes would catch the motion. Then he uncapped the liquid and let it wash over his body, starting with his chest and then drifting up to his head. He wanted to take his time to spread it properly, but he also had to hurry. The invisibility that Green Till provided only lasted for thirty seconds before it began to fade. So, with only a hope in his heart, he set off, running towards the pyramid. His legs were cramped from holding the same position so long, his arms stiff from the cold, but he shoved it down as he thought about what was at stake.

It was pathetic. Halfway there, the Green Till began to fade. He expected to be skewered by an arrow at any second, his body filled with pain. But the injury he had expected did not come. He looked up, expecting to see the Valkyrie swooping down upon him, their spears raised. But they were not there—their roosts were empty.

"*How am I still alive?*" the Raider thought. He glanced back and spotted the powerful warriors, all of them crowded around the spot he had previously been.

"*The Faerie Fire…they saw the flame spots and flew down to check it out,*" the Raider thought. He smiled and continued to run, his speed picking up the more his body warmed. Then he was at the base of the pyramid, his hands shaking as he poured the rest of the Green Till onto his head and back. He did not have time to see how well he was hidden; instead, he focused all his attention on grabbing the vials at his side. He pulled them out one by one, uncorking them slowly. Once the vials were open, he was careful not to slosh them around too much. Dragon Fire, once exposed to the air, was extremely sensitive. One wrong move and he would disappear before he knew he was even gone. Of course, creating an explosion was the whole point of the chemical mixture, but if not done correctly, it would not have the needed effect.

He poured a red vial into a clear one until it turned a hint of yellow. He then carefully twisted the bottle counterclockwise. He had practiced this part of the operation so much that he could do it with his eyes closed. But as adrenaline coursed through his veins, as his shaking fingers reached for the next vial, he began to wonder if his panic was giving way to carelessness. Whether he had done it correctly or not, it was finished, and he packed it against the base of one of the corners of the pyramid.

"*It's done,*" the Raider thought.

But he did not have time to revel in this victory as a voice called out from behind him. "Raise your hands slowly, or you will be cut in two."

He turned around slowly, raising his hands. As he moved, he smoothly grabbed two small, dark vials from his chest.

"Drop your weapon!" one of the Valkyrie yelled.

The Raider smiled as he obeyed, and the two glass bottles fell to the floor, releasing Liquid Darkness into the air. Despite the Raider moving with lightning speed as night filled the room, a spear entered the space where he once stood, grazing his side and leaving a deep cut behind. The pain was only an afterthought as his body began to run up the side of the pyramid, arrows tracing his steps as he moved.

A normal creature would have lost all of their vision, but the Valkyrie proved the exception. They could still see hints of the target in front of them, and they proved it as they swung their weapons with unmatched efficiency. If the Raider had not been agile, he would have been cut down a dozen times over. As it was, he could barely keep ahead of the attacks, his lungs burning from the effort. With the Bunsin Cream spread on his eyelids, he had a slight advantage over his opponents, but not enough to get careless.

He climbed to the peak of the Pyramid, which was so high that he outdistanced the spread of Liquid Darkness. At the top of the pyramid, he stepped out of the cloud of blackness, drawing two weapons, one a Nunshun Stick, a weapon of the Assassins of the Midnight, the other a short Crossbow.

The first Valkyrie cut through the smoke, her wings spread majestically as she moved, a pair of short swords in hand. She would have swooped in, but the Raider fired the Crossbow at the Valkyrie first, aimed straight for her chest. With surreal speed, she twisted to the side, the needle missing her by inches, and dipped back down into the Liquid Darkness. The needle continued on toward the smooth wall in the distance, a thin cord trailing behind.

When she emerged again, the other two Valkyrie were with her, their wings sending forth a billowing wind. Facing one of the Valkyrie Elites head-on was a death sentence—three, that was just being redundant. Luckily, that was not the plan. He pulled a thread on his side, uncorking several potions at once, creating a spray of energy that propelled him in the opposite direction. He used the Nunshun Stick to latch onto the string left behind by his needle, and he was off, his body whipping away like a flag unfurled during a tornado. It was efficient but not graceful, and when he reached the other side, his body would have splattered against the wall had he not activated a potion of Polix Saliva. It smelled worse than advertised as it covered him in a thick, snot-like substance. He bounced off a far wall and back down the cord. But the potions still propelled him forward, knocking him into the wall for a second time, and despite the Polix Saliva, his head hit hard. He was sure he would have blacked out completely had he not been wearing a helmet.

He pulled the release cords on the potions propelling him

forward, sending them shooting off into the distance and over the cliff face.

He took a moment to process what had just happened. "It worked. I can't believe it worked."

Then he heard the Valkyrie not far behind, their wings working furiously to span the considerable distance. They moved at a pace that defied their bodies, and soon they were only a few dozen yards away. But then Dragon Fire exploded, filling the room with a cacophony of noise and flames. The Raider was thrown to his back, his ears ringing. For several long moments, his vision went blurry, and he could tell he was close to complete unconsciousness. A raw buzzing in his ears made all other sounds disappear.

When his senses returned to him, he realized he had vomited on the floor. Slowly he looked up, wiping his mouth as he did. The Valkyrie were gone, thrown by the explosion of Dragon's Fire.

He pulled himself off the ground, forcing focus into his eyes. "*Get up, you fool. Time to go.*" He began limping for the exit. He only had moments before more Valkyrie would be coming. But it was already too late, and although he did not stop to check the damage below, he grinned, knowing that his plan very likely had succeeded.

Chapter 1

The Isles of Balinbar

"What do you know about the floating isles of Balinbar?" Hawthorne asked, her voice taking on a no-nonsense tone.

Jason shrugged. "The ones that are above the English Channel?"

"Yes," Hawthorne answered.

"They are a chain of twenty islands or so located just south of England and above the English Channel, each one is a few miles wide," Sharlindrian answered, her voice holding the same matter-of-fact tone as the EarthWorks official in front of her. "The biggest island is close to fifty or so miles wide. The islands are controlled by four different factions, the most powerful of which are the Valkyrie."

Hawthorne scooted closer. She was unaccustomed to having someone answer one of her questions so accurately. Still, she had to take the Elf down a notch, just to set the right tone. It was her role to know everything, and she wanted to make sure the others knew that. "Not quite, but close. They are actually southeast of England, but yes, they do float a few miles above the water. There are close to twenty Clans on the islands, but they all support one of four major factions—the Valkyrie, the Cicurians, the Nords, and the Ynglings. During the war with the Brood, the Valkyrie supported Kara'Kala, while the other three loosely supported the Triumvirate. In truth, I believe they would have supported the Vampires had there not been a war going on at the time."

"Why would anyone support the Vamps?" Swiftrunner asked.

"For protection," Hawthorne answered. "The Valkyrie once controlled all of the islands, and they were…sometimes hard to get along with, to put it lightly, which planted the seeds for separation.

They were good rulers, just strict. Rules are their sort of religion. With the fall of Kara'Kala and the rise of the Vampires, the other islands were given just the sort of opportunity they needed to declare their independence."

"So are the Vampires supporting these other islands now?" Evalee asked.

"And if they are, are they planning on attacking the Valkyrie?" Nickle added.

"Well, this is where it gets interesting," Hawthorne replied. "About the same day you five were slapping each other on the back for beating the Vampire Queen, the Valkyrie's Vault was attacked—"

"—What is that?" Jason asked.

"I was about to explain—" Hawthorne began.

"—But why didn't you," Jason persisted.

"Because you interrupted me," Hawthorne said, her voice taut. "The major commerce of the Isles of Balinbar is Lightning. The vast majority of those on the Isles are employed as Storm Chasers. These crazy people head out into the midst of storms and collect Lightning. It's a perilous and tough job but extremely lucrative."

"Who do they sell the Lightning to?" Jason asked.

Hawthorne was about to answer, but Sharlindrian spoke first. "Every magical city beneath the surface uses Lightning in some fashion or another. EarthWorks itself uses Lightning to power the Gravitational Spells that keep buildings the right orientation."

"Why?" Nickle asked.

Hawthorne quickly jumped in, cutting the Elf off before she could speak. "Lightning is very powerful and much cheaper than other sources of magic. It's a perfect power source for that kind of spell. It's easy to deploy, as it only has to be released along the base of the buildings, and it finds its own way to where it is needed. EarthWorks purchases the vast majority of its Lightning from the Valkyrie."

"But they were Kara'Kala supporters," Jason interjected.

"Two hundred years ago," Sharlindrian pointed out.

"Yes, two hundred years ago," Hawthorne agreed. "The war with the Brood is over, and it's time to move on. Besides, the Valkyrie proved very powerful and reliable allies in the war against the Vampire Queen."

"So, what happened to the Valkyrie's Vault?" Nickle asked.

"Someone, who I believe is a member of the Assassins of the Midnight, located the Vault, broke in, and attempted to rupture the containment area for the Lightning, which could've started an unstoppable and cataclysmic reaction that would have melted down for a few minutes before finally obliterating a portion of the island and all those nearby."

"Those Midnight Assassins don't mess around," Jason said.

"It's Assassins of the Midnight," Hawthorne corrected. "Luckily, a week before, the Valkyrie Crown Prince had just taken on the project of reinforcing the containment cell with Orion metal, which gave it just enough protection to prevent a complete disaster."

"What connection does this all have with the Vampires of Nordum?" Swiftrunner asked.

"Well, my contact on the island—" Hawthorne began.

"You can just say his name," Jason said. "It's Locke. We all know the guy."

Hawthorne swallowed, forcing patience into her features. "This is where my contact and I differ in opinion. He doesn't believe it was a member of the Assassins of the Midnight. It was made to look like one of them, but there were enough amateur mistakes to provide ample doubt. Whoever did break in, showed a mix of agility and magical power that was more akin to a Vampire. He believes it was one of the Vampires from Ethilian's inner circle, all of whom are rumored to be hiding out on the Frozen Peaks, the island of the Nords."

"And what do you believe?" Sharlindrian asked.

"I believe that the Nords hired an Assassin of the Midnight to do the job. But, whoever it was, definitely had help. The Vault was too secure for anyone unfamiliar with it to come that close to succeeding. Someone in the innermost circle of the Queen of the Valkyrie must have helped."

"So you think it was an inside job?" Evalee asked.

"Precisely," Hawthorne answered. "Possibly one of the

privileged servants or even one of the Valkyrie Elites—the guardians of the Queen and their Lightning Vault."

"So you want us to find out who is behind the plot?" Nickle asked.

"More precisely, I want you to find out if it was an inside job," Hawthorne replied.

"This sounds awesome!" Evalee squealed. "We get to travel to the Isles of Balinbar!"

Jason stepped back, surprised by the High Faerie's sudden outburst of emotion. "Why so excited? Do they have some cool things to see there or something?"

"I didn't know it existed until now," Evalee replied. "But it sounds fun. I can't wait."

"Fun is not how I'd describe your mission," Hawthorne clarified. "But this must be sorted before open warfare breaks out. Already, several in the ranks of the Valkyrie, including the King, want to declare war against the Nords. The Nords are known to hire Assassins of the Midnight on occasion, so it is not that far-fetched. Fortunately, the Queen of the Valkyrie is more levelheaded than her war counsel, so she's not rushing into anything. But I don't know how long she can prevent war."

"What will happen if war is declared?" Swiftrunner asked.

"It will divide the islands, creating a massive breakdown in the supply chain. Prior to war, most islands will move out their Lightning supply to a safer location. In times of emergency, the Valkyrie will transport it through the Tube to EarthWorks, giving us about a six-month supply. But if the war drags on much longer, it will lead to massive energy shortages that could have some deadly consequences."

"Not to mention the lives lost in the conflict," Sharlindrian added.

"Of course. A war of that scale would not look good for the Tri'Ark's publicity. We have sent emissaries to both the Nords and the Valkyrie, but it has done little to help."

"And what exactly do you want us to do?" Nickle asked.

"You each will be given a specific job that will increase your chances of finding the traitor among the Valkyrie," Hawthorne said. "If we can stop the leak, it will likely prevent any more adverse incidents."

"But Jason and I were planning on returning to Tortugan," Nickle answered. "The work release you signed off on is about to run out. Our third year at Tortugan has only been going on for a few weeks."

"Your work releases just got extended."

"I don't know," Jason said with a sly grin. "Third year at Tortugan is a special year. I was really looking forward to…that stuff we were going to learn…."

"Third year is when you learn Blacksmithing," Hawthorne answered.

"I know," Jason said. "I really had my heart set upon it."

"You will still be studying it—just not at Tortugan."

Jason shook his head. "What if we aren't very good at it. We'd have to hire tutors to teach us, and who knows how much that would be. The cost for supplies alone would likely bankrupt the whole team."

Hawthorne cracked a smile. "Have you met Shemway Darkfiend? You talk just like him."

Jason frowned, clearly insulted by her words. "Well, I don't know about that. All I'm saying…."

"You will continue to receive double pay," Hawthorne answered.

"That's it?" Jason insisted.

"I'm not running a charity," Hawthorne replied. "What I pay you comes from my personal funds, not the Tri'Ark. So, it does have its limits."

"Still, we are risking our lives…." Jason replied.

Hawthorne steepled her fingers, considering the Dwarf's words. "If you find the leak, I'll throw in a one hundred kilo bonus to be split by all of you."

Jason's eyes widened as he considered the amount. "Well…that probably…should work."

"But I have a lot to do and only a few days to do it," Hawthorne continued. "If a few of you could help me secure supplies, it should get you on your way that much quicker."

"When do we leave?" Nickle asked.

"Three days from now, I hope. I still have to make arrangements with the Captain. If all goes well, in three days, you five will be off to the Isles of Balinbar. Hopefully, it will be enough to stop the coming war."

Chapter 2

Among Piddlers

Nickle's legs shook as his eyes began to open. He had pushed himself harder than ever before, Vicinerating with all four of his friends at once from the Tube station in the Chrysler building in New York to another part of the city. A wave of exhaustion swept over him, almost pulling him to the floor.

"Are you all right?" Jason asked.

"I knew I should have Vicinerated too," Evalee answered. "I could have at least taken Sharlindrian with me."

"You didn't know…where we were going," Nickle said through a wheezy breath. "It's a lot harder….Vicinerating to a place you've never been…."

"True," Evalee answered, her voice falling low. "Where are we, by the way? What is that awful smell? I thought you said you would take us to see the Piddlers?"

"It smells like Thieftian magic," Sharlindrian said.

"More like urinal cakes," Jason added.

Nickle nodded as he unlocked a bathroom stall door, leading them into the men's bathroom at Yankee Stadium. Several guys glanced their direction, startled by the five friends pouring out of the stall. Swiftrunner was last, as he had to adjust his rear body into that of a Satyr before he headed out. Evalee added to his magic, adjusting the Cennarian's legs with a clever illusion so they looked like a set of Human legs.

"Follow me," Nickle said, leading the group towards the bathroom exit. Three of them obeyed, leaving Evalee behind. The High Faerie was intrigued by everything around her. She flushed one of the urinals, watching the water disappear down the drain. She did it again and again, intrigued by the process. It was utterly unremarkable except for one thing—she knew that since this was a Piddler device, it had nothing to do with magic.

"By the Summer Solstice," Evalee declared. "What is this thing for? What does this do?"

One of the men in the bathroom looked up, surprised by the questions, not sure if the young woman was joking or not.

"Is this for drinking?" Evalee asked no one in particular.

Before anyone else could answer, Nickle appeared, grabbing the High Faerie by the hand. "Come on, Evalee, time to go."

"She seems a bit lost," a man said with a Boston accent.

"It's her first time at a game," Nickle whispered back.

He grabbed her hand, dragging her out of the bathroom.

"But I haven't seen anything yet," Evalee said. "Why bring me to a place if…." But her words stopped short as she stepped outside the bathroom and into Yankee stadium. Her eyes went wide as she took it all in. Piddlers were everywhere, wearing Yankee baseball caps and jerseys.

"Where are we?" Evalee asked.

"This is a baseball game," Nickle replied as he continued to pull her through the stadium. Within moments, they stepped out into the upper bleachers. "Now, I wasn't able to get the best seats, but they shouldn't be the worst either." Nickle occasionally glanced at several tickets he held in his hand, trying to find the right seats. "When I came here a few days ago, no one else was here. Let me think…they should be somewhere off to our left. Dang, this is a lot more confusing than I thought it would be."

"How do Piddlers find anything in all of this chaos?" Sharlindrian asked.

"It's all numbered," Nickle said. "All right, here we go. I think our section is right next to us. Follow me."

Only Jason obeyed. The other three were too busy studying the Piddlers all around them. They had never seen such a large collection of non-magical creatures in a single location. A man wearing sweatpants and a Yankee's shirt squeezed by, shaking his head at the three onlookers. He had one hand on the back of his sweats as if it was needed to keep them up. Another man talked loudly on a black cube, explaining in detail how the quarterly business report appeared misleading. Sitting in front of them was a large family, all wearing matching t-shirts.

Nickle eventually realized that only Jason had been following, and he had to double back. Just as he did, a man carrying an assortment of hotdogs, nachos, and drinks squeezed by. Evalee only stared in disbelief at the stack of food.

"Where do we get some of that?" the High Faerie asked.

"At the concession stand," Jason answered.

"And is there a limit to how much you can buy?" Evalee asked.

Jason and Nickle exchanged a worried look. Finally, Jason answered. "Let's…just find our seats first."

They eventually did make it to their seats, but it was not before Sharlindrian had tugged on someone's wig, curious by the patch of fake hair, and Swiftrunner had accidentally stomped on a ketchup packet, spraying a few fans in the crowd.

Nickle let out a long breath as they sat, already exhausted by the day's events. Jason sat on the opposite end, blocking in the others.

"Ok," Evalee said. "This is too exciting—and I haven't even Vicinerated yet. When do we get food?"

"Ummm…," Nickle replied. "Whenever you want. You just have to make sure and pay with dollars." The Dwarf pulled out a wad of cash from his pocket, uncrumpling a few bills.

"That's how they pay for things?" Evalee asked. "With paper? You know how easy it would be to make your own money?"

"Well," Nickle shrugged, "that would be illegal. Plus, it wouldn't be that easy…."

A moment later, Evalee had a stack of bills in her hands. "Too easy. I could make this all day."

Nickle pushed the High Faeries hand down. "That's a great illusion, but we don't want to draw attention. Most Piddlers have never even seen a stack of bills like that, let alone held one. Here just take some of my money…."

Before the Dwarf finished his sentence, the High Faerie was gone.

"Evalee?" Nickle asked. The High Faerie appeared not long after with a mound of food in one hand and a massive, caffeinated drink in the other.

"Go easy on the drink," Nickle said. "I don't know how it's going to affect you…."

Evalee already had her lips around a straw and was chugging

the drink as if it would be taken away from her at any moment. Then she transitioned to eating nachos, a wide grin on her face. "Sharlie, you've got to try this! It's like liquid gold." She passed the tray down to Sharlindrian, who took it carefully, as if she had just been handed a porcupine.

The Elf dipped the tiniest chip in the cheese and tasted it. Then she ate an entire chip, then two. "Swiftrunner, have you tried these golden chips?"

"They're disappearing so quickly," Swiftrunner replied. "I didn't think I'd have a chance to." He took a chip and dipped it in nacho cheese. After taking a bite, he narrowed his eyes, considering the taste. "Not bad. Tastes a bit like Yellowkin flowers mixed with vine sauce." Before long, the three of them were all competing for who could grab the next chip faster.

"Don't forget the guy on the edge," Jason said.

"I got your back," Evalee said with glee. She then turned to Nickle. "Hey, I need more money."

"Here's a hundred, but make sure to bring back some change...." Nickle started to say, but before he could finish, she was gone, having Vicinerated back to one of the concession stands. When she appeared again, she had a stack of nachos and hotdogs in her hands that was so high it reached her chin. "Who wants golden chips?"

She began to hand out chips in so much earnest, she actually passed a few trays to some random people in the crowd. The five friends dined on soft drinks, hotdogs, and nachos. Evalee seemed especially cheery. The mix of caffeine and Vicineration appeared to put the High Faerie on a heightened level of happiness. It was refreshing to see her act like her former self. Nickle had begun to wonder if she had been changed forever with Atlantia's spell.

Evalee then spotted Dandy, the Yankee mascot, dancing to an upbeat song at the front of the stadium. The enthusiastic figure was so funny to Evalee that she could not help but release a deep belly laugh. Eventually, the noise caught the mascot's attention, who then began to gesture toward Evalee in the way of an invitation.

Before Nickle could stop her, the High Faerie was next to the dancing figure, doing her best impression of a Piddler's dance. It was super awkward and funny at the same time, unleashing a level of laughter that echoed through the stadium. Within moments, Evalee and the mascot were locked in an epic dance-off. The mascot was good—there was no doubt about it. Whoever was behind the mask had years of training and even more of practice. But Evalee was not to be outdone. She moved with an unearthly and captivating cadence. Her natural talent, coupled with a dangerous amount of caffeine running through her veins, allowed her to make up moves no one had ever seen before. Soon the audience was divided down the middle—half cheering for the mascot, the other for the High Faerie.

It seemed pretty even, but then at the height of the competition, Evalee revealed her Faerie wings and took to the air, shooting out a beam of colors as she did. The crowd cheered as if this had been a planned spectacle. Then Evalee disappeared from sight, reappearing next to Nickle a moment later.

Evalee was breathing heavily from the dance-off, but she sported a smile that would not fade.

"Nice moves," Nickle said. "But do you mind hiding your wings again? We don't want to draw attention."

Evalee placed a hand over her stomach. "Sure."

"Thanks."

"Piddlers sure know how to party. Baseball is a crazy game."

"Technically, the game hasn't even started," Nickle answered.

"What?" Evalee asked as she sat up in surprise. "How long have we been here?"

"Ten minutes," Nickle answered.

Evalee suddenly looked at her drink as if it were poison. "What is in this?"

"It's called caffeine," Nickle answered. "And, it can make even the most stalwart of Piddlers jittery."

"Jittery?"

Nickle only laughed in reply.

The baseball game started a few minutes later. It was a great game by all definitions. Both teams played even better than expected—yielding several home runs. Evalee, however, had fallen asleep by the end of the second inning. Swiftrunner helpfully used his magic to extend their seats, giving them much more leg room and allowing Evalee to stretch out. By the end of the third inning, Swiftrunner had changed their seats, even more, turning them into comfortable recliners. Since the High Faerie was asleep, she could not maintain the illusion surrounding Swiftrunner's legs, and they reverted to that of a Satyr. But Swiftrunner was quick enough to modify his pants so they were much baggier and could cover his lower body. Nickle vaguely wondered why Swiftrunner did not just change his legs to be like Human legs. The Dwarf made a mental note, saving the question for later.

While Evalee slept, Sharlindrian took an empty seat on the other side of Nickle, a small smile on her lips. They sat and talked about mostly nothing for the majority of the game, catching up on all the missed conversations they should have had during the last several months.

"When this is all over," Sharlindrian whispered, "Evalee will claim that baseball is her favorite sport. But, if anyone ever asks what baseball is, she's likely going to say it's like a mix between a buffet and dance competition."

Nickle gave a subdued laugh. "Oh, Evalee. She can make even the most mundane moments seem exciting."

"You know," Sharlindrian said. "She would follow you to the ends of the Earth if you asked her. I've never seen anyone so loyal in my life."

"Well, I'm glad she's part of our team."

Silence fell between the two of them for a few moments. In front of them, a baseball player took a swing at a pitch, missing only by an inch. The empire called a strike. Nickle was surprised to realize that they were already in the bottom of the eighth inning.

"What's wrong, Nickle?" Sharlindrian asked slowly as if considering her words. "You're different—more serious. Ever since we fought that Vampire Queen, you haven't been the same."

Nickle turned to his long-time Elf friend, not sure how to answer. The more he stared, the more his mind began to pull at the memory of a conversation between him and Tiberian. He tried to ignore it at first, but the more he did, the more real the memory became. A coldness rippled down his body. He could just barely see snowflakes at the edge of his vision. His breath came out in a puff of cold, white smoke. Tiberian's explanation of who Ethilian really was repeated through his mind.

"Nickle...Nickle," Sharlindrian said. "See, that's what I'm talking about. You keep drifting off."

Nickle nodded, opening his mouth to speak, trying to force words to leave his mouth. He needed to tell Sharlindrian...it was the right thing to do. "*She needs to know,*" Nickle thought. "*She deserves to know.*" But then he began to think about what else he should tell his friend—and not just Sharlindrian either. They had a right to know—to know what he really was. To know that Nickle was formed by magic that most would consider evil.

Just then, there was a sudden cry from the audience. Sharlindrian and Nickle looked up, just barely catching a glimpse of a baseball hurtling down towards the ground. It seemed to fall especially quickly, as it had an arrow sticking clean through it. The ball was destined for a homerun, but the extra weight now sent it spinning to the ground.

Even before they looked at the Cennarian, they could guess what had happened.

"You owe me a Kilo," Swiftrunner said, a finger pointed at Jason's chest.

"What a shot," Jason said, still stunned by the archery performance. "You have a real talent."

"Thank you, little buddy," Swiftrunner said, "but just because you recognize my skill doesn't mean you're getting out of paying me that Kilo."

"That was a good shot, but I don't think I owe you a Kilo. It looked more like a graze than a direct hit. We'd have to look it over to be sure."

"Whether I grazed it or not, I still hit it," Swiftrunner defended.

Nickle approached the Cennarian, his eyes wide. He was in full panic mode. He lowered his voice, hissing like a snake. "Where did you get that bow? Put it away."

Swiftrunner shrugged. "I had it slung to my back and used magic to make it blend in. I always have it with me. You know that."

"Put it away," Nickle repeated in earnest. "Not many Piddlers are used to seeing a bow at a baseball game."

"Relax," Swiftrunner said. "I was discrete. I adjusted my surroundings, so no one saw me shoot it. Plus, I've already changed the arrow, so it came apart like a bunch of threads."

"But you knocked the ball right out of the sky," Sharlindrian answered. "People are going to notice that. Piddlers don't shoot things out of the air with arrows."

"Really?" Swiftrunner asked. "My bad. I've been itching to do it this whole time. I thought it was remarkable how everyone was showing so much restraint."

Nickle let out a long breath, standing up as he did. Despite his tone, he actually appreciated the distraction from having to answer Sharlindrian's questions. "Well, we better get going before it gets too late. Hawthorne has a list of things for us to do tomorrow."

Chapter 3

The Docker Quarter

Nickle had never been to this side of EarthWorks—the Docker Quarter. It was an enormous space, but flying craft and workers made it appear much smaller. Massive circular tubes were floating in the air while being loaded and unloaded on floating barges. The barges were bigger than anything Nickle had seen in EarthWorks, much bigger than the Dwarf Warships that the Silver Army used. They were used to transport goods from the surface to the large cities below. The space was crowded with workers, who were busily heading in every direction or concentrating on various tasks. A group of Hamadryads were pulling apart a crate by magically changing it into flowers, revealing several barrels inside. They had the upper torsos of Humans and the lower bodies of deer. Above them, a Dwarf rode a giant cylinder as it floated through the air. The squat man appeared to be guiding it in the correct direction. A giant was picking up large stones and loading them onto a tube equipped with a cargo bay. Nickle saw almost every creature he had ever seen before, including a group of grey Trolls playing a game on a small table that involved fiery cards.

Nickle nodded to a passing Goblin, who had a Stone Tablet in hand. The Goblin shrugged his shoulders, not understanding the Dwarf's gesture. Instead of nodding back, the creature narrowed its eyes, almost as if it had just been insulted.

"I'm just saying hi," Nickle replied.

"Hi?" the Goblin answered, his chest stretching tight with muscles. He had a black tattoo of a moon shrouded in shadow on his shoulder. Nickle recognized it as being a tribal tattoo, but he was unfamiliar with what tribe it was affiliated with. But he was not as focused on the tattoo as much as he was on the curved cudgel at the creature's side.

The Dwarf and Goblin stared at each other as an awkward

silence descended between them. Finally, Nickle spoke, his voice low. "Just…you know…being friendly."

"Just keep walking, shorty," the Goblin answered coldly. "We don't got no time for golly dropping."

Nickle looked incensed. The insult had not only been unoriginal, it was also inaccurate as he was a good foot taller than the green creature. If anything, he should be calling the Goblin "shorty."

Swiftrunner nodded towards the worker. "It's his first time on the docks."

"Well, keep moving four legs," the Goblin answered, his chest now inflated and eyes narrowed.

Swiftrunner grabbed the Dwarf around the shoulders, directing him away from the Goblin and towards a far dock. "Dust demons and dirt devils, just let me do the talking. People down in the Docker Quarter aren't known for their cheery attitudes or manners."

"Geez," Nickle said. "What's got him all uptight?"

"They just have a different way of doing things down here," Swiftrunner replied. "As the saying goes, 'If you want to know what someone really thinks of your new hat, just ask a Docker.'"

Nickle nodded.

"But," Swiftrunner added. "That's not always a bad thing. These people will tell you how it is—good or bad. If you want to know what they think of you, they'll probably tell you before you even have to ask. It kind of comes with the job, you know. It's hard to transport thousands of pounds of goods throughout EarthWorks unless people say what they mean."

"I was just being friendly," Nickle grumbled.

"To a Docker," Swiftrunner said. "That just comes across like you're about to ask them for a favor."

"How do you know you're way around down here?" Nickle asked.

"My first job in EarthWorks was as a Docker," Swiftrunner answered. "It paid great, but Dockers don't usually care for Cennarians."

"And why is that?"

"We're just not city folk, I guess," Swiftrunner answered. "These people are always rushing—never appreciating anything around them. It's a very different way of thinking, and Cennarians have a hard time adapting to it. Can't say I enjoyed the job much."

They walked through an arched passageway before running into an open-air market. The food came in a series of distinct smells that wafted over them in surging waves. Sometimes it smelled amazing; other times…not so much.

"Ooh," Swiftrunner said, his pace picking up slightly. "They're selling Borginian Belly Grass. Nickle, you'll have to try this just for gallop's sake." He trotted over to a table selling a mix of grasses and herbs. Nickle joined his friend a second later and perused the vender's wares. It looked like a bunch of grass clippings and pruned branches. As he studied it closer, he could distinguish slight differences in texture and color of the different clippings. Across the vendor's table was a young, attractive Hamadryad with a set of small horns. She smiled at the newcomers, displaying more friendliness than Nickle had seen since arriving in the Docker Quarter.

"Hello, sweet friends," the Hamadryad said with a distinct country accent. "What can I help you two with?"

"Two bushels of Borginian Belly," Swiftrunner said. "My Dwarf friend here has never tried it before."

"You two are friends?" the Hamadryad questioned, her eyes linking the two newcomers together.

Nickle and Swiftrunner exchanged a look before nodding.

"Yeah," Swiftrunner said.

"Like actually friends? You're not just working together on something?"

Nickle folded his arms. "We're best friends. Why?"

"Now I've seen everything," she answered as she scooped several grass clippings into two triangular cups.

Nickle let out a long sigh as he looked at the grass. Since he had first met Swiftrunner, the Cennarian had persuaded him to try several things—all of them tasted like grass. Sometimes the grass was a little spicier, other times, it was more salty, but it all tasted like grass.

The Hamadryad handed one to the Dwarf and the other to the Cennarian. "That will be twenty grams."

"Oh, dang," Swiftrunner said. "I must have left my medallion behind. Do you mind, little buddy?"

Nickle frowned but did not protest further. He pulled a gold medallion from around his neck and held it next to a tablet on the counter. A mist of smoke emerged from the tablet and stripped off twenty grams of gold.

"You've got some expensive blood," Nickle said.

"For Borginian Belly Grass, you're mistaken," Swiftrunner said. "This is the finest turf from here to the surface."

Nickle looked at the grass and then back to Swiftrunner.

"Go on," the Cennarian replied.

Nickle did. It tasted like grass. Grass that had the slight flavor of lemon and lime—but it was still grass. Grass that had cost him twenty grams of gold.

"Was I right, or was I right?" Swiftrunner asked.

Nickle nodded, thinking of a reply. "You were right. This is defiantly Borginian Belly."

Swiftrunner grinned. "Yeah, isn't it great?"

Nickle shoved the rest of a blade of grass in his mouth just so he had an excuse not to answer.

They stopped next to a metal railing while they consumed their grass, taking in the sights and sounds of the Docker Quarter. Initially, to Nickle, it appeared to be just pure chaos. There seemed to be no rhyme or reason why certain ships would approach and dock while others would just hover. But the more he studied it, the more smoothly it appeared to flow.

Nickle spotted several Atlantean statues that were being unloaded from a barge, each one was easily twelve feet tall. They looked as fierce as the ones they had seen on their journey through the city of Atlantis, but they appeared somewhat smaller in the expansive docking station.

"Where did those come from?" Nickle asked.

Swiftrunner also noticed the marble busts. "Impressive, aren't they? As soon as they raised New Atlantis, they began to sell and export some of the artwork. It's mostly being shipped to museums and rich collectors. The proceeds are being used to rebuild the city."

"The Atlanteans have their work cut out for them," Nickle answered. "That city was huge."

"I heard that New Atlantis is much smaller than the original."

"I'm sure that's because they only have access to half the power of the Eye."

Swiftrunner frowned as he finished off his last blade of

Borginian Belly Grass. The Cennarian looked longingly at his friend's bushel, subconsciously licking his lips as he did.

"You can have mine," Nickle said, handing over the grass.

Swiftrunner refused at first, but it did not take much convincing before he finally gave in.

As their conversation died, Nickle felt himself paying closer attention to an emotion he had hardly noticed before. There was a tightening of his ear drums. Magic…was being used. This was not unique, of course, as magic was being used all over the dock as freight was being moved. But, something was different about this magic—it was odd, almost uncomfortable, like a pebble caught in one's shoe. As Nickle focused in on it, he began to look around, trying to spot the source.

"What's wrong?" Swiftrunner asked.

"I don't…know," Nickle answered, his mind distant from his words. Then he looked up to see a crate of stones ten feet above them, hovering in the air as it waited to be unloaded. In that instant, Nickle knew what it was—the Mystic magic that was being used to elevate the pallet was being eroded, like a knife cutting through a supporting rope.

Nickle's eyes went wide as he realized the danger. He grabbed Swiftrunner by the shoulder and Vicinerated, appearing twenty yards away. Just then, the pallet of stones crashed into the floor of where they had just stood, sending up a plume of dirt and debris.

But the destruction did not end with one pallet of stone. As the Mystic magic broke, it affected the others around it, reversing their gravity. More palates began to fall, crashing into the ground like bombs being dropped, releasing a torrent of destruction. Nickle Vicinerated again, grabbing two people that were in the path of destruction and moving them to safety. People scattered from the area in a panic. Pallets continued to fall. The noise was deafening; the layer of smoke was thick and overwhelming. A final crate high above careened towards the ground, impacting so hard it sent forward a concussive wave.

Nickle reappeared next to Swiftrunner. He placed his hand over his mouth, protecting his face from the dust. The Cennarian did the same. After the last pallet fell, an eerie silence filled the Docker, all eyes turning to the mess. In only moments, this part of the Docker had completely changed. It now looked more like the ruins of an ancient city than the busiest port in EarthWorks.

An official-looking Satyr approached the pile of rubble. "Anyone injured? Everyone alright?"

There were only a few grunts and grumbles in return, but there were no cries for help. No one appeared to have been injured. Surprisingly, despite the shock of it all, people quickly returned to what they were doing before, acting as if this sort of thing happened regularly. A minute later, several dozen Goblins appeared and began to clean up the rubble.

"We almost got squashed," Swiftrunner said, his voice falling low. "What was that? How did you know to Vicinerate out of there? What happened?"

Nickle shook his head, searching for the right words. But he actually had no idea what had just happened. He shook his head again. "At least no one was injured. That could have been really bad."

Swiftrunner nodded. "I'm liking this place less and less. Come on. Let's just do what we came to do."

"Sounds good to me," Nickle replied.

Without another word, Swiftrunner led the way deeper into the Docker. The further they walked, the darker and more shady people seemed to act. Adrenaline was still pulsing through their bodies, and they made good time through the docks.

"You sure this is the right way?" Nickle asked.

"I'm as sure as barley on a bright sunny day."

"Umm…just so we're clear…that means yes, right?"

"As right as a double notched arrow."

Nickle sighed.

Swiftrunner finally led them to a thin frigate with an abundance of sharp, jagged edges. They both began to walk up the gang plank, their hearts pounding in their chests. Hawthorne had given them instructions on where to go, but she had failed to mention how intimidating the trip would be.

A giant Rock Troll stepped into their path. "And who are ye?" The creature was as large as a boulder, its yellow eyes set in a grey face. It had bat-like ears that twisted around in search of noise. Since Nickle's trip down into Atlantia, he had learned a lot about Trolls, and he now knew that besides their name and grey skin, they were nothing like Rock Trolls. Rock Trolls preferred crowds—especially ones that were eager to fight. They were not the most coordinated creatures, but they supposedly could take a solid hit and hardly be phased.

"Travelers...looking to secure passage," Swiftrunner said, his voice trembling ever so slightly.

The Rock Troll did not appear amused. "This ain't no charter boat. These are the rigs of Cap'n DeathDealer, the Assassin of Lord Kimble and his entire entourage."

Swiftrunner smiled. "Yeah, that's who we've come—"

"—Best you move along, little beasties, lest the Cap'n lays eyes on ye and decides you'd fetch a fine price on the Isles of Balinbar."

Swiftrunner leaned forward, uttering the secret phrase that Hawthorne had given him. "The sky is only as high as one can go."

The Rock Troll was still not impressed, but he did not protest further. He stood like a stone for a few moments, his expression severe. Finally, he stepped aside. "Fine...but, the Cap'n ain't in the best of moods, yah hear. You can't blame me if the Cap'n gets an itch to cart ya'll off as merchandise. At your peril, proceed to board."

Swiftrunner frowned. "We could just wait out here if you want—"

"—Now ye makin' demands? Ye be a bold Cennarian to be making demands of the Cap'n," the Rock Troll said.

Swiftrunner exchanged a look with Nickle, who simply nodded. The two friends studied their surroundings as they walked onboard. It was a large vessel but not quite as wide as a Dwarfian Warship. It seemed to be made more for speed than combat, but to be fair, it also had an impressive array of cannons. But the ship was in rough shape. Its wood planks were worn down by a combination of weather and time. The sails were a patchwork of random clothes, and the rigging had turned grey and was fraying. The crew had the same worn but experienced appearance. There were twenty in total, not nearly as many as Nickle would have thought, but more than enough to give him the chills. A Satyr with a peg leg stared at them carefully, one hand on a cutlass at his side. An Orc with several axes strapped to his back picked at his two large canines with a bit of wood. A Human dressed all in black leaned against the ship's cabin, his body lined with an array of potions.

Nickle wanted to nod, but he was unsure if that was the correct response. So, he just stood there, pretending that his eyes could not focus on anyone or anything in particular.

Finally, the Rock Troll broke the silence, pushing open the cabin door. "In there."

"There?" Swiftrunner questioned. "There's barely any light."

"You want to meet with the Cap'n or not?"

"I can see well enough," Nickle said. Without another word, he stepped through the door and into the darkness. Swiftrunner was only half a second behind, as he was not too eager to be left on the deck with the crew.

The floor squeaked as they walked down a narrow hallway and past several smaller doors. They finally reached the last door, which was marked with the words "Cap'n Courters."

"You sure about this?" Swiftrunner asked, grabbing the Dwarf's shoulder before he could rush in.

Nickle shrugged. "Hawthorne wouldn't have sent us here if she didn't trust him."

Nickle then knocked. Once. Twice. No response. The two friends again looked at each, but this time, they were not alone. A third person had silently stepped between them, their face shrouded in darkness.

Swiftrunner yelped. Nickle stepped back into the wall.

The Cap'n's face was shrouded in a dark hood that concealed their features. After a few awkward moments, the Cap'n spoke. "What are you two barnacles waiting for? Get inside."

Nickle obeyed quickly, grabbing the handle on the door and stepping through it backwards. The other two quickly followed. Nickle tripped over several discarded bottles and landed hard on the ground, one hand landing on something soft, the other on something sticky.

As the Cap'n entered, several luminescent vials of blue liquid lit up, filling the room with bright, albeit inconsistent light. Nickle's first impression was not good. The room was messier than his shared apartment with Jason, and that was saying something. Nickle looked down to discover that one of his hands had landed in a half-eaten pie.

"Ugh," Nickle whispered, wiping his hands on his greaves as he righted himself.

The Cap'n removed a long cloak and hood, throwing it against a hat rack that tipped over. Long flowing obsidian hair whipped out, perfectly framing the figure of a beautiful woman.

"You're a woman," Swiftrunner said in surprise.

"Very observant, horseman," the Cap'n drawled. She then collapsed onto a chair positioned on the other side of a desk and kicked up her feet.

"What happened here?" Nickle asked. "The place looks ransacked."

The Cap'n frowned, turning her attention to the cloak and hood she had just discarded. Using a clever mix of Mystic magic, she raised the cloak into the air until it was only inches away from Nickle's head. Then in a flash, she drew a knife from some unseen pocket and threw it across the room, pinning the cloak against the wooden wall with the blade. The dagger wobbled for a second before settling in, acting as an improvised hanger.

"There," the Cap'n said. "I've cleaned up a bit. Happy? Or should I spend more time flinging daggers across the room until you're satisfied?"

Nickle's eyes traced up the wall to the dagger, which was only inches from his head. "No," he squeaked, his voice higher than usual. "No," he repeated. "Just surprised, is all."

"Surprised," the Cap'n said in a drawl. "Have you never been on a Privateer vessel?"

Nickle shook his head.

"Then why should you be surprised if you didn't know what to expect," the woman answered.

"Well...," Nickle said, looking to his friend for help, "I guess...you're right. That's a good point."

"It's an excellent point," she corrected. "Now sit down before I throw both of you out."

Nickle and Swiftrunner were eager to obey, but unable to find a chair. The Dwarf approached a mound of property, hoping to find a seat underneath, but no such luck, as it was only a stack of books covered in clothing. Swiftrunner had a little more success, using his Transformation magic to adjust a mound of rubbish into a couple of chairs.

The Cap'n eyed the new furniture with disdain but did not comment on it. Instead, her right hand pulled a flask from a drawer, and she began to take large swigs of whatever was inside. Once finished, she wiped her mouth with the back of her hand.

"So, what brings a little lost Dwarf and a confused looking

Cennarian to my cabin?" the Cap'n asked. "Are you looking to sell some cookies?"

"Cookies?" Nickle replied. "No. We were sent here by Hawthorne."

The captain threw a dagger across the room, hitting a partially hidden target. "Don't mention her name. You were told to use the moniker H and nothing else. What's the point of secrecy if you can't keep things secret."

"Oh, I just assumed we could trust you," Nickle said.

"Don't assume anything."

"Oh, ok," Nickle answered. "Well, we're here to book passage onto your ship. We have dust. Can you help us?"

"I don't think you'll have enough dust to afford my services," the Cap'n answered, pulling another dagger from an unseen location. She used this one to clean her nails. "What is the destination?"

"Balinbar," Swiftrunner answered.

"Which one of the islands?" the Cap'n asked. "And yes, before you ask, that does make a difference."

"The Island of the Valkyrie," Swiftrunner continued.

"What would the cargo be?"

"There will be five of us, plus our bags," Nickle submitted.

"Don't forget our supplies," Swiftrunner added. "We have three pallets of stuff."

"What's inside the pallets?" the Cap'n asked.

"That's our business," Nickle answered.

The Cap'n clicked her tongue. "That will cost a lot more then. Tell H to deliver the crates to my ship by tomorrow. But this will not be cheap."

"We can pay if you can get us there," Nickle answered. "I mean if you can get us there without attracting any attention."

"Listen, little Dwarf, I'm the best at what I do. You will not only arrive there promptly, but the world will be none the wiser you were ever on my ship."

Nickle pulled his head back. Something was so familiar with the words that it was like déjà vu. "What's your name?"

The Cap'n narrowed her eyes and tightened her chin. "Cap'n DeathDealer."

"No, what's your real name?" Nickle persisted.

"DeathDealer."

"So, when you were born, the first name to pop in your mom's head was DeathDealer?" Nickle pushed.

"What does it matter, dirt-digger," the Cap'n growled.

Nickle suddenly smiled, unexpectedly finding himself with the upper hand in the conversation. "And here you were, lecturing us about not giving up details."

"What details? What are you talking about, little Dwarf?"

"Swiftrunner, do you see what I see? Look at the hair and build; look at the perfectly symmetrical face."

"Yeah," Swiftrunner said, "now that you mention it, I think I see what you mean." This, of course, was not true. The Cennarian had no idea what the Dwarf was implying, but his friend had never led him astray before, so he thought he would just play along.

Nickle let the silence fill the room before adding one last piece to the puzzle. "Your last name is Darkfiend, isn't it?"

The Cap'n's expression changed ever so slightly, giving her away. She stood up, her hands tucked behind her back. "Very perceptive, Dwarf. Hawthorne said you were intelligent, but she failed to mention that you were clever. My real name is Shannon Darkfiend. Now you understand why I don't use it. It just has no zip to it, does it?"

"You're a Thieftian, aren't you?" Nickle said. "What is Shemway to you? A cousin? A sibling?"

"He's my baby brother," the Cap'n said, her voice falling low. "And I am not a Thieftian, not by trade anyway. By reputation, I am a feared assassin that terrorizes the Eight Winds."

"You kill people for money?" Swiftrunner said. "That's horrible."

"It's more about the reputation, not the money."

"That's even worse."

"Oh, get off your high horse," the Cap'n said. "Actually, killing people is bad for business and goes against my Thieftian heritage. As all Privateers know, spilling blood will get you respect, but it will also cost you gold dust and make you enemies. And I am all about making money."

"But...as an assassin," Swiftrunner said, "not killing people is bad for business. That's literally your business."

"Let me explain it this way," the Cap'n said, returning to her seat. "What if I made up a name, a character, an identity. Then I used that identity to rob and steal and intimidate others."

"People would be angry at you," Swiftrunner replied.

"They'd be angry at the character I've created, yes. If you push them too far, they may even try and hire a ruthless Privateer captain to get rid of them. So that's where I come in."

"So you assassinate the character you created, solving the problem," Swiftrunner said carefully.

"Yes."

Nickle shifted in his chair. "And since the person isn't real, you don't make any additional enemies. And either way, you're getting paid."

"Exactly!" the Cap'n said with a laugh. "The best part is that I don't actually have to kill someone. Have you ever tried to get blood out of cotton? It's abysmally difficult. So, I get to plunder, blame it all on a fictitious character, assassinate that character, and pick up my reward for solving the problem. I became a renowned and ruthless Privateer assassin without making nearly as many enemies as one would think."

"Now I'm starting to see the resemblance to Shemway," Swiftrunner said.

"How is my baby brother, by the way?" the Cap'n asked.

"He plays for the Harbingers," Nickle said with a shrug.

"Does he now? I assumed he would be too intimidated by germs in the locker room to play a team sport. Oh, baby ShemShem. He was certainly the odd one in the family—always kept everything so freakishly clean. But enough about that. We need to talk about your situation. Nickle, you should not have come here—not out in public."

"How did you know my name?"

"Because you're not the only perceptive one," the Cap'n replied. "You're lucky you weren't killed at the docks this morning."

"That was an accident," Swiftrunner answered.

"No, it wasn't," the Cap'n answered. "Take it from a fake assassin; that was an attempt on your life, Nickle. Hawthorne is a fool for sending you down here, among the cutthroats and thieves. The Dockers are full of decent and hardworking folk, but they also have more than their fair share of roughnecks and criminals."

"She actually sent Swiftrunner," Nickle answered. "But since I wasn't doing anything at the time, I told him I'd go with him."

"It's not safe for you to walk around EarthWorks," the Cap'n answered. "At least while you're down here, I suggest you keep a low profile."

"Who would want to hurt Nickle?"

"I don't know, but someone just tried," the Cap'n answered.

"Dang, change my name and call me a donkey," Swiftrunner said.

"Not sure how that applies to the situation," the Cap'n answered. "But whatever makes you feel better. So, let's get this business done and get you on your way."

"How soon can you take us to Balinbar?" Nickle asked.

"In three days, as the light is beginning to fade, I'll meet you at the edge of EarthWorks, in the area where the Tube is just beginning to enter the city."

"There's nothing over there," Swiftrunner said.

"Exactly. Will your little group be ready by then?"

"Yeah, I think so," Nickle said.

"You'll need a good cover story," the Cap'n answered. "It will cost more, but I can arrange all of that."

"Hawthorne…I mean, H, has that all figured out."

The Cap'n let out an annoyed growl. "Well, Hawthorne, despite being completely boring at times, has a decent mind. You can trust her to get it all in order. Now, I have a lot to do—so, away with you."

Chapter 4

The Island of the Valkyrie

Jason felt his stomach turn into a lead ball as the ship took flight, forcing him to grab a railing for support. His friends around him did the same. He looked to Nickle, who in turn glanced at Evalee, Swiftrunner, and Sharlindrian. The ship rocked back and forth as the Cap'n charted a steady course for the surface. It would take hours before they emerged, at least several days longer before they reached the Isles of Balinbar owing to several planned stops the Cap'n had arranged. It seemed the ship could travel faster, but it would use more magic to do so.

It had been three hectic days gathering the items on Hawthorne's list of supplies, but now, supposedly, they were ready for the voyage. They all had their separate roles to play, as indicated by the different clothing they were wearing.

Sharlindrian was dressed as a High Lord servant, her clothing fine but also faded with time. Transformation makeup covered her ears, rounding their appearance. She wore a black dress coupled with a white apron.

"Ooh," Sharlindrian whispered, one of her fingers pulling at a loose string. "I can only guess what she has in store for me."

"Don't take it personally," Jason answered. "At least you're not dressed like a shopkeeper." The Dwarf was dressed in a red, collared shirt and draped with a dirty, leather apron.

"I'd rather be a shopkeeper than whatever she has planned for me," Sharlindrian said. "I bet I'll be running errands for some rich family. They're the worst."

The other four looked at the Dark Elf, not missing the irony.

Sharlindrian narrowed her eyes into slits. "Don't say it. Anyway, what are Nickle and Evalee supposed to be? You're certainly dressed much better than the rest of us."

"I don' know," Nickle answered. "Hawthorne gave us a little book on Valkyrie Palace protocols to read through. Maybe we're to be tutors?"

"Are you serious?" Sharlindrian said, her voice becoming shrill. "Nickle, you don't even know what a fork is used for."

"Yeah, I do," the Dwarf replied. "The fork is the thing that holds the napkin down on the table."

Sharlindrian's mouth dropped open ever so slightly, unsure if Nickle was joking or not. The other three broke into laughter, easing some of the tension.

Jason gave Nickle a fist bump. "That was a good one."

The Elf let out a long sigh as she turned to Swiftrunner. "And what did the all mighty Hawthorne assign to you?"

"I'm guessing a messenger of some sort," Swiftrunner said.

"Well," Jason replied with a prolonged sigh. "If I'm a shopkeeper, I just hope whoever I work for isn't a jerk. That will make all the difference in the world."

"How long do you think we need to play this charade?" Sharlindrian asked.

"Maybe a few weeks," Nickle suggested.

"I'm just excited to see the Isles of the Balinbar," Evalee said. "I hear the Valkyrie are wonderful people."

"Hmmm…wonderful is not how I'd describe them," Sharlindrian replied. "Intense is the word I'd use."

"What are they like?" Evalee asked.

"The Valkyrie have a unique class of women warriors," Sharlindrian answered. "They are powerful and fearless—if their legends are to be believed."

"But they have wings, right?" Evalee persisted. "Like me."

"Different, but yes," Sharlindrian answered.

"And the men?" Nickle asked. "Do they have wings too?"

"No," Sharlindrian answered. "They mostly work in the Lightning trade, as many people in the Isles of Balinbar do. There are some men warriors and some women Lightning traders, but not many, for whatever reason. Most likely tradition."

"And the other islands?" Jason asked. "What do you know about them?"

"Well, the Cicurians own an island chain called The Climb,"

Sharlindrian replied. "Don't ask me why it's called that, but it is. They are very territorial and don't allow anyone on their island without express permission. Then you have the Balkinian chain, home of the Nords. These Humans are masters of Ice magic, which is similar to Elemental but more focused. Most of their homes are made of ice, as well as their tools. And finally, you have the Ynglings. They only control two islands, but they are some of the bigger ones located in the center of all the rest. For this reason, the Ynglings consist of all kinds of people, including Nords and Valkyries, but they are usually the ones that have been thrown or chased out of other islands."

"You're just a walking encyclopedia, aren't you?" Jason said. "How do you know all this stuff?"

Sharlindrian blushed. "As soon as I found out where we were going, I looked it up."

"Still, it's impressive," Jason persisted.

"Do you know how the islands were formed?" Nickle asked.

"No one knows exactly," Sharlindrian answered, a distant expression on her face. "But there is an ancient song that has been passed down from generation to generation among the people of Balinbar."

The other four looked at her expectantly. A few moments passed before the air turned awkward.

Sharlindrian blushed again. "Oh, you want me to…sing it? Here? Right now."

Jason dropped his pack on the deck and laid down, making himself comfortable. "Sure, we've got nothing but time."

Everyone else seemed to take their cues from Jason, and soon all of them had turned their packs into makeshift pillows.

"Well," Sharlindrian answered. "I've never been known for having a singer's voice. And I'm not entirely sure of the tune, although I have heard it before." She half hoped this would get her out of singing, but no such luck. Her friends simply stared at her.

"Ok," Sharlindrian said. "Here it goes."

Tu la ru la laddie
Tu la rea la lee

When land was new,

and the Earth not old.
In a valley green,
Where all was told.

In the time when the ocean,
was as sweet as the sea.
There was a land,
full of the free.

Tu la ru la laddie
Tu la rea la lee

But in the flames a Demon was born,
His heart as black as night.
He raised the Gru Ren Sheen from the Earth,
Who destroyed all in sight.

Balinbar would not be consumed,
Nor his people would run.
So with his power, he raised the land
Saving all from the burning sun.

Tu la ru la laddie
Tu la rea la lee

"That was beautiful," Evalee said. "You have the voice of an angel."

"I wouldn't say that," Sharlindrian said, still slightly embarrassed.

"What's the Gru Ren Sheen?" Swiftrunner asked.

Nickle felt his chest tighten. A wild panic spread up and down his limbs. Without even thinking, his mind replayed Tiberian's words when they were being held captive by the Vampires. *"You're not like the Gru Ren Sheen—you were just made in a similar process."*

"No one knows," Sharlindrian answered. "They were created by Aldrick thousands of years ago. Supposedly, they were so frightening that after they were destroyed, it was outlawed to even talk about them. And now, people have forgotten everything except their name."

"That's scary," Evalee interjected.

"Well," Jason said. "How tough can they be? They got wiped out."

"Well, look what came aboard," a voice said from behind the group. They all turned to the noise and saw the Cap'n. She was dressed all in black, two cutlasses at her side. On her head was a western-styled billycock hat. Her leather-gloved hands were perched on her hips, as if she was on the peak of a mountain overlooking an opponent.

"Hey, Cap'n," Nickle said.

"Don't hey Cap'n me," she replied. "If you're going to take a spot on my ship, you will work for it. Between helm and stern, no hand sits idle while I'm the captain of the Argos."

The five friends exchanged looks, unsure if this was a joke or not.

Nickle noticed that several crew members were carefully watching, so he stepped closer, whispering in the Cap'n's ear. "But we paid a bunch of dust for the trip."

"True," she whispered back. "But my crew doesn't know that. And like any crew on a Privateer ship, if they see something odd, they'll talk about it. Your cover will be blown—your story will leak out among the bars of Valenburg."

"So, what did you tell them?"

"That you managed to pay for some of your ticket, but that you will have to work off the rest of the price, of course," the Cap'n said with a wink.

"Are you doing this because I figured out you're Shemway's sister?"

"Hmmm," the Cap'n said. "I don't think so."

The Cap'n then turned to the other four friends, her face lighting up with a new fire. "Stow your gear down below and report to Mr. Helmick. If you've never had a blister on your hands, you're in for a shock."

***

"You call that swabbing the deck?" the Cap'n asked, her voice pitched. "My crew would do better if they took turns spitting on the floor." The crew cheered at this, enjoying the fact that the Cap'n's attention was not on them for once.

Nickle and Sharlindrian were stuck swabbing the decks with a set of bristly brushes. The other three friends were somewhere else, performing some other mundane task. They were only halfway done, and Nickle's back and fingers were already sore from use.

The Cap'n leaned closer to Nickle's ear. "Actually, you're doing a phenomenal job. Much better than any of my slaggin' crew would do. Are you using some kind of magic?"

"I put a fire Rune in the bucket and heated up the water," Nickle replied. "The hot water seems to do the trick." This was true, but not the whole story. While he scrubbed, Nickle began to use Alteration magic to repair the boards. Without hardly trying, his vision widened, allowing him to see the magical threads of the world, as he had done while on the Blood Spire. Then he began to mend the severed ones, returning the thread to its former glory. Once he realized what he was doing, he redoubled his efforts, bringing in the threads and forging them together. It was different work than he had done before but far more rewarding. Soon, the deck was not just clean, it was brand new.

"What else could I repair with Alteration magic?" Nickle thought to himself.

"I should have hired you months ago," the Cap'n said.

Nickle gritted his teeth. "*We* are the ones paying you, remember?"

"Yes," she answered. "But, you also paid upfront, which means even if you walked away from the deal now, you wouldn't get any of your dust back. So now I have all the leverage. What a bargain you are getting. Not only am I giving you a ride to the Island of the Valkyrie, I'm also giving you life lessons. You're truly receiving the better end of the deal."

Nickle rolled his eyes. By the time they finished swabbing the deck, they had made it to the surface of the Earth by traveling through one of the busiest tunnels. It was a grey, cloudy day—the kind of day that threatens rain but never follows through. The ship continued rising above the Earth until it broke through the top of a raincloud and sunlight poured over it. From there it continued its course to the east, heading over the ocean.

The first day was by far the worst. The Cap'n seemed to be attempting to work them to death. The ship and crew visited three different surface cities along the way, each time trading some of their wares. By the second day, the Cap'n appeared to relax a little, and Nickle and his company were not given too much to do besides washing dishes. Between the five of them, they were able to clean up rather quickly, allowing them plenty of free time.

They spent most of their time on the deck, lounging in the sun, enjoying the breeze that whipped through the air. The crew of the Argos was a lively group, always joking and jesting. Jason fit right in, talking to them as if he had been on the deck for years rather than days. He spent his time learning how the ship operated, which used a magic that was much different than the Dwarf Frigates. Evalee spent her time using her Faerie wings, flying around the vessel, enjoying the breeze as it pushed her hair from her face. It was rare for anyone to see her use her wings as she usually kept them hidden by Magic de Danaan.

On the fifth day, just after eating lunch, one of the crew members in the crow's nest shouted down below. "Land ho!"

This sent a rush of energy through the five friends, who sprinted to the front of the ship. At first, they only saw a hint of the floating island, which was obscured by a mess of clouds. But as they passed through, the mountain came into focus, revealing a mix of eye-popping greens, blues, and reds. The island was enormous, stretching further than they had first imagined, and was covered in rich vegetation. At the center of the island, both above and below, were two mountain peaks. The peak below was longer and pointed straight down to the Earth. The peak above was more rounded at the top and crested with a blanket of snow.

As Nickle studied the approaching island, he realized how fast their ship was traveling. More vessels came into view, some leaving, some docking at the island. It quickly became apparent that this was a very busy port.

The Cap'n took the helm, a smile on her face. The more congested the airway became, the more Nickle hoped the ship would slow down. But no such luck with the Cap'n at the helm. If anything, she seemed to speed up. To her credit, she was masterful at piloting the vessel, avoiding several collisions by only feet. To his surprise, Nickle realized that the crew was just as apprehensive as he was.

"Cap'n," said the Rock Troll. "Perhaps...we be slowing down now."

"Negative, my First Mate," the Cap'n said with a laugh. "We have paying travelers on board that need to get to where they're going!"

Just then, the Cap'n turned the ship upside down, barely avoiding being pinched between two other, larger ships. The magical gravity kept them on their feet, but the effect was disorienting. The ship banked hard to the right before righting itself again.

Sharlindrian's face was turning green with the movement. Jason's did not look much better. Besides the Captain, Evalee was the only one that appeared to be enjoying herself. Everyone else was reviewing their life's decisions, just in case they died.

Finally, the Cap'n activated the rear brakes, twisting their ship and momentum around, allowing them to slide right into a space along one of the docks. The Argos bumped gently against the side before stopping completely.

The Cap'n leaped from the upper deck, a smile flashing across her face. "Welcome to the Island of the Valkyrie!"

Chapter 5

The City of Valenburg

"Well, hop to," the Cap'n said. "We don't have all day. Trim the sails and remove the cargo we shouldn't be carrying. The Valkyrie inspector will be here shortly, and we *will* be ready by the time they arrive. So if I see anyone lagging, I will flog them myself!"

This sent a flurry of movement among the crew. The gangplank was extended to the island, and cargo from down below began to surface.

The five friends just stood there, their balance still uncertain. Now that they were not afraid of the Cap'n crashing into something, they were able to take in the whole of the city. It was noisy and busy, with every sort of creature imaginable. Along the docks were small shops and restaurants. The air had a misty smell—like that of newly fallen rain.

"It's the Lightning," the Cap'n said, now standing behind them.

"What do you mean?" Sharlindrian asked.

"That's what that smell is," the Cap'n answered. "Lightning. The main product collected and traded at the Island of the Valkyrie is Lightning. And Valenburg is the biggest city on the island. So, no matter the time of day, you can still smell the aftermath of it. We ourselves were in the middle of collecting Lightning when H sent for me."

"I had no idea so many people traded in Lightning," Nickle said.

"Indeed," the Cap'n answered. "Don't worry about your freight. I'll make sure it's delivered to the right location. Now, get off my ship."

Nickle turned to thank the Cap'n, but she was already off, yelling at one of her crew. He instead turned back to the group. "I can't decide if I like her or not."

"She's not so bad," Jason said. "No wishy-washy language. Straight to the point."

"She's Shemway's older sister," Nickle said. "I didn't want to tell you during the trip, so it didn't create any tension."

"I knew it!" Jason exclaimed. "From the moment I met her, I hated her—and now I finally know why."

The other four laughed at this.

"Well, come on then," Sharlindrian said. "We better get going before the Cap'n tries to charge us more money for the ride."

"Or assigns us additional chores," Swiftrunner added.

The group deboarded carefully. The gangplank had rope railings, but it occasionally would shift in the wind, sending up panic through the friends as they walked.

Evalee looked over the edge, squinting her eyes as she did. "I can barely see the ocean below us! I can't believe we're up so high."

"Please don't mention that," Jason mumbled. The Dwarf hugged his bag as if it was trying to get away, his eyes straight forward and focused on something in the distance. His steps were slow and precise, as if he had to make sure the next step was there before he continued.

It took twice as long as any member in the Cap'n's crew, but as the five of them finally stepped onto solid ground, Jason's body filled with relief. He was tempted to kneel and kiss the cobblestone below, but the pressing crowd around him made it impossible. Swiftrunner took the lead, using his height advantage and large frame to force himself through.

The docks were massive, much more elaborate than they first imagined. They were on the upper level of three docks, each of them at least a hundred feet in height. Unlike the Cap'n's reckless approach, the rest of the ships approached in orderly lines, waiting patiently for an opening along the dock. This was so different than the chaos of EarthWorks.

The people were dressed differently too. Many wore fur coats lined with red and gold lace. The majority of them were large, burly Humans with long black beards, several sporting dark tattoos. But there was a diversity of other creatures as well. All of the Valkyrie there were male, which seemed odd to Nickle.

After some persistence, they were finally able to break through the main crowd and step onto a side road. The group passed several small shops, one selling pieces of magically made art. The art was as impressive as it was mesmerizing, constantly changing colors the longer one stared at it.

Then they finally saw a female Valkyrie for the first time, standing next to a wall that circled the city. She was elegant and beautiful. A pair of brilliant white wings sprouted from her back. She was a warrior by all definitions of the word. Her golden weapons looked positively lethal and glimmered in the light of the sun. She carried a spear in one hand, a circular shield in the other. At her waist was a curved falcata blade.

Jason could not stop himself from staring. "A winged Valkyrie. I've never seen one before."

Then something crashed right in front of them, sending a plume of dust into the air. A Valkyrie had landed right before them, her wings stretched up high. She wore a golden helmet that exposed little more than a set of beautiful eyes. She carried no shield but wore a golden breastplate and set of greaves that stretched to her knees.

"What is your business in the city?" the Valkyrie demanded, her voice taking on a severe tone.

"Easy, Vlanish," the other Valkyrie whispered. "You'll scare them off if you talk like that. The little one looks like he's about to cry."

Jason stepped to the front, taking control of the situation. "We've got papers. We should be good." Jason handed his work release permit to the woman, who briefly scanned it.

She then looked up, her eyes narrowed. "Papers can be forged."

"Sure," Jason answered. "But these ones aren't. Come on; we've had a long day."

The other Valkyrie approached, taking Jason's papers from the first. "This one is to work at a new shop. They're in order. Let him pass."

"Tell me," the first Valkyrie said. "Why would anyone leave the big city of EarthWorks just to come to Valenburg and work at a shop?"

"I have my reasons," Jason said, not even flinching for a second.

"Let him through," the Valkyrie with the spear said once more.

"His papers check out."

The first gnashed her teeth and turned to the other. "We are on high alert—that means we take our time to scrutinize outsiders."

"Great," the other Valkyrie said. "And now a line is beginning to form. You want to stay late checking passports again?"

"I'm just doing my job," the other replied. "Fine, proceed, Dwarf. But stay out of trouble, or I will carry you to the edge and drop you off myself."

"Don't worry," Jason said as he pushed through. "I'll behave."

The other four were scrutinized as well, though not nearly as much. It was not long before they passed the city walls and entered the city proper. The buildings were thin and tall. The limited space on the island encouraged everyone to build up instead of out. They were built with a mix of stucco and large timbers, coupled with thick terracotta tiles. The streets were straight and immaculate. Not a piece of trash could be seen anywhere. It was a stark contrast from EarthWorks, which had roads so crooked that it almost seemed intentional.

Jason pulled out a map that Hawthorne had given him. After studying it longer than everyone thought was necessary, he finally looked up, pointing in a westerly direction. Jason took the lead as the rest followed behind.

The people were just as orderly and clean as the city. Everyone that was going in one direction traveled on the same side of the road, which was odd getting used to at first, but it soon proved much more efficient. The signs for businesses were also much more subdued, as if there were strict rules at play that regulated their size and use of colors. The effect would be considered boring by any resident of EarthWorks, but it created a uniformity that added to the clean aesthetic of the city.

After eight blocks, Jason consulted the map again. This time he took even longer than before. He finally looked up and pointed back in the direction of the docks.

"You're cute when you're concentrating," Sharlindrian said. "But, please give me the map."

"I got this," Jason said.

An awkward silence ensued as Sharlindrian and Jason locked eyes.

Finally, Nickle spoke. "Hey, it wouldn't hurt just to have a second pair of eyes on the map, right?"

Jason slowly inched the map over to the Elf, who took it with a flurry. After briefly studying the parchment, she pointed north towards a massive castle at the center of the city. "I'm pretty sure we head that way."

Jason nodded. "Yeah, that way will probably work. It might take more time, but it will work."

"Maybe we should take a Taxi'Lator or something," Nickle said. "Or whatever is equivalent in this city."

"We only have ten blocks to go," Sharlindrian said.

"Plus, we'll get to see more of the city," Evalee added, eager as always.

They again headed off down the road. It happened slowly, but eventually, Sharlindrian took the lead, charting a route that guided them directly to where they needed to be. They all dropped their packs when they arrived and stared at the building before them. It was an ancient but well-built building. Inside was nothing but dust and cobwebs.

"This is the shop you're going to be working at?" Swiftrunner said to Jason.

"I guess so," Jason answered.

"Looks like the only thing you sell is dust and cobwebs," Evalee answered.

"Well, let's get off the street and see what it looks like on the inside." He pulled a rusted key from his pocket and placed it in the lock. It took a few moments of wiggling it back and forth before something clicked, and the door slid open.

Jason walked around the mostly empty shop. A chill swept through the room, bringing a few of the cobwebs to life.

"This place needs some serious cleaning," Sharlindrian said.

"What do we do now?" Evalee asked.

"I guess we just wait for Hawthorne's contact to show up," Jason replied, dropping his pack on the floor. "I bet any one of you it's Locke, though. I bet we'll both be working in the shop."

"I think Locke is too recognizable for such a public position," Sharlindrian said. "He has to stay in hiding most of the time. He's a wanted man."

"He'll be here," Jason said through a grin.

"Don't count on it, Dwarf," said a voice from the shadows.

Jason whipped around, his hands balling into fists. He

subconsciously began reaching for his axe, forgetting he was not carrying one.

"First," the voice continued. "Prove to me you are the people that are supposed to be here."

"I have the key to get into the shop," Jason answered.

"Anyone could have stolen the key," the voice replied.

"Well, it's me, Jason Burntworth. You must have heard that we are coming."

From the shadows, a figure appeared, grabbing Jason around the throat. "Stay back, all of you."

Nickle took a step forward.

"I'm warning you," the stranger replied. "Right at this very moment, I'm pointing a needle at your friend's throat. This needle has been dipped into Harpy's blood and mixed with Shillian Root. That is a lethal combination. One prick from this needle, and he'll be dead before you can even call out his name."

"Ok," Jason replied, raising his hands defensively. "But how does that solve anything?"

"If you can answer a question, I'll know you are truly Jason Burntworth. If not, you'll die here and now, Dwarf."

"What question?" Jason asked.

"What is the funniest video in the world?" the voice replied. Just then, as if on cue, several Stone Tablets set up around the room began playing a video of Jason locked in epic combat with a Demon. The Demon punched the Dwarf in the stomach. A moment later, Jason vomited onto the Demon.

Jason dropped his hands, his expression falling. "Shemway? What are you doing here? You shouldn't be here."

Shemway was too busy laughing uncontrollably to answer. The Thieftian began hitting the wall as he laughed. "You should've seen your face...."

"Shemway, this is an important mission," Jason insisted. "Where's our contact? Where's Locke?"

The Thieftian kept laughing for several seconds longer. Jason tried to get an answer from him, but it was all in vain. Finally, Sharlindrian reached out a hand, picking Shemway up with a wave of Mystic magic. Shemway was able to resist a portion of the spell, but since the BlueStar had been combined with her body, she was now a force to be reckoned with.

"Easy, Elfling," Shemway said. "I'm just having a little fun."

"Answer the question, Shemway," Sharlindrian replied. "Where is Locke? Where is our contact?"

"Locke?" Shemway said. "I have no idea. But as far as your contact, that would be me."

Jason began shaking his head. "What? No, I don't think so. That's impossible."

"Sorry to say, little lad," Shemway said, "but I'm the Shopkeeper…and you…you are my assistant."

"Not happening," Jason said.

"You don't have to call me 'sir' all the time," Shemway answered with a roguish smile. "Just when there are customers in the shop."

"Not happening," Jason repeated.

"Tell us what is really going on here," Sharlindrian said.

"That is a longer conversation," the Thieftian replied. "One that will require chairs and a bottle of wine."

Chapter 6

Base of Operations

Shemway drained two cups of wine before he filled a third and washed his hands at a nearby water basin. They had walked down to the basement of the shop, and it was almost like stepping into a new world. All the dust and debris present upstairs was completely absent down below. The contrast was so stark, it almost felt like they were in a different building.

The basement was furnished with several couches, dressers, an armoire, and a wet bar. Shemway slipped a new shirt on, throwing the old one in a far corner. Then he fell heavily into a soft leather couch, kicking his feet up on an end table as he did. He closed his eyes as if he just had the most exhausting day.

"Why'd you change your shirt," Evalee asked.

"It's filthy up there," Shemway said, his eyes still closed. "Not to mention how dirty all of you are."

"Hey," Jason said, slightly offended. "We've been on the road."

"My nose already told me that," Shemway answered.

Jason's jaw tightened. "Don't push me, Thieftian. It's been a long day."

"So, what is this place?" Evalee asked.

"Headquarters," Shemway replied. "Base of operations, if you will. It will be a shop by day and where we plan at night. Sharlindrian and Evalee, you will share a room in the attic. Swiftrunner, Nickle, and Jason will share a room down here, next to mine. Oh, and your gear arrived before you did. How did that happen?"

Sharlindrian and Jason met eyes before she quickly answered. "We were...delayed. Where's our gear?"

"The pallets are against the far wall," Shemway replied. "But, it will have to remain here unless I approve otherwise. The city is already on edge, and a bunch of Dwarves roaming the streets in full battle

Tines will likely bring a lot of unwanted attention on us."

Jason and Nickle rushed to the pallet, attacking it with animal zeal. They pealed the crate like an orange, scattering slats of wood everywhere.

"Are you trying to make the biggest mess possible?" Shemway asked. "That crate is reusable if you don't tear it to pieces."

Nickle and Jason looked at each before they both shrugged, returning to their work. The crate had already suffered too much damage to be salvaged. Soon they were handing out armor and weapons to their friends.

Jason picked up his set of Dark Elf armor, a smile on his face. "I'm glad to see you."

"Well, give it a kiss and tuck it away," Shemway said. "You won't be wearing that unless absolutely necessary."

"So you keep saying," Jason answered grumpily.

After sorting through their armor, they dropped their gear in their appropriate quarters. The attic had been cleaned and cleared, providing the girls ample space for all of their equipment. The boys were not so lucky. There were only two bedrooms in the basement, and Shemway had already claimed the larger of the two. The other was small and awkwardly shaped. A bunk bed was against one wall, a single bed against the other.

After several minutes, they returned to find Shemway with another glass of wine in hand.

"So," Sharlindrian said, her arms folding across her chest. "Hawthorne was obviously leaving out a lot of details when she recruited us. Tell us what this is really about. Why am I dressed like this? Did she assign me to be a cleaning lady or something?"

Shemway stirred, took a swig of his wine, and placed it on a coffee table in front of him. "Very perceptive, young Elf. Your role is an important one, as you will be cleaning the houses of the Müllers, the Nilssons, the Kinnunens, and…the…oh, what is that last family name. I guess it doesn't matter now. You'll learn it soon enough."

"Why?"

"Two reasons," Shemway said. He then paused, not responding for a while, allowing the tension to rachet up. "First, two of those families require someone with a talent in Mystic magic. Mystic is rare among the isles—almost looked down upon really. You see, they don't care for Elves much up here. But, and this is the important part, these wealthy Houses are all suspects of mine. Each one has their own motives for wanting war. The Saarinens...that's it. That's the House I had forgotten before. They specifically manufacture and sell many of the Warships. War could be very profitable."

"But Hawthorne said they tried to blow up the entire island by starting a chain reaction with the Lightning," Sharlindrian said. "If they took out the island of the Valkyrie, then there would be no need for anyone to make any ships."

"That is Hawthorn's theory, not mine," Shemway said. "I don't think they were trying to destroy the island, just damage the confidence in the Valkyrie's ability to protect the Lightning Reserves, which would destroy the local economy and give an advantage to the other three competing factions."

"Why do you say that?" Nickle asked.

"The intruder made too many mistakes," Shemway replied simply. "It was made to look like an Assassin of the Midnight was hired for the job, but after looking over the reports Hawthorne provided, it was clearly an amateur. Someone who had a great knowledge of potions but little practical experience."

"That's a mighty fine risk," Swiftrunner said. "Just to gain an economic advantage. They could've just as easily destroyed the island." The Cennarian had slumped onto a couch, his body looking uncomfortable.

"Well said, horseman," Shemway said, raising his glass. He moved a little too eagerly, and a drop of the crimson liquid splashed onto the wood floor.

"What about me?" Jason asked. "Why am I here? Why am I dressed like a shopkeeper?"

"Assistant," Shemway corrected.

"Right," Jason answered. "At least Sharlindrian's job makes sense...she'll have access to the personal chambers of very powerful people, but what am I supposed to learn as a shopkeeper assistant."

"How to stock the shelves?" Swiftrunner suggested.

Jason gave the Cennarian a scornful look.

"Ahh," Shemway said. "Now that part of the plan is pure genius."

Jason rolled his eyes. "That's the part you came up with, isn't it?"

"Of course," the Thieftian replied. "Over the last few months, rumors of war have increased the security on the entire island. The tighter security has made it downright impossible to sneak in potions necessary for any kind of mischief. No unauthorized magic is permitted in or out. If the Nords did hire an Assassin of the Midnight, and they are still here, or even if it's an amateur wannabe, they will need obscure and unique ingredients to create the potions they need. And we, my friend, are a new shop featuring just such items. Like honey to a fly, we'll suck them in and trap them. Or rather, I will. You'll be cleaning the shelves and making sure they sparkle."

"So why are you in charge?" Jason grumbled.

"I got here first."

Jason looked like a volcano that was getting ready to erupt. Nickle quickly stepped in, changing the subject. "And what about Evalee and me?"

"You are to be assistants to the Prince and Princess of the Valkyrie, a high honor indeed," Shemway said. "Never has a High Faerie ever been granted such a privilege, much less a Dwarf. Hawthorne believes that someone within the inner circle of the ruling family was responsible for the attack or, at the very least, aided whoever did the deed. There were certain things about the attack on the Valkyrie Vault that only the royal family and their advisors were aware of."

"What about Swiftrunner?" Jason asked.

Shemway looked to the Cennarian. "You, my friend, will be a messenger. If you perform your task well, you'll be promoted to carry the correspondence to and from the Valkyrie Palace."

"They don't use photo callers up here?" Swiftrunner asked.

"No, they don't," Shemway replied. "They don't trust them—especially not now. Photo callers are easy to hack into—that's why our friend Locke always preferred to use good old-fashioned letters."

"So, I just carry letters?" Swiftrunner asked. "That sounds easy enough."

"Should be," Shemway said. "They've never had a Cennarian courier before—few Cennarians have even visited the Isles of Balinbar. So, they typically use Satyrs to carry their messages. If you can be fast, you should quickly rise in rank and position. Do that, and they will trust you with the most important messages."

"You're sayin' I can go as fast as I want?" Swiftrunner asked.

"As fast as you can manage," Shemway agreed.

"This is awesome."

Sharlindrian and Jason had their arms folded across their chests, deep frowns set on their faces. As the conversation progressed, their moods seemed to sour even more.

"At least somebody is happy," Sharlindrian mumbled.

"If that's everything then," Jason said. "I better start unpacking."

"Well, not exactly," the Thieftian answered. "You still have your education to consider. Hawthorne has assigned you several books to read and study as part of your work-release program. Just because you're here doesn't mean you can forgo your education."

"What?" both Jason and Swiftrunner yelped.

"And since you were galivanting around in Atlantis," Shemway said, speaking over the interruption. "You all have some work to make up. If we are to keep up the ruse that you are all really on work release, we will need to be able to prove it through your studies. Prepare yourself for long days and even longer nights."

Chapter 7

A Visit from an Old Friend

Nickle could sense the Scathian long before he revealed himself. He sent a mental impression, pushing it out as simply as if he was speaking. *"Locke, you can come out. They've all gone to bed."*

Still, it was a long while before Locke entered the shop's basement, pushing his way through an open window. The large man struggled to squeeze inside, despite the ample size of the window. "You're getting better with the Magic of the Mind, much better. When did you first know I was here?"

"I sensed you back on the docks when we landed," Nickle answered. "And I knew it would not be long before you showed up here." The Dwarf greeted his old friend and mentor with a warm handshake. But then his tone changed. "But what are you doing here? This city is on high alert, and the Valkyrie don't seem to mess around. I imagine you're just as wanted up here as you are in EarthWorks."

"True," Locke grunted, his hand clenching his side.

"Are you all right?" Nickle asked quickly. "What happened? Come into the light of the fire."

The Scathian complied, shuffling forward. As he stepped closer to the fireplace and his figure was illuminated with light, the Dwarf could not help but gasp.

"You're injured. What happened? Are you being pursued?"

Locke landed hard in a chair, his expression tightening as he did. He gave a low growl as he repositioned himself.

"Let me see the wound," Nickle said. "How bad is it? What happened?"

"I was Demon hunting. Managed to track one of them down to the Teutoburg forest—except it wasn't just one I ran into. I was able to subdue them quick enough, but not before they were able to give me this."

"Two of them were able to do this to you? Did you have to take on your Demon form?"

"Ever since the Blood Spire, I've had to avoid that. After the battle, it took me several days to revert back to a Human—it's getting more difficult every time."

"Let me see the wound."

Locke did not respond for a while, but Nickle's gaze did not let up. Finally, the Scathian pulled back his hand, revealing a deep gash along his side that cut through his armor.

"Locke," Nickle said quickly. "That looks deep. You need a Healer."

"I just need to rest."

"Sharlindrian is right upstairs. It won't take a second to get her...."

"It can wait," Locke said. "I needed to talk to you first. Plus, as a Scathian, with enough focus, I can speed up the healing process."

"Why haven't you already?"

"Keeping the Demon within takes...energy."

"You need to slow down. You can't hunt all of them down by yourself."

"I only have two left—and then it will be finished. I will have caught them all."

"Who is left?"

"Captain Black and the Listener."

"Those are the most dangerous," Nickle answered. "You can't do it alone."

"I can," Locke growled, a momentary anger narrowing his eyes. "And I will."

"It's not your fault they escaped."

"Perhaps. But who else is going to put those beasts back in their cages? As soon as they fled EarthWorks, the Tri'Ark turned a blind eye to them. The Atlanteans? The Orcs? The Witches of Stobbin? None of them care about Demons running around when Vampires now take to the skies. Don't worry about me. I've had worse and survived just the same."

"Then why are you here?"

"To take you away from here."

Nickle pulled his head back, surprised by the response. "Me?"

"It's not safe here. Hawthorne should have known better than to send you out here, at the edge of the Vampire Queen's influence."

"What are you worried about? I'm operating under an alias. Nobody knows I'm up here."

"I'm worried that there are people here that want to end your life."

"My life?"

"Tell me what happened on the docks a few days ago."

"How'd you hear about that?"

"News still reaches me."

"It was an accident."

Locke shook his head. "No, it wasn't."

"Was it the Cap'n who told you?"

"That doesn't matter. What matters is that you are safe. You are constantly putting yourself out there—risking too much to save others."

"Who do you think tried to kill me?"

Locke paused for a moment, deciding whether he wanted to share additional information about the incident. Finally, he spoke. "It was a group of Orcs working on the Docker that were responsible for the attack. Apparently, they were still angry at you for splitting the Eye of Atlantia with the Atlanteans. I don't think it was planned so much as they simply saw an opportunity. The more you put yourself out there, the more enemies you will make."

"Is that why you hunt the Demons? Because you think they might be coming after me?"

Locke did not answer.

"Listen, Locke. I'm here trying to prevent war among the Isles of Balinbar. The Vampire Queen is up here somewhere, growing her forces. I'm here to finish what we both started. She has to be stopped."

"But not at the peril of your life."

"All of my friends are here—risking their lives just as well as me."

"It's different with you," Locke said, his voice rising in volume.

"Why?"

"I don't know. I just know it is."

Nickle let out a long sigh, his mind going back to his conversation with Tiberian while he was being held captive. Locke was right—something was different about him. But he doubted Locke would be too excited to find out he was made in a process known as Soul Carving. A dark and unwelcoming thought entered the Dwarf's mind. *"If he knew…would he try to kill me?"*

Locke studied the Dwarf closely. "You know something. Don't you?"

Nickle looked up but did not respond.

Locke seemed to take this as an affirmation. "What do you know? Did Ethilian tell you something?"

Nickle opened his mouth to speak but shut it again just as quickly. He turned away from the Scathian and focused on the flames in the fireplace. He could feel the Scathian trying to pry into his mind and search for answers, but he had taught the Dwarf too well. His mind did not give anything away. As a Scathian, Locke could always try and force his way in, but the process could severely injure or even kill the target—for this reason, this technique, known as the Fau Ung, was strictly forbidden unless in the most dire of circumstances. Even still, Locke began to doubt if he would be able to overcome the Dwarf's mental defenses, even with as little training as he had.

"What do you know?" Locke repeated.

After several long moments, the Dwarf turned back around. "I know I need to find Greggory McDooble."

"McDooble? What for?"

"Do you know where he is?"

"No, he disappeared years ago. No one has seen him…since you were conscripted into the Silver Army. What does he have to do with this?"

"He has information that I need."

"I can try to track him down for you, but you will need to do something for me."

"I'm not leaving Valenburg," Nickle answered. "I can't abandon my friends or my mission. Just as you have taken it upon yourself to hunt down every last Demon, I can't walk away from this mess with the Vampires. I just can't."

Locke clenched his jaw. He knew that at this point, there was no reason to continue. He stood, his body regretting the quick movement. "Well then, since you've made up your mind, I better head for the door."

"Wait," Nickle said. "Locke, I...I also have something to ask of you."

Locke let out a long breath. "Asking for favors now?"

"Can you continue to teach me the Scathian art?" Nickle asked. "I appreciate all the instruction I received while in Atlantis, but I need more."

"You've already risen as high as you can without beginning The Ten Trials—and I'm not sure if you're ready for that."

"I am, Locke."

The Scathian considered these words for a long while, his eyes locked intently on Nickle's miscolored ones.

"If you want to protect me," the Dwarf said. "The best thing you can do is give me the tools to protect myself."

"What if the process breaks you—I've seen it happen before. I don't know if you're ready."

"If I'm not now, I never will be."

"Are you sure?"

The Dwarf nodded.

The Scathian considered it for a moment more before finally shaking his head, a final decision being made. "I'm sorry. You're too young. You're just not ready. A Scathian must first master their body before they can master the mind. New recruits go for weeks without food or sleep—just so they can better hone their skills. It's a painful process, one that is challenging in the best of circumstances. Just stay alive, protect your friends, and when this is all over, maybe we can talk about this again."

"Fine."

Locke turned to go, heading out the way he had come. "I'll stop by in a week just to see how things are going up here."

"One more thing," Nickle said.

"What's that?"

"Sharlindrian is almost down the stairs. She's coming to heal you."

"How did she...," Locke began. "Wait...did you use Scathian magic to wake her?"

"I asked her to come down."

"And she was all the way upstairs?"

"She was in the attic."

"Really?" Locke said, trying to remove the amusement from his voice. This was no simple feat, as it would have taken weeks of study for a Disciple of the Scathians to master a mental projection that was so far away. Transmitting your thoughts was much more complex than reading them, and to do so through several floors and furniture was impressive.

"I haven't tried it before like that, but it seemed to work."

Sharlindrian descended the final step into the basement. "Why… am I down here… in the middle of the night? Oh, Locke…it's you. And you're injured! What happened to you?"

Chapter 8

The King and Queen of the Valkyrie

In all his life, Nickle had never worn a shirt as stiff as this. It was like it was made of wood rather than cotton. Three distinct collars ran the length of his neck, each one slightly different in size and revealing a different color. His shirt was white, his cuffs red, the seams of his clothes black.

Evalee appeared a second later, stepping out of a large changing room. She wore similar clothing, her hair tied tightly into a bun, as was the fashion of the Valkyrie. She had been instructed not to hide her wings, and she blushed ever so slightly as Nickle looked them over. They were slender and seemingly made from silk.

"Why do you hide those all the time?" Nickle asked.

"You've been to EarthWorks," Evalee replied. "People blame the blackouts on the Faeries, and with my wings showing, people can pick me out as being a High Faerie."

Nickle smiled. "Well, just so you know, you never have to hide your wings for my sake."

They had both arrived at the Palace early that morning, long before the sun had begun to rise. There were no Taxi-Lators in the city of Valenburg. Instead, they took a pigeon-drawn carriage to the servant's entrance, which was located at the rear of the Palace. As they rode along, their eyes went wide with wonder. The Palace grounds were impressive, to say the least. They passed large bushes that were cut into various shapes and fountains that were steepled with fierce-looking winged warriors.

No sooner had they arrived at the servant's entrance and exited the carriage when they were ushered right in. The Valkyrie were nothing if not orderly, and before long, Nickle and Evalee had been given a locker for personal possessions and additional pairs of clothes.

"Duty and humility," a pale-looking Valkyrie said as they

changed. "You must always remember your duty and always demonstrate your humility." She was an ancient woman, her hands and arms flecked with aging spots. Two majestic wings stretched from her back, carefully tucked behind her shoulders. The wings looked like they had once been white but had turned grey with time. Her posture was rigid and formal, akin to the many statues they had seen on the Palace grounds.

"Duty and humility," the Valkyrie repeated.

"Duty and humility," Nickle replied.

"Duty and humility," the Valkyrie said for the third time.

Nickle stared back, unsure if she wanted him to repeat the phrase again. Luckily, Evalee appeared before too long, and the Valkyrie ushered them into a long hallway. The deeper they went into the Palace, the more ornate it seemed. The ceilings were vaulted and crowned with intricate molding. Red and white carpet sprawled across the floor, upholding a wide array of statues, paintings, and planters. The air was filled with the scent of cinnamon and spice.

While the Valkyrie led them down the hall, she continued to speak in a stern tone. "You two have the high honor of serving the High Lord Prince and future Queen of the Valkyrie. This is no easy task, and I'll warn you once, if I hear you fail in your duties, you will be removed with prejudice no matter who you are or what stock you come from. You will find yourself headed back home before you can mumble an apology. Is that understood?"

"Sure," Nickle said.

"Right-io," Evalee answered.

The Valkyrie turned around. "My title is Mistress of the WestWing. You may also call me just Mistress or Ma'am. Understand?"

"Yes, Mistress," the other two replied.

The Valkyrie continued. "Your resumes we received from the Tri'Ark were impressive, to say the least—otherwise, you would not have merited this position. But for both of our sakes, don't mess this up. You were both provided reading material that discussed the protocols of High Court. Were you able to study and commit them to memory?"

"Umm...most of it," Nickle answered honestly. "It's not too different from the customs of Tiran 'Og."

"The most important thing to remember," the Mistress said

quickly. "Is when you meet the Queen, you will kneel and bow low. You will stay in this position until you are acknowledged." The Mistress of the WestWing continued for several long minutes, explaining in great detail the proper way to address and approach the royal family.

They finally entered a waiting room just outside the Great Hall. A myriad of officials and Palace staff waited, all of them as silent as a collection of rocks.

Nickle exchanged a worried look with Evalee. Initially, he had felt fortunate for the assignment he was given, but now, he was not so sure. The Valkyrie were nothing if not serious—so different from the EarthWorks officials he had met.

Then they were ushered through double doors and into the Great Hall. The room had a cathedral ceiling lined with paintings of a large-scale battle. It depicted a Valkyrie army, led by a beautiful woman in a golden crown, attacking several flying frigates. It certainly sent a message to all those who came to High Court: mess the Valkyrie and get your butt kicked.

Pillars circled the room, each made from a different stone or metal. As they progressed down the Great Hall, they became more refined, more elegant. It was all illuminated by the glow of yellow torches that were fueled by magic.

At the far end of the room, three steps led to an ornate platform. On this platform was a throne like no other. It was formed from a solid piece of black obsidian. It was not a work of art or symmetry, having been formed by Lightning rather than carved by hand. The throne stretched up far higher than necessary. It was polished in places, along the seat and hand rests, but rough and fractured in others.

Nickle and Evalee took a position to the right of the throne, among several other high servants and Attendants, all of whom stood in a tight formation.

The Valkyrie that had been their guide whispered one final piece of advice. "These are your spots. Make sure you are here at this time every day." Then she was gone, disappearing through the doors they had entered.

They waited and waited, hardly daring to move. Nickle began rocking back and forth between his toes and heels. The movement was barely noticeable, and it kept his legs from falling asleep.

Then a set of trumpets sounded, startling both Evalee and Nickle so badly they almost ran for the door.

A Valkyrie warrior spoke to the room. "Presenting the High Queen of the Valkyrie, Lady of the Wind, Protector of Valenburg and its people, the Shield Bearer of the Oaths of Old, Ruler upon the Obsidian Throne, Victra Petrov Godfrey."

Every knee bent, every head bowed.

With wings spread wide, the Queen of the Valkyrie entered, a spear and shield in hand. She appeared to be a cold, ruthless woman, forged in the crucible of war. On her brow was the same golden crown as seen in the painting high above. She wore golden armor and greaves that shimmered in the light of the room. As she sat on the Obsidian Throne, she tucked her wings behind her back. Her spear was placed on one side, the shield on the other. The weapons appeared to fit perfectly into unseen slots on the throne. Once seated, she gestured with her left hand.

The same Valkyrie as before then spoke to the room. "Presenting the King of Valenburg, the Wielder of Lightning, the Father of All, Boris Godfrey Boyar the Third."

A large-chested man rippled with muscle entered the room, his body covered in furs. He sported a trim black beard that was braided with beads. He lacked armor and weapons but appeared no less deadly. He seemed to have been a great warrior at one time, but age had finally caught up with him, as evidenced by his wider paunch. He took a seat on an ornate throne that was positioned off to the side.

The Valkyrie warrior spoke a third time. "Presenting Princess Jaylyn Godfrey, Heir to the Obsidian Throne, and Prince Yaroslav Boyar."

Two siblings entered the room, their heads held high. They held all the power and privilege in their eyes of their position. Nickle could not help himself. He glanced up, catching the eyes of the Prince. He quickly looked down and away, afraid that he had just been caught breaking protocol. The two siblings sat in smaller, ornate chairs on the opposite sides of the King.

"All rise," Victra Petrov Godfrey said.

All the servants, messengers, and emissaries stood, creating a cascade of shuffling that filled the hall.

"On this eighth day of Octovian in the year of seven hundred and eight, let us begin Court," Victra said.

Boris stood and dramatically turned to the Court, his long fur coat sweeping the floor as he moved. "Then may I, my great Queen and wife, start with a proposal most important."

"Not now," Victra said. "As we have pressing matters of state."

"This matter involves our security, and under our laws, it must be addressed."

"You addressed it yesterday and the day before. Husband, why waste the ears of the Court on things we already know."

"We have been wronged," Boris said, his deep voice falling to a growl. "Not three weeks ago, we were attacked. Likely, the attack was conducted by a member of the Assassins of the Midnight. I believe this Assassin was hired by the Nords, as they have been known to deal with that dark group in the past. Our Hunters have confirmed sightings of Vampires near the Balkinian chain—sound proof that the Queen of Vampires is indeed in league with the Nords.

"The Assassin they hired tried to rupture the Lightning and create a cataclysmic explosion, possibly destroying Valenburg and our people in one mighty blow. This violates an unspoken law between all of the Isles. Even when we have been at war with the other islands, they have never attacked or sabotaged our Lightning Reserves. Before any conflict, both sides have always given time for the Lightning to be shipped off the islands, thus preventing the needless destruction of our lands and the loss of life. But this attack violated that unspoken agreement and did just that. This is a serious act of war, and we must respond to it."

The room filled with a mix of shouts and jeers. The majority of the noise appeared to be coming from a contingent of men and women wearing blue sashes.

When the noise died, Victra turned to her husband, her voice cold and calculating. "It is an act of war, as the High Court has already agreed. But who is the enemy? Who should we attack? The Nords? You used words such as 'likely' and 'possibly.' If we are to respond, we need to do so with a clean conscience. I will not invade a sovereign nation over something that is 'likely.'"

"Then, O' my Queen, at least issue a trade embargo," Boris said, turning to the crowd, his hands raised for dramatic effect. "Let them suffer as they tried to make us suffer." The Blue Sashers erupted with another raucous cheer.

"Again, I echo what I have said the last several weeks. I *will* not condone actions that will lead to a war with an enemy we have not yet identified. Our Hunters are investigating the incident, and they will reveal the truth of the matter. How we respond will be based on facts, not supposition."

Boris' jaw tightened. "Whether you want war or not, war has come to us. We stand ready, Ruler of the Obsidian Throne, to destroy all those who oppose the Valkyrie." For a third time, the Blue Sashers yelled. This time it was accompanied by a low, steady chant, "Raise the King. Raise the King. Raise the King."

Victra's body tensed, her fingers tightening around the armrests. The Valkyrie Elite all around her sensed her mood and moved closer, guarding their Queen with a protective zeal. Victra raised her hand, demanding silence. It was slow in coming, but finally, the room did grow still.

"Let me be clear," Victra said firmly. "I will defend our people from all enemies at home or abroad. While breath still enters my lungs, while my heart still beats, my first responsibility will be to protect our people—even if I have to protect them from ignorance. We will trust our Hunters and let them do their job. And, if we find out who attacked, then we will hunt them down with the fury of the Valkyrie!"

This time, the entire crowd of onlookers cheered, raising their fists in the air, several of them shouting the Queen's name.

These words from the Queen seemed to silence the Blue Sashers, at least for now. The Court's attention turned to other, more mundane matters of state.

For both Nickle and Evalee, Court was at first exciting, then tedious, and finally boring. For an entire hour, they listened to information provided by messengers or plaintiffs regarding specific problems or complaints. But they were not alone in their boredom. The Princess appeared just as bored, her face drooping like a melting candle as Court progressed.

Upon seeing this, Victra excused them and their Attendants. Evalee and Nickle, along with ten other servants, exited the room through a door located just behind the throne.

As soon as the doors shut behind them, Jaylyn turned to her entourage. "Wow. It gets worse every day. It's like mother wants me to collapse from boredom."

"She released us early," Yaroslav replied. "Be grateful you got out early. A full day of Court was scheduled for today."

"Well, she excused me early because she knew I'd be dead by the end of it," Jaylyn answered. "And then who would fill the Obsidian Throne? She saved my life so I could preserve her legacy."

"It's your legacy too," Yaroslav answered. "In due time, it will be your throne. And then, no one will have the authority to excuse you early."

Jaylyn narrowed her eyes at her brother. She was about to respond, but she caught sight of Evalee's wings first. She ran to the High Faerie, pushing through her Attendants. "So it is true. They did hire a High Faerie attendant. And look. Your wings are so beautiful—like a tapestry of silk."

Evalee smiled, unsure of how to respond. "And…yours too…I mean, Heir to the Obsidian Throne."

"Oh, we're not in Court anymore," Jaylyn answered. "You don't have to be so formal." Jaylyn looked to be around sixteen. She was short for her age, but her brother made up for it by being extra tall. Her hair was as black as night and silky smooth, the way Sharlindrian's used to be before she became a Dark Elf.

"Oh, ok," Evalee answered.

"What is your name?" Jaylyn asked.

"Evie," Evalee answered.

Jaylyn remembered her manners, turning to Nickle next. "And yours?"

"Michael," Nickle answered.

"Are you a Dwarf?" Jaylyn questioned.

Nickle nodded.

"By the Winged Stars, how lucky are we, Yaroslav, to meet such interesting people?" Jaylyn answered, her voice taking on a gleeful tone.

"They are our Attendants," Yaroslav said, his voice falling low. "Not our guests." The young man was pale-skinned and thin. He had intense dark eyes that would lazily flick about the room, intimidating the most confident of Attendants.

As he met eyes with the Dwarf, something caught in Yaroslav's throat. The young man opened his mouth to speak, but no words came out.

Nickle looked to Evalee, unsure if he had done something wrong.

"Who are you?"

"Michael," Nickle answered.

"Your eyes," Yaroslav said. "They're like...Kara'Kala's."

"Yes...," Nickle answered.

Awkward, silence fell over the hall. Yaroslav turned to the other Attendants. "The rest of you are excused for your regular duties."

The other servants bowed low before exiting the hall.

Yaroslav nodded to Evalee and Nickle. "Come on. Let's show you the Palace grounds."

"Oh, now you find them interesting?" Jaylyn said. "You're such cloud buster."

Yaroslav ignored his sister and gestured down the hall. "So your name is Michael? How in the world does a Dwarf end up with eyes like Kara'Kala."

"Honestly," Nickle replied. "I don't know what to tell you. I was born with them, and nobody stuck around to answer any of my questions."

"So you were an orphan?" Yaroslav asked. "Like the Demon Lord himself. Fortune has favored you."

"I wouldn't describe it as fortune. My father died before I was born, and my mother died while giving birth to me."

"How intriguing," Yaroslav said.

"Well, look how quick the wind changes," Jaylyn teased, walking with Evalee a few paces behind the two boys. "Yaroslav is obsessed with learning everything he can about the Demon Lord."

"He brought the world to its knees," Yaroslav said. "Not only is he the one that founded Atlantia and EarthWorks, but he unified us under one leadership. I can't help but admire that sort of mix of ingenuity and bravery. He is the only one to humble the Elves in a millennium."

"You don't know what you're talking about," Jaylyn answered. "You haven't even seen an Elf."

"I don't have to see them to despise their arrogance," Yaroslav replied, his voice chiding. "They are the main buyers of our Lightning, and yet, they never send an Elf emissary. I suppose they are too good to be mingling with the Valkyrie."

"Can I ask a question…oh, great and…wonderful Heir to the Obsidian…."

Jaylyn laughed. "You're funny. But you don't have to use my title when it's just us. I'm serious. Now, what's your question?"

"Why do only the female Valkyrie have wings?" Evalee questioned.

"Is it not that way with the Faeries?" Jaylyn asked.

"No, both the men and women have wings."

"Hmmm. Well, legend says that in the battle against Aldrick, the Demon Lord, the people of the Valkyrie were getting desperate. They had already taken to their floating islands in the sky, but as the conflict grew, the smoke from below choked out the sky. So they prayed to Yuri, the God of war, asking for help. By the time Yuri visited, the Valkyrie were too busy digging into the earth to make shelters. When the God of War told them to come out, the King of the Valkyrie yelled out of the tunnel, 'If you want to bless us, bless our backs while we dig.' A little incensed, Yuri decided to do just that, but he only blessed the backs of the women since it was a man that insulted him. So he turned our women into fierce, winged warriors. The women then joined together and fanned their wings, pushing the smoke away from the floating Isles of Balinbar and saving the people."

"That's just superstitious nonsense," Yaroslav said.

"It is part of our lore," Jaylyn answered.

"Lore is to make disobedient children obey, nothing more,"

"I think it's a wonderful story," Evalee chimed in. "Is that why only women are warriors?"

"That's why they think they are the only warriors," Yaroslav said. "The men fight as well, just not with wings. We fight from our flying ships, our Finches, Falcons, Ospreys, Owls, Hawks, and Eagles. While the women attack from above, we meet the enemy head on, cannons blazing, our ships aimed straight for the enemy. Michael, have you ever seen a battle between flying frigates? There's nothing quite like it."

"You haven't seen one either," Jaylyn said.

"I've watched the recordings," Yaroslav answered. "I've studied the battles. Come now, sister. At least allow me that. There hasn't been a major armed conflict between the Isles of Balinbar since before we were born. So how could I see an air battle?"

The four of them entered a large living room. Both Yaroslav and Jaylyn sat down on several soft couches. Nickle and Evalee stayed back, unsure of what to do.

"Oh, go on," Jaylyn said. "Have a seat."

"I'm sorry...and I hope this doesn't sound like a stupid question...but I don't even know what we are supposed to do," Evalee said.

Jaylyn laughed. "It usually takes the new personal assistants some time to adjust to their roles. Mother thinks it's good we meet and mingle with creatures outside of the Valkyrie. She thinks it will make me a better ruler. So, you are here, simply to be here."

"Where are we?" Nickle asked.

"This the EastWing, the area of our domain," Yaroslav said with a grin. "We don't spend much time here, though. Life is pretty busy in the royal family." Then he snapped his fingers, an idea suddenly popping in his head. "Oh, I want to show you something, Michael. A man like you might appreciate this sort of thing." He shot up as if he had remembered something important and headed towards a far door. Nickle followed close behind, glancing only once at Evalee as he did.

"We're staying behind," Jaylyn said. "I can't stand that place."

Yaroslav pushed open the door, and a row of torches lit up the room. The Valkyrie was grinning ear to ear as Nickle entered. A thick and pungent smell of linseed oil hit his nose. The massive room was filled with creatures. For a few moments, the Dwarf thought they were all alive. Several of them moved and breathed, but when they did not do anything else, Nickle assumed they were all just statues of some kind.

"Wow," Nickle said. "You hunted all of these?"

"A few of them," Yaroslav said. "Father doesn't care for hunts, so he doesn't often let me go. So, I buy most of these carcasses from the Privateers who come to trade with Valenburg. Then I make them come alive with my potions. It's quite the process." Yaroslav guided Nickle past several bears, a boar, and an elephant that kept raising its trunk into the air, before they finally arrived at a table.

"This is where I process the creatures," Yaroslav explained.

There were three workbenches shaped in a "U." One of them had the remains of a lion pelt on it. Another had a series of potions and bottles tucked in drawers and on shelves. The collection of potions was the largest Nickle had ever seen—even more extensive than Shemway's collection.

"This is impressive," Nickle said. "And you need all of these potions to make your animals come alive?"

"No," Yaroslav said. "Each one requires a Tanning Potion to cure the skin, and then a Filling Potion to give it form. But the rest of the potions are used to create different effects. Some will make the animals move back and forth, while others will make them breathe fire. With the stock I have here, I can get them to do just about anything. Father also buys me the best ingredients, and so I don't think there is anyone on the island that can stuff an animal better than me."

"How did you learn how to do all of this?" Nickle asked.

"You want to try?" Yaroslav asked with sudden excitement. "I can teach you."

Nickle really did not care to touch the skins of dead animals. Between the sight and smell of the room, he had become a little nauseous, and he thought it would only increase the more potion bottles were opened or animals handled. But this was who he was now—an attendant for the Prince of the Valkyrie. It seemed like a pointless position. What were wealthy aristocrats supposed to know about Assassins of the Midnight?

But, he had a job to do. So, he turned to Yaroslav, a smile on his face, and said the last thing he wanted to say. "Absolutely."

Chapter 9

Lady Fiurda

Sharlindrian Avish MeithDwin stood at attention, a mop in hand, her long blond hair tied up with a handkerchief. Standing beside her were several hopeful girls, all of whom were trying to unsuccessfully imitate Sharlindrian. Despite only wearing black eyeliner, she had a beauty and confidence that made her stand out like a rose among a garden of lilies. They were standing in a plain room with white walls. Along one of walls was a series of cubbies holding every cleaning tool and solution imaginable.

"What's your name?" a short girl with red hair whispered to Sharlindrian.

The Elf turned to the voice, surprised to find someone speaking to her. Besides her four friends, she had spoken to only a few people since she had become a Dark Elf. The Dark Elves embraced silence more than conversation.

"Of course," Sharlindrian thought. *"She doesn't know I'm a Dark Elf. If she did know, it's doubtful she would even look at me, much less speak to me."* Dark Elves had a dual reputation for being quiet and extremely deadly—something that did not endear them to others. To join the Dark Elves, she had to take the Oath of the Wind, which compelled her only to speak when necessary and, even then, to use as few words as possible. In their unique culture, it was more important to find a few precise words rather than vomit out everything that came to mind. This practice turned tradition was in direct contrast to the High Elves, who loved nothing more than to run their mouths.

Sharlindrian had taken the Oath without a second thought—thinking her life was already over at that point. But her friends had given her new purpose, and more and more, she found it harder to stick to her Oath. Of course, without another Dark Elf nearby to reprimand her, no one would know. But it felt wrong to disrespect one of the traditions of the people that had taken her in.

"My name is Ginger," the girl persisted. "What's your name?" Ginger was a light-skinned freckly-faced girl with an easy smile, her eyes twinkling with the spark of life. Sharlindrian's eyes used to twinkle like that.

"Alice," Sharlindrian replied. She hated using the name Hawthorne had assigned her. As a Dark Elf, she had learned to value what little she possessed—most of all, her name. Jason had taught her that. Now she was trading it away as most people trade simple trinkets.

"That surprises me," Ginger answered. "You don't look like an Alice."

For a few moments, the Elf panicked, thinking that she had somehow given herself away. But Ginger did not seem to notice and kept on talking. "I've known a few Alices, all of them tall and skinny. Except for one who was shorter and skinny. Not that I am saying you're not skinny, 'cause you are, just not supper thin, you know?"

Sharlindrian glanced at the girl's shoulders, not seeing the wings of the Valkyrie. "So you're not from the island?"

"Oh no. A Valkyrie would never be allowed to clean a house for the wealthy. I'm an Atlantean by birth, but I've spent time all over the world chasing a better life. Valenburg pays better than anywhere else, so I'm lucky enough to be here. Despite having to deal with… Lady Fiurda."

Sharlindrian smiled at the girl's dramatic expression. "Who is Lady Fiurda?"

"She's coming now," Ginger said. "Just keep your eyes down and your temper in check."

Sharlindrian let out a long sigh. She began to worry that if keeping her temper in check was a requirement for the job, then the ruse might be a lot harder than anticipated. Still, she needed Hawthorne's steady income more than she cared to admit, and she doubted the politician would continue to pay her if she got fired on her first day of being a spy. She would have to take a page out of Nickle's book and bite her tongue.

"Line up, line up," said a tall woman in a fancy dress that did not quite fit. Without even thinking about it, Sharlindrian assessed the clothing quickly. *"If she tailored the top and let out the lower back, it would fit much better. But what a dreadful combination of color."*

"I see we have some new girls today. Well, I am Lady Fiurda. I will be the one responsible for overseeing your work. Now, I have very high standards. We clean the homes of some of the most important people in Valenburg. If it does not match my expectations, you will find yourself in the unemployment line. If you don't like that, I will let it slip that you are insubordinate and unruly, making it impossible to get a job anywhere else—at least one that pays a decent wage." Everything from the way the woman stood to the tone she used suggested that she should be obeyed.

"Am I understood?" the Lady demanded.

"Yes, my lady," the group of girls replied.

Lady Fiurda stopped pacing in front of Sharlindrian, her eyes giving her a critical scan. "My, what a beautiful thing you are. Hard to believe, but I was beautiful once—like you. But beauty often fades with hard work, as you will soon find. Even so, I doubt you will work here long enough to find out."

Sharlindrian did not dare meet the eyes of the woman. The woman's tone and voice had such a biting edge to it that she was afraid that if she did look up, she might very well say something rash.

Lady Fiurda waited for a response, but since none came, she turned back to face the group. "Good, now onto assignments. Rachel, Justina, and Lea, you are assigned to The Müller estate. Jamie, Yolinda, and Lisandra, you are off to the Nilsson family guest house. Ginger and Alice, you are off to the Kinnunen. Now, hurry up. If I catch you slacking, you'll regret it."

With this, the girls headed off to perform their assignments.

"You'll need a duster and a bottle of the blue solution," Ginger said through the corner of her mouth. "I'll grab the key. Put down that mop. They have one there that they let us use, and it's much better—it's magical, and you never have to wring it out." Within seconds, the two girls had grabbed their cleaning supplies and were off at a run.

"Why are we running?" Sharlindrian asked.

"Kinnunen's estate is a few blocks from here," Ginger answered. "I'm sure Lady Fiurda wanted to test you and see what you're capable of."

The Elf thought it was odd that they needed to hurry. The sun would not even rise for another hour. But the pace kept their bodies from getting cold, so she did not complain—at least not much.

By the time they arrived at the servant's entrance, Ginger's hands were shaking, either from the exhaustion or the cold. She fiddled with the lock, dropping the key once before cursing and trying again. This time she successfully unlocked the door, allowing them inside.

She took off her coat and tossed it in a small cupboard, her voice rushed. "If you start on the kitchen, I can handle the bathrooms."

"Why are you in such a hurry?" Sharlindrian asked. "We have all day to clean, right?"

"You really have no experience in this, do you?" Ginger replied. "We are here all day, but that doesn't mean we can clean all day."

Suddenly, understanding dawned on Sharlindrian. In her former life, she rarely ran into the cleaning staff, and when she did, it was at odd hours. She had never understood the implication of that before, but she realized it now. They were supposed to clean when the occupants were sleeping or away. It seemed that to the wealthy, even the sight of an individual cleaning was beneath them.

"That's fine," Sharlindrian said, heading down a hall to the left.

"It's the other way," Ginger said.

"Oh, right," Sharlindrian answered. She found the kitchen moments later. It was nothing short of a disaster, with dishes piled high in the sink, countertops with drips of food, and garbage all over the floor. It seemed difficult to imagine that all of this was made during one meal. With a sigh, she set to work, activating a Water Rune and Fire Rune that were inscribed into the side of the sink. Water filled the basin quickly as she looked for a rag to wash the counters. She found one, dipped it into the water, and began scrubbing.

But it was a terribly slow process. She had never used a washrag before, at least not over a surface that was so large and messy. She kept spreading more of the mess than she was picking up. Once the countertop was clean, or rather clean-ish, she began picking up any extra plates not in the sink, exposing a lot more food on the counter that she had previously missed.

"I should have washed the counters last," she hissed. Another wave of panic passed over her as she realized how much time she had wasted already. She began washing the dishes, but she was clumsy with the scrub brush. It kept slipping from her grip. *"I'm a warrior, not a maid,"* Sharlindrian thought. *"Give me a sword. Give me a Demon to take on, but not this."*

After cleaning a third of the dishes, Ginger appeared, carrying a bucket in one hand and a sponge in the other. "What's taking so long? You should be done by now."

Sharlindrian turned around, her shoulders falling ever so slightly. "It took a while to tackle the counter."

"The counter looks horrible," Ginger said. "There are whole sections that don't even look washed."

"That's where the plates were when I moved them."

"That's why you should always wash the countertops last."

"Well, I know that now."

Ginger shook her head. "You've never done this before, have you?"

Sharlindrian let out a long sigh. "No."

"You lied on your application then," Ginger answered. "There's no way you would have gotten this job if you didn't' have at least five years of experience. Oh, this is bad. I have to tell her."

Sharlindrian went to Ginger, her eyes taking on a rare intensity. "You can't. I need this job too much."

"But we're so far behind," Ginger answered. The longer she spoke, the more panic seeped into her voice. "I need this job too, and if Lady Fiurda sees the state of the kitchen, we're finished. This is all supposed to be done before the Kinnunens wake up."

"Calm down," Sharlindrian said. "As a friend of mine has taught me, there's always a solution. We can do this."

"How?"

"What else needs to be done. I might not be apt at the kitchen, but I might be able to help elsewhere."

"The living room needs to be picked up," Ginger replied. "But that's the hardest part. That's why I was saving it for last; so that both of us can do it. It's too much. We're finished. Two years I waited for an opening for this job, and now that's all gone."

"You work on the dishes," Sharlindrian said, her tone oddly calm. "I'll take care of the living room."

"It's impossible."

"Just wash, and we'll get through this, ok."

"Ok," Ginger said as she took a deep breath. "Ok, I'll do the dishes…while you clean…the entire living room…by yourself."

Sharlindrian nodded as she headed to an adjacent room, her hands outstretched. It was worse than she feared. *"How can one family make such a mess in one evening?"* she thought distantly. There were toys scattered everywhere—amongst the couches, floors, and shelves. Flecks of popcorn and ketchup littered the ground, adding color to the oak floors.

The Elf stumbled over some toys as she headed to the center of the room. "You can do this, Sharlie." She closed her eyes, focusing on her Mystic arts. As her mind focused, she could sense each object in the room, sense its size, weight, and purpose. Then she began to raise her hands in the air, calling forth her power, reversing the gravity of everything in the room. Slowly it all floated up, but not all at the same speed. Lighter objects floated more quickly. With her enhanced power from the BlueStar, she was able to differentiate between small toys and dirt.

She then began funneling the dirt towards the trash and the toys into a wood bin. The next layer floated up and it was a more complex mess of food pieces, large toys, trash, writing pads, and quills. It took tremendous concentration, but she sorted them all in her head, sending them in four different directions. She repeated the process again and again, letting everything float around her until she figured out where it needed to go.

When she opened her eyes, the room was spotless. Even the ketchup stains on the floor had been removed.

Ginger was at the edge of the living room, her mouth slightly ajar. "What kind of magic was that? I've never seen anything like that."

"Oh, that," Sharlindrian said as she lowered her hands. "That was just a little Mystic trick I've been practicing."

"Why didn't you do that in the kitchen?"

"I didn't want to break the dishes—plus, I really didn't know what I was doing in there. The living room is easy enough to figure out."

"You just saved us."

"Well, we still need to finish the kitchen. Can you show me how to do it properly?"

"Of course, that's easy," Ginger said, a faint smile on her lips. "Doing what you just did—now that's something special."

"With a little dedication, anyone can learn how to use Mystic magic."

Ginger turned towards Sharlindrian, taking her hands. "Can you teach me? As an Atlantean, we always had tools infused with magic, but we never really did magic ourselves."

"If you can teach me how to clean, I can teach you the little Mystic magic that I know. Deal?"

Ginger's face broke into a full grin. "Deal. When I was a young girl, all I ever dreamed about was learning Mystic magic at an Academy and becoming a Healer."

"What's changed?" Sharlindrian asked. "You can still do that."

Ginger let out a long sigh. "Oh, dreams are things given to little girls so they can deal with a harsh reality."

"That's the most cynical thing I've ever heard," Sharlindrian replied.

"I don't have the name for it—and likely, the talent either."

"What does a name have to do with it?"

"You are so funny," Ginger said with a little laugh. "You act like you don't have to play by the same rules everyone else does. No Academy will let me attend with my last name. I don't come from a family of wealth and prestige."

Sharlindrian felt a deep pain in her heart at the mention of last names. She once was a MeithDwin, part of one of the most powerful families in the world. She could have done anything—gone anywhere simply because of who she was. For several months after her own people shunned her, she had believed that all of that had been taken away—that she was indeed worthless. And it took a dear friend, who would not abandon her, to show her that she could do great things even without her last name.

"No," Sharlindrian said. "The world does work that way in part, but there is also an important part of merit. For example, if you had to have some delicate procedure performed on you, would you elect the Healer with the more important name or a Healer that has proven exceptional talent again and again."

"The more talented Healer, of course."

"Exactly," Sharlindrian said. "You, Ginger, with time and dedication, can rise to a level that is more respected than someone with a fancy name."

"Wow," Ginger said. "You...are like really inspirational. Have you always been this sure of yourself?"

Sharlindrian laughed, dodging the question. "Oh, and by the way, I also don't do any Hexation magic. Will that be a problem?"

"You should have indicated that on your application."

"But I didn't," Sharlindrian replied with a sly smile.

Ginger giggled. "No, with your skill in Mystic magic, I don't think it will be a problem."

They returned to the kitchen, cleaning with a new speed. Ginger was so talented at cleaning, it was like its own magical power. Soon, the kitchen was sparkling with a new sheen.

"It's finished," Sharlindrian said.

"Just in time too," Ginger said. "The Lady should be here anytime for inspections."

"She inspects our work this early in the morning?"

"Not always," Ginger said, rolling her eyes. "But since you're new, I'm sure she will want to see how we did."

Just then, the servant's entrance opened and shut.

"Same as before," Ginger said. "Stay here, keep your eyes down, and only answer questions that she asks, ok? If you do that, we just might get through this day."

Within moments, Lady Fiurda came around the corner, her hands behind her back like she was a drill instructor. She was thorough in her inspection, carefully taking notes on a clipboard as she went. She finally looked at the two girls standing at attention in the kitchen, her jaw taut.

"It's passable," Lady Fiurda said. "But I did find some dust on one of the kitchen doors. And one of the mirrors in the bathroom had a spot of water on it."

Ginger curtsied. "Thank you, my lady. We will make sure we address those concerns next time."

Lady Fiurda drew closer to the smaller girl, her teeth clenched. "You are such a wretched-looking thing, aren't you? Firey red hair mixed with freckles." She waited for a response, but none came. "Well, you two better get off to the servant's area. Valhalla knows how the Kinnunens would react if they saw what sort of wretched thing cleans their house. Now, get going."

Sharlindrian felt a flash of anger rise through her chest. They had completed their job in the required time. Now, this woman had to bring them down a notch for no reason in particular. She was about to protest, but Ginger seemed to sense the tension and left the room in a rush. Sharlindrian followed soon after, locking eyes with Lady Fiurda for a split second as she did. The Lady followed shortly after, exiting the way she had come, leaving the two girls in the servant's area.

Then they waited like a set of scared mice. Half an hour later, the Kinnunens started to awake. They had a massive family, as evidenced by the noise they made coming down the stairs.

"I'm surprised they don't have servants to help the kids get ready for school," Sharlindrian said in a whisper.

"Oh, they do," Ginger answered in the same low tone.

"So it's only us they don't want to see," Sharlindrian said, a new venom in her voice. "The other servants get to prance around like part of the family, and we have to hide away like somebody's dirty laundry."

Ginger laughed briefly before covering her mouth. "You're so bad."

"It's just ridiculous," Sharlindrian answered. "Our job is harder because we have to hide away. We could be cleaning, but we're here, wasting our time instead." Sharlindrian reflected upon her own experience. She had not realized how difficult she had made the life of some of her servants with her outlandish demands. She was nicer than most Elves, but that was a very low bar. And yet, whatever she requested, they had always done without hesitation or complaint. She had not even known their names. It was considered bad manners to ask their names, so she never did. Something that in this moment, she regretted. Many probably knew her better than her father. She had several Attendants as well, although she did not prefer to have people standing around, answering to every whim, so she often had them standing by in the servant's area—away from the rest of the house.

"Oh, one day, I hope to be a Family Attendant," Ginger said with a sigh. "I hear that sometimes, the family gets so attached to their Attendants, they treat them like family—no arduous chores, no insults, no hiding in the shadows."

"Why do you let Lady Fiurda insult you like that?"

"She's my boss."

"That doesn't mean she can treat you like that. We did what was required. She doesn't need to demean us for doing a good job."

Ginger laughed again, this time, it was much more subdued.

"Alice, you are something amazing, someone cut from a different cloth. I've never heard any of the other girls talk like you."

"Lady Fiurda is a fool. A true mark of a good person is how they treat individuals who are lower in station to themselves."

"Who told you that?"

Sharlindrian's mind flitted to an image of Jason Burntworth. Even in her mind, he was sporting a cocky grin. "Just a friend. In any case, since we have time while we wait for the family to leave for the day, why don't we start your first lesson of Mystic magic."

"Really? Are you serious? Right now?"

"You'll have to get a Relic or Totem to be able to do it, but we can practice the technique now. Now, take a deep breath and clear your mind."

Chapter 10

Shemway's One Stop Alchemy

"No, no, no," Shemway said. "I said Liquid Darkness upfront. That's our big seller and has the highest profit margins. We only need to sell a few of those a day, and it pays for the whole operation."

"But aren't you worried about someone bumping into the display and knocking one to the floor? It could be a disaster. We'd have to shut down for at least an hour."

"Luckily, there aren't enough Dwarves living on the island to pose a serious threat," Shemway answered. "Put it up front. That's where it goes."

Jason whispered something inaudible as he proceeded to obey, repacking the small vials so he could move them to the front.

It had been a long, rough morning for the Dwarf. He had spent the majority of the time cleaning the front room. He tried using a few Wind Runes, but they ended up moving the dirt around rather than cleaning it. It did, however, eliminate the need for dusting, so that was something. He then washed the windows, swept the floor, and wiped down the countertops. After that, he spent even more time moving the inventory up from the basement to the first floor. After an hour of lifting the heavy merchandise from the basement to the first floor, Shemway asked him why he was not using the Lifter.

"Lifter," Jason said. "What's that?"

"It's a small room that enables you to reverse the flow of gravity, so it takes you to the upper floor."

"You have an elevator in here, and you didn't tell me. I've been carting this stuff up here for half the morning. And why aren't you helping me? What have you been doing?"

"Working on the sign," Shemway said with a flourish.

Jason walked over to the Thieftian, glancing down at the artwork. It read simply, "Shemway's One Stop Alchemy."

"How come it only has your name on the sign?"

"Because you're supposed to be undercover."

"Why do you get to use your real name?"

"Because I'm a Thieftian. No one cares what I do or what side I'm on. Now, get back to work. I'm not paying you to stand around."

"Technically, Hawthorne is paying me."

After having to move the Olive Onions a fourth time, which is an essential ingredient when brewing an aging potion, and while Shemway returned to the basement, Jason was able to take a closer look at what they were actually selling. On one side of the shop there appeared to be more normal ingredients, or at least, things that Jason could actually identify. There were Newt Eyes, Frog Livers, Bat Wings, and Duck Saliva. But the further he progressed around the room, the stranger they became. There was Ghost Tongue, Pepper Soul, Biting Snowflake, Polix Entrails, and SunKist Baby Rum. Most of it smelled pretty rank, so Jason took it upon himself to install a few Runes on the ceiling that circulated the air out a window. The Runes would have to be replaced every few days, but since Jason was a master of Runes, this was not a major commitment.

"What in the world are you hanging those up there for?" Shemway asked.

"To keep the air fresh. Your ingredients might draw our target to us, but it's just as likely to drive them away. Some of this stuff stinks."

"Well, take them down."

"I ain't going to take them down before you even try to see if they're working."

Shemway walked closer, standing under one of the Runes. "There, I've tested it." He sniffed the air, and surprisingly, he did not retch from the smell of the foul ingredients. He sniffed again, this time a little deeper. "Fine. They don't work, but you can keep them up anyway. Make sure you put one above the Blundin Fungus. For some reason, it gives off an awful smell between one and two in the afternoon."

They took a lunch break at noon, eating dried fruit in silence before returning to work. When the shop was completely cleaned and stocked, they opened the doors. The first customer to come in was a mother and a small boy. Within seconds of being in the store, the small boy went straight to the vials of Liquid Darkness and knocked one of them to the ground, blacking out the shop. They had to shut down again and clean for the next few hours, scraping the black chalky substance off the walls and floor.

At three, they opened their doors to the public again, this time, the Liquid Darkness was placed in the back of the shop and was locked away in a clear chest.

"This is it, my boy," Shemway said. "We are truly titans of industry. Entrepreneurs on the ocean of capitalism!" He slapped Jason on the back, and a remnant layer of Liquid Darkness filled the air.

Jason grinned broadly, a warm feeling in his chest. "This is awesome. We're going to be rich."

Then they waited, grinning like a set of idiots. Time around them seemed to slow. They were energetic individuals who were used to taking action rather than waiting for something to happen. Soon, the two pulled up stools and waited some more.

Then a person hesitantly walked in. Jason and Shemway rushed the woman, their mouths spreading wide in enthusiastic smiles. Both the Dwarf and Thieftian spoke simultaneously, the volume of their voices competing with each other. For a few brief moments, the woman thought she was being mugged.

"What you lookin' for!" Jason asked.

"How may we serve you!" Shemway added.

The woman was so frightened she backed out of the shop, her hands trembling as she went. Once outside, she sprinted down the road and out of sight.

"I think we might have come on a little too strong," Shemway said.

"Are you sure she wasn't just going to get her friends?" Jason asked. "We've got some great prices."

"She was terrified," Shemway replied. "How about this. One of us watches the front of the shop while the other keeps themselves busy in the back."

"All right," Jason answered. "I'll take the first shift in the front."

"I don't think so. I'll take the first shift."

"It's ok. I can manage. Why don't you take a break?"

"Look down at your chest. Do you see your name tag? What does it say after shopkeeper?"

Jason's body deflated. "It says 'Assistant.'"

"And yet, on my name badge, it only says Shopkeeper."

"Fine. I'll be in the back if you need me." The Dwarf stomped off, mumbling under his breath. He entered a tiny office and fell heavily into a swivel chair. He closed his eyes, holding as still as possible. He briefly contemplated taking a nap—he had nothing else to do. Of course, he could start studying the textbook Hawthorne had sent him—that is what he should be doing in his downtime.

"How does Nickle do it," Jason thought. *"How does he just sit there? I wonder what he thinks about?"* He tried to mimic his friend, focusing on his breathing. There had been several times he had seen Nickle concentrating so hard, he did not move for hours. He took a deep breath and then let it out. He did it again before it all fell apart.

"Nope," Jason said. "That's about my limit." He stood, scanning the small but extremely clean office. Shemway had turned it into an apothecary. It had a cutting board, all sizes of vials, mortar and pestle, raw ingredients, and several cauldrons.

"Let's see what we can make with these." The Dwarf pulled out a carefully cared for book labeled "Thieftian Trade Potions" from a bookshelf. He flipped to the table of contents. "Yeah, now that's what I'm talking about. These are the sort of potions we need to be selling. And if I can add a little Runic magic to a few of them, it just might add a unique flair that will make all the difference."

He worked for two hours straight, using all the potion-making knowledge he had learned from Shemway and his natural affinity for Runic magic. The result was eleven vials of a substance that had never been invented before, all of them slightly different colors. The little office was now a mess of spilled liquids, half-used ingredients, discarded vials, and misplaced books. But Jason hardly noticed, he was too excited by his new creations. He carefully scooped them up and headed back into the shop, a wide grin on his face.

Shemway was still by the door, his posture mimicking that of a melting candle.

"How's it going?" Jason asked.

"Slow," Shemway replied. "We've had a few lookie-lues and someone that actually tried to pickpocket me."

"Have we made any gold dust?"

"Yes, but not in an honest fashion."

Jason looked to the Thieftian, surprised by the response. "I'm...not sure what that's supposed to mean."

"Never steal from a thief," Shemway answered simply.

"Well, never mind that," Jason said excitedly. "Our luck is about to change. I've done it. I've brewed something that no other potion shop has ever seen before."

Shemway stepped closer. "What is it?"

Jason started putting them on a display closest to the door. "A Gel Bright."

"By the by, that is a horrible name. What can it do? Increase your speed? Make you slippery to the touch?"

"Well, maybe. I'm not sure. The base potion I pulled from your Thieftian book. Something called Gel Skin."

"Yes, it makes your skin slick, allowing you to slip past enemies easily. But it has limited application. No one in Valenburg is going to want that."

"Well, that is just how the potion started," Jason replied. "Then, I improved upon it even more."

"Improved?"

"Yes, I kept drawing different Color Runes on the surface of the potion. Once one formed, it sank to the bottom. Then I drew another Color Rune of a different color and repeated the process several more times."

"What do Color Runes do?"

"They change things different colors. But only graffiti artists ever use them since you can't exactly control how much of something is turned into that color."

"So what in the world is this potion supposed to do?"

Jason winked. "Watch this." He grabbed one of the potions and studied it for a moment, working up the nerve to drink it down. Then he did so in one quick gulp. He felt a tingling sensation that spread from his stomach to his limbs. It was an odd feeling—both warm and cold, both soothing and irritating.

"I don't see any difference...," Shemway began. But then, something did change. Different colored Runes on Jason's skin began to appear, adjusting in size and brightness. An orange Rune flashed across his face, a blue one soon followed on his chest. The effect was mesmerizing.

"Great," Shemway said. "You've managed to turn yourself into a light show. What is the practical application of this potion? What is the point? No one is going to pay gold dust for that."

"Sometimes potions don't need to have a purpose besides being fun."

Shemway folded his arms, his eyes narrowed into critical slits. He opened his mouth to speak, but before he could, five young adults entered the shop. They were dressed in the red and white uniforms of a nearby school, two of them had wings. By the way they stood and acted, they appeared to be from wealthy families.

"What is wrong with your skin?" the tallest of the kids asked.

"It's called Gel Slider," Jason announced proudly. The kids all had a hard time looking away from the Dwarf as different colors flashed across his skin.

"How long does it last?" one of the winged females asked.

Jason looked to Shemway.

"What, me?" Shemway said. "You're asking me? Well, the Gel Skin usually lasts for two hours." He then turned to the kids, his voice falling to a lecturing tone. "But this is just an experimental batch we are testing. Take it to the back, Jeffery."

"How did you do it?" the tall kid asked.

"It's a combination of Thieftian and Runic magic," Jason answered enthusiastically. "And this is the only location you can buy it at. We brew it in the back."

"How much is it?" asked the winged girl.

"Eight…I mean ten grams a vial."

Shemway scoffed at the price but then was interrupted by one of the kids.

"I'll take all the ones you have in stock."

Jason looked to Shemway and grinned. "All of them, you say?"

"All of them," the kid replied.

Shemway directed the kid to a white tablet. The boy took out a gold medallion, and the tablet stripped away one hundred grams of gold. He then boxed up the ten vials and handed them to the youth, who retreated out the door with his friends.

Shemway grinned. "We're going to be rich."

"I'm going to be rich," Jason corrected.

"But we're partners."

"What does it say on your name badge?"

"Shopkeeper."

"And what does it say on mine?"

"Shopkeeper Assistant."

"That doesn't sound much like partners."

"Fine, you can take the title of Shopkeeper."

"That's a start," Jason said, his hands now behind his back. The tone and cadence in his voice very much mimicked the way Shemway talked as he negotiated prices.

"If you want my trade secrets, we need a fifty-fifty split."

"Sixty-forty," Shemway said.

"That works, as long as I get the sixty side."

"But I'm the one who knows how to brew the Thieftian trade secret potions."

"And how many of those did you sell today? Oh, and one last thing. My name goes on the sign too."

"You're not even using your real name right now."

"Then my fake name goes on the sign."

"Why do you even care if your fake name is on the sign. That isn't even your real name."

Jason folded his arms. "That's my offer."

"All right. Here is my counteroffer. You have to also teach me Runic magic."

"Only if you teach me more Thieftian skills—and I'm not just talking about potions. I want to learn how your tools work; how you find out information; how you can sneak in and out of places without being noticed."

Shemway straightened up as if he was trying to intimidate the Dwarf. But Jason never backed down from a challenge. Finally, the Thieftian stuck out his hand. "Fine. Deal."

Jason took it, a bright red Rune highlighting his face as he did. "Good. You're not going to regret it."

And for precisely twenty minutes, the Thieftian did not regret it. But then he stepped into the small office in the back and about passed out from the sight of the mess.

Chapter 11

Meeting of the Minds

"Here's your Blacksmithing book," Nickle said, handing a red-bound book to Jason. "I don't know how you couldn't find it. It was just under your bed."

Jason let out a long sigh. "Oh, that's where it was. Dang. I must have just missed it."

The five friends had gathered in the shop's basement, several books on their laps. They had already been in Valenburg for a week, but it seemed much longer. Between their various tasks, their spying activities, and their homework, there was not much time left in the day. Sharlindrian looked particularly worn; her hands wrinkled from using wet rags.

Jason took a seat next to Nickle, who was already pouring into the book on Blacksmithing. Evalee and Sharlindrian were sitting on a couple of bean bags just opposite them. Swiftrunner had been kind enough to use his magic to make a set of bean bags for the girls out of the available hardbacked wood chairs. He also adjusted a chair into a Cennarian stool and sat next to Jason, a broad grin on his face.

"Why are you so happy?" Jason asked.

"I'm glad you asked, little buddy," the Cennarian said. "My job is awesome."

"I'm glad somebody likes their job," Sharlindrian said, her eyes drooping from the want of sleep. She had a large book of Mystic magic on her lap, but her eyelids began to close each time she read it for too long.

"What's so special about your job?" Jason asked.

"I get to run all day," Swiftrunner said.

"Sounds like a nightmare," Nickle whispered.

"Becoming a Letter Runner is no joke," Swiftrunner said. "They have it set up like a competition. We all started as trainees in the

Minor League. At first, they only gave us small letters to deliver, most of them scattered throughout the town. Then they try to push us and see who is the fastest. I'm pretty sure all of us had to deliver the letters to the same addresses, just in different orders. They are trying to weed out the slow and inefficient. Well, guess who was the number one Initiate this week?"

"Since you're the only Initiate I know of," Jason replied. "I'm going to guess you."

"That's right. They said I set a new record. Now, I'm off to the Mid-leagues."

"Who are you competing with?"

"Mostly Satyrs, Pest'Lins, and a few Cicurians. There were a bunch of Orcs, Humans, and Goblins in the first few days, but they all got weeded out. They couldn't keep pace with the rest of us."

"I'm surprised it's so competitive," Evalee said.

"Oh, they've taken the competition to a whole new level," Swiftrunner said. "They pay us a ton of dust if we hit the daily quota, more money than I'm getting paid from Hawthorne, in fact. Letter Runners are like Cracken' Tumbler players in EarthWorks. Once a year, they have the Race of the Gods where Letter Runners from around the world come to compete in the world's longest foot race."

"So, next week you start the Mid-leagues," Jason said. "What's that going to be like?"

"I think we'll actually start delivering real letters, but the competition will be intense. Oh, man. I love it. I'm loving this as much as you enjoyed Cracken Tumblr, Jason."

"Yeah, those were the good ol' days," Jason said, his voice sounding distant. His eyes locked onto a far wall as he recalled the time he was the team captain of the Rough Skins at Harbordeen.

"It's only been half a year since then," Sharlindrian said with a laugh. "I'm not sure if that qualifies as the 'good ol' days.'"

Evalee burst out laughing.

"Well, maybe not," Jason said. "But it was certainly a lot of fun." He briefly thought of all the friends he had made during his time at Harbordeen.

"Study time is over," Shemway said as he walked down the stairs. He threw a large folder on a center coffee table, sending sheets of paper flipping through the room. All eyes went first to the folder and then to Shemway. The Thieftian was still wearing his name tag, something that was not missed by Jason.

"Hey," the Dwarf said. "Your name tag says, 'Head Shopkeeper.'"

"Of course, it does. Someone has to be in charge."

"That doesn't sound like we're partners. You can't just make yourself 'Head Shopkeeper.'"

"Part of our deal was that I allowed you to change your title to Shopkeeper, and so you have. There was nothing to indicate that my title would also remain Shopkeeper. But that is beside the point. We need to get down to business. We're not here on vacation. We've got a spy to catch."

"Tell me about it," said a sleepy Sharlindrian.

"We've got to find out who attempted to blow up the Valkyrie Lightning Vault," Shemway said, undeterred by the interruption. "Time is slipping away."

"Yeah," Nickle said. "Things are pretty intense in the Palace. Every day, as the Court begins, the King makes a big speech about how they need to go to war against the Nords to show their strength."

"They don't even know who is responsible yet," Sharlindrian said through a yawn. "That'd be like shooting an arrow in the air and hoping it hit the person who was guilty."

"What's worse," Evalee added. "Is that the Blue Sashers—that's the party that supports the King's plea for war—are gaining support. It won't be long before they are the majority in the Court. The Queen of the Valkyrie is losing control of the situation, and who knows how long she can maintain it. So far, she has been able to quell everyone's fears by saying that her Hunters are hot on the trail of the perpetrator and that they will soon be brought to justice."

"That reminds me," Nickle said. "Who here knows about our mission? Have the King and Queen been told who we are and what we're doing? When she says that her Hunters are looking into it, is she referring to us?"

"In part," Shemway answered. "Hawthorne and the Queen arranged for us to be here. Queen Victra knows we are here and what we're trying to do, but she doesn't know who we are. She wants to keep it that way, so it doesn't taint the investigation. I believe she suspects that Nickle and Evalee are working for us, as it is extremely odd for a

High Faerie and Dwarf to be assigned as Attendants to the Prince and Princess. But the King, for his part, has no idea. He is a simpler creature, one that sees everything as being strictly right or wrong. He's a great battle tactician and warrior, but that makes for a horrible politician. So, what leads do we have?"

An awkward pause fell over the room. Shemway met everyone's eyes in turn. "What about you, Nickle?"

"The Prince is kind of a weird kid," the Dwarf replied. "All he wants to do is get dead animals and stuff them, so they look alive again. We use such an odd mix of potions every day that my hands end up smelling like shoe leather."

"Not really a lead," Shemway said. "But certainly an interesting tidbit. Swiftrunner, anything on your end?"

"No," the Cennarian replied. "I won't start delivering real letters 'til next week. If I do good that week and make it to the Big Leagues, I might be entrusted with the letters sent to and from the Palace. If something is interesting in the mail, I should spot it then."

"Ok," Shemway said. "Until then, your job is to make sure you make it to the Big Leagues. What about you, Sharlie? Sharlie?"

All eyes turned to the Elf, who was now fast asleep.

Shemway frowned for a second. "We'll have to debrief her tomorrow. Did she mention anything of note before she nodded off?"

"No," Evalee said. "At least, not about the investigation."

"Well, as far as the shop goes, we've had a lot of customers and a few who stick out. We've placed a few Rune Trackers on those individuals of note but haven't learned much since then. Thanks, Evalee, by the way, for drawing a map of the city so we can track their movements."

"It wasn't any trouble at all," Evalee said. "It gave me an excuse to Vicinerate above Valenburg so I could see the entire city at once."

"The map is laid out in the second bedroom of the attic, by the way, so be careful not to step on it if you wander up there for whatever reason," Shemway said. "All right, does anyone have any suggestions? Anyone? No? Well, until we get any new leads, keep your eyes peeled and your ears sharp."

Chapter 12

The Plain of the Mind

Nickle could sense the Scathian a mile off, his mind a mix of rage and contempt. It was Locke, he was sure, but he was in bad shape. As the Scathian made it to the rear window, Nickle called to him, surprising the large man.

Locke looked up at first, his eyes flashing with rage. When he saw Nickle, his gaze turned to annoyance. He was not used to people seeing him before he saw them. The Dwarf gestured to the back door, ushering Locke inside. As the large man approached, Nickle was almost overcome by the rage boiling inside the man. To his trained mind, it appeared almost as strong as a smell.

Nickle gestured down the stairs. He was about to speak, but the Scathian's anger crescendoed, silencing any potential conversation. When they reached the bottom floor, Locke reclined in a chair, his eyes shutting, his body relaxing. Nickle did not interrupt as the Scathian went through a series of mental exercises, calming his nerves and releasing the tension. Slowly, the rage ebbed and receded like a tide going out to sea.

Finally, Locke opened his eyes.

"It's getting harder, isn't it?" Nickle asked. "It's getting harder to keep the Demon at bay."

Locke clenched his teeth, a wave of momentary anger rising in his throat. He pushed it down, refocusing his mind. "Yes. It's never been like this before. Ever since I took on my Demon form when I fought the Baroness, it's been increasingly more difficult. A few times, I've lost control completely."

"Like what happened as we entered Atlantis," Nickle added.

Locke did not answer for a while. He finally took another long, calming breath before he spoke. "Yes. Something has changed. Something primal. I've been a Demon for two hundred years, but it takes more restraint on any given day now than it used to take for an entire month. I can barely sleep at night for fear my dreams will turn to nightmares, and I'll wake up a Demon."

"I can sense you coming a mile off. Your anger makes you shine like a beacon. What do you think has changed?"

"I don't know," Locke said. "But if it continues to get worse...something will have to give. As of now, I've given up on finding Captain Black and the Listener—it's just too risky. A battle with them could very well...push me over the edge."

"What might happen then? I mean, if you can't control it?"

"I don't know," Locke replied, his voice edged with frustration. "There are a few Demons who cannot take on a Human form, perhaps because they can't control their anger. It's a vicious cycle. The more you give in to it, the more control it has over you. I think just being around other Demons has resurfaced some of my old hatreds." Locke let out a long sigh. "But that's not why I'm here. I'm here to pick up any information you might have developed."

"Hawthorne has you running messages?"

"For now, until I have better control over the anger. It's therapeutic, really. Giving me a mindless task that involves no confrontation has helped me gain better control."

"Well, unfortunately," Nickle said. "We haven't made much progress. Things are moving in the right direction—we're all solidifying our positions in Valenburg—but I can't help but feel we're looking for a needle in a haystack."

"Needle in a haystack?"

"Oh, that's just a Piddler phrase. I guess you'd probably say looking for a Gremlin in the Emerald Tunnels."

"Piddlers have such odd phrases? Why would a needle be in a haystack?"

"Well, if you had one person who was a seamstress and another person who was a farmer...."

"If you can make up random scenarios when you're coming up with your idioms, you could make a common Piddler phrase about anything. Gremlins actually live in the Emerald Tunnels...that's why it makes sense."

Nickle cocked his head to one side. "Yeah, I guess so. It makes sense to them though."

"But that's not why you're nervous."

"Nervous?"

"Your mental defenses might have developed so much I can't read your mind, but I still can sense your emotions."

"I've got to appear in the High Court tomorrow," Nickle said. "That always makes me nervous."

"That's not it."

"Fine," Nickle said. "You're right. I am nervous. I need to ask you something, and I'm afraid of how you might answer."

"What's that?"

"I need you to put me through the Scathian training."

"This again. Why are you in such a rush to suffer? The Ten Trials are no joke."

"Because we don't have time to wait."

"What are you talking about? You have nothing but time. Dwarves live for six thousand years, or so I'm told. Longer if you don't burn yourself out. But what good are you to anyone if the Scathian training breaks your mind? What if it messes you up so bad you can't recover? I've seen it, Nickle. I'm not making this up."

"Could it kill me?"

"No, I wouldn't let it go that far, but it might snap your mind. Do you understand? It's designed to push you to the very edge of insanity. Only then can you harness the powers of the mind."

"I'm ready. I can handle it."

"I've made up my mind on this. The answer is no for right now."

"You said last year that I was learning the Scathian techniques far faster than anyone else you've seen before."

"True."

"Then why not see how far I can go?"

Locke let out a long, exaggerated sigh. A tinge of anger flared in his chest before he pushed it back down. "No, it's too dangerous."

"And there's nothing I can do to change your decision?"

"No, Nickle. Hector told me to protect you. I'm not about to throw you into deep water without knowing you can swim."

Nickle nodded resolutely. "Somehow, I knew you'd say that." He walked over to Locke, patting the old warrior's shoulder. When he did not remove his hand a moment later, Locke looked up, his eyes narrowed. Then in a flash, the Dwarf slid his hand to the side of the Scathian's head. He had seen Tiberian do this technique to the Atlanteans, and now he pretended to copy the magic, acting as if he had pushed his mental force into his friend's mind. Locke's eyes went wide as he raised his mental defenses. But the attack he expected to come, the mental energy that usually followed this technique, did not happen.

But Nickle was no fool. He knew he could not overcome Locke with Scathian magic, so he instead reverted to Alteration. He peered into the warrior's head, seeing the threads of his mind, seeing the cords that kept him alert. Then he pinched those threads, and Locke fell unconscious, his chin resting on his chest. It was an extremely complicated technique that took several long seconds to work, one that he would not be able to do without being so close to someone. But he had practiced it a few times on Jason, and it had worked like a charm every time he tried it before.

"I'm sorry, old friend," Nickle whispered. "I need that training." He then pulled an ancient box from his pocket that glimmered red like a ruby. After Locke had refused to train him the first time, Nickle had Vicinerated to several shops in EarthWorks, looking for an item he knew he had seen before. It took a while, but he finally found it. The Plain of the Mind—he only hoped it worked as advertised.

"This better work," Nickle whispered. "After spending two hundred kilos of dust on this." Then he activated the Hex in the Plain of the Mind, which opened up the box. He closed his eyes, now free to wander through the subconscious of Locke with little resistance. It did not take long to find the memories he needed—they were in the darkest depths of his brain, in the place where mental scars are tucked away. He then put the Plain of the Mind next to Locke's head, and the box, in turn, copied the memories. The whole process took only seconds, but he was so nervous about being caught or Locke regaining consciousness that it felt like hours. Nickle then turned his attention to the latest memory, the one right before Locke was knocked out. Instead of copying this one, he ripped it out completely, locking it away into the Plain of the Mind.

He almost completed his task there, but then he reflected on the conversation he had just had with Locke. His friend, although he would never admit it, needed help. Locke was struggling to keep his emotions in check, something he had never struggled with before. Nickle did not know much about the mind, so he feared he might do more damage than good if he messed with things too much. But he felt confident he could at least change one thing for the better. As he sensed the source of Locke's rage, he began to pull at it, ripping away all the anger that broke away easily. This took much longer than the two tasks before, and he was unable to keep track of how much time had passed.

Once finished, Nickle also tucked the rage away into the Plain of the Mind. He wanted to take it all, but it seemed too intertwined with the Scathian's personality. There was no telling what sort of damage he could do if he drastically adjusted things.

Once done, Nickle pulled back, surprised at how easily the task was accomplished. The Goblin who had sold Nickle the Plain of the Mind had been hesitant to let it go. A Hex of this much strength, if misused, could very well cause real damage to someone. But then Nickle nodded to a wheelbarrow that contained two hundred kilos of gold dust, and all hesitation in the Goblin disappeared in an instant.

After Nickle bought it, the Goblin explained in great detail how to properly use it. It was designed to absorb the memories of the wielder, not another person. But, Nickle figured, since Locke had taught him how to enter someone's mind, he should be able to sort through other people's memories. It had been a gamble, but it had paid off.

Nickle patted his friend again and readjusted his pillow, trying to make the large man as comfortable as possible. He looked entirely too big for the couch, but his expression was much more peaceful. This lessened the guilt building in Nickle's chest.

The Dwarf looked at the box, which had closed of its own accord. He knew this had to be done. But he could not help but feel bad. Tiberian had sunk Atlantis using the same justification, and it left a bitter taste in the Dwarf's mouth.

"This is different," Nickle whispered. "No one was injured."

Then Jason burst from his room, stubbing his toe on the door. His hair stuck every which way, like the back of a porcupine. "Morning, Nickle. Oh hey, Locke's here. Where did he come from?"

"I let him in, and before I knew it, he had fallen asleep," Nickle answered.

"Huh," Jason replied, yawning as he stretched his arms out.

"Well," Nickle said awkwardly, hiding the Plain of the Mind behind his back. "In any case, I've got to get running to the Palace. They want us there before the rooster crows."

***

Since Tortugan had drilled punctuality into his head, Nickle was never late for anything. For Evalee, however, promptness was a different matter entirely. Time was more of a suggestion than a concrete concept to a Faerie. Luckily, Sharlindrian was like Nickle and would always get Evalee moving in the morning.

This morning, however, even Sharlindrian slept in. But thanks to Vicineration, Nickle and Evalee arrived before they were even missed, appearing abruptly in the changing room. They could not Vicinerate directly into the Palace, but there was a small area in the servant changing room that was missed by the Vicineration preventing Totems, a security oversight that neither Evalee nor Nickle were too eager to share with anyone else.

The Mistress of the WestWing was somewhat startled to find them dressed and ready for the day. She had relished in the idea of getting the two young Attendants in trouble, and despite a watchful eye, she never saw either of them enter the Palace grounds. Ruthfully, she inspected them before allowing them to head off to Court.

Besides the King wanting to declare war, the High Court was exceptionally dull. It seemed that once a year, they had an accounting of all the royal commodities in storage, and it happened to be today. Luckily, the Queen dismissed the Prince and Princess earlier than usual.

Princess Jaylyn Godfrey was all smiles as she walked out. Evalee fed off the young girl's energy and was soon smiling just as wide. As usual, besides four Valkyrie Elite bodyguards, the rest of the Attendants were dismissed, leaving Evalee and Nickle to trail behind the Prince and Princess.

"I'm so glad we're out already," Jaylyn huffed, leading the other three down the hall. "Seriously, how can anyone listen to someone rattle off numbers and expect to stay awake."

"Oh, sister," said Yaroslav. "Numbers are what keeps us in power."

"I highly doubt that," Jaylyn argued. "Wouldn't you agree, Evie?"

Evalee almost did not respond, still not used to her fake name. She made up for it in earnest, nodding vigorously. "Of course, my lady."

"See," Jaylyn smiled. "You're outvoted."

"She's your Attendant. Of course, she agrees with you," Yaroslav said. "Michael, back me up on this."

Nickle stepped forward, inserting himself into the conversation. "The Prince is absolutely right. Numbers…and such…are truly important to…defense and…math."

"My goodness," Yaroslav laughed. "You call that backing me up? But in all seriousness, the first number that was read was our Lightning Reserves. That is the source of our power, wealth, and prestige. Reading the commodities every year is not about figuring out what we have, it's about letting the other powerful families know how much they need us. It keeps them in line, beholden to the Godfreys."

"Oh, Yaroslav, when are you going to realize that not everything is about maintaining power. I do feel, brother, that it is becoming quite the obsession."

"It's my obsession that saved the Lightning from certain destruction," Yaroslav asserted.

"What do you mean?" Nickle asked, momentarily forgetting himself. "I mean…I'm sorry…I don't mean to overstep."

"It's all right, Michael," Jaylyn said. "It's common knowledge that there was an attack on our Lightning Vault a little over a month ago. The whole island is talking about it. Luckily, Yaroslav had the ingenious idea to reinforce the Vault with a new kind of metal only months before the attack, saving all of our lives. The island could have very well been ripped in two."

"Don't be dramatic, sister," Yaroslav said. "It doesn't suit you. But yes, the reinforcement in the Vault protected the Lightning, saving us from a crippling shortage that would have decimated the Valenburg economy."

"You don't think it would have ripped the island in two?"

Evalee asked.

"Not likely," Yaroslav replied. "To create an explosion with Lightning you need the right catalyst. From what I heard, the intruder used Dragon Fire to try and ignite the Lightning, which burns way too hot and expands far too quickly. You would need a mixture like Orange RipTide to get the right effect, something that burns hot but doesn't expand quickly. But, in the end, it all worked out. Mother didn't even want to tell me where the Vault was. So distrustful, even of me."

"Don't be offended, brother. No King or Prince has ever been told where the Vault is kept. That secret is only kept by the Valkyrie Elite and the Queen."

"Well, it's lucky then that she finally did," Nickle added.

"Yes, it is," Yaroslav said, his voice sounding bored.

They passed through double doors that opened up to the lounge. Nickle glanced over at the door that led to all the stuffed animals, and his stomach momentarily turned. He hated the smell of all the potions in the room, not to mention all the creepy animals slowly moving with hints of life.

With the training Locke had already given Nickle, he could have easily peered into the youth's mind and seen exactly what made him tick. Even now, he could sense a deep-seated anger buried underneath his calm demeanor. But if Nickle pried any deeper, he would likely not succeed. Already he sensed some mental resistance from both of the royal twins. Likely they had been trained to repel mental intrusions from a very young age—something that only the very wealthy could afford. Even if he succeeded in garnering some information, the mental invasion would leave a trace. It would be a simple task for a mental Purveyor to find the evidence of the intrusion. If it was linked back to him, it would be very bad, likely jeopardizing all the lives of his team.

"I'm going to lay down," Yaroslav said. "My head is still burning from the two animals we stuffed yesterday. I don't know if it is the new batch of Polix Saliva or the Faerie Fire we used to embalm them, but it still has my head in a tizzy."

"You could just stop stuffing dead animals altogether," Jaylyn suggested sweetly.

"I'm an artist, Jaylyn. If I were to stop, who else would make the most life-like dead animals in Valenburg?"

"I'm not sure that is a title to strive for."

Yaroslav rolled his eyes before walking towards his bedroom, his two guards following closely behind.

Jaylyn looked at Nickle and Evalee in turn. "Sit down, you two. I've never seen a set of Attendants that took so long to get comfortable."

Evalee grinned. She was really starting to like Jaylyn's apathetic approach to her royal life. She sat next to the Princess. "I'm sorry. We're just so glad to be here that we don't want to mess it up."

"If you had messed up, you'd no longer be my Attendant."

Evalee laughed.

"I'm serious. I've had Attendants last less than half an hour."

"Oh."

"But you're still here," Jalylyn said sweetly. "So, you're doing something right. Anyway, I want you two to tell me all about EarthWorks."

"You've never been?" Nickle asked.

"No, but I hear it is delightful," Jaylyn answered. "But first, we need food. I was in such a rush today that I didn't have time for breakfast."

"Me too!" Evalee said.

"Oh, bother. Yaroslav already dismissed the other servants. I'd send one of the Valkyrie Elites…but mother never allows them to leave my side. I guess we'll have to take a trip to the kitchen."

"I can go," Evalee said. "I know where the kitchen is. What do you want?"

"Oh, you're too kind," Jaylyn said. "Just grab whatever looks appetizing to you—I'm sure High Faeries have excellent taste."

Evalee ran off. She would have Vicinerated, but the inner Palace had Totems prevented that kind of magic. But she was quick enough, sprinting down the hall.

"You don't talk much," Jaylyn said to the Dwarf.

Nickle shrugged. "I guess not. I've got four friends, all of them are pretty social."

"You seem even more subdued today than usual. Why is that?"

Nickle's memory briefly flashed back to Locke, who he had left on the couch unconscious. A palpable guilt burned through his mind. It had been a rash action, one that he would not have taken had he thought there was another way. Worse, he actually got away with it. He was half hoping Locke would have stopped him. Maybe then the Scathian would finally realize how important all of this was to him. To add even more to his guilt, he planned on using the Plain of the Mind tonight.

"There," Jaylyn said. "You're doing it again. Your mind just wanders off. You're like my brother when he's mixing his potions and stuffing his dead animals. Come sit closer."

Nickle obeyed, sitting on a chair next to the couch.

"Don't be shy," Jaylyn repeated. She patted the seat next to her on the couch, the spot that Evalee had vacated when she left to get the food. "Sit here."

Nickle complied.

"Now, tell me about EarthWorks," Jaylyn said.

Nickle was slow in talking, but he eventually picked up momentum. He explained the different structures, the various magical races, and some of the city's problems. Jaylyn proved an excellent listener.

Finally, as Nickle began losing steam, he began drawing on bits of advice that came to mind. "Oh, and don't eat the Goblin Burgers."

"Goblin Burgers?"

"Especially before battle."

Jaylyn looked at the Dwarf for several seconds longer, trying to decide if he was joking or not. She then burst into laughter, filling the living room with the cheerful noise. She was soon laughing so forcefully, she had a hard time breathing. She grabbed a pillow, covering her mouth and muffling the sound. Moments later, she pulled the pillow down, coming up for air, and the noise returned.

From down the hall, Evalee could hear the raucous laughter. She was carrying a platter of food, complete with crab rangoons, lobster bisque, sandwiches, various meats and cheeses, and a white cheddar dipping sauce. When she finally spotted the source of the noise, she was surprised. Nickle had taken her seat and was now sitting next to Jaylyn, who was laughing with the Dwarf like he was the funniest person in the world. She hesitated at the edge of the doorway, afraid she was walking in on a private moment. And then...Jaylyn reached up and put a friendly hand on Nickle's shoulder.

An emotion that the High Faerie had never felt before burned through her body, filling her veins with pure adrenaline. Her eyes narrowed.

"*Curse their private moment,*" Evalee thought. She rushed in, the food rocking precariously back and forth on the platter. When she reached the two people on the couch, she did not bother with pleasantries. She instead just sat down between them, forcing the two apart.

"I brought your food," Evalee said with a false pleasant voice. "I hate to interrupt all this laughter, but crab rangoons are your favorite."

"The tray is frozen," Jaylyn said.

Evalee looked at the tray for the first time since stepping into the room. Everything was coated in an inch of ice.

"Did you pull these from the freezer?" Nickle asked.

Evalee did not have a good answer; her chest was still tight from the burning emotion that whipped through her body. "It…wasn't like that when I grabbed the tray. The chef had set it out under a Warmer Rune. Why?"

"Well, do you mind going and getting another one?" Jaylyn asked sweetly. "I don't mind ice…when it's in my drink."

Both she and Nickle laughed.

The emotion in Evalee's chest returned, narrowing her eyes. "Sure. I can get another tray. Nickle, do you mind coming and helping me?"

"Oh, but then I'll have no one to talk to," Jaylyn protested.

Evalee's eyes went wider. "Nickle…come with me now." The High Faeries' voice was so tense, it startled the other two.

"Sure," Nickle answered. He then turned to Jaylyn. "We'll be right back. I'm sure there was just a mix-up in the kitchen."

"Ok, but don't doddle," Jaylyn said. "My ribs are starting to poke through my dress I'm so hungry."

Nickle forced a laugh before heading out of the room with Evalee. As soon as he was out of earshot, he turned to her, his face serious. "What happened to the tray?"

"I…don't…really know," Evalee answered. "It wasn't frozen when I grabbed it."

"I know it wasn't. *You* did that to the tray. You blasted it with Elemental magic. That's impressive stuff."

"Something came over me," Evalee said, her voice trembling. "I don't' know what happened. One moment everything was fine, the next...I dunno. It was like that. Something was tearing in my chest, making it hard to breathe. Something...happened. Do you think she'll kick us out of the Palace? Did I just fail our mission?"

"It's ok," Nickle said. "No one was injured, and I don't think Jaylyn had any idea what really happened. I've used magic I did not intend to on more than one occasion. It can shake you up a bit."

"But how?"

"It's Elemental magic," Nickle said. "I'm sure of it. Remember Atlantia's gift? Anger. Something must have set it off in you. What were you thinking about?"

Evalee paused to consider her emotions. She had no idea what it really was—she had never felt it before. "I don't quite know. How can anger be a gift? Anger is not a gift." The High Faeries' fingers tightened around the tray, sudden rage overwhelming her. "Why did I get the crappiest of the gifts?" Just then, the ice thickened on the tray.

"Just breath," Nickle said. "In through the nose, out through the mouth. I can teach you how to control your emotions, but for right now, you just gotta keep it together."

"You promise?" Evalee said, her voice tense. "I've never had to deal with this emotion before."

Nickle stopped walking and grinned, locking eyes with Evalee. "Of course. I'll always be here for you."

The thought of spending time with Nickle eased the tension in her body. She took a deep breath, relaxing even more. Slowly, the dark emotion running through her chest dissipated before it died completely. By the time they reached the kitchen, the ice had disappeared.

"Well," Nickle said with a smile. "Might as well grab a different tray after walking all of this way."

Evalee smiled back. "Thanks, Nickle."

Chapter 13

The BlueStar

When Sharlindrian reached the Müller Estate, their cleaning assignment for the day, Ginger was not there. This was certainly odd, as she had left for the estate long before Sharlindrian did. Lady Fiurda had kept Sharlindrian back and lectured her on the process of becoming a full-time staff member. It was a pointless, cutting speech, one no doubt meant to humble and control her.

Sharlindrian looked around the cobblestone courtyard, hoping to see her sitting on a wall and resting her feet. The Müller Estate was massive, consisting of a well-manicured lawn, a main house, a stable, some sort of sports arena, and two guest houses. Luckily, they only had to clean a few rooms in the main house. The rest would be cleaned by several others, who had probably already entered. But she felt confident that Ginger would have waited outside for her.

Then the red-headed girl did appear, but not in the condition she expected. She had a small cut above her eye, and her hands were held behind her back by an Elf. Three more Elves and a Thieftian came into view, stepping around the corner of the house. In the lead was Victor Andlemires. He was perfectly handsome, his clothing immaculate in the dim light of the pre-dawn. A light smattering of makeup highlighted his features. His appearance contrasted sharply with Sharlindrian's simple clothing. Sharlindrian readily recognized the other three, Flueren Bashulins, Alexander Mevish, and Tirillian Gabon.

"Well, well," Victor said. "Look what we have here. The little birdie that flew the coop found a nest among the commoners."

"Are you sure it's her?" said Alexander Mevish. He was the one holding Ginger's hands behind her back.

"Let her go," Sharlindrian demanded, her commanding tone causing momentary hesitation among the others.

"It's her," Victor replied. "She's just shaved her ears down with

Transformation makeup. But I recognize that arrogant and demanding tone anywhere. Look how low you've fallen. Sharlie, what are you doing? Cleaning houses? I guess there are worse professions."

"Let her go," Sharlindrian repeated. "That's not a request."

Victor turned to the Thieftian, handing him two large medallions of gold. "Here is your payment, as promised."

"Pleasure during business with you," the Thieftian answered. "If you ever need my services again, please, contact someone else. Now that all is complete, I'll take my leave."

"Don't' you want to stay and watch the fun?" Alexander asked in a sweet voice.

"No," the Thieftian answered, giving a subtle wink at Sharlindrian. "I've seen what this one can do." Without another word, he shot a Crossbow into the high reaches of the Estate and whipped out of sight.

"Then take your money and run, you coward," Alexander said to the disappearing Thieftian.

"We won't hurt you…much," Victor said, his tone becoming coarse. "Give me what is mine. The BlueStar has been in my family for a millennium. I lent it to you as a promise of our future, but since you spat in the face of that future, I've come to collect it."

"I was a MeithDwin when you presented it to me, Vicky," Sharlindrian answered. "Your dispute is with them."

"You are the one that has it," Victor said. "Where is it, Sharlie?"

"It's gone."

"Something like the BlueStar doesn't just disappear. Where is it?"

"I don't have it."

Victor stepped closer, a hand on the hilt of his sword. "Enough games. My honor is in question until I return the BlueStar."

"Your honor was in question the moment you tried to kill a Dwarf because he was better at you in a game," Sharlindrian answered.

Victor slowly drew his blade; the other Elves mimicked the movement. Ginger was tossed to the side. She stumbled over a planter and fell into the bushes.

"Don't kill her," Victor said to the other three Elves. "After seeing how she lives, that would be doing her a favor. And she deserves no mercy from High Elves." He then turned back to Sharlindrian, who had not even moved since the swords had come out. "Just remember, I tried to be reasonable, Sharlie."

"My name does not belong in your mouth," Sharlindrian answered. Then she rushed in, surprising her quarry. She had used Mystic magic to reverse her gravity towards the Elves, making her move with a speed that blurred her features. A fist collapsed into Alexander's throat, another clocked Tirillian across the head. Each time she used her magic to magnify the impacts.

Victor stabbed at her legs, but his movement was so slow. He had been weighed by Mystic magic. He immediately began resisting the magic and used his own spell to speed up his movements, but it was out of sync with his body, creating more harm than good.

Sharlindrian was now in the middle of them, creating devastation everywhere she turned, using her Mystic magic to alter their gravity, throwing them off balance. They were as sand before a momentous wave. She swept Tirillian's feet from beneath him and hit Flueren so hard in the wrist that it shattered bone. With a yell, she dropped her sword and cradled the wound, stepping back as if she now faced a monster.

Sharlindrian returned to the position where she had started. "Vicky, this is your chance to simply walk away. Heal your wounds and leave. I can't give you the BlueStar because I don't have it. Look for it elsewhere before this little game becomes something much worse."

The other Elves all looked to Victor, who was holding a broken nose. His nose slowly reformed into its perfect shape as Alexander sent over a healing wave of Mystic magic. Within moments, the wounds they had accumulated were healed, their swords back in hand. They were raised defensively now, so different than when this first started.

"Let's go," Flueren said. "She doesn't have it."

"She's a maid," Victor hissed. "She cleans houses to afford the rats she consumes. We are the children of High Elves. We are from the most powerful families in the world. Regroup and raise your blades. We are children of Elvenduur."

With this battle cry, they charged in again, all restraint gone. Alexander began creating Light Lances and casting them forward, barely missing their target by inches. Sharlindrian's immense Mystic power allowed her to slow down each of the projectiles just enough to dodge. It was an incredible show of force, and it was not wasted on the other four.

The Elves came from all angles, using their combined force. They were talented students of the Mystic Arts, of that, there was no doubt. They were top of their class and praised by their teachers as being prodigies. But Sharlindrian had become a woman of war—forged in the Dark Woods and trained by one of the greatest Elves of all time, Tiberian MeithDwin. She had learned close combat from Dwarves, she had learned how to guard her mind from a Scathian, she had learned how to wage war from Dark Elves.

She disappeared using the Shadow Stride technique that Tiberian had recently taught her. She did not vanish completely, but in the dim light of the early morning, it was just as good. When she appeared again, she floored Victor and then Flueren. Alexander's blade was sliced in two by a Light Lance. It was not even a close fight; she had been toying with them before. Now she unleashed all of her fury. Soon, Flueren was knocked unconscious. Alexander joined her side not long after. Tirillian was sent pitching into some thorny bushes.

In a desperate move, Victor Exsiliogated behind his opponent. But his mind had momentarily disconnected from his body, giving Sharlindrian all the time she needed to take him to the ground.

Victor's eyes widened at the pain, his teeth clenched.

Sharlindrian stood over him. "Just remember, this is what you chose."

"How?" Victor asked, his voice struggling with disbelief.

Sharlindrian healed his bones, removing the pain. "You, like your race, judge value based on what you see, on the wealth a person possesses, but the value of a person is not defined by what they wear or own. It's by who they are on the inside." She used her Mystic magic to pull the Elf to his feet. "Now, grab your friends and leave. Return to your large mansions and your rich tables of food, and never seek me out again. If you do, it will not end well."

Victor lowered his head, refusing to make eye contact with Sharlindrian. He grudgingly obeyed, heading off to his friends, healing them just enough so they regained consciousness or could use their legs again. And then they were off, leaving their swords behind.

As they disappeared off the estate grounds, Ginger joined Sharlindrian's side. "That was amazing."

"It was a distraction," Sharlindrian answered. "Now we've

really got to hurry if we're going to finish before inspection."

"Can't we at least acknowledge how awesome you are?" Ginger said.

Sharlindrian laughed. "You're funny. But seriously, we need to move. Gather up the swords and hide them in the bushes. They should fetch a fine price at a pawn shop."

"Won't they be even angrier you've sold their swords?"

"Oh, they will recover them, I'm sure of it. They'll send out servants to scour all of the shops in Valenburg until they are found and then pay a price a hundred times more than we will get for them. But, it will fetch more than enough dust to buy you a powerful Mystic ring."

"My own ring? Are you serious?"

"Almost everything you saw me do," Sharlindrian said. "Is something you can learn to do yourself. So could the Elves that I fought. The difference is, they were not willing to pay the price that I already have. You, Ginger, don't have to settle for what you are told you can do. What you can achieve is decided simply by what you are willing to do to achieve it."

***

Sharlindrian limped across the mansion's bedroom, pain crippling her movement. Despite her impressive display, she was not unscathed. One of Victor's lunges had pierced her in the upper leg, leaving behind a trail of blood. It was certainly not the worst wound she had received in her life, but it was now becoming annoying. She was falling behind schedule. Luckily, Ginger had doubled her efforts, working twice as hard.

Despite the queasy feeling it gave her, she had used her Mystic magic to stop the bleeding. She could not heal her own wound, as it was challenging for any wielder of Mystic magic to do so, even for her.

She entered the primary bedroom to find it a mess of blankets, pillows, discarded food, clothing, and dishes. She used her magic to arrange everything in the room, pulling dishes into a pile, pillows to the bed, dirt and debris in the trash.

But then she noticed something odd, something that she only picked up because she was trying to manipulate every loose item in the room. She could sense several objects behind a wall. She at first thought she was just detecting items in the closet, but this was not the case. The closet did not extend all the way back to the wall she was scrutinizing.

She closed her eyes and pulsed with her Mystic magic, making the items behind the wall tremble. She could get a sense of metal and weapons, a helmet reinforced with magic. She tried to sense any magical triggers or traps, but she detected nothing. Sharlindrian pulled back, ashamed to be snooping, but then she realized that was the whole point of what she supposed to be doing, and the guilt disappeared.

"There's a hidden compartment," Sharlindrian said in a whisper. She approached the wall slowly, studying it from multiple angles. Something magical ran from the back of the wall to the bust of a man nearby. It was like an invisible string that was so faint, she could only detect it through absolute concentration.

Her hands fumbled with the head, finding a Rune tucked behind the ear of the statue. Once pushed, three notes sounded. At first, it seemed like nothing happened, but then the wall began to disappear, revealing the mask of a Demon Guard. But this was not only a mask like those she and her friends had found while at Harbordeen; this was a complete set of polished armor, as if it might be needed for battle at any moment. It was primarily red with black accents. Two large butchering blades hung at the waist, each sharpened to a razor's edge. It was crafted with the finest skill and lined with unfamiliar and ancient Runes.

As she studied the armor, she again sensed that something else was in the room, as if other articles were just beyond her reach. She closed her eyes and concentrated, finding another secret Rune just behind one of the blades. She pushed it and two notes sounded. The armor swung out like a door, and the wall behind melted away like evaporating water.

She stepped inside, and a torch magically sprang to life, illuminating a long tunnel. To either side of her were dozens of red sets of armor, each with accompanying butcher blades and circular shields.

"For the sake of Ivishdor," Sharlindrian said. "There's enough armor here to field a small army." She found herself counting the sets of armor as she continued. Then the hallway split in two different directions. She glanced to her left and saw a series of stairs heading down into the darkness.

She looked back at where she had come from, trying to ensure no one was following. Most of the family members had left for the day. Only Ginger and Sharlindrian had been assigned to clean the upstairs rooms, a monumental task because of their sheer size, but not impossible between the two of them.

Regardless, Sharlindrian had to hurry. She hesitated for a moment, deciding between going down the stairs or heading back. In a rush, she ran down the stairs and into the dark. She activated her Shadow Stride ability as she walked, making her almost disappear entirely.

The stairwell was more extensive than she would have ever thought. Likely, she was underground by now. After a few dozen steps more, she entered a massive cavern with walls that curved up into a dome high overhead. Like the hallway above, torches automatically activated, providing ample light for the room as she entered. It was a throne room of sorts, with several additional passageways branching off in various directions. At the far end of the chamber was a massive throne carved from bone. Above that was a red tapestry bearing an ancient white symbol of evil.

Sharlindrian's voice trembled as she realized what it was. "The sign of the Demon Brood." She looked around, a new panic settling in. She then tried to Exsiliogate out of the room, but it had been embedded with Totems that prevented her. So instead, she returned the way she had come, heading back up the stairs in a rush.

As she reached the primary bedroom and reset the secret door, she was able to think through everything she had just seen. The hundreds of sets of *new* armor. The lethal weapons. The empty throne.

Her thoughts brought her to one final conclusion that turned her stomach. *"These people aren't just reminiscing on the rule of Kara'Kala; these people are planning for his return."*

Chapter 14

Just Jump

"It should work," Jason said. "The line in the middle is a little thin, but that should do it." The Dwarf leered over the Thieftian's work, judging it as harshly as possible. Despite Jason's efforts to humble the Thieftian, Shemway had a natural talent with a Dwarf Stylus, producing perfect Runes on only his third or fourth attempts. His excellent penmanship transferred seamlessly to Rune making.

"All right," Shemway said. "I'll thicken up the next one I do."

Each morning between the time everyone left for the day and when the shop opened, the Dwarf and Thieftian took turns teaching each other their magical arts. By the first day, Shemway was able to craft Color Runes so perfectly that he could assist in producing the Gel Slider, which had become their number one selling potion. Even with both of them crafting as much as they could, they still ran out of stock each day.

"How's your Crossbow coming?" Shemway asked.

"It's...well," Jason replied. "I potion treated the string and flight groove easy enough, and it's holding up in the tests, but something keeps going on with the Crossbow limbs. I've potion-treated them three times now, and usually, they are either too brittle or flexible. But this last time, I think I finally got the right mix down."

"It's not an easy task," Shemway agreed. "But it is the most important part of the Crossbow. Let me see."

"Well, it's not done...."

"Don't be stubborn, Dwarf. I can't help you unless I see it."

"I don't want to show you until...."

"This Crossbow, if done correctly, can be used to support your weight. It can be used to pull you out of danger and past almost all obstacles. It is often said that potions are what a Thieftian uses to break into the vault, but it is the Crossbow that gets them there."

Jason sighed. "You're not going to wait for me to finish it, are you?"

"I don't want you to die using a faulty Crossbow," Shemway said. "Who would I pick on if you were gone?"

Jason pulled out his Crossbow from a cabinet. "Now, I've followed your plans exactly, and then…I made a few improvements."

"What in the world…," Shemway said, his hand taking ahold of the strange contraption. "Improvements? You've gone with a completely different design."

"No, the design is the same. I just added a mix of Runes and reinforced several of the vulnerable spots. I noticed early on that the Rope Wheel has to endure the most pressure. So I reinforced it with that tightening solution you made, but then I added additional supports and Runes."

"How much weight are you trying to hold with this?"

"I bet I could hold ten thousand pounds."

"Ten thousand pounds? How much weight do you plan on gaining in the next few years?"

"Well, Dwarf Tines are pretty heavy, so I wanted to be sure it'd hold me. But then I thought, why not push it even further."

"You're needle would never hold that weight."

"The old needle, yes," Jason said, a sly grin creasing his features. "But this one, I think so." He pulled out a needle the size of a pencil—double the width that usually was shot from a Thieftian Crossbow.

"You like to push the limit, don't you? Did you soak it in the Transformation Powder and dip it in the Clinging solution?"

"Yeah, twice."

"Hmmm…it could work. The needles are designed to become part of the structure when they hit an object. That is why there is no damage left behind—something that is critical to a Thieftian avoiding detection. When you hit the release, it sends a slight shock up the cord temporarily breaking the connection with the target and allowing the needle to fall free. How is your potion belt coming along?"

"Finished them."

"Them?"

"Yeah," Jason said as he retrieved a few leather wrist bands from the same cabinet as before. "Instead of a belt or bandoleer, I decided to go with two sleeves that wrap around my arm. I can adjust them too, just in case I'm wearing my Tines."

Shemway inspected them skeptically. "Thieftians never use wrist carriers to hold their potions. They are too fragile. One good hit to your arm, and who knows what might happen."

"But I plan on reinforcing my potions with Strength Runes. Plus, I plan on wearing my Rune belt, so I don't have room for a potions belt too."

"Why can't you just try something before you immediately begin changing it?"

"I dunno. It's my nature, I guess. But it will work."

Shemway smiled. "You willing to bet your life on it?"

"Sure...wait...you mean that figuratively, right?"

"I mean it how I'm saying it. You willing to bet your life on it?"

Jason shrugged. "I guess so."

"Then here. Take this. Consider it an early birthday gift."

Jason opened the package, his face spreading into a wide grin. "Are you serious? Shemway, this is awesome."

"Yes, my boy," Shemway said with a smile.

"You got me actual Thieftian garb."

"That is as authentic as it gets. Endued with Blundin Fungus to make you as silent as death; dyed in the Potion of the Mother Night so it bleeds Liquid Darkness, allowing you to blend into the shadows; and infused with a Potion of Liquid Fall, slowing you down if you ever trip over a cliff. Two thousand millennia of Thieftian minds have made this garb what it is today—so don't go trying to improve upon it."

"Shemway, this is...I mean to say...thank you."

"And, after we close up the shop for the day, you'll have a chance to test it out."

"Wow...wait...what's this," Jason said, his fingers finding a small piece of paper. "This is an invoice. Are you charging me for this? You said it was an early birthday present."

"Everyone knows the best birthday gifts are the ones you pay for yourself. Besides, you don't have to pay...I'll just dock it from your wages."

"Oh, thanks," Jason grumbled.

***

"Ok, jump," Shemway said, his voice full of amusement.

"Jump?" Jason questioned.

"Yes, jump."

"I'm not so sure that's the best idea...."

"Just jump."

Shemway and Jason had rented a small two-person ship for the evening. It was a simple vessel with only one sail between them. At the rear of the ship were a few levers that controlled elevation and pitch. Shemway operated the vessel with a shaky hand, shooting them away from Valenburg and towards the largest mountain on the island.

Jason loved the trip over to the mountain, his hair blowing in the wind. For the first time, he was able to see the whole of Valenburg, which was an impressive sight. There were several other smaller cities in the distance, but nothing compared to the capital.

Then Shemway parked next to a sheer rock face, smiled, and told Jason to jump.

The Dwarf looked down. It was easily a two-hundred-foot drop, but it could even be more than that, as he was never good at judging distances from this high up. Suddenly, his Thieftian clothing seemed entirely inadequate for the situation. With a good set of Dwarf Tines, he could survive any fall. It would be painful and likely damage his armor, but he would survive. Thieftian garb was cool and all, but it felt like a regular set of clothing.

"You want me just to jump? And then what?"

"Then shoot your Crossbow into the rock above and swing along the face of the cliff. If you shoot it right, you should be able to run along the cliff and gain momentum, which will give you time to shoot your Crossbow into the next location."

"I don't know if I've ever told you this, but I'm scared of heights."

"No use being scared of heights," Shemway said with a handsome grin. "It's the impact with the ground you should be scared of. Listen, my friend, if you want me to train you in the Thieftian art, you will have to do it as we do it. I made my first Crossbow when I was twelve. The next day, my father took me to the Cliffs of Insanity to test it out."

"Twelve?"

"I was a late bloomer."

"And what happens if I miss?"

"You fall."

"Yeah, I know that part."

"At this height, you will have a few seconds to retract your Crossbow and try another shot. If that one fails, you'll have to default to your Wind potions. Pull one out from your fancy wrist bandoliers and let one drop. It will fall faster than you will, trust me. Once it ruptures, it will slow your fall until it's like you've jumped off something a few feet from the ground."

"Won't my Thieftian clothes stop me from falling?"

"Your Thieftian clothes are called a Shin Hon. It will slow you down, but you'll still break bones upon landing. I don't recommend it. Your Crossbow is attached to a cord that is tied around your waist. So if it leaves your grip, reach for the cord at your side instead of trying to chase around the device. Now, you remember how to operate your Crossbow?"

"Yeah," Jason said, pointing at a few of the buttons. "This one shoots the needle; this button retracts it quickly; this one retracts it slowly; and this one detaches the arrow."

"You're forgetting one," Shemway said as he stepped closer.

"That's all of them," Jason laughed.

Then the Thieftian pushed Jason over the edge. "It's the one that makes you jump." He laughed to himself, relishing in the family joke. It was so much funnier being the one to say it than the one hearing it.

Jason's body tumbled through the air, his lungs tightening like steel cords. He pointed his Crossbow and fired, hoping that it would land true. It did strike something far above, slowing his fall. Unfortunately for Shemway, the thing that Jason shot was the vessel that they had been riding in.

The sudden weight shift sent the ship pitching towards the cliff face. Before Shemway knew what was happening, he was thrown over the side. He was quick to react, retrieving his Crossbow and firing, hitting a rock cluster high above.

Shemway spotted Jason, who was holding his Crossbow like it was a life preserver and he was on a sinking ship.

He lowered himself until he was even with the Dwarf. "You've lost your momentum. Number ten of the Thieftian Code—always keep your momentum, especially when you are on the Crossbow. Since you shot straight up, you lost all of your kinetic energy when you stopped. You will need to detach and anchor somewhere else that has more of an angle. If you lose your momentum, your enemy will pick you off as easily as one swats a fly."

"You pushed me," Jason accused.

"I told you to jump at first, but when you didn't, I had assumed you had forgotten how."

"Why don't Thieftians use two Crossbows," Jason said. "That way, you can swing from one to the next."

"It would make you too dependent on them. You need your other hand to hold a weapon or potion. If you trained with two, you would forever need two."

"So," Jason said. "Now that I'm stuck hanging here, what do I do?"

"You will need to regain your momentum. Pull out a Gale Potion from your fancy bandolier. Then hold it in your palm and point it in the oppositive direction you want to go. When ready, crush the vial, or I guess in your case, you're going to have to activate the Strength Rune you inscribed on it."

Jason obeyed, pointing away from the rock face.

"Wait…don't point it that way…," Shemway began.

But the correction came too late and Jason ruptured the vial, shooting him directly towards the rock face. The Dwarf bounced twice off the rock face before he swung back to his starting position, a little more dazed than before.

"When ruptured, the Gale Potion will do just that, provide a sudden burst of air. Your Shin Hon will absorb that wind and translate it into momentum. But you never want to shoot yourself into something solid, like a cliff. Use the potion to gain elevation, which will give you a few seconds to shoot and readjust the Crossbow. Then at the apex of your swing, you will have a second to detach and reshoot your Crossbow."

"Ok," Jason said, replaying the information in his head. He briefly went over the buttons on the Crossbow before finally nodding. "Here we go then." He pulled out a second vial, this time pointing it straight down. With a word, he activated it and was shot into the air. He detached the Crossbow and fired again, anchoring himself to a rock ledge not far above him. As he fell, the cord of the Crossbow tightened, suddenly sending him whipping forward in a wide arc. He briefly had to run along the rock to prevent himself from being torn to pieces. Then he fired again, this time aiming a little better. His momentum translated into the swing perfectly, making it seem like a seamless operation.

"That's it," Shemway shouted. He then went after the Dwarf, using two potions to rocket him through the air. He swung past the Dwarf in a perfect mix of agility and speed. "Now begin to gain altitude!"

"*Altitude*," Jason thought to himself. "*All I'm trying to do is stay alive.*" But after a few more swings, he began to obey, focusing on gaining height at the end of each swing. There was a learning curve, as Jason's body quickly found out. More than once, his body was sent spinning against the rockface. But the Shin Hon seemed designed specifically to protect against this sort of abuse, and each time he emerged terrified but unscathed.

As the minutes gave way to hours, the times Jason slammed into a rock outcropping diminished. Soon, he was racing Shemway across the mountainside. By the time the two of them returned to the ship, Jason was seething for breath. Even Shemway was a little winded.

Jason slapped the Thieftian on the back. "That was awesome."

Shemway looked ruthfully at the dirt print on his shoulder. "Yes…truly invigorating. After a few training days like this one, you almost might not be terrible."

Chapter 15

The Order of BlackCreed

Nickle almost did not go through with his plans. Locke's warnings of the Scathian training echoed in his ears, putting pause in his mind about the use of the Plain of the Mind. But then Sharlindrian had returned that night, giving everyone a debrief of what she had found in the Muller's estate. Her final words reverberated in his mind long after. "They aren't just collecting old relics of the past, they're actively preparing for the return of Kara'Kala."

The conversation had then evolved into the need for group training, something that they had not done since the Dark Arena. Sharlindrian quickly took charge, much to the chagrin of Jason. They soon decided to start waking up even earlier each day and training for an hour.

Nickle spoke little the rest of the night, pretending to study his big book on blacksmithing. But in truth, his mind was far from how to quench a blade and endue it with Runic magic.

After conversation and studying died, everyone retired rather early, due in no doubt to their new schedule.

Jason was the last to leave, giving his friend a supportive squeeze on the shoulder. "Don't stay up all night."

"Yeah, I'm just going to finish this chapter," Nickle answered. He then sat there for an hour, building up his courage, waiting for the noise in the shop to die down. The fire slowly disappeared before he placed a few Blaze Runes inside the hearth.

Nickle took out the Plain of the Mind. It was oddly warm. Then he took one last breath before he put it to his temple. Then the world around him disappeared as he was pulled into a distant memory. It was so real, Nickle looked at his hands, trying to separate reality from memory, but they seemed indistinguishable. He was taller, much taller than normal. His build broad but less muscular and scarred than he would have guessed.

"*I'm in Locke's body,*" Nickle thought. "*Just as he was over two hundred years ago—unscarred and untested.*" Of course, this had been the plan all along, but he was still surprised that it had worked.

"Pick up the pace," said a large man with a grizzly beard who was leading the pack. "If you don't make it to the top of the Lonely Spire before the storm sets in, your body will freeze in the cold."

Nickle was walking on a narrow path that crested the top of a mountain. To either side of him were sheer cliffs. A fall from this height would mean certain death. In front and behind him were dozens of other Initiates, all of whom were wearing thin black shirts and pants. He worked his body hard, pushing through the cold. An artic wind whipped by, stealing his breath. The cold was so overwhelming at first, he could only wheeze in and out with quick breaths.

"Your mind is the key to staying warm," the large man continued. "If you can't stop your fingers from getting frostbitten, you will never be a Scathian. Pull your heat to your body's core—rely on your training."

Nickle obeyed without thinking, feeling a flush of warmth through his body. He recalled Locke's lessons, focusing his mind on generating heat in his body. He pushed aside all emotions, pushed aside the pain in his lungs, the frost developing on his fingers.

"Give up now," the man continued. "And we will give you blankets; we will give you food. Give up now and you will survive. We have fires burning a little way down the trail. Give in and you will be filled with warm drink and food."

No one took the man up on his offer—at least for the next half mile. But slowly, the cracks in the resolve of several of the warriors began to appear. The signs of it were easy to spot. Uncontrolled shaking against the cold. A slight hesitation between taking the next step. Eyes down and on the path rather than looking forward.

Soon two hundred Initiates became one hundred and then ninety. Two hours later, by the time they reached the peak of the mountain, there were only seventy left. They were all tough men and women, those who would not be broken by the freezing air.

"I am R'Lung, Supereon of the Order of the BlackCreed Faction," said a tall woman, her face shrouded in a metal mask. "This process is meant to separate the weak of mind from the strong, the fragile of spirit from the bold, the clumsy from the talented. Survive on this peak and earn your First Stripe. If you see me again, I shall be your sister."

"Form a circle," one of the other Scathians said to the Initiates.

There was a scrambling of movement as everyone hustled to obey. Occasionally, Nickle's concentration would break, allowing the cold to seep into his body and penetrate his chest. He forced it out, clinging to the calm his mind so desperately needed.

Only one Scathian remained with the Initiates that night. She was a tall woman, one that had barely spoken since they set foot on the mountain peak. She used magic to start a small fire, one that was fueled by a pile of freshly cut wood nearby. The yellow flames looked so tempting, so tantalizing. The fire represented warmth—warmth that could be used to heat their bodies while their minds rested.

The test was easy enough to figure out: leave the circle and join the Scathian at the fire, and forfeit your chance to join the Order. For the first three hours, no one moved, each one concentrating with all their mental power to prevent their bodies from hypothermia. They had all been trained in the cognitive techniques necessary to survive; otherwise, they would not have been selected. They had all been sharp students, handpicked from the best academies. But it was not so much their talent being tested as it was their will.

Finally, a burly Initiate with a broad chest stood, his hands frozen to the front of his chest, and joined the Scathian at the fire. He was promptly rewarded with a blanket and warm food. Seeing this, four more Initiates left the circle and joined their companion. Slowly, the numbers dwindled until only fifty of the toughest remained.

It was more difficult than Nickle would have ever imagined. He initially thought that Locke was overexaggerating the Ten Trials, that Locke simply wanted to save Nickle a few bruised knees. But the Scathian had not been using hyperbole—this challenge was designed to shape minds, but it also had the real possibility of breaking them first.

He had to maintain an absolute focus; otherwise, his body would begin freezing within seconds. He shoved everything else in his mind far into the distance. The Isles of Balinbar; the Assassin of the Midnight; the Prince and Princess; his friends. All of it became as distant as the mountain peaks all around him.

As the night progressed, his resolve deepened. He would not die here, and he would not succumb to the lure of the flames.

When the sun began to rise, the warmth seemed so foreign to him, like elements from a former life. It gained in height, cascading the mountain range in a beautiful sight. The Dwarf might have cried, but his eyes were too dry to shed tears.

As the sun became completely visible, the woman sitting at the campfire stood, approaching the Initiates that remained. She patted each one on the shoulder, affording a quick smile. "Rise, my brothers and sisters, for you, are not Initiates anymore, but Disciples to our order. Rise, and bask in the light, for it is a new day, and you have earned your First Stripe."

Nickle slowly stood, his eyes taking in the scene all around him. There were only forty-five of them left—each one appeared as solid as stone. The Dwarf felt a slight burning on his left forearm, and he glanced down. A black line magically began appearing on his skin.

"You have passed the First Trial," the woman continued. "But you still have nine more. Before you are sent into the next four trials, you must take upon the Oath of the Unbound. You must swear to be unbound by the taste of food, water, or sleep. Break your Oath before you complete the Fifth Trial, and you will no longer be a Disciple."

The woman went to each Disciple, letting them spill the Oath. Finally, it was Nickle's turn. Somehow, either by hearing the others or just intuition, he knew what he needed to say. "By my Honor, I will not eat, drink, or sleep, until I overcome the Fifth Trial or am consumed by it."

"Good," the woman answered. "Grab your swords from the wooden chests by my campfire. Now your training really begins… Nickle…Nickle."

The Dwarf stirred, shaking his head as if pulled from a daydream.

Evalee stood before him, her sweet smile lighting up the room. "Nickle, it's time to train." He was back in the shop's basement in precisely the same position he had been in before.

Nickle shook his head again. "Train? Why are we training in the middle of the night?"

"It's not the middle of the night, it's early morning. Please tell me you got some sleep."

"Yeah," Nickle answered, looking around him as he did. He could see Jason padding up in his Dark Elf armor. Sharlindrian was sheathing a sword. "I got…loads of sleep. I'm good."

She gave him an encouraging smile before heading off to dress in her own armor.

Nickle swallowed, surprised at the reality before him. He was so lost in Locke's memories, it took him a while to adjust to the temperature and lighting of the room. Then he happened to glance down, a slight itch running across his hand. A black mark now crossed his forearm, just as it had while in Locke's memory. It was the First Stripe of the Scathians—the mark that he was now a Disciple.

"What's taking you so long?" Evalee asked as she adjusted her armor.

Nickle's eyes snapped up. "Nothing."

The High Faerie stepped closer and lowered her voice. "You better gear up. Sharlie is not in a great mood today, and I'm pretty sure she's going to put us to task."

"I wouldn't expect anything less."

Chapter 16

The Land of Ash

Nickle had Vicinerated to this spot many times before. It's where he went when he needed to clear his mind and renew his focus. He had just endured a long day of training, Court, stuffing dead animals, and training again—this time with the Scathians. So, he was hoping to get at least a few moments of peace and quiet. But that is not what he found. The land was changing—and it was happening far too quickly.

He looked over the edge of a massive cliff, his back to the lush green valley of the Land of the Beasts. His eyes were set on the grey sand before him, which slithered and turned like waves of living serpents. But he knew that was far from the truth. The Blight was absent of all life—devoid of all magic. And yet it moved, creeping over the land, consuming trees, mountains, rivers, lakes. All was choked out as the grey tide progressed. To touch it for too long meant death, as it would strip away a person's magical powers, strength, and eventually soul.

While he was attending Harbordeen, he had visited this very place. This was the location where he had chased down a Snipe with a group of Cennarians and convinced it to take its medicine. Now it was nothing but a wasteland. The Blight had progressed even more than he had first feared it would, and besides the Cennarians, few even talked about it. Those who did were labeled "alarmists" and were censored from public discourse. The problem was so great, no one seemed willing to acknowledge it even existed. And so, the officials of EarthWorks went about solving manageable problems, such as food or Lightning shortages, or congestion in public transportation systems.

He had come here to get away, to breathe the fresh air that was so abundant in the Land of the Beasts, but seeing the land now—seeing how far the Blight had progressed—removed all hope of finding solace. Even now, the Blight was halfway up the steep mountainside upon which he stood.

An intense curiosity hit him as he stared at the land below. *"What is causing the Blight? Is it something that is happening naturally, or is some magical race doing something that is causing it to spread?"*

He locked his eyes on the border of the grey ash and Vicinerated to that location. He was overcome by the lack of feeling—the sheer void of the land before him.

The ash suddenly shifted towards him, sensing his magical presence, like a moth drawn to a beacon of light. Limbs began to appear, forming from the decay and rot of things left behind, reaching out for the Dwarf, pulling at the power that wafted from his body. Even standing this close could be fatal for some. He remembered clearly how Evalee had Vicinerated to the edge of the Blight to warn Nickle. She was only able to utter two words before losing consciousness.

A grey tentacle reached beyond the borders, inching its way closer to the Dwarf. Nickle sliced it in two with his axe. It fell to the ground and reformed into three more evil appendages that pursued him.

"There has to be a way to solve this," Nickle said in a whisper. He reached out, his right-hand drawing closer to the Blight. He hesitated for a second, pulling his fingers back. But then his hesitation gave way to resolve, and he touched the Blight. As skin contacted ash, his mind was transported somewhere else.

It was dark, even for him. His wrists were in pain—horrible burning pain that pulsed up his body in waves. He looked down, half expecting to see the Blight covering his skin. But instead, he noticed his hands were red. He was a Demon. He was Kara'Kala. He was shackled with fiery chains around his wrists, stomach, and legs.

Somehow, he instinctively knew these chains would not be able to hold him for long. He pushed with his tremendous power, fighting against the restraints. It sent pure agony up his body—but he ignored it as if the pain was not new to him. He pushed harder.

"He's resisting!" shouted a voice from outside the darkness. Nickle knew that voice. It was Hector Brannon.

Then he realized he was in a cell of some sort—one that was being transported. Memories came back to him—the battle of the

Three Stones, facing off with the Masters of Magic, the betrayal of Chemos—his once most faithful friend.

A wave of magic was sent inside the cell, increasing the power of the restraints and forcing a nauseating pain up his spine. A foul rage climbed up his body and manifested itself in an unearthly growl. He gave in to the hate and rage, allowing it to give him more strength. One of the cuffs was about to snap—he could feel it, feel his power overcoming the device.

"Tiberian," Hector said from outside the small cell. "I need your help. Stop fiddling with that thing and lend me your power!"

"I'm here," Tiberian replied.

A new wave of magic reinforced the restraints. The pain was so sharp that Nickle stopped resisting.

"Put it down," McDooble said. "That should work. Is the FireWall ready to be erected?" The cell was dropped hard, and Nickle hit his head on the Rune enhanced metal above. Instead of injuring his head, the containment cell was dented by his horns.

"I was working on it when Hector called me over," Tiberian grumbled.

"I'll keep him contained, but hurry," McDooble said quickly. "Even as he is, even like this, I can't hold him for long. Get that FireWall working!"

There was frantic movement outside the cell, more voices joined the mix. It seemed to be a coalition of all magical creatures. Minutes ticked by, and Nickle continued to test his restraints. Once or twice, he almost broke free. The more time that passed, the more the rage coiled in his heart like a serpent. He wasted no words and instead turned inward, focusing on harnessing all of his power.

"Hurry!" McDooble yelled.

"Just a minute," Tiberian said, his usual playful tone gone. "Almost done. Are the Wailers in position? I can get the spell started, but unless they can maintain it, it won't be long before it comes crashing down."

"They're in place!" said a distant voice.

"By the Ears of Ivishdor, I hope this works," Tiberian answered.

Then Nickle felt something twist inside his stomach, a wrenching pain that washed over him in inconsistent tides. He could sense a great magic being summoned—a massive wall of flames rising from the Earth in such a scale and size as never had been seen before. The magic required for such a spell was unfathomable, as thousands of voices rang out in harmony, summoning an impenetrable prison. It burned upwards and formed into a massive wall, reaching the ceiling far above, spreading out from there. It was suffocating. His breaths were shortened to infrequent and desperate gasps. He tried to revert to his Human form, as the flames would not affect him as badly then. But the cursed shackles around his legs and wrists prevented the change.

"No!" Nickle screamed. He could feel the weight of the trap he was in, feel all hope fleeing. He would only have one chance to escape, and it would require all the strength he still possessed.

"Get ready!" Hector yelled. "I'm opening up the box."

Then light began to pour in as the four walls of his cell began to peel back, removed by a mix of Transformation and Mystic magic.

"Steady," Tiberian said.

As he was able to see more, he realized he was in a larger, more permanent cell made from Asminian stone that was reinforced by Fire Runes. Surrounding him were the Masters of Magic and several of their Disciples, their hands raised in defense. His eyes darted around the room, catching sight of a door only ten feet to his left. If he did not make it out that door, all hope was lost. He closed his eyes and held still, saving all his strength for one final effort.

"Sharon, remove his shackles one by one and replace them with his permanent restraints," McDooble cried.

A Disciple stepped forward quickly, obeying her Master's command. Nickle could sense the pure terror in the young wizard's emotions. "*She should be afraid,*" Nickle thought.

As soon as the first shackle was free, Nickle's eyes opened, and he pushed out, sending an explosive wave of Mystic energy, driving all those in the small room against the walls. It was so sudden and powerful that the others were completely caught off guard. He used his freed hand to attack the shackle on his left arm. It seared his flesh with unrelenting pain, but he ripped it free, growling as he did. Next, he broke open a chain around his right leg and began working on his final restraint.

But he had not moved quickly enough.

His enemies finally regained their wits and attacked, crushing him with one burning spell after another. He fought on, his iron will pushing him through the agony. He made for the door but was stopped short as Chemos pushed in, his two swords in hand. The Demon Lord was stabbed twice before he lashed out with a claw, leaving a horrific wound on his once friend's face. The wound went from Chemos' right ear to his left eye, traveling in a wicked and bloody "L." The scar would remain for the rest of the man's days, despite all the Healer's attempts to make it fade.

But then a thick chain was locked around his legs, another on an arm. This sent flames ripping through his blood and forced him to a knee. His breath came up short. He was choking, his lungs burning for air. As he tried to take a deep breath, another shackle was added to his body, and then another. Soon he appeared more metal than beast. The chains pulled him to the ground, each one leaching the strength from his body.

"No!" Nickle yelled. "Release me...or I will end you all."

A large shackle was placed around his waist, completely seizing up his lungs.

"It's finished," Hector said, favoring his right arm. "Everyone out."

The rest obeyed, filing out, leaving Hector alone with the Demon. He stepped closer, a look of pity in his eyes.

"You and I...know...," Nickle said, forcing the words from his lethargic mouth. "You can't...maintain this prison...you waste too much of your magic." He roared, unable to deal with the pain that ripped through his body.

"You're right, my son, as always. Even now, your mind still impresses me. I have failed you, and now you must pay the price."

"I...will return...," Nickle said. "I will...destroy everything."

"Yes...," Hector said, his voice falling low. "And that is why I must take one last thing from you."

***

Nickle pulled back, his brow beaded with sweat. He was no

longer a Demon, no longer seeing the world from Kara'Kala's eyes. He was once again a Dwarf at the edge of the Blight. His energy slipped from him, and he fell to a knee. Where he had touched the dying land, life began to reappear, pushing away the dead ash. It spread like a ripple across a pond, changing the grey back into green grass, rocks, and bushes. It spread for ten feet before it stalled and stopped. It stayed that way for a few seconds, a portion of the land once again reclaimed, but then it started to be absorbed again by the flowing ash.

Seeing the land dying right before his very eyes made Nickle feel sick. He placed a hand over his stomach and stepped back. He tried to Vicinerate, but the Blight had taken too much from him. He stumbled away, walking twenty feet before doubling over and vomiting. He was so exhausted—beyond exhausted.

"That was a bad idea," Nickle whispered to himself. He found his feet again and pushed on, trying to get as much distance from the cursed land as possible. The further he walked, the more his strength slowly returned. Within an hour, he was able to Vicinerate back to Valenburg. He raided the downstairs fridge, throwing open the doors like he was trying to free a prisoner. He reached passed the Artic Runes that kept it cold and grabbed a goat skin full of water. He put the bladder against his head, enjoying the cooling waves on his skin.

"My goodness," Sharlindrian said from a couch. "What happened to you?"

Nickle turned around, surprised he was not alone. He was a mess of sweat and dirt, his cheeks stained with ash. "Oh, I'm sorry. I was hoping no one was awake right now."

"They won't be for much longer if you keep up that noise," Sharlindrian said in a good-natured gest. "What's wrong? You look like you just fought off a poltergeist. What have you been doing?"

Nickle looked at the water flask, tempted to take a drink, but he pushed the urge down and instead turned to the Elf. "I...well....I mean to say...." He struggled to speak for a few more seconds before she cut him off.

"Fine," Sharlindrian said. "Keep your secrets, but I can't help you if you don't tell me what they are."

"What's all this?" Nickle asked, hoping to change the subject.

"Classic Nickle," Sharlindrian said. "Always looking to get everyone else in the room to talk more than him."

Nickle collapsed into a seat next to Sharlindrian, his eyes scanning all the articles she had spread over the coffee table. "What is this? These are all about the Vampire Queen."

"A little research project is all," Sharlindrian answered. "When I was…a MeithDwin, I knew all the wealthy and powerful Elf families. If I did not know an Elf's name, I at least knew them by reputation. But it's odd. I know I don't run in those circles anymore, but I thought I would have at least heard a rumor or two about who Ethilian really is. Where did this incredibly powerful Elf come from? How come no one seems to know? It seems all the information about her has been scrubbed from the history books. I've been down to the Library, and besides recent articles, there is nothing about her."

"Perhaps it's best not knowing," Nickle answered simply.

"You are so cryptic sometimes," Sharlindrian said with a laugh. "What is that supposed to mean?"

Nickle frowned. His body was exhausted. His mind ached for sleep, but he knew he could not give in. He turned to his friend, his eyes distant. It was at that moment that he decided that he would not tell Sharlindrian about Ethilian—at least not now. *"It would do nothing but give her pain, and she's had enough of that already,"* Nickle thought.

He smiled, realizing that his friend had asked him a question and he had yet to answer. "If you knew all about your enemy—knew their struggles, their hopes, their dreams, it might be that much harder to face them."

"I never thought about it that way," Sharlindrian said.

"I'm just saying that sometimes, the past might be better left in the past."

Chapter 17

Race to the Big Leagues

Swiftrunner stretched his hindquarters, his face the image of concentration. He had been in the Mid Leagues for several weeks now, his reputation and skill increasing every day. His climb for position and prestige had been nothing short of incredible. It usually took months for someone to get an opportunity at the Big Leagues, but here he was, surrounded by thirty hopeful Satyrs, most of whom he had never seen or met before.

They were standing on the highest hill in the city of Valenburg, just south of the Palace grounds. Before them, among cobblestone roads, lay thousands of houses and shops, each one a possible destination for their letters and packages. All he had to do now was place in one of the top five spots. Then it would be official—he would be an Elite Letter Runner, charged with delivering the most important packages to or from the Palace.

He felt a prod to his shoulder. He turned, annoyed by the interruption to his routine. There was a Satyr before him that was beyond beautiful. Her face was a mix of makeup and mystery. Out of her long, flowing brown hair protruded two perfectly shaped horns.

For a few seconds, he completely forgot what he was doing, his mouth dropping ever so slightly. Then he finally spoke. "Did you...umm...need something, darling?"

"Yes," she said sweetly. "I need you to lose."

"Not likely."

"Oh, it is more than just likely—it's inevitable," the Satyr replied. At these words, the rest began to gather around, their chins taut, their eyes narrowed. Apparently, Swiftrunner's reputation had not endeared him to any Satyrs. A few of them made soft "maaa" sounds, like a herd of goats circling up to protect themselves from wolves.

"You tell him, Liliana. This is our turf."

"You see," continued the Satyr. "For the last several decades, Elite Letter Runners have always been Satyrs. Through our efforts, the people of Valenburg receive their most important packages."

"There can't be any harm in one little Cennarian joining your ranks," Swiftrunner said with his country accent.

"One...no," Liliana said sweetly. "But if you dominate the race today, it will draw in more. Soon one will become two, two will become four, four will become...twenty-four."

"I'm not sure you did the math right on that last one."

"This is my point, horseman," Liliana said, jabbing Swiftrunner in the chest several more times. "We cannot let you win. It would jeopardize hundreds if not thousands of Satyrs' livelihoods. People will start looking for Cennarians to deliver the mail. That can't happen."

"Listen," Swiftrunner answered. "I enjoy this job, but I won't be here long. I'm just on a work release. Even if I make it to the Big Leagues, I won't be there for more than a few months."

"You are not listening," Liliana said. "You cannot be allowed to win—you shouldn't even have made it past the Mid-League. You were up against some of the fastest Satyrs."

"And I beat them fair and square," Swiftrunner said.

"Yes, you did, but it was mostly luck. So, don't get prideful, lest your luck disappears. Accidents have been known to happen on the streets of Valenburg to those who are not lucky."

"Accidents?"

"Walk away now, and we'll let you stay in the Mid-Leagues. You'll make decent money, and we'll leave you alone."

"But you aren't the one who decides who competes in the Leagues," Swiftrunner challenged. "Those decisions are made by Valenburg officials."

"You won't be competing in any league if you end up with two broken legs."

Swiftrunner pulled his head back, unsure if he had heard the Satyr correctly. She was so intense that the Cennarian had no doubt she meant business. He might have even walked away right then and there had he not had a mission to accomplish. And his friends were depending on him. This thought strengthened his resolve.

He turned away and stepped up to his position on the starting line, his eyes narrowed as if he was looking into the sun.

"So be it, you arrogant Cennarian," Liliana said.

As the Satyrs joined Swiftrunner on the starting line, a Valkyrie woman appeared, her face flushed red from exertion. She was quite a bit different from the other winged warriors Swiftrunner had seen in the past. She was completely out of shape, a small paunch evident as it hung over her belt. A Valkyrie would have never been allowed to deliver the mail, as that would be seen as being beneath them, but apparently, they could be in charge of the people who did.

"I am one of the deciding officials for today's competition. Each of you will be given a series of letters for delivery. All of them will be marked with the same addresses in the same order, but that doesn't mean you all need to take the same paths. There are two important elements in this race: speed and accuracy. The first five to deliver all seven letters and cross the finish line at the docks will be allowed to join the Big Leagues."

While she spoke, a Human handed out seven letters to each contestant. Most Satyrs put the letters in a little leather fanny pack while Swiftrunner stowed his in a Cennarian Shoulder Satchel. Jason had called it a purse at one point, but that was ridiculous. Besides being roughly the same size and shape as a purse and having one shoulder strap, it looked nothing like a purse.

Swiftrunner glanced at the two Satyrs next to him; one of which had a set of ram horns. They smiled at him mischievously, as if he was the butt of a private joke.

"May you be accompanied by speed and endurance," the Valkyrie said. Then there was a loud bang, and they were off, sprinting down the road in a flash. Satyrs had a tremendous acceleration, far better than any other land creature. A dozen Satyrs pushed for first, each one throwing elbows at their competitors. One unlucky Satyr was clocked in the chin, sending him spinning off to the side into a large trash bin. Swiftrunner glanced back, repressing a laugh as two goat legs poked out the top, wildly kicking in the air.

The Satyrs were also incredibly agile, running up the sides of walls and leaping over obstacles with ease. Their hooves made a tremendous sound as they clattered down the cobblestone, seemingly warning all those further down the street of the wave of creatures approaching.

This went on for four blocks, then five. All the while, Swiftrunner kept towards the back of the pack, waiting until the Satyrs fell into a rhythm and pace. Once they did, Swiftrunner made his move, kicking his speed up several notches. This is how he had won all of the courier races before, finding a rhythm at the beginning of the race and making sure he stayed in first. He had always been fast, even among the Cennarians. It had been his endurance that always suffered, but thanks to Atlantia, that was no longer a problem.

By the tenth street, he was in the lead, just like all the other races. But then he heard an odd noise. A flute mixed with the sound of the wind cut through the air. As soon as it did, a root erupted from the ground, temporarily snagging the Cennarian around the rear leg. Swiftrunner fought against the root, kicking free a second later.

While he was distracted, however, three Satyrs passed him, Liliana in the lead.

"Stay in the back, Cennarian," Liliana screamed. "This is not your race!"

This encouraged Swiftrunner all the more. "All right. Time to stop playing." His body regained its speed quickly, and soon he was nipping at the heels of the leading Satyrs.

"He's back," one of the goat men called.

Liliana glanced back and frowned, surprised by how quickly the Cennarian recovered. From a pocket, she pulled out a whistle and put it to her lips.

Swiftrunner had heard about this kind of magic; he had even seen it on an occasion or two. Satyrs were known to have a talent at Musification—the power to control nature with music. Specifically, music that was created by wooden flutes. But he had never seen anyone use it so proficiently. Nature was challenging to control in the best of times, and usually, spells like this were unpredictable and wild.

Liliana winked before blowing three sweet notes. Again, a root burst from the cobblestone and reached for Swiftrunner's legs. This time, however, the Cennarian was ready and leaped to the side, barely dodging the finger-like appendages.

The other two Satyrs mimicked Liliana, pulling out flutes from their leather fanny packs. They played different notes, but they had a similar effect.

Roots began to explode from the ground like mines, forcing

the Cennarian to twist and turn in multiple directions, dramatically slowing him down. But the magic seemed to take its toll on the leading three Satyrs, forcing their movements to slow as they had to increase their concentration on the notes they played. This gave the rest of the Satyrs a chance to catch up, all of whom were bearing flutes and looking at the Cennarian like he was responsible for canceling Christmas.

Music came at him from all different angles, forcing dozens of roots from the ground. He was dodging them pretty effectively until he ran right into a pigeon-drawn carriage. His sudden stop made him a perfect target for the roots, which began wrapping around him like boa constrictors. Satyrs encircled him, using their wooden flutes to great effect. Soon, he looked more like a massive plant than anything else.

The Satyrs all slowed, impressed by their handy work, giving each other hoof stomps.

Liliana approached slowly, a devious smile on her lips. Swiftrunner could barely see her through a crack in the roots. "As I told you before, Cennarian. This race belongs to the Satyrs."

With that, she took off, heading down the road with her pack of Satyrs.

"She's crazy," Swiftrunner said. He briefly struggled against the roots, breaking a few of them as he did. At that pace, he could fight his way through, but it would take several minutes.

"But if she's allowed to use magic, so can I," Swiftrunner said. He then used Transformation magic, turning himself into a tree and then into a massive cat and then back into a tree. The change in size snapped the roots in a flurry.

Once again, he was back on the road—far behind the others. He was able to deliver his first letter and then his second without any complications. By the third drop-off, he was finally catching back up to the rest of the Satyrs. They were running at a much slower pace, their energy all but depleted. This part of the race came down to endurance—something that Swiftrunner had an infinite supply of.

As the Cennarian passed the Satyr in last place, the goat bleated out a warning to the others. "He's back! The four legs is back!" These few words stole the creature's last bit of strength, and it came to a stop, completely exhausted.

All the others looked back, startled not only to see Swiftrunner, but also to see he was not even winded. Sweat did not trickle down his brow and back like the others. He looked just as fresh as when they had first started.

"Get him!" Liliana commanded.

The music notes returned, but this time, the Satyrs were much too winded to use it effectively. Roots exploded from the ground, but they were not well aimed like before. The Musification seemed to drain their energy, and soon, seven of the remaining fifteen Satyrs were too tired to continue.

Swiftrunner felt his chest begin to burn with unnatural heat as if something had lit his heart on fire. He could win this race. He would win this race. He slowly took the lead, relief flooding over him. But it did not last long.

From the tops of houses, Satyrs by the dozens began to appear, carrying flutes in their hands. These new creatures were not even competing in the race.

"Stop him," Liliana wheezed.

This was all the encouragement the creatures needed. They began to jump from the buildings, shooting down like missiles from the sky. One of the creatures latched onto Swiftrunner's face, refusing to let go. The Cennarian transformed himself into a boulder and rolled right over the creature. It was so seamless, it seemed scripted. Then two more Satyrs leaped down upon him, pulling him in separate directions. A third landed on his back. The Cennarian was strong enough to continue, but his speed was very much diminished.

"Easy now," Swiftrunner said. "Now, this is two wheat buckets shy of being fair. C'mon now. Who is hanging on to my tail?"

One enthusiastic Satyr cranked hard on Swiftrunner's ear, pulling him right into a shop window. Glass shards exploded everywhere as merchandise was kicked up.

Liliana retook the lead, waving a sweet goodbye.

Not long after, Swiftrunner emerged from the shop. Only one Satyr still clung to his back, but Swiftrunner momentarily turned the creature into a pile of mud, something he felt suited the situation. He galloped down the road, the warmth in his chest spreading. It felt like it was ten degrees hotter than when they started. His limbs burned more than they ever had before, but he pushed it down and rode on, his competitors only yards in front of him. At the next turn, Swiftrunner was able to take the lead and deposit his fourth letter. The Satyrs were right behind, shouting out curses and jeers.

"You haven't won yet, four legs!" Liliana cried.

"These people are crazy," Swiftrunner said. He pushed harder, giving himself a comfortable lead. Slowly, the Satyrs fell into the distance, and he let out a sigh of relief. But Liliana's words had him on edge. He nervously glanced down each side of the street, looking for goat-legged cheaters. It was not long before he spotted one far ahead, looking down from a building.

"It's another ambush," Swiftrunner whispered to himself. "These people are more persistent than a couple of horse flies. I've got to take a different route." He knew the streets well, knew that the most direct path lay in front of him. But if he wanted to avoid trouble, he had to take a route the Satyrs were not expecting.

So, he suddenly banked left, riding down a long alley. As he approached a stone wall, he changed his legs to that of a Satyr and leaped over. By the time he landed again, he was back into his original form, galloping out into an open road. As expected, the Satyrs were not there, but the path cost him precious time. He pushed himself to his top speed, barreling past the people of Valenburg. The heat in his body was starting to become unbearable. It felt like he was in the midst of a desert with nothing but the sun above him.

Up ahead, he could see a woman watering her plants with a watering can. Just the sight of it made his tongue feel as dry as sawdust. He grabbed it from the woman's grasp and aimed the spout at his mouth. Trickles of water dripped out from the dozens of holes in the nozzle, teasing more than quenching his thirst. After getting a mouth full of water, he dumped the rest over his head. Steam as thick as a hot shower rose off his body.

"What in tarnation is going on?" Swiftrunner said as he looked at the steam coming off his skin. He did not have time to consider the full implications of what was happening to his body. So he pushed on, saving the thought for later. Before long, he joined back up on the right path just in time to cut off the Satyrs and deposit the fifth letter.

"You slimy four legs!" Liliana said to his back.

He could not help himself. He smiled. For some odd reason, he was starting to like the girl. He mimicked her goodbye wave as he sped off. Before long, he had deposited the sixth letter.

"Yeeha!!" Swiftrunner yelled. "Only one more to go!"

As he galloped, flames began to appear from his hooves, briefly burning patches of ground. The Cennarian was so focused on the road ahead of him, he did not even notice the flames.

He was so far ahead of the other Satyrs that nothing short of an army could ruin his chances. At the seventh letter drop, however, there appeared to be just that—a group of thirty Satyrs, all with clenched fists or flutes.

Swiftrunner slowed down, ducking into an alley behind a small grocery store. As he did, he realized his shirt was on fire. "Dirt devils and dust demons, what is going on here!" He ripped his shirt free and tossed it to the ground where it still burned in earnest. He patted his arms and face, ensuring the rest of him was not in flames. Surprisingly, his skin had not been burned, but his whole body felt as hot as a boiling pot of water. Luckily, his Cennarian Shoulder Satchel survived unscathed.

He glanced around the corner, eyeing the seventh drop. "How can I make it past all of those crazies?" He was still at least a few minutes ahead of the others. "Think, Swiftrunner. You're so close. You can't just give up now." He thought about just charging right in, perhaps even turning himself into a boulder before making contact.

"Wait just a fletching second. I can become a Satyr. Ha! What prairie was my mind wandering in? Hope this works." He messed up his hair with his hands and used the remnants of his charcoaled shirt to give it a darker hue. He looked wild, perhaps even a little unstable. He stepped out from behind cover, his lower body now that of a much chubbier Satyr.

Compacting his entire frame into a much smaller body was difficult, but he made it work. He was still much bigger than your average Satyr, something he had no way of changing, but he felt confident it would not draw as much attention as the fact that he was no longer wearing a shirt.

"I've just got to give them something else to focus on," Swiftrunner said to himself. He then picked up his pace, running towards the group of Satyrs in a panic. "He's coming! The Cennarian is galloping in. Get ready!"

He kept shouting and waving his arms in the air. The closer he got, the more riled up the rest of the Satyrs became. He finally reached the group, and they let him right in.

"What's he wearing?" one of the Satyrs asked.

"A blue shirt, I think," Swiftrunner answered. "I didn't pay attention to that. But he's got brown hair and is strikingly handsome—for a four legs. But be careful, he's got devil tricks like I've never seen before. I think he set my shirt on fire. Best be ready for the incredibly handsome brute. He can't be more than a minute behind me."

And with them looking down the road, Swiftrunner slipped the final letter into the drop box. He should have left it at that, sneaking away and then heading for the finish line. Instead, he pulled out a Dwarf Stylus and began drawing Water Runes on every surface he could. Jason had spent long hours teaching him the correct form, and the effort paid dividends now. He put a few on the cobblestones at the back of the mob, a few more on a light post close by, several more on pillars that ran along the streets. The whole thing took several minutes to complete, but as he did, three Satyrs came around the corner, Liliana in the lead. They had obviously pushed themselves harder than they ever had before, as they were wheezing like a pair of asthmatic cheetahs.

Swiftrunner grinned as he saw them, saying the word of power that activated all of the Water Runes at once. Waves shot out in every direction, sweeping up several of the Satyrs, most of them making goat sounds as they were swept away.

When Liliana looked up, her loyal band of Satyrs were all floating by. A dozen yards in front of them was Swiftrunner, a roguish grin on his face. He had turned back into his Cennarian form and reared up on his hind legs. Then he was off towards the finish line.

She tried to find a second wind in her body, but she was so exhausted, the only thing she could hope to do was maintain her steady pace. By the time she placed her seventh letter in the drop box, Swiftrunner had crossed the finish line, much to the amusement of a crowd of people who were waiting for him.

She crossed the finish line a few minutes later, her hand over a cramp at her side. Swiftrunner was surrounded by a myriad of creatures who all congratulated him, patting him on the back. It seemed that Orcs, Goblins, Circurians, and Humans were all eager to see that it was not a Satyr who had come in first.

"You," Liliana said, her teeth clenched.

Swiftrunner slowly turned around. The air became tense as the noise died all around them.

"Yes," Swiftrunner said, his chin taut. "What about me?"

For a few brief moments, the Cennarian was sure she was about to slap him. Her beautiful features were so tense, her stare could have cracked stone. But then, to everyone's surprise, including her own, she straightened up and kissed him right on the lips.

"Good work, horse boy," she whispered in his ear. "The Satyrs always gather at Billy's Goats after the tryouts for the Big Leagues. Since you're first, you will be the guest of honor. Be there by seven. Bring a friend…if you have any."

Chapter 18

Summer Solstice

"Your story isn't making any sense," Jason said. "This woman tried to kill you, correct?"

"Yes," Swiftrunner answered.

"She sent a swarm of Satyrs after you, correct?"

"Yeah, they jumped all over me and pushed me into a shop. At one point, they had me all wrapped up in roots."

"All that makes sense," Jason said. "They wanted to win. But what doesn't make sense is why we are going to hang out with the people who were willing to cheat just so you couldn't win. What if this is a trap? What if they are going to prank us?"

"That's why you're here," Swiftrunner answered. "If any Dwarf can get us out of a mess, it's you."

"Great, thanks," Jason mumbled.

"And then," Swiftrunner said, only partially listening to his friend. "She kissed me right on the lips. Right in front of everyone."

Swiftrunner had returned to the shop in a daze. He had won. He was now in the Big Leagues. He then told the first person he saw everything about the race. Admittedly, it was not the best story he has ever told, as he kept jumping all over the place and adding obscure details. Regardless, he somehow convinced the Dwarf to go with him to Billy's Goats. They had showered, changed, and were on the road not long after, heading towards the obscure restaurant set in a part of the town dominated by Satyrs.

"Where's Nickle, by the way?" Swiftrunner asked. "I think he'd get a kick out of seeing all of these Satyrs."

"Tell me the part again where your shirt burst into flames," Jason said. "You think that was the Satyrs?"

"No, their magic doesn't work like that. I didn't know at the time, but after thinking about it for a little bit, I think that is the result of Atlantia's blessing."

"You mean curse," Jason said, rubbing the Rune of Power inscribed on his chest. "Every time I use this Rune of Power, it just about cripples me with pain afterwards."

"Yeah, but it's pretty cool you're like super strong for a little bit. You picked up an entire statue like it was a club and smacked the Vampire Queen. I bet she won't forget that anytime soon."

"But then I'm as fragile as a baby. It feels like a thousand red hot needles being shot into my heart."

"Well, at least you don't have a chance to set your shirt on fire."

"True."

They stopped before a decent-sized building that had the words "Billy's Goats" in big vibrant letters written across the front, which sharply contrasted with most of the buildings in Valenburg, as it was against regulation. Loud music wafted to their ears from inside the building.

"Well, I think this is it," Swiftrunner said.

"Very likely."

"We best be riding in before the dinner bell breaks."

"Sure," Jason answered.

The Cennarian took the lead, stepping inside, the Dwarf not far behind. It was packed with Satyrs of all sizes and colors. There was a bar on their right, several tables and booths on their left. At the front was a well-used stage draped with all sorts of Elite Letter Runner Bandoliers, many of which had been signed. A band at the front played a mix of exotic flutes and bass drums.

Only a few noticed the newcomers, but that soon changed as silence fell over everyone that saw them. The silence spread like a disease soon infecting the whole place. Even the band stopped playing, annoyed that the entire audience started to turn away.

"I think…we better leave," Jason whispered.

"Not a bad idea…," Swiftrunner said, slowly inching towards the door.

Then Liliana approached from behind, squeezing the shoulders of the two newcomers. "Oh, don't leave. You've just got here." She pushed them in and waved to the rest of the Satyrs. "It's fine. They're with me." With these words, the noise returned in earnest, everyone refocusing on the conversations they were having.

"Are we safe here?" Swiftrunner asked.

"You're cute, but don't tell me your dramatic," Liliana said. "Let me grab you a table."

"Where?" Jason asked.

She ignored the question and instead led them through the middle of the restaurant and to a booth. It was occupied with five Satyrs, but at a snap of her fingers, it was vacated without another word. One of the Satyrs stayed behind to clean up a few food trays.

"Looks like a booth just opened up," she said sweetly.

Swiftrunner had to readjust his body with Transformation magic to fit. Jason sat next to him, his hands occasionally drifting down to where his Rune belt would typically hang. It was not there, of course, but he could not stop his hands from doing it anyway.

Liliana snapped again, getting the attention of the bartender. She then did some sort of sign language before turning back to Swiftrunner and Jason. "This round is on me."

"Are you like…the owner or something?" Jason asked.

"Owner, operator, financier, and everything in between," Liliana said with a wink. Just then, two more lady Satyrs appeared. One had short, cropped hair that was dyed blue, the other had long blond hair with pink tips. They were both beautiful but preferred dark makeup. Without a word, they squeezed in next to Liliana, who greeted them with a nod.

"Who are these handsome strangers?" one asked with a flirtatious tone.

"This one," Liliana said, nodding to Swiftrunner, "took first in the tryouts for the Big League. First time in over twenty years that it wasn't a Satyr. Oh, what my father would say about that. But he did win fair and square."

Swiftrunner coughed as she said the word, "fair."

Liliana laughed. "Oh, don't let your hooves get chipped. Yeah, there was a little foul play on our part, but you still won in the end. So it made your victory even more rewarding, correct? It made the whole thing so much more exciting. Let me ask you something."

"Let me ask you something first," Swiftrunner said, his jaw set. He was not going to let this Satyr push him around, even if this was her place.

"Go ahead."

Swiftrunner coughed, surprised that his demand was so quickly agreed to. He strained his mind for a question. Luckily, the drinks arrived at the same time.

Jason eagerly took his drink in hand. It looked like a delicious mix of crushed ice and a frothy red liquid accented with several blades of grass. He took a quick swig. It tasted like Sangria mixed with sprite, an odd combination that was balanced out by the bland blades of grass. The Dwarf thought it was ok, but Swiftrunner acted as if he had just discovered how to transport his tongue to heaven. He was so absorbed with the drink, he had forgotten entirely to ask his question.

Finally, Liliana brought him back around to it. "Your question?"

"Yeah," Swiftrunner said, putting the drink down. "Umm…who is Billy?"

The three Satyrs laughed.

"Seriously," Liliana said. "That's your first question?"

The Cennarian shrugged.

"Billy was my father," Liliana said. "For the first ten years of my life, it was just him and I against the world. He always dreamed of starting his own place, one where he could build a refuge from the world. But it was never to be." The Satyr looked at her drink, suddenly emotional. She shook loose some distant memory before continuing. "So after he was gone, I came here, looking for work. And wouldn't you know, I found it as an Elite Letter Runner. I lived like a pauper for five years, saving all of my earnings before I had enough of a down payment for Billy's Goats. Silly name, really, but that was what my father wanted to call it. Now, my turn. How did you win?"

"I've always been fast," Swiftrunner said, taking another drag on his drink. "This drink is fantastic, by the way. Is the recipe a secret?"

"No changing the subject," Liliana said. "I answered your question, now you have to answer mine. How did you win? You must have been in a dead sprint the whole time. I'm one of fastest Satyrs from here to the surface, and I've never, not in my whole life, seen anyone finish the tryouts for the Big Leagues so quickly."

"I'm sure those on the Big Leagues could beat me," Swiftrunner said.

"All of those runners were *from* the Big Leagues," Liliana said. "It's petty, but we couldn't let you win. So, we pitted you against our very best."

"Well, I must have had just a good day," Swiftrunner said, finishing off the brew.

Liliana sat back, folding her arms across her chest. "Keep your secret then."

"So what can I expect in the Big Leagues?" Swiftrunner asked.

"Better pay," Liliana said. "Better assignments."

"Is anyone going to...try and sabotage me?"

"No," Liliana hissed. "You're in the Big Leagues now. No one will mess with you. You might get a few requests for autographs, but that's about it. You're a celebrity of sorts, as most people in Valenburg haven't ever seen a Cennarian before."

They talked for several hours, enjoying the company and the variety of served drinks. Jason bought the next round and Swiftrunner after that. Liliana's friends were much nicer than she was, or at the very least, they were much less intense. Occasionally, Liliana had to step away for a bit, attending to some task or dealing with some problem. But after making the rounds, she would always return. They talked on and on about the internal politics of the city of Valenburg and how certain laws limited the opportunities for Satyrs.

At midnight, Liliana smiled. "You two are in for a treat."

"What's that?"

"Well, every year, the tryouts for the Big League are on the eve of the Summer Solstice, which is the most important holiday to any Satyr. On this day, we remember the past by rebuilding it."

Jason looked to Swiftrunner, but he had no clue what the Satyr was talking about. "How do you celebrate?"

"I can explain it," Liliana said. "But it would ruin the surprise. Come on. Our ride is probably here."

***

It was soon apparent that the Satyrs had no intention of sleeping that night. Swiftrunner and Jason had followed Liliana and all the other Satyrs to three flying frigates parked right next to Billy's Goats. All vessels were supposed to land at the dock, but the Satyrs did not seem too keen on obeying the rules. It took several minutes to load all the Satyrs, but as soon as they did, they headed off, pitching down and away from the Isles of Balinbar.

The cool breeze felt especially chilly as they dived through the clouds and towards the land below.

"Where are we going?" Swiftrunner asked.

"You're impatient, aren't you?" Liliana replied.

It took an hour before they reached their destination, but it did not disappoint. They could not get too close, as a crowd of Satyrs had now congregated around several large and ominous stone pillars.

"This is Stonehenge," Jason said.

"Stonehenge?" Swiftrunner asked. "Isn't that a Piddler location?"

Liliana shook her head. "Piddlers have no idea what this place really is or why it was built. They spend all of their time giving tours through here but have no idea what this place is all about."

"So, what's the purpose?" Jason asked.

Liliana led the way closer to the stones, pulling out a flute from a pocket in her shirt as she did. As they approached, they heard music being played from different parts, each taking on a different melody. At first, the music was a little disjointed like two breezes competing for dominance in the sky, but as more joined in, it became seamless. Jason and Swiftrunner could feel ancient magic at work, one that raised the hairs on the back of their necks and sent a chill through their bodies.

Then a Satyr appeared on the top of one of the tall rocks, his body moving to a lively jig. The Satyr began to play a sweet melody that started to unify all the other flutes, pulling the distinct sounds together into melodic harmony. The music was so infectious that no one could hear it and not be affected by it. Satyrs began to dance, their flutes in hand.

Soon the air itself was sucked into the song, spinning around all the creatures, leaving a trail of leaves and dirt. The water soon joined in, rising from the earth, sometimes taking shapes, sometimes just floating in the air in trails of mist.

When the Earth joined in, a deep bass was added to the song. The dirt beneath their feet began to move, sending rocks rising from the ground into other pillars. Stonehenge did not remain how it was, but instead became what used to be—a banquet hall for the Satyrs and all their kin. Tables sprang up, a roof formed above, and food appeared in such abundance that Jason's eyes went wide. More pillars formed and reached for the sky, creating separate rooms and adjoining halls, all of them centered around the original stone circle. Vines, bushes, and trees grew in seconds, decorating the space in an artful nature.

The music persisted, pulling at the heartstrings of all who heard it. It became a beautiful melody that occasionally took on a surprising tone or cadence. It was a ponderous song, both epic in scale and personal in nature.

"What is this place?" Swiftrunner asked.

Liliana smiled wide. "This is how the world was formed, under the watchful eye of the Satyrs. Once a year, the Earth gives us the power we once all had."

Stonehenge became something beyond scope, beyond measure, becoming more opulent than the fanciest courts in the world.

"And all the food," Jason asked tentatively. "Is it for eating?"

"Just wait," Liliana said, setting her flute back to her lips.

The music turned more frantic, and things happened more quickly, as if they were on a schedule and they were running late. Then in a fantastical moment, the song crescendoed into one final note. All the Satyrs looked up at their creation, a massive building upheld by their efforts. They were tentative at first, making sure that the magic had taken.

A lone Satyr approached, his flute still in hand. He walked up several stairs to the center of Stonehenge and carefully looked around, examining the work. Then he raised his hands in the air, and the crowd of Satyrs exploded into raucous cheers. All civility was put on hold as everyone rushed forward towards the food.

It became a banquet like no other with every food and dessert ever before conceived. Jason quickly got caught up in the moment and ran forward. He first looked for a plate to stack his food on but then quickly realized there were none. He then defaulted to the local customs, which seemed to be to simply eat with your hands.

Jason bit into a massive chocolate cake. It was so delicious he took two more bites in quick succession. Two Satyrs opposite the table were attacking a gigantic turkey leg. He then spotted a mound of chicken wings that were glazed to perfection. Jason made a stop there before continuing down the table to a series of potato wedges with melted cheese. Despite all the Satyrs feasting, the line of food never ended.

"Swiftrunner!" Jason said, looking for his friend. "You've got to try these Beignets!" He had never known what a Beignet was or even heard the word for that matter, but it seemed the magic had provided his mind with the correct term for the dessert. Jason looked around for his friend, surprised that he was not standing right beside him. He finally did spot the Cennarian holding hands with Liliana at the edge of the building. He was laughing at something she said, his eyes locked on hers, as if he could not see the mound of fantastic food beyond them.

"Ugh," Jason said. "Well, I guess that leaves more for me."

Chapter 19

The Eagle's Nest

Jaylyn smiled at Evalee, her face shining in the sun. "Technically, I should be in my art class, but my teacher always insists on painting still lifes. Why paint a bunch of bottles and dead flowers when all of this is happening?" She gestured dramatically to the port in front of her.

"What is this place?" Evalee asked.

"This is the Port of Marseille," Jaylyn answered. "Only the army and those on official business can use it. Isn't this a lot more fun than sitting inside and watching paint dry?"

Nickle was taken aback by the swarm of military ships in and around the port. There were dozens tied to long wooden piers that hung over the edge of the floating island. More still floated higher up in the sky. It was impressive by any measure, even matching the might of the Silver Army. The flying vessels all came in different shapes and sizes, most of them painted white with gold trim.

Nickle and Evalee exchanged a worried look.

"What?" Jaylyn asked.

"This is amazing, but can we be here?" Evalee said in a whisper.

"I'm the Princess, future heir to the Obsidian Throne," Jaylyn said. "No one questions where I go unless my brother is around. He's the only one that would dare tell mother that I was where I wasn't supposed to be. But he's out sick—again."

"Does he get sick a lot?" Nickle asked.

"He claims to be sick all the time," Jaylyn said. "But I doubt he really is. Right now, Yaroslav is supposed to be inspecting the Eagle's Nest, the control tower in the Port of Marseille, but once again, he skips out on his duties."

The lively girl led the way, trailed by Nickle, Evalee, and six Valkyrie bodyguards. Since they were not in the Palace, she had to have three times the guards, and they could not be the standard Palace Guards, but from the Valkyrie Elite. Each one carried a round shield, spear, and falcata sword.

Nickle could not help but stare at the ships. Ever since he saw Dwarf Frigates in EarthWorks, he was amazed by the craftsmanship and ingenuity of the Dwarves. He had thought that there were no finer fighting vessels in the world—that is, until he saw the ships of the Valkyrie. They were large but thinner, built for speed and agility. They had fewer cannons but more sails, no doubt choosing flexibility over firepower. He was almost positive the Silver Army had many more ships, but if the fighting forces were equal on both sides, he really had no idea who would win in a fight. If Jason were here, he would have said the Dwarves all the way, but Nickle was not so sure.

Certainly, the cannons of the Valkyrie would not be nearly as effective as Rune Cannons, but perhaps they had different magical innovations that made up for this.

To the right of the port was a training ground, a large square area seeded with vibrant green grass. Several hundred Valkyrie Elite wielded spears, shouting in unison as they performed a specific slashing maneuver. It was both awe-inspiring and intimidating.

"I train almost every day," Jaylyn said. "But mother has never allowed me to train with the Valkyrie Elite like she did when she was my age. I should be out there with them, earning their respect. But mother flatly refuses, breaking several hundred years of tradition."

"That's because," said a voice from behind. "She's afraid you will beat up her Elites too much."

Jaylyn turned around, her face twisting into an easy smile. "Sosha, I was hoping to find you here." She ran forward, taking the powerful woman in a quick embrace.

"And who are these two?" Sosha asked.

Jaylyn pointed to the High Faerie and Dwarf. "This is Evie, she is a High Faerie from the Blackwoods Forest, and this is Michael, a Dwarf in the Silver Army."

"Such esteemed guests," Sosha said with a low bow, giving them more respect than was customary.

"Sosha is the General of the Valkyrie Elite," Jaylyn said.

Nickle and Evalee studied this newcomer carefully. She had smile wrinkles around her eyes and mouth that seemed to contrast the sharp features of the woman before them. If Jaylyn was not around, Nickle very much doubted that this woman would be seen smiling.

"What are you drilling today?" Jaylyn asked.

Sosha joined Jaylyn's side as they walked the parade grounds. "We have a fresh batch of recruits, part of your mother's New Defense Initiative. The Valkyrie Elite is to be doubled."

"Doubled?"

"Sometimes the best way to prevent war," Sosha said. "Is to prepare for one."

"That doesn't make any sense," Jaylyn answered.

"Ask your Dwarf friend. He has the eyes of a warrior."

Jaylyn laughed. "Michael? No, I don't think so."

"We shall see," Sosha said. "But we need a demonstration, as is demanded by our traditions when the Princess comes to the training grounds."

"But they're busy training."

Sosha grinned as she whispered, "It inspires them to see their future Queen. Give them a chance to earn your favor."

Jaylyn let out a long sigh. "Fine."

They walked down several steps until they reached the training grounds. As soon as Jaylyn's foot touched the grass, two whistles rang out, calling all winged warriors to attention. Every head bowed, and every knee bent before the Heir of the Obsidian Throne. To her credit, Jaylyn blushed as red as a cherry before nodding to Sosha.

The General let out a sharp, high-pitched whistle. Evalee could not tell the difference between the whistle before and this new one, but it seemed clear enough to the Valkyrie. The warriors immediately stood, their hands behind their backs. It was so in sync that the movement itself was impressive. The Valkyrie all wore matching golden breastplates and helmets, each rimmed with horns and two wings. They wore white greaves and golden boots.

"Our noble Princess wishes to have a demonstration. Are there two among you who are worth your title?"

Without hesitation, the two fiercest women stepped forward, raising their spears high, accepting the challenge.

"Good," Sosha said.

The two women faced each other, bowing low, performing an ancient ritual before their mock battle.

"You mistake, trainees," Sosha said. "You are not to face each other, otherwise, I would have had you trade your real weapons for training ones. You are to face me."

The two women looked at each other, unsure if this was a test.

"If you hesitate now," Sosha said. "You shall not leave this training ground a Valkyrie Elite. Attack me."

This was all the prompting the two women needed. They lunged forward, their weapons cutting through the wind. But Sosha was now in the air, using her wings and an Elemental Wind shot from her hands to propel her into the sky. She twisted around with surprising agility, dodging two pathetic attacks. The other Valkyrie moved in again, attacking with an animalistic fury, their spears shining with the reflection of the sun. They used Wind spells to accelerate their movements, shooting them towards or away from danger.

It was a fighting style that neither Nickle nor Evalee had ever seen—a game of agility and movement. But, as the new Initiates used their wings only to gain height and fly, Sosha used hers as weapons, sweeping the legs out from one and knocking a spear away from another.

The General twisted around, shooting dust into the air, temporarily blinding her opponents. It was over in three more moves, the two recruits were knocked to the ground, their weapons discarded.

Despite her rank, Sosha went to each one, pulling them back to their feet. They touched foreheads, whispering to each other as they did. "Well fought, Valkyrie."

"You must be getting old, Sosha," Jaylyn teased. "It took you over ten moves."

"That was only to show you how talented this rising generation has become," Sosha answered. She turned back to the lead instructor and whistled. Without another word, the Initiates were back in rows, their weapons in hand.

The large Valkyrie turned to Nickle and Evalee. "What do you think?"

"It was wonderful," Evalee said. "Interesting mix of styles. I wish I could learn to fight as you do."

Sosha smiled at the High Faeries' enthusiasm. She instantly liked the young woman—as almost all who met her did.

"I've never seen a fighting style like that—a mix between

precision and speed," Nickle answered.

"But...," Sosha prompted.

"But...," Nickle drawled, unsure if he should complete the thought. "But you leave yourself open when you're leaping into the air. Against two opponents, if you can keep track of both of them, you should be fine. But in the middle of battle, your opponents can come from anywhere."

"You see, Jaylyn," Sosha answered in triumph. "Both this Dwarf and High Faerie are warriors."

Jaylyn frowned, an annoyed expression on her face.

"If you still don't believe me," Sosha said. "Then answer me this. Why has the Dwarf barely looked away from our warships since coming to the Port of Marseille?"

"I'm just curious, ma'am, how they work," Nickle answered. "As a member of the Silver Army, I've ridden in the Dwarf Frigates quite a bit, but these are like nothing else I've seen. You have so many different kinds of ships."

"And each one with a different purpose," Sosha drawled. "Whereas you Dwarves only have three different kinds of ships, you limit your tactics."

"How many types of ships do you have?" Evalee asked.

"Twenty," Jaylyn answered before Sosha could. "But many of them are simple variations of other ships. There are six primary ones."

"Can you name them all, Heir to the Obsidian Throne?" Sosha asked.

"First, you have the Finches, small agile ships used for scouting. Then you have the Falcons, lightly armored but fast ships armed with a small complement of cannons. The Owl, a heavily armored troop transport. The Hawk, a medium armored frigate with a full complement of cannons. These are used for bombarding enemy structures. And the Eagle, the largest and most heavily armored of any of the armada."

"You forgot one," Sosha said.

Jaylyn bit her lower lip. "Did I? Which one?"

"The Osprey."

"Oh, that's right," Jaylyn said quickly. "The Osprey carries small vessels that can be deployed into battle."

"That is a lot more than we have," Nickle said. "We pretty

much just use the Dwarf Frigate for combat. They're slow-moving but heavily armored and lined with sixty cannons, twenty on each side and ten at the stern and helm."

"Our Eagles only have fifty cannons," Jalyn said sheepishly.

"But we have the Ulanova, the largest warship ever crafted," Sosha said, a cruel smile on her lips. "It holds over one hundred and twenty cannons."

"Really!" Jaylyn and Evalee said together. The two girls blushed and looked at each other, giggling from their excitement.

"Can we see the ship?" Jaylyn asked.

"I'm afraid not right now, it's being inspected," Sosha said. "But in a few weeks, I will need to take the ship out for a patrol. You two can see it then."

Jaylyn frowned but did not protest.

They talked for a few minutes more, but the interaction ended in a rather anti-climactic fashion as another Valkyrie appeared, whispering in Sosha's ear.

The General turned to her audience. "Your mother summons me, Jaylyn, and at the risk of offending you, I beg your leave."

"Of course," Jaylyn replied.

As Sosha headed out, Jaylyn led her precession in the opposite direction, away from the training of the Valkyrie. The Port of Marseille was even more massive than Nickle and Evalee first imagined. They turned a corner and discovered an entirely new section they had not even known existed.

Jaylyn playfully nudged Nickle in the shoulder. "Impressed?"

For some reason, Evalee felt a flash of anger ripple through her body. Nickle had been training her to control her emotions, and she had progressed well enough, so she was surprised at how quickly a rage shot through her chest. She was not even sure why she was angry. She liked Jaylyn. But at that moment, she wanted to punch her in the face. She let out a long breath, releasing the tension in her chest, forcing her clenched fists back open.

Evalee inserted herself between Nickle and Jaylyn, pretending to trip over some object. "I'm so sorry…Jaylyn, what is that massive tower?" It was a massive circular structure. It was less of a tower and more just a big building. Each floor was lined with windows for offices for various Valkyrie officials.

"That's the control tower, better known as the Eagle's Nest," the Princess answered. "That is the one that my brother is supposed to be inspecting—"

Before she could finish, several large explosions erupted, sending a deafening sound echoing through the docks. A massive plume of smoke leaked out of the sides of the tower, filling the air with choking vapor.

Jaylyn, Nickle, and Evalee hit the ground, their ears ringing.

The Princess' eyes were wide, her hands over her chest, her breath coming up short.

Nickle looked up, trying to spot where the explosions had come from. The source seemed to be on the opposite side of the tower, but he did not think about it too long, as a massive crack in front of them appeared.

"It's coming down," Nickle said through the confusion. He turned to the Valkyrie Elite, all of whom had huddled around Jaylyn. "Get her out of here. The tower is collapsing right on top of us."

The warriors did not need another prompting. Within seconds they had taken flight, taking the Princess with them.

Evalee stood, her eyes narrowed. "If that thing crashes down, it will kill hundreds of people. What do we do?"

"You start moving the people," Nickle said. "I'll see if I can slow it down."

"Just be careful," Evalee answered. Then she was gone, Vicinerating off into the distance.

Nickle took a deep breath and focused, using his Alteration magic so he could see the threads of reality. Millions of colorful strings filled his vision. The problem was immediately apparent as hundreds of thousands of threads on one side of the tower had suddenly been severed in an explosion. He could stitch them back together if he had enough time.

"I just need to slow it down," Nickle whispered. "People need time to get out of the way." Then he set to work, his hands outstretched, pulling the threads together. But the collapsing tower had already gained too much momentum. Every thread he connected instantly snapped. The building was tipping more and more toward Nickle and the dozens of ships tied at the port.

"I guess I'll have to try something different," he hissed. Instead of grabbing one thread, he grabbed dozens, pulling them together in a rush. These stayed connected a little longer before snapping, momentarily stalling the tower's collapse. He tried again and again, fastening the cords as quickly as possible, but it was not enough.

"Come on, Nickle," the Dwarf said, his voice growing tense. "You can do this."

The tower continued to tip, gaining momentum with each passing moment. It seemed like a hopeless task. His body was already so exhausted from the lack of food and sleep. The strain made his hands shake. He began to think about his own survival, about Vicinerating away from the area.

"No," Nickle replied with new determination, shaking off the fear. "Evalee needs more time. The people need more time." He focused his mind, digging deeper for power. He felt a familiar warmth rising in his body—this time, he knew exactly what it was. Mystic energy flowed out of his heart and through his limbs, illuminating him with white light. While one hand continued to use Alteration magic and fix the threads of reality, the other pointed above, pulsing out a wave of Mystic magic, capturing the tower in a luminescent glow.

Nickle immediately felt crushed by the strain of the magic as the tower continued to fall. The momentum slowly dissipated, but he could not stop it completely. Foot by foot, the gigantic behemoth descended upon him.

The pressure on his body was so great, his lungs would not work properly. Beads of sweat trickled down his face, his cheeks flushing red. As the strain proved too much, he was pushed to a knee, cracking the concrete upon impact. Still, he held on, fighting frantically for every second, not surrendering to the tremendous weight. His head started to spin, his thoughts becoming distant. Blackness slowly closed in all around him.

"Come on!" Nickle yelled, surprising even himself with the intensity of his words. "Just a little more."

The structure moaned as it slowed down even more. Nickle pushed his last bit of energy into his magic, his hands quivering from the effort.

But then, the tower stopped falling, robbed completely of its momentum. The Dwarf relaxed his right hand. It had stopped. The building hung at a precarious forty-five-degree angle, casting an ominous shadow across the dock that almost swallowed Nickle.

Evalee appeared at his side a second later, her eyes full of wonder. "What did you do, Nickle?"

"I stopped it, I guess." He tried to stand but fell back down. He was still too weak. Evalee finally pulled him to his feet, sending a wave of lightheadedness through him.

"What did you do, Nickle?" Evalee asked again.

This time the Dwarf looked around, trying to spot what the High Faerie was referring to specifically. The base of the tower was no longer just stone. A mix of black tentacle-like roots poured out of the ground, mixing into the structure in a seamless design. Stone gave way to furniture which gave way to rock and debris. While he was focused on stopping the tower with Mystic magic, his other hand had been busy threading together the damaged parts of the building. But it looked wrong, like something out of the home of Atlantia. They were all items that had been forced together.

"I used Alteration magic to reconnect some of the threads," Nickle replied.

"That was amazing," Evalee said with a smile. "When did you learn how to do that? And did you use Mystic magic to stop the tower from falling? I didn't know you wore a Mystic Relic."

Nickle looked to his sweet friend, a friend who had been nothing but loyal to him for years. He wanted to tell her—to tell her everything that he knew about who he was. But, if he did, it would endanger everything they were trying to protect. It would put a wedge between them, forever driving them apart. Faeries were noble creatures, pure of heart and intention. If she knew what he was, it would push her away.

"*Or would it,*" Nickle thought. "*Would she abandon me if she knew what I was?*"

Luckily, he did not have a chance to answer the questions as a crowd of Valkyrie began to approach.

"We better get out of here before the locals ask too many questions," Nickle said. "Come on."

Chapter 20

A New Alliance

"First they attack our livelihood, then they attack our line of succession," the King roared, his voice easily filling the Court. The Blue Sashers concurred with this assessment, shouting long after it was appropriate.

The Queen stirred on her throne, her grasp of the situation fading. Two days ago, she could have stopped this rant with a simple word, but now she was powerless against it. The people would hear their King's cries for war.

"The Crown Prince had been scheduled to visit the Eagle's Nest," the King continued. "Had he not fallen ill earlier that day, he could have been killed. Can there be any doubt that this was an assassination attempt? He is not in the direct line of succession, but an attack on the royal family is an attack on all of us."

Again, the crowd roared.

Nickle and Evalee stood at their regular positions, just behind the seats of the Prince and Princess, ready to attend to their various needs. Nickle's body was drained, pushed to the limit. He wanted so much just to eat and sleep that it created a physical pain in his muscles. He had lost count of how many days had gone by since he had started his Scathian training. It would be easy enough to figure it out, but he purposely did not. He licked his lips as he smelled the food far off in the kitchens. But he pushed it down. He would not violate his Oath.

The magic he had expelled the day before had been far more than he thought himself even capable of. He had used Mystic magic two times in the past without even knowing what he was truly doing— once when he was fighting McBrian and again in the Grindlemire obstacle course. But this was different. He had studied how to use Mystic magic. Even more importantly, he had seen Sharlindrian do it. So when it came to the tower falling, it all came as natural as a baby bird first learning to fly.

The Queen's teeth clenched as she turned to Sosha. "Tell me what your Hunters have discovered with the investigation into the attack at the Eagle's Nest? Who is responsible?"

Sosha stepped forward, her armor covered in ash and sweat. She had not slept since the incident, directing the salvage and rebuilding operations. It had been a monumental effort to right the tower while at the same time repairing the damage. There had been some discussion about just completely tearing it down and rebuilding it, but that would take months, and since it was vital to their military operations and war could break out any day, it needed to be repaired quickly. It required two hundred ships to lift the structure while ground crews worked to rebuild the foundation. This took even more time as they had to chop through the odd, black tentacles that had sprouted from the ground and prevented the tower from falling.

"We've determined that there were three separate explosions," Sosha said. "All of them have characteristics and traits consistent with Dragon Fire, the same potion that was used weeks ago in an attempt to rupture our Lightning Reserves. What's more, several witnesses have reported that they saw a figure dressed all in red. He or she had prominent tattoos on the back of the neck and forearm, which are common among the Assassins of the Midnight."

"So it is true!" the King cried. "The Nords must be responsible."

"Let her finish!" the Queen roared. "We are not a rabble of cutthroats. We will have order, or we will not hold Court at all."

At a look from the Queen, Sosha continued. "There are many Assassins of the Midnight all around the world. At this time, we have no evidence that this Assassin is working for the Nords."

"Were there any attempts to arrest this criminal?" the Queen asked.

"Yes, but the…individual proved…adept, using a few potions to slip passed our warriors and evade capture," Sosha said. "On a personal note, if I may approach, Queen of the Valkyrie."

The Queen nodded, and the General stepped closer, taking a knee before the Obsidian Throne. "Twice, we have been attacked. And twice I have failed to protect your family. I have disgraced my position and your title. With your leave, oh great Queen, I will cut off my wings and retire in disgrace."

The Court filled with scattered shouts and jeers.

"We are on the cusp of war," Queen Victra yelled. "And you would now try to surrender your spear? When I need you the most? Stand, Sosha, General of my Valkyrie Elite, and raise your head. If you desire honor, then hunt down those responsible and bring them to me."

For once, the Blue Sashers roared their approval for the Queen's words. She was relieved by this, as she half thought they would call for Sosha's removal, or at the very least, for her punishment.

For the briefest of moments, she had regained some measure of control, and she would use it the best way she knew how. "Bring in the Atlantean Ambassadors."

Nickle and Evalee exchange a curious look.

Two Valkyrie warriors opened the great doors at the end of Court, allowing in a host of blue-clad warriors. There were six of them, all of them calm and confident.

Nickle and Evalee recognized the man in the lead. It was Major Q, the leader that had led the Atlantean forces in Atlantis. He looked just as he had before, although a few more medals were affixed to his armor. He strode in, nodding to the Queen.

"All must kneel before the Obsidian Throne," one of the Valkyrie growled, a spear held at her side.

"Of course," Major Q said as he went to a knee. "I do apologize as I am not familiar with Valkyrie protocol."

"Quite all right," Queen Victra Petrov Godfrey answered. "We can excuse minor mistakes in customs as our people are forming a new friendship."

"Thank you, most gracious one," Major Q said, standing as he did.

The Queen also stood, addressing the Court. She needed something to distract her people's demands for justice, at least for a while. She hoped that the Atlanteans might prove to be the distraction she needed. "There are some here that cry for war, as to be expected. There are some here that yearn to right the wrongs, as do I. But we must make sure it is a war that we can win. We have the mightiest armada of all the fleets in the Isles of Balinbar; we have the greatest warriors; we have true and tested leaders. But the Nords are not fools, and I very much doubt that they will wish to start a war they cannot win. It is likely that the Vampire Queen has allied herself with the Nords. If we are to survive, we too must make allies. May I present to you, Major Q, the Atlantean Ambassador who is to oversee a new peace treaty between the powers of the land and sky."

"Thank you, Queen of the Obsidian Throne," Major Q said. "The pleasure is all mine. The last Queen I was in front of was the Queen of the Vampires on the peak of the Blood Spire, and it was a very different experience to meeting you."

"Did you fight her in battle?" Queen Victra asked.

"Well, no...not exactly," Major Q answered dolefully. "She fled just as soon as I arrived. It would have made for an epic struggle though, one likely set to rhyme and verse."

"Have you heard of the ballad of Grimfang the Grand?" the King asked.

"It sounds vaguely familiar," Major Q said. "I'm trying to recall, but I think I saw Grimfang there, somewhere towards the back."

"Grimfang," the King roared. "Truly a great warrior and Orc. The Ballad says he was the first over the wall, his weapons raised."

"There were a few that made it over the wall around the same time," Major Q said. "Hard to keep track of who specifically was over the wall first in all the confusion. If I didn't beat old Grimfang into the fortress, I can't imagine I was too far behind."

The Queen turned and faced all those in her High Court, deliberately spending more time staring down the Blue Sashers. "The Atlanteans have agreed to aid us in our cause, bringing us new weapons and soldiers to fight if needed. They have sent us three air vessels to be led by Major Q himself, as well as a compliment of soldiers and cannons. If it comes to war, we will not stand alone. Even now, I have a special envoy entreating the closest magical cities—the Orcs of the StoneRidge Mountains, the Trolls of Hellshire, and the Goblins of Tyrin. If the Vampire Queen is truly among the Isles of Balinbar, then it will be together that we will defeat her and her minions."

"Well said," Major Q replied.

"Now, I must have some words in private with the Prince and Princess," the Queen ordered.

The noise grew louder as everyone bowed low and headed out various exits. As they departed, Nickle could not help but notice how much bigger the room appeared to be. The Dwarf and High Faerie turned to go, but they were stopped short by a few Valkyrie, who wordlessly gestured for them to stay. The rest of the attendants left.

Nickle gulped. He had a feeling something like this was going to happen. He shared a nervous look with Evalee, who simply smiled. It seemed impossible to make the High Faerie worried.

The Queen descended the steps of her throne, her features cruel and unforgiving. She first looked to Evalee and then Nickle, giving them piercing stares that stabbed into them like spears. "You two…are not what you seem. Hawthorne sent you?"

Evalee and Nickle did not react, unsure of how to answer.

"There are no listening charms in this room," Queen Victra said. "Your words are safe in here. Are you working for Hawthorne?"

"Yes," Evalee answered.

"When I asked for help, I wanted it to be in the form of members from the Magic Response Team," the Queen said. "I need to figure out who is attacking us and what they are after. But she said she would send something much better—the very best she had to offer."

The King looked insulted. "You went to a foreign people to beg for help? You debase yourself, my love. We do not need help from outsiders. We are Valkyrie."

"My dear husband," the Queen said softly. "We are warriors, we are fighters, we are Storm Chasers. But we are not investigators. We are not spies. If we make a misstep and attack an enemy blindly, we will fail. We need to know the truth before we take action." The Queen turned back to the Dwarf and High Faerie. "So… are you the best she has to offer? Or was she lying to me? In exchange for her assistance, I gave her a major discount on an entire year's worth of Lightning. So, I repeat, was she lying to me?"

Jaylyn took a step forward, her voice in a panic. "They saved me. That tower could have crushed me."

"You should have never been there," Boris said, his voice cold. "You must adhere to your schedule for that very reason."

"Easy, father," Yaroslav said, matching his King's tone. "No one knew she would be in danger on the docks. I doubt even the Assassin knew she was in the area. If they did, and she was the target, there are far more effective ways of assassination."

"My Valkyrie Elite would have never allowed that to happen," the Queen said firmly.

Jaylyn gestured to Nickle and Evalee. "These two saved hundreds of lives who were either in the control tower or who were on the ships it would have smashed into. You saw what they did."

"Yes, I did," the Queen answered. "And I don't understand it. Things make me nervous when I don't understand them. How did you stop the Eagle's Nest from falling?"

Nickle swallowed.

"Who are *you* really?" Queen Victra asked.

"We're here to help you," Nickle answered. "Hawthorne is trying to keep the whole world from coming apart, and we're working with her to accomplish the same goal. I don't know if we are the best she has to offer, but our group was able to defeat the Vampire Queen, split the Eye of Atlantia, and prevent the Orcs and Atlanteans from fighting each other in an all-out war."

"So that was you?" King Boris growled. "We heard... rumors."

"Yes," Nickle answered simply.

"But why are you here, in my Palace?" Victra asked.

"Hawthorne thinks that, given all the information, the culprit is someone on the inside," Evalee said. "Or at the very least, they had help from someone on the inside. Someone that had intimate knowledge of where the Lightning Vault was located and how it was protected. Someone who knew how the Valkyrie Elite fight and how they would react."

Yaroslav laughed. "The Valkyrie Elite are the most loyal set of warriors ever to grace the sky. They obey without question. If you are suggesting that one of them could be working with the Nords...."

"We still don't know if the Nords have anything to do with this," Victra said, an annoyed tone in her voice.

"Mother, if they keep trying to kill us and we do nothing, eventually, they will succeed," Yaroslav said, taking a step closer to his father. "You must take action. You must not let this go unpunished, or you encourage more attempts."

"That is enough," Victra said, her eyes narrowed.

But Yaroslav continued without pause. "At the very least, move our Lightning Reserves to safety. Ship them down to EarthWorks to protect our island from another surprise attack."

"Enough!" Victra roared. "I will not be lectured by my own

son in my Court. It's bad enough my husband has drawn a hard line in the sand, I don't need it from you too. If I move our Lightning Reserves, it will be because we are at war. And we will not go to war with someone unless we know who we are attacking and why."

Yaroslav straightened up, taking the rebuke from his mother hard. His hands clenched into fists. "So be it, but know that your seat of power becomes weakened each day these offenses go unpunished. Who knows how much more time you will have on the Obsidian Throne." The young man turned around, heading for the door, a major breach in protocol.

The Queen contemplated summoning her guards and having him dragged back. But since there were no witnesses to the offense, it was much easier to forgive. Still, she did not care for the insolent tone in his voice.

"He is impetuous," Boris said. "Forgive him."

"As are you," Victra said.

"But, he is also correct," the King continued. "You have a seat of power, but to remain on it, my love, requires a show of force. Even if the Nords are not responsible, we must treat them as if they are. We must send a message to our enemies, as we have done in times of old, that the Valkyrie cannot be intimidated."

"I need more time," Vitra said, her voice taking on a bitter edge. "Let my Hunters gather solid information, and we will punish the actual culprits." She then turned to Nickle and Evalee, casting an austere glare. "If you are as valuable as Hawthorne seems to suggest, then prove it. Get me the information I need, or all of us will suffer because of it."

Chapter 21

Hitilanda the Horrible

Business was booming at Shemway and Jeffrey's One Stop Shop Alchemy. Each day, dozens of kids would line up, waiting to see if a new potion was being released. Jason had expanded their line of elixirs to include Hair Explosion, Fool's Beard, and several types of disguise potions, which he entitled "Insta-Disguise." Technically, they did not work that great since they tended to make a person look more like a monster than anything else. But they were easily deployed by simply throwing them into the ground. Shemway changed the potion's name to "Monster Makers," and they became another instant success.

Jason invented more Rune-influenced potions, each one just as pointless but entertaining as the next. As the weeks passed, their list of clientele grew. Soon, Flying Traders were stopping by and negotiating to purchase large batches of the stuff.

"What are you going to do with your share of the money?" Jason asked one day before the shop opened up.

"I'm going to spend it," Shemway replied.

"Yeah, but on what?"

"Is nothing private to you?"

"I'm a Dwarf in the Silver Army. Privacy ain't exactly what they're known for."

"And what great and noble item will you spend your money on?"

"I'm going to buy my first set of Tines, one that has a quick Rune Recharge Time and set with a primary Strength Rune. They've also been coming out with these new Wind Runes placed in the back that can give you a burst of speed. I might even take them by the Gnomes of Tiran'Og and see what they can do to enhance it."

Shemway nodded. "Uh-huh."

"You're not even listening," Jason answered, slightly offended.

"Yes," Shemway answered, turning around. He had a Dwarf Stylus in his left hand and was busily etching the top of a potion. "That is a very accurate assessment."

"Seriously, what do you spend your money on?"

"On things that matter."

"Hey, wait a minute," Jason said, pointing a finger at the Thieftian's chest. "Your name badge says, 'Shopkeeper in Charge.' That's a much better title than, 'Head Shopkeeper.'"

"You said you wanted 'Head Shopkeeper.' Will you never be satisfied? Instead of worrying about my managerial duties, why don't you get back to practicing your stealth? You're falling behind my quota."

Since Jason had begun his Thieftian training, he had been practicing his pick-pocket skills, something that Shemway insisted was invaluable to the trade. Jason practiced on the customers that walked into the store, swiping items with nominal value, such as candy or quills. But he always felt so guilty that he would slip it back into the customer's pocket before they left.

Shemway, however, did not have this moral restraint. A piece of parchment on the wall kept track of their successes, and Jason was left far behind.

"Yeah, I'm not sure I want to swipe candy from kids anymore," Jason said.

"There is an ancient Thieftian phrase that goes like this: 'You cannot learn what you don't practice.'" Shemway said. "The prize is not the candy, it's the skill. Learn the skill, and it will be a prize for your entire life."

"I see the value in it, I just don't know how I feel about it. You know. If it was something important, or if I was taking something from someone bad, that'd be one thing. But, I'm lifting mostly candy from teenagers."

"Their teeth will thank you later."

"And you won't let me count it if I put it back. That should count twice."

"Stealth is built on taking, not on putting back. If you were a Thieftian, you would be lifting pockets by the time you were four."

"I still don't agree with that parental choice."

"Well, in any case, let's open the doors and let in the public.

There is gold dust to be made."

Jason complied, opening the front doors. As predicted, a few eager customers were waiting outside, most of whom were children that would rather be tardy to school than have to wait in line that afternoon.

Jason completed the purchases while Shemway worked the sales floor. They were a good team—something that neither of them would ever admit.

At noon, a thin average-sized man entered the shop, his back straight, his posture militant.

"Major Q?" Jason asked, his eyebrows arching.

"Oh, if it isn't the little Dwarf lad, Dime or Quarter," Major Q said. Behind the Major was his faithful Lieutenant Joey Jacobs. They wore clothing that starkly contrasted with the Valkyrie.

"Oh, I'm not him…but sure," Jason said. "It doesn't matter, really. What are you doing up here?" He was about to remind the Major of his real name, but he remembered he was incognito. Technically, his name was now Jeffrey. So why correct someone with a fake name when they are already using your wrong name.

"Big stuff, Quarter," the Major answered. "Big stuff. Our High Chancellor has forged a new alliance with the Valkyrie. She had the Valkyrie modify three of our ships so they could be airborne. In exchange, we're here to provide military support."

"Things getting that bad up here?"

"I don't know the politics of the Isles of the Balinbar, but I do hope so. Nothing tests the steel of a warrior like a battlefield, where heroes are born, and songs of fortune are written."

"You heard about the new ballad 'Grimfang the Grand?' It's one of the most popular tunes up here."

"Yes," Major Q replied coolly. "I've…heard it sung…once or twice."

"It's all over New Atlantis," Lieutenant Joey added. "Can't walk more than ten feet without hearin' it."

"Yes, Joey," Major Q grumbled. "Well, we best finish our browsing and return to the ships. Who knows when we will be called to arms at a moment's notice."

Jason nodded. "Well, great seeing you two. Stop by sometime soon."

The two Atlanteans went in different directions, and one ended up bumping into the other. Major Q finally shuffled past and out the door, followed by Joey.

The rest of the day became a blur as customers arrived and potions were sold. As the sun set, Jason's friends began to return. First, Swiftrunner and then a very exhausted Sharlindrian. Finally, Evalee returned, a large basket in hand.

"Look at the all the cake the Palace is just giving away!" the High Faerie squealed. Jason and Swiftrunner did not need much more of a prompting to start digging in. Soon, they had plates topped with white cake with a crème ganache.

"Where did you get this?" Swiftrunner asked after placing a second slice on his plate.

"In the metal bins along the servant's entrance," Evalee answered. "It's fantastic. To think that this has been there this whole time."

Jason's fork stopped halfway to his mouth. "What do you mean this whole time?"

"Metal bins?" Swiftrunner asked. "You mean, like garbage cans?"

"Well, I saw it yesterday and didn't know if someone had already claimed it. But, it must not belong to anyone anymore because it was still there today."

"What sort of markings did the bin have on the side?" Swiftrunner asked carefully.

"Hmmm," Evalee said carefully. "Yellow…squares or something."

Swiftrunner put his plate down. "Evalee, that's the royal garbage."

"Ugh," Jason groaned, putting his plate down as well.

"Is that not…something you do?" Evalee asked.

"No," Jason answered.

"How very wasteful," Evalee answered. "So, how do they get rid of their trash here?"

"Well, in EarthWorks," Swiftrunner said. "The Cennarians typically use their Transformation magic to turn it into butterflies that fly back to a designated location where it's incinerated by massive Fire Runes. Up here in Valenburg, I have no idea. But, either way, it's best not to pick up food that's been tossed out."

"Oh, ok."

"Where is Nickle, by the way?" Jason asked. "You guys usually return home together."

"He…," Evalee said carefully. "Well…he told me not to tell you two."

Swiftrunner and Jason exchanged odd looks.

"Not tell us?" the Dwarf said.

"Why ever not?" Swiftrunner said.

"He's…testing himself," Evalee answered.

"Testing?" Jason and Swiftrunner said at the same time.

"I've said too much," Evalee replied.

"Where is he?"

"By the docks, in the Low District," Evalee answered. "Now, I really have said too much. Oh, he'll never trust me again. He only told me just in case he didn't come back tonight. I don't know what he's doing."

"That's where Billy's Goats is," Swiftrunner said. "I wonder if he went there?"

"No time to think of your girly friend," Jason answered.

"Maybe she can help us find him," Swiftrunner suggested.

"You guys can't go look for him," Evalee said. "He'll know I said something for sure. He's been acting so strange lately, who knows how much he'll be offended."

"What do you mean acting strange?" Swiftrunner said.

"He's more quiet than usual, even when we're in a conversation," Evalee answered. "And he never eats or drinks in front of anyone anymore. What do you think is going on with him? Jason is more likely to be the irresponsible one and sneak off—not Nickle."

Jason thought about it for a second, reflecting on the last several weeks of mealtimes. Nickle, without exception, had always excused himself from the table before the meal got started. "I got a bad feeling about this. We better start looking for him."

"He's going to be mad at me," Evalee hissed.

"You stay here," Jason said, "just in case he comes back. And if we run into him, we'll just say we were looking for Swiftrunner's girlfriend."

"You have a girlfriend?" Evalee asked. "Since when?"

Swiftrunner turned as red as a prize tomato. He shrugged sheepishly.

"It was love at first fight," Jason said, saving a wink for his Cennarian friend. "Actually, it's a weird story. He will have to fill you in later." He then turned to Swiftrunner. "Let's get going."

"You want to grab, Sharlie too?" Swiftrunner asked.

"She went to bed early," Evalee answered. "Her job runs her ragged."

"Well, we better get moving," Jason said. "Hopefully, he's still in one piece."

***

Nickle looked across the wet street, seeing the dark and dingy bar he knew had to be the right spot. He was wearing a dark cloak that had been enhanced with Essence of the Night, an expensive potion that Shemway had brewed for him specifically. Whatever darkness was around, the cloak actually pulled closer, blending the wearer into the background.

The building was in an exceptionally poor condition, its paint peeling, its wood beams splintering. The sign above was faded and worn to the point where it was barely legible.

It had taken several days of sitting on the docks and reading minds before he slowly closed in on the possible location. After watching the place for a while, he witnessed hundreds of Storm Chasers, each with thick gold medallions in hand, enter the establishment, and then several hours later, these same crowds of people left, albeit with much less money. All that was left to do was get inside.

He was now in the Low District, a rough part of town that was beholden to one as long as they had money to pay. Three doors down was Billy's Goats, a location that Swiftrunner and Jason frequented more and more each week.

"This will work," Nickle said to himself, his voice low. His stomach twisted into knots. His idea had been a long shot—one that was so bad, he dared not say it out loud.

"This will work," he repeated.

He had first heard about the Fighter Pits from Yaroslav, who had alluded to him that he had actually been to a few of the fights on more than one occasion. Of course, this kind of public brawling was illegal, but, as the Valkyrie believed, it was also necessary. So a blind eye was turned to the brawling, as long as it was not out in the open.

The Dwarf steeled his nerves and walked across the road, glancing behind him as he did, acting like many of the other patrons he had seen entering the establishment. He entered to find it occupied by only a few people, all of them in deep conversation with drinks in hand.

Nickle put his hand on his stomach, fighting down a slight nausea at the musty smell of the room. The pangs of hunger were so intense, he momentarily lost himself. He refocused his vision and continued, heading past the bathrooms and to the back. He knew this was the right way; he had sensed the mental energy of the others that had taken this same path.

Then he ran into Gulgar, a massive Orc with two large tusks, one chipped, the other pierced with a silver ring. Behind him were a set of Goblin twins with a matching pair of nasty-looking and Hexed-infused daggers. And if that was not enough, there was Bonleon, a half-giant endowed with incredible strength. Bonleon was not as tall as his ancestry might suggest, but he had more than his fair share of strength. He preferred a pair of Lightning Knuckles, which sparked when they contacted someone's face.

Nickle decided that the best thing he could do was just pretend like he belonged. So he kept walking, nodding to each of the guards in turn.

Gulgar raised a thick hand, blocking the Dwarf from stepping any further. "Don't think so, litl' Dwarf. Let me see the Sheen first?'

"Sheen?"

"If you don't know what it is, then you don't have it," Gulgar growled.

Nickle briefly scanned through the Orc's mind, picking up the image of a luminescent tattoo placed under someone's forearm. Like the thought he had just received, he turned his arm over, allowing it to be inspected. "Of course, I know what the Sheen is."

Gulgar looked to the Goblins, who looked skeptical. One

finally came forward, passing a red dagger over Nickle's arm. Nothing happened. From the brief image Nickle had seen in the Orc's mind, he knew that if he had the Sheen, it would have lit up like Christmas lights."

"Get out of here, Dwarfy, before we cook yah," Gulgar said. "And if I ever see you in here again, I'll have Bonleon sit on your head, yah hear!"

The other three jeered, gritting their teeth in solidarity.

The Dwarf backed away, his hands up. "Sorry, I just thought...."

"You didn't think," Gulgar said. "That's the problem. Now get walking before we break your legs."

The Dwarf obeyed and turned around, his nerves getting the better of him. Three steps later, he stopped next to a doorway. *"I can't give up now—not when I am so close."* His chest tightened again, anxiety flitting through his body. Instead of continuing on, he shut the door that led back out to the street.

"What's he doin'?" Bonleon said in a foolish voice.

"Oh, you're going to regret that," Gulgar said.

Nickle slowly turned around, his jaw set, his mind focusing on the other creatures in the room. Within moments, he had intruded into each of their brains, seeing their weaknesses, their strengths, their fears. They had neglected to protect their minds, and it was almost like they were inviting Nickle to mess with them. If a skilled Purveyor later examined their minds, it would be obvious as to what he had done, but it did not matter. He would not be coming back here.

"I'm a very important person," Nickle said through a mental impression. *"Don't you remember me, Gulgar?"* At the same time, the Dwarf began implanting false memories into the guards' brains, each one had Nickle at the center of some great event.

Gulgar kneeled. "My king, how may I serve you?"

The other three also bowed, slamming their fists against their chests.

Nickle sighed. This was harder than he thought. He wanted to be important, but not *that* important. He tried again, making the memories seem somewhat less grand. Still, Gulgar bowed low and saluted. His third attempt was much more successful.

The Orc approached Nickle, slapping him on the back, a grin

on his face. "Oh, if it isn't…you…you slippery dog. Been so long since I've seen yah. What brings you to this part of the world?"

"Oh, Gulgar, you know why I'm here," Nickle answered with a cheerful grin. "Where else could I go to see the best fights in all of Valenburg."

"True enough," the Orc answered.

"But…I don't have my Sheen," Nickle whispered.

"The likes of you don't need it," the Orc answered. "Just tell them that you're personal friends with Gulgar the Grouch. And if anyone doubts it, send 'em my way and I'll set them straight."

"Thanks," Nickle said with a grin.

One of the Goblins gestured with a twisted dagger. "Right this way."

Nickle nodded as he headed down two flights of stairs and into the darkness below. The more steps he descended, the more grimy and gritty the walls appeared. After passing through another set of doors, he stepped into a massive room packed with cheering creatures waving different colored rags in the air. At the center of the room was a clear-shaped magical sphere. Two fighters danced in the middle, exchanging a series of strikes in marshal combat. It seemed readily apparent that whatever the sphere was made of prohibited the fighters in the middle from using most types of magic.

Nickle went to sit down, but it was so packed there were no seats available. But, with a bit of mental persuasion, two Satyrs suddenly realized they had somewhere else to be, leaving a space wide open for the Dwarf. He sat down and simply observed everything around him.

The noise was deafening, the cheering endless. He blocked most of it out of his head, only allowing important bits to filter into his ears. Very quickly, he began to learn the rules of this underworld.

At the center of the arena was a Valkyrie named Hitilanda the Horrible, and she was dominating the arena. She was a massive creature, rippled with muscles and scars. Her once white wings were tattered and worn, as if she had been flying during a hurricane. She was a warrior; of that, few could doubt. Those that did doubt her skills and challenged her in the arena were quickly subdued. Three Orcs started the night by issuing their challenges. They were abnormally large creatures, almost as broad as they were tall, even more burly than the Valkyrie herself. But what they had in strength, Hitilanda made up for in speed.

"Who can beat Hitilanda the Horrible!" a magically enhanced voice announced from out of nowhere. "The undefeated champion of the ring for three nights in a row!"

Nickle looked around for the source and finally found it. A Leprechaun on a raised podium was standing at the far end of room, his animated movements matching his voice.

"Any takers! Twenty kilos of dust to the winner. Twenty! You could use it as a down payment on your own ship. You would be the captain. Imagine that." The Leprechaun knew his audience well. Several in the crowd began discussing the idea with their neighbors, trying to figure out if they would have any chance of defeating Hitilanda the Horrible. Wisely, no one stepped forward, or at least, no one that anyone noticed.

Nickle had begun walking to the center, his body still draped in the dark cloak. He made it all the way to the entrance of the arena before anyone took notice. As he began walking up the wooden steps to the sphere, the audience realized what was happening almost at once. People began to whisper, trying to decide if the child-sized creature had just gotten lost on their way to the bathroom or if they intended to issue a challenge.

Finally, the Leprechaun spoke. "Is that a challenger? Or did someone's kid get separated from their family?"

The audience roared with laughter.

"Come on now," the Leprechaun said, enjoying the attention from the audience. "Let's see who is under the cloak?"

Nickle pulled the cloak from his shoulders. He then folded it and set it carefully to the side.

"A Dwarf!" the Leprechaun roared. "You think you got a chance at winning, shorty?"

Nickle looked at the little man dressed in green and gold finery. In a loud and commanding voice, he spoke the words that were required. "I challenge Hitilanda the Horrible and do so of my own free will and choice."

Usually at this point, the audience roared with applause; this time, they only gapped. Nickle was nothing in size compared to the Valkyrie. It was like a grape standing before a grapefruit. There were a few cries of protest, but they were all ignored. A door in the magical sphere opened, allowing Nickle inside.

Then the audience cheered, enthralled by the unexpected scene. Hitilanda the Horrible was not as amused. She began to hurtle insults at the Dwarf, trying to throw off his concentration.

But Nickle was not listening. His focus was absolute. He narrowed his eyes at the fighter that stood before him.

He needed this challenge. His body craved it, demanded it. Every night for four weeks, he had endured the grueling Scathian training, his mind being tested at every turn. For four weeks, he had not eaten, slept, or even had a drink of water. He survived solely on his mind's ability to ration his body's food supply to keep him from starving. It was a mental task that took tremendous attention every minute of the day. He had earned his Second Stripe as he descended the peak of the Lonely Mountain. To earn his Third Stripe, he had to willingly drink **The Serpent's Kiss**, a poison so potent it is rumored that a single drop is enough to kill a hundred people. For his Fourth Stripe, he had to use his mind to channel all of his strength into his muscles to lift the Boulder of Bawdier. He had earned four of the Ten Stripes, but the Fifth Stripe could not be reached without facing an actual opponent.

Nickle did not hear the sound that initiated the combat; he instead relied on his opponent's movements to dictate his actions. Hitilanda moved with a grace that defied her large stature. Within moments, she was attacking Nickle with all the fury of her kind.

The Dwarf ducked and dodged, his honed mental skills giving him a slight edge and allowing him to barely avoid each crushing blow. He shuffled his feet out of the way, off lining before turning back to his opponent. The Valkyrie roared in frustration, jumping high and attacking with her wings. Nickle was nicked in the arm, but only just barely.

A minute went by, and still, the Valkyrie could not land a solid blow. She became somewhat reckless as her frustration grew. Nickle had yet to even try and throw a swing, much less land one. Slowly, her proper fighting stance gave way to a manic rage.

It was then that Nickle hit back, attacking with a rabid fury. The Valkyrie was hit in the ribs and leg, dropping her to the ground. A third and fourth blow struck her across the cheek and shoulder. She swung out her wings in desperation, but these were easy enough to duck under. When he came up again, he released all the strength he had into a final blow into the Valkyrie's chest, pitching her against the arena wall.

Hitilanda the Horrible hit the magical barrier hard, knocking her unconscious, her body slipping to the floor. It all happened so quickly that the audience did not know how to react. One moment, Hitilanda the Horrible was chasing the Dwarf around the arena, the next, she was crumpled on the ground like a bird who had just had its wings clipped.

Nickle looked down at his left forearm just in time to see a black stripe appear on his skin. It was the Fifth Stripe, the last one he would receive on his left arm.

"It worked," Nickle said breathlessly. "I can't believe it worked."

He exited the arena, recovering his cloak from the ground seconds later. Still, no one reacted. He walked over to the Leprechaun and picked up two large gold medallions from the prize table.

"Thank you," Nickle said in a dry, dusty voice.

By the time the Leprechaun found his voice, Nickle was halfway to the exit. "Looks like we have a winner! The Dwarf of Devastation has conquered Hitilanda and is now our new reigning champion! All hail the new champion!"

This brought the applause that was so absent before. But it was wasted on Nickle as he was already heading back up the stairs. When he reached the ground floor, however, he ran into something he had not expected. The two Goblin bouncers from before were knocked unconscious. The Giant was reeling from being struck in the face, and the Orc had Jason in a headlock.

"Jason?" Nickle asked.

"There he is," Jason roared. "I told you he was here! Let go of my head."

Gulgar still held Jason in a headlock. "Sir, you know this Dwarf?"

"Yes, Gulgar, release him," Nickle said, sounding harsher than he meant. "Jason, what are you doing here?"

Jason rubbed his neck after he was released. He first looked to Nickle and then to Gulgar, not quite understanding the connection between the two.

Finally, Nickle grabbed his friend around the elbow, dragging him out of the room. "What happened?"

"I was trying to fight my way to you," Jason replied simply. "I was doing pretty good too, took out two of the Goblins. And the Giant was a lot softer than he looked. But that Orc's got a mean streak in him."

Nickle led the way out of the dingy bar and into the main street. "Why were you trying to find me?"

"I thought you were in trouble."

"I'm fine," Nickle said. "It's all under control."

"What are you talking about," Jason said. "You're cut on the right shoulder. You're bleeding."

Nickle had not realized it before, but when the Valkyrie had nicked him, it had cut his skin right open. It was a long cut but shallow. "Oh, I didn't even realize that."

"What were you doing?" Jason demanded. "Liliana said that one of the Satyrs saw you enter that dingy bar an hour ago. She said that there is a secret fighting ring beneath the surface."

Nickle listened carefully as he stopped at a mobile food cart that sold strange pieces of meat wrapped around long, pointy sticks. "Whatever these are, I'll take thirty of them."

"Thirty?" replied the older man from behind the cart. "Are you sure?"

"Make it forty and an extra-large drink too."

"Forty it is," the man answered.

The man took payment and began handing out sticks of meat to the Dwarf as quickly as he could. With little ceremony, Nickle began to eat the meat as fast as possible. Ten heartbeats later, he was already on his third stick of meat.

"Don't you even want to know what kind of meat that is?" Jason asked.

The cart owner looked up, opening his mouth to answer Jason's question, but Nickle stuck up a hand first.

"No, please don't tell me. Let me just enjoy it."

Around twenty sticks of meat later, Nickle began to slow down, a lethargic energy seeping into his body with each bite. He turned to his friend, his face pale. "You want one."

"No," Jason answered, his temper getting the better of them.

"I want a few answers."

"Ugh," Nickle answered, placing a hand on his stomach. "I guess I'll take the rest to go."

"Sure thing," the cart owner chirped.

Once the food was bagged, he continued to walk down the street, his left hand still over his stomach.

"Pigeons," Jason said. "It was pigeon meat."

"Ugh," Nickle repeated. At the next trashcan he passed, he was about to toss the bag, but Jason stopped him.

"You're just going to throw the rest away?"

Nickle nodded.

"Well, I'll have at least one in that case," Jason said, taking the bag from his friend. But then he suddenly changed his mind, realizing that he was still angry. "No, wait. I'm still mad at you." He tossed the pigeon meat towards the trash, missing by a good foot.

"At me?"

"Yeah, what is going on with you?" Jason asked. "Sneaking off. Not letting the rest of us know what's happening. Skipping dinner. Going down into dark and dirty fight clubs. What were you doing down there?"

Nickle let out a long sigh. "Now that I've earned my fifth stripe, I can finally talk about it. You want the long version or the really long version."

"As long as it's the truth, I don't care."

Nickle sat down on a stone bench carved like a giant bird. His friend refused to sit, his arms crossed. Then he started at the beginning, leaving nothing out. He told Jason about stealing Locke's memories and then reliving them. He talked about the different challenges, about fasting from food, sleep, and drink, and how the first Five Trials were designed to push a candidate's body to the extremes.

"But, I came across a problem," Nickle said, his voice distant. "In the Fifth Trial, you have to face an opponent in your weakened, starving state. You have to defeat them using only the mental skills you've honed in training. But when I tried to do that from Locke's memory it didn't work. It had to be a real challenge."

"So you weren't just watching the fights; you were actually fighting in them?" Jason said, his voice in pure shock.

"Yeah."

"And you won?"

Nickle revealed the two gold medallions on his neck. "Twenty Kilos."

"What?" Jason said. "They paid you? Nickle, you can't be going around fighting in shady places like that. They wouldn't pay you that much unless there was a real chance of getting seriously injured."

"Yeah, I know."

"Do you?" Jason asked. "Why are you doing this? Locke didn't think you were ready. People can be broken in two by the Scathian training—their minds just snapping under the pressure. In any case, you don't even have someone to guide you. There's no one to warn you if you're in too deep."

Nickle stood, a momentary anger flashing through his body. "I don't have time to wait."

"Time? What are you talking about? You've got nothing but time. You're only in your third year of training."

"That's just it. I don't have time."

"Why?"

"Kara'Kala is going to break free from his prison."

"What? When?"

"I don't know," Nickle answered, his voice low. "It could be five years from now, it could be fifteen, but he will break free."

"How can you possibly predict that?"

"Tiberian told me while we were locked up in cages on the Blood Spire. He thought he might die in that fortress, so he told me more than he wanted or planned to. As the Blight grows and spreads, absorbing magic from the Earth, the FireWall becomes a little more unstable, a little weaker. And one day—one day very soon—it will not be able to hold back the immortal tides of darkness. Kara'Kala and his Demons will break free."

"And the Tri'Ark will fight them and put them down as they did two hundred years ago."

"Not this time," Nickle said in a whisper. "The world is weaker than it has ever been, it's magic is depleting. Every week, I Vicinerate down to the Lands of the Beasts and see how much the Blight has progressed. It's not spreading in inches or even feet, but in hundreds of yards, consuming everything before it, turning the land to ash."

"The Tri'Ark is working on containing the Blight."

"No, they're not. And worse, they've given up even trying to anymore. They're so focused on preventing EarthWorks from falling apart that no one but the Cennarians and Faeries are talking about it. It's not even discussed in the papers, not in the Tri'Ark Councils, not among EarthWork officials. At this rate, the Land of the Beasts will be destroyed within twenty years, its magic consumed by the Blight. This is the same kind of Blight that destroyed the Orc's homeworld, and once it depletes enough magic, it will destroy our world too, turning it into nothing but a ball of ash and blood."

"What does the Blight have to do with Kara'Kala?"

"I don't know, but it can't just be a coincidence that the Blight started spreading much more rapidly when he was in charge of EarthWorks."

"This is not your fight, Nickle," Jason said.

"Of the Three Masters of Magic that stood against Kara'Kala, only two are still alive. One of them, Tiberian, is so weak that he can barely stay awake for more than a few hours at a time. The other, Greggory McDooble, has disappeared. The Tri'Ark is falling apart. EarthWorks is falling apart. They won't be able to stand against Kara'Kala."

"And so what? You can? You can't take him on. That's why the Silver and Calameer armies exist."

Nickle turned away, his eyes distant. There was a long pause before he spoke again, his mind torn between two decisions. "Jason, I want to tell you something. Can I trust you?"

"You know you can," Jason answered.

He turned back to his friend, a strange sadness in his eyes. "I wasn't born so much as I was built. My body was pulled together by different elements of magic and then fused together."

"What are you talking about?"

"I was made through the same process used to make Gru Ren Sheen."

"Yeah, I'm not buying it," Jason said, his voice attempting to jest.

"Look at me, Jason. Think of everything I've done in the past, everything that I can do. Look at my discolored eyes. When I was in Tortugan, twice I used Mystic magic to get myself out of a bind—without training or even the use of a Relic. While I was at Harbordeen,

I learned how to Vicinerate—something that should be impossible for anyone but Faeries. In Atlantis, I began to master the Scathian arts—something a Dwarf has never done."

"You've just got some talent, that's all," Jason said, trying to convince himself.

"You don't believe me," Nickle answered.

Jason opened his mouth to speak for a second before shutting it. Then he looked around, making sure that they were alone. He cleared his throat before starting again, this time his voice a whisper. "Do you know what would happen to you if that were true? Do you know what the Tri'Ark would do to you?"

Nickle nodded. "Yes."

Jason did not know how to respond to the simple and direct answer. So, he just patted his friend on the shoulder, searching for the right words. "Well, don't worry about that. I wouldn't let them do anything."

Nickle let out a long sigh, as if a weight was being taken off his chest. "So, you believe me?"

"Of course, I believe you."

"Thank you. You have no idea how difficult it's been keeping all of that in."

"Hey, if you can't share a secret with your best friend, then who can you share one with. Although, I wish your big secret was something like…I adopted a puppy and I need help keeping it hidden from Shemway."

Chapter 22

A Bright Future

Over the last several weeks, the rigors of cleaning houses left blisters which eventually turned into callouses on Sharlindrian's hands. It was rewarding, in a way, turning something disorderly and messy into something organized and clean. She was now in the Nilsson Manor, a wealthy family heavily involved in the Lightning Trade. They were a massive family with just under a dozen kids, and the parents did not show signs of slowing down as Mrs. Nilsson was expecting a new baby any day.

They were also supporters of Kara'Kala, as proven by a hidden set of armor Sharlindrian found in the basement. The secret compartment was not nearly as expansive as the Kinnunen's Estate, but the armor had been well maintained. It seemed that at least half of the wealthy families in Valenburg still collected Relics from the age of the Demon Brood—something that secretly terrified the Elf. She had been raised to think that Kara'Kala was evil incarnate. It seemed disheartening that a normal-looking family could keep anything connected to the Demon Lord. But she had to remind herself that the people alive in Valenburg today were not the same people alive during the reign of Kara'Kala. So who knew exactly why they kept the items they did.

Sharlindrian was upstairs, carefully using her Mystic magic to arrange a home office. Usually, her magic made things easier, but today, she was so distracted, she zipped a letter opener past her leg, leaving a small cut behind.

Sharlindrian frowned, her face annoyed at the pinching pain. She bent down, holding a finger against the cut. It was not long but deep, and soon blood began to drip down her leg. "Ginger, can you help me with this? I need a cloth."

Ginger appeared a second later, pulling a white cloth from a pocket. "Here you go."

"That was quick," Sharlindrian said.

"I was just walking down the hall when you called, Sharlie."

"So, you've taken to calling me by my real name?"

"It's such a pretty name," Ginger answered. "I can't help but say it when no one is around. So what happened to your leg?"

"I wasn't concentrating hard enough when I was using my magic, and a letter opener sliced my leg."

"Can you heal it? Oh, I've always wanted to see someone heal a wound."

"It's hard healing yourself. Only a few can do it without becoming sickened by the process. So where does the interest in healing come from?"

"Oh, it's foolishness."

"Come on, Ginger. At least give me a story to listen to while I wait for the bleeding to stop."

Ginger laughed. "Oh, all right. When I was a little girl, while some girls and boys were playing house or battling with swords, I was always pretending to be a Healer. I'd fix up my stuffed animals, taking away their aches and pains, sealing up their cuts and bruises. I always thought I'd be a Healer one day."

"Why didn't you?"

Ginger laughed. "Sharlie, I clean houses. I could never do that."

"Why not?"

"Well...I'm not you, for starters. You're so confident and dynamic. You're perfect with Mystic magic. The way you took care of those Elves was amazing."

"Ginger, if you have the desire, all you lack is the proper training."

"But even if I saved all my wages for the next five years, I'd hardly have enough to attend a proper Healer school.

"Perhaps," Sharlindrian said. "But, there is nothing stopping me from teaching you for free."

"Now?"

"I can't let my leg bleed all over the white carpet, can I?"

"But who is going to heal you?"

"You."

Ginger blushed. "Me? I could never do something like that."

"Yes, you can. Do you have the Mystic bracelet that you bought?"

"Of course," Ginger said, pulling up her left sleeve. "It's so pretty that I never take it off."

"Well, we paid a good price for that Relic. You've been able to change the gravity of a few things, but now let's give it a true test and see how it can heal."

"Are you sure I won't like…make it worse. I've never done this before."

"If people only do things that they have already done before, then no one would learn anything new. Trust me, I once instructed a Dwarf on how to heal, and if he could do it, I'm pretty sure anyone can. Now clear your mind. Push out all thoughts and emotions—become a blank slate just as we practiced."

"That's easy enough. That's what I do when I clean."

"Now, Healing is very much like cleaning a house. You just have to put the right things in the right spot and then wipe clean any dirt."

Sharlindrian slowly guided the young woman through the steps of removing the pain, sealing up the veins, and connecting the skin back together.

"I'm genuinely impressed," Sharlindrian said. "No hesitation. No fumbling mental impressions. You're a natural."

"Oh, I'm sure it's just the Relic."

"The Relic is just the vehicle, you are the person who has to steer it to the right location."

"What is this?" a shrill voice said as a sharp-eyed woman entered the room. "Lounging about? Sluffing your schedule." It was **Lady Fiurda**. She was dressed in an immaculate brown suit. It was simple, but the lines were as crisps as a leaf in fall.

"No, ma'am," Ginger said quickly. "We were…."

Lady **Fiurda** slapped Ginger across the cheek, instantly silencing the young woman. It was not a powerful blow, but it did have a sobering effect.

Sharlindrian shot to her feet, her eyes narrowed. "I cut my leg, and she was helping me mend it.'

"Mend it?" Lady **Fiurda** said with a laugh. "The girl can barely keep up with her workload."

"We clean faster than anyone that works for you," Sharlindrian answered.

"Watch your tone," Lady Fiurda answered. "Or you'll get the same as Ginger."

"Go ahead then," Sharlindrian answered. "Hit me."

Lady Fiurda was so offended she did not know how to react. She resumed her proper posture, studying the blond woman before her.

"We're the best cleaners you've got," Sharlindrian said. "We clean twice as much in half the time. That's why you're here, isn't it? You want to figure out how we get it done so quickly."

"I just want to make sure you're cleaning with the same quality as everyone else," Lady Fiurda answered.

"You've seen our work," Sharlindrian answered. "You know what we do."

"Watch your tongue, you insolent girl," Lady Fiurda said. "You will address me with respect, or you will find yourself in the unemployment line. If you cross me, you will not be able to get a cleaning job from here to New Atlantis, do you understand?"

"I will gladly treat you with the same respect you afford Ginger," Sharlindrian answered.

Then Lady Fiurda took a swing at the Elf's face, one that had a lot more power than what was used against Ginger. But Sharlindrian had expected the attack. She adjusted the gravity of Lady Fiurda's hand, making it hit the Elf's face with four times the strength. Sharlindrian had leaned into the blow, gritting her teeth in the process. The impact was so terrific that it instantly broke Lady Fiurda's wrist, sending pain rippling down her body.

Lady Fiurda backed up, rubbing the fingers of her other hand over her injured wrist as if trying to understand what had just happened. She was so shocked, she did not know how to react. So, she just stood there, stumbling on her words. She could not accuse Sharlindrian of attacking her, since she had been the one to hit the Elf, as evidenced by a bright red mark on her cheek.

"We are your best cleaners; that's why you always send us to the most important rooms," Sharlindrian said. "We will continue to be your best cleaners, but you need to respect us and our space. You hit Ginger again, and you won't need to fire us because we will be gone, taking any of the others with us who don't care for your treatment. You might have a lot of influence up here, but how do you think your business will be affected if half of your cleaning staff suddenly walks out on you?"

Lady Fiurda slowly straightened up, her back going as rigid as a board. She fought down the pain, trying to regain her poise. "You are such a pretty girl. Such a waste. You might have actually been someone, but you don't have the brains for it, I imagine. So you find yourself here, cleaning the toilets of those people that actually have meaning in their lives. To survive, you must clean, your hands being worn down, your sweet curves eventually disappearing. And one day, I promise you, as you clean a bathroom for the thousandth time—a bathroom that is bigger than your house—you'll look in the mirror and see how wretched you've become. That is all your future holds in store for you."

With this, Lady Fiurda left, a sly smile on her lips.

Sharlindrian was so angry, she almost punched a wall.

Ginger had pulled back from the conflict, her eyes filling with unfallen tears. When Sharlindrian looked at her, she gave a gentle smile. "I don't think the Lady Fiurda will bother us again."

"Are you sure? I thought she was going to fire us on the spot."

"No," Sharlindrian said. "People like her only act tough, but inside they are a mess of nerves and insecurities. She took things too far, and if she makes a big deal of this, she knows I will too. She just attacked one of her employees, and I doubt that would bode well for her reputation. I doubt she will look at us from now on, much less conduct surprise inspections."

"You think so?"

Sharlindrian touched her tender cheek gently. "Yes, I think it worked out for the best. And look, I also have another wound for you to heal."

Chapter 23

An Old Friend

Swiftrunner never had a job that he was so good at and liked so much. Each day was like his best day. The people of Valenburg were not the most welcoming at first, but most had just never seen a Cennarian, let alone had their mail delivered by one. But upon meeting and talking to him, almost everyone was entranced by Swiftrunner's country accent and easy-going nature.

The children would often meet him in the street, shouting out his fake name, challenging him to a race. He let the kids almost win every time, but by some miracle, he would just barely pull ahead at the last second.

He received more money than any job he had ever had, and to earn it, he only had to do the one thing he absolutely loved—go galloping through the streets. He had to be careful, however, so as not to push himself too hard and light himself on fire, thanks to Atlantia's gift.

Since he had started dating Liliana, the Satyrs had accepted him as one of their own. They even began talking about how good he might do in the Race of the Gods.

And then his mind drifted to Liliana, his beautiful girlfriend. He really did not know what she saw in him—he was just a simple Cennarian from the country. She, however, was something different entirely. She had been one of the most successful Letter Runners in her time. Her success and intuition lead to her purchasing and running a very fruitful restaurant. She was even talking about expanding and starting new restaurants in other cities. And she had done all of it before the age of twenty, something that seemed beyond impossible to him.

He had delivered his mail quicker than usual that day, giving him plenty of free time in the afternoon. He only had one package left, and it did not need to be delivered for a few hours. This package was odd. It was sent from the Palace, but instead of being ornate and marked with the symbol of the royal family, it was wrapped in simple brown paper. Instead of being addressed to a name, it was being sent to "Prisoner 1173, Mortory Prison Grounds, Patomose Island."

So instead of dropping it off directly, he took a trip to Billy's Goat, a place that was quickly becoming his favorite destination in the world. He stepped inside, a broad grin on his face. The Satyrs all greeted him in a chorus of jeers, raising their glasses and shouting salutations.

Liliana heard the noise from the back and found a mirror, ensuring her makeup was in order before stepping into the front room. She planted a sweet kiss on the Cennarian's lips before gesturing to the back. "And what brings you here today?"

"Do I need an excuse to visit you?" Swiftrunner asked.

Liliana giggled as she grabbed his hand and pulled him back to the rear office. In direct contrast to the rest of the restaurant, it was messy, with disheveled papers, half-eaten plates of food, and an array of quills, ledgers, and books. Liliana slumped into a leather chair while Swiftrunner took a seat on a couch. It was not the most comfortable, but it could at least accommodate his larger frame.

"How's work going?" Swiftrunner asked.

"Dreadfully boring," Liliana said. "Today, I've been dealing with acquisition orders and sales receipts."

"Sounds as rough as a swarm of sand flies in June," Swiftrunner said.

"Do you just make up those sayings, or do other Cennarians actually say them too?" Liliana asked, a devilish smile on her lips.

"I'm not creative enough to make them up myself," Swiftrunner said.

"I'm not sure if I believe you. In any case, what is that package you're carrying?"

"Oh, this," Swiftrunner answered, throwing it to the Satyr. "It came from the Palace, and I'm shipping it out later today. But, I wanted to bring it by as it seemed odd. It's addressed to a prisoner on Patmose. You know anything about it?"

Liliana twirled around in her chair while she studied the package. "I don't...think so, but I know someone I can ask." She pushed a button on her desk, activating a bleating goat sound that carried through the restaurant. Within moments, a Satyr server poked their head inside. He was a handsome Satyr with muscular arms. As he stepped in, he had a broad smile for Liliana, but at the sight of Swiftrunner, it quickly faded, folding his arms across his chest.

"Bobby, do me a solid and find out what the other Letter Runners know about this package and who it is addressed to," Liliana said as she tossed the box to the Satyr.

"You got it, deary." The Satyr turned around, sparing a glare for Swiftrunner, and exited out of the room.

"What's his deal?" the Cennarian asked.

"Oh, Bobby," Liliana said with a sigh. "Good lad, just been a bit on edge since we broke up."

"How long ago was that?"

"Same day we met," Liliana said with a sweet voice.

"Oh, that's…awkward timing."

She smiled and stepped closer, smoothing back Swiftrunner's hair. "But don't worry. He won't stray from his task. Are you hungry? Oh, I am. I can put in an order for us?"

"Sure, as long as Bobby isn't the one preparing the food," Swiftrunner answered. "That'd be as foolish as asking a pig to prepare you some eggs with a side of bacon."

"Where do your people come up with such colorful metaphors?"

They talked for an hour solid, the time slipping away quickly. When the food arrived, they enjoyed the taste of Zoysia Grass dipped in Cheddar Fondue. When Bobby returned, Liliana was cuddled up next to the large Cennarian, her hands in his.

Bobby turned as red as a ripened tomato before throwing the package at Swiftrunner. "Found what you're looking for, four legs. One of the Letter Runners has gotten a similar package from the Palace on a few occasions. They thought it strange too, so they asked around. It turns out that the prisoner receiving them is going to have a long stay on Patmose."

Swiftrunner shifted sideways, breaking his hands free from Liliana's grip. "Were you able to find out the name of the prisoner?"

"Yeah, it's a Dwarf, if I remember right. I think he goes by the name Thornhead…Thornhead Back'Break."

Chapter 24

The Island of Patmose

It took most of the day to travel to Patmose in a light frigate. Then they had to take a smaller vessel to the actual prison grounds, as the island was located in the middle of the Mediterranean Sea. The land was cold and grey; signs of a recent downpour were evident. A powerful wind carried a scent of distant dying grass and struggling bushes. For the most part, the island was barren of any signs of life, except for the occasional bird overhead. They passed a few small homes, all with white walls and flat roofs. Most of them appeared to belong to fishermen.

"Why didn't you just Vicinerate us there?" Jason asked.

"I've never been there before," Nickle replied. "Plus, transporting two of us would be a difficult task over such a long distance."

Jason had already asked this question, but he was hoping the answer would change. The fair for the ride was pretty steep, not to mention the tab for the onboard food. Jason had lived up to his Dwarf heritage, consuming all the food placed before him, but that was before he found out he had to pay for each item. After that, he was in a permanently bad mood.

Nickle remained mostly silent during the trip. His mind enjoying the respite from the Scathian training.

When they arrived at their destination, they immediately felt cheated as the ship dropped them off on the top of what appeared to be a deserted part of the island. Long blades of white grass whipped in the wind as they studied their surroundings.

"There's nothing here," Jason said.

"Come on," Nickle gestured with his head. He could sense several minds a few hundred yards down beneath them. The two Dwarfs descended the side of the mountain towards a cut below.

Without Nickle's guidance, Jason would have been hopelessly lost, no doubt completely missing the entrance to the prison. It was hidden well, tucked in against the mountain side. The two Dwarves had to resist the Magic de Danaan around the entrance before they could finally see it with their own eyes—even then, it was easy to miss. A simple iron door set into the side of the mountain.

Jason approached, unsure of what to do. "I guess we knock?"

Nickle shrugged his shoulders. They both approached the door before Jason gave it several sturdy knocks, each one sounding ominous and foreboding.

"Are we sure we can trust this information?" Jason asked.

"Swiftrunner swore by it," Nickle answered. "He said Liliana double-checked the information to be sure."

"And are we sure we can trust her? I mean, just how those two met sounds like the beginning of a bad romance novel."

"I wouldn't know," Nickle said. "I've never read a romance novel."

"Yeah," Jason said quickly. "Me either. I'm just guessing that's how a typical romance novel would go. You know, where they first hate each other and then they're madly in love. Like that movie 'Pride and Prejudice.'"

"I wouldn't know that either," Nickle answered. "I haven't watched the movie."

"Yeah, I definitely haven't seen it either," Jason answered. "Besides, the book is better anyway." He hit the door again, and suddenly, a latch opened up, revealing green eyes and feathers.

"What do you want?" the creature asked, its voice clipped and harsh.

"We're members of the Silver Army here to see a prisoner," Jason supplied.

"Who authorized that?" the voice asked.

Jason turned to Nickle, his voice falling to a whisper. "Who authorized that?"

Nickle patted his clothing as if he was looking for something. "Ummm…authorization?"

"This is one of the most secure locations on the surface," the voice answered. "Did you really think you could just walk in here and demand to see someone?"

"Just a second," Nickle answered. The Dwarf disappeared in a flash.

"Where did the little guy go?" the voice squeaked.

"He does that from time to time," Jason replied. "He'll be back. Umm…he must have forgotten the authorization paperwork."

Nickle did not return for several minutes. By the time he did, Jason had sat down on a rock several yards away from the door.

"Where'd you go?" Jason asked. "I thought you were going to just manipulate his mind or something."

"They've got anti-Scathian charms all over this place; I can feel them blocking almost all my mental energy. It's complicated magic to create, but it seems like something absolutely necessary. It protects the prisoners as well as the guards from each other. Besides, we know Hawthorne, one of the highest-ranking government officials in EarthWorks. It took a while to find her, but I got it."

"Got what?"

"Permission to go inside."

"What?"

Nickle nodded. "Yeah, it took a little convincing, but she finally came around to the idea when I mentioned this is a potential big lead." The Dwarf walked over to the door and knocked.

Before long, the latch opened up, and the same two eyes appeared. "You two again—"

Nickle held up a yellow sheet of paper with an embossed symbol on the bottom right. "By order of Jane Hawthorne, One of the Five Seats, who sits on the Tri'Ark Council, we have been granted permission to see prisoner 1173."

The eyes reviewed the paper, not quite believing what they were seeing. "Blimey, you do have permission. Hey, Jeremy, check this out. I've never seen someone granted permission to visit one of the inmates on the thousandth deck."

"There's no way that's true," Jeremy replied. "Give it here."

Nickle passed the document through the tiny peephole. The latch shut a second later. The Dwarves exchanged worried looks, each one wondering if it was the best idea to simply give away their permission slip through the door. Finally, the door started to creak as if heavy machinery was being moved. It popped open not long after, slowly swinging wide.

Nickle was first to step in, followed by Jason. The door had looked deceptively small in the mountainside. As they entered and walked past it, they could see it was several meters wide and was reinforced with a myriad of Runes and Hexes. The walls were thick, lined with a layer of metal, flames, stone, ice, and another layer of metal, all of it replete with Repulsion Runes. Before them stood two Circurians, one had the head of a Jackal, the other that of a Hawk. Their bodies were impressively muscular, as were all Circurians, and lined with a unique set of golden armor and weapons that shimmered in the room's low light. The armor was not as protective as Dwarf Tines but seemed to give the wearer more flexibility. It looked Egyptian in design and was enhanced with its own magic. Jason had never seen Cicurian armor before, and he could not help but study it in earnest.

"Who made that armor?" Jason asked.

"This armor was—" the Cicurian with the Hawk head began to say, but then the Jackal interrupted.

"No, Boddy," Jeremy answered. "No questions…no answers."

"Right," Boddy replied. "You're right."

Then the two guards approached the Dwarves with a series of Rune inscribed tablets, checking them for hidden weapons or magical items.

"Put these bracelets on," Boddy said, handing each of the Dwarves two stiff rings.

Nickle instantly recognized them as being Byzantine cuffs, except these were not linked together with a chain.

"They will prevent you from doing magic, so don't even try to use it," Boddy said. "They cost a fortune to make, so don't bang them up. No Vicineration or Exsiliogation is allowed or possible, as the prison is lined with Totems. Ain't nothing breaking into Patmose uninvited and ain't nothin' leaving without permission."

"Come on," Jeremey said. "Best we get this done before supper is served. Old Back'Break gets a bit of a temper if he skips a meal." Jeremy led the way down a non-descript tunnel and to a lift. The lift rocked back and forth as the Dwarves stepped aboard. Boddy also stepped aboard, leaving Jeremy behind. Then the shaft began to shake as it was slowly lowered into the darkness below.

"This is Piddler tech," Nickle said, observing the pulley high above.

"This once was an old mine shaft," Boddy said, "or so I was told. Got abandoned though."

Jason clung to the side rail until his knuckles turned white. "And how far are we going down?"

"Until we stop," Boddy answered.

Jason swallowed, eager to change the subject. "Tell me…what sort of magic do Cicurians use?"

Boddy rubbed his bill for a quick second before answering. "You've never heard?"

"I just need something else to think about right now," Jason answered.

"We can take on our Bestial Form, giving us increased strength, power, and magical resistance. There's a good reason we get picked for gigs like this. I can turn into a Hawk."

"I bet that's handy," Nickle said.

Boddy leaned forward, winking as he did. "It's a lot cooler than being able to turn into a Jackal, that's for sure."

The lift drifted gently back and forth as they went, squeaking all the way. When they finally stopped, Jason let out a sigh that was loud enough to be mistaken for a gust of wind. Boddy then exited and placed a hand on a cabinet, which popped open a second later. From inside, he took out two Runes, each the size of a Nickel.

"Shrinking Runes?" Jason asked.

"Yeah," Boddy answered. "If you want to see the prisoners, you've got to shrink down. It makes it easier to control the inmates when they're only six inches tall."

They were used to swallowing the Runes, so they did not even ask for water. Before long, they were only a few inches tall. The guard pointed to a small set of doors against the wall, which opened as they approached.

They ran into two Beast'Heads, one a Frog'Head, the other an Eagle'Head. They looked remarkably like the Cicurians except being only six inches tall. Their armor was made of beetle parts, and their weapons that of cricket legs. The Dwarves were again searched for magical weapons or tools. Finally, their Byzantine cuffs were checked to ensure they were functioning correctly before being sent on. The security measures increased the deeper they walked into the prison.

After passing two more security doors, they stepped into a massive room where they took Restorative Runes, returning them to their former height.

As Nickle thought through the process, he realized the genius of the setup. Only one side had Shrinking Runes, while the other had Restorative Runes. Even if a prisoner could escape to this point, they would be unable to fit through the tiny doors on the floor.

Then they entered the area of the prison cells, each one lined with thick, heavy bars, all of them reinforced with Runes and Hexed for good measure. They passed by a cafeteria and a weight room before they ended up on another lift that took them down several dozen yards. The security was far beyond what either of the two Dwarves expected.

Finally, they were escorted by a Circurian with a Tiger head to the cell of prisoner 1173. "Back'Break...you've got some visitors." The guard pointed to two chairs bolted to the floor before leaving the room.

Jason and Nickle did not sit and instead peered into the cell, trying to see the Dwarf that had once been the Elected Chief Warlord of the Silver Army. But the dimly lit room appeared to be empty. Then something lunged forward, grabbing the bars of the cell, startling both Nickle and Jason so badly, they just about ran in the opposite direction.

Thornhead laughed, a resounding noise that echoed off the cold stone walls of the room. "Oh, this is interesting. I just finished my day of hard labor, and this is how they reward me, with a visit from two of the greenest Tenderfoots in the Silver Army."

Jason shoved down his apprehension and took a seat, Nickle did the same.

Thornhead looked thinner than before, his body more defined with muscle. All the fat he had gained while being the leader of the Silver Army had melted away with the past few years of hard labor. He seemed stronger, his eyes more intense. Byzantine shackles were secured on his wrists and connected with a thick chain.

"Tell me what must be going wrong in EarthWorks for you two to come visit me," Thornhead said. "You two are the first Dwarves I've seen since I've been here. I had a hundred good friends in EarthWorks, each one was trying to gain my favor for some political or military position. But since being here, not a one has come by."

"Your name came up," Jason began. "We thought you might

know something about some trouble brewing on the surface."

"So, it's not in EarthWorks. Where could it be then? In the Valley of the Trolls…no? What about on the plains of Kansas…Rinacons are usually on the prowl this time of year…no? Well then, it has to be something to do with the people of Androm or the City of Ni'sheen."

"It is something to do with the Isles of Balinbar," Jason answered.

"Ahh, in the floating isles," Thornhead answered, his voice full of awe. "But, before I answer anything, tell me one thing."

"What's that?"

Thornhead dropped his friendly demeanor, revealing his teeth in a feral rage. "Why in the world would I help you two? I was so close…so close to setting everything right. And you two snatched it away from me."

"Technically, it was just Nickle," Jason said.

"Hey," Nickle protested.

"But let's not split hairs," Jason continued. "We work for Hawthorne now, the same person that pushed your sentence from twelve hundred years to two thousand. Do you want to know why it's in your best interest to help us? If you do, we'll take all the information you give us and present it to Hawthorne. If it helps us, it could very well help you get a reduced sentence. How does two hundred years less sound to you?"

"It sounds like you don't need the information too badly."

"Well," Jason said. "If you give us good information, it could be even more. Hawthorne—"

"—Hawthorne don't mean a lick to me, lad. Tell me what you want to know, and I'll tell you how much it's goin' to cost yah."

"Who is communicating with you?"

"I don't have any idea. They don't give me any letters. You're in the most secured facility on the surface. You think they give me anything?"

"Well, who would be trying to communicate with you from Valenburg?"

"The Island of the Valkyrie?" Thornhead said, scratching at his mangled beard. "The Valkyrie were some of the most stalwart supporters of Kara'Kala. Grand warriors in their time. It could be any one of them."

"Give us names."

"Show me the package," Thornhead said in a low grumble. "It's already been scanned for magic. It can't do no harm here."

Jason looked to Nickle, who simply nodded. They really had no other option at this point.

He then tossed the package to Thornhead, who studied it carefully, turning it back and forth in his hands. "I'm guessing you two already tried to read it—otherwise, why would you be bothering to bring it to me." He opened it up, revealing three circles of red in the middle of a white paper.

"What does it mean?" Jason asked.

Thornhead stared at the color in cryptic disbelief.

"What does it mean?" Jason repeated.

"It's a call to arms," Thornhead answered simply. "Someone is trying to reestablish the Demon Brood."

"That's it?" Jason asked.

"Who?" Nickle asked. "Who is trying to reestablish the Brood?"

"I don't know," Thornhead replied. "I just know what it means. They didn't bother to sign it."

"That's all you can tell us," Jason said in a huff. "Come on, there must be more to it than that."

"The Demon Brood was the most powerful force in the world, laying low every army sent against it. It was only by chance that it was defeated at the battle of Three Stones. Establishing the Demon Brood is no idle matter."

"Who would send it to you?" Nickle persisted.

"Those who are trying to recruit me to their ranks," Thornhead said darkly.

"But you're stuck in here," Jason said.

"For now," Thornhead replied. "But you, Jason, of all people, are on the wrong side of all of this."

"What are you talking about?"

Thornhead tossed the letter at Jason's feet. "You haven't figured it out yet? Oh, lad, you're in for a shock."

Jason shook his head. "Isolation has not done you good, old Dwarf. Come on Nickle. This was a waste of time." He stood up, heading for the door.

"You still have the burn under your left arm?" Thornhead said in a whisper. "I was actually the one that gave it to you. Your father asked me to do it."

Jason stopped a few feet from the door and turned around slowly. "How do you know about the burn? Enough games, Thornhead. What do you know?"

"I know that of all people, you should be the last one to fight against Kara'Kala," Thornhead whispered. "In fact, your parents died trying to free the Demon Lord."

"That's a lie. My parents died in Brazil while on assignment for the Tri'Ark," Jason yelled.

Thornhead laughed, amused by the intensity of Jason's voice. "The Burntworths were killed in Brazil, but you, my boy, are not a Burntworth."

Jason stepped forward, grabbing the prison bars. "What are you talking about? What do you know?"

Thornhead only laughed in reply, his voice echoing down the long halls of the impenetrable prison.

Chapter 25

The Ulanova

"A tour?" Sosha answered with a playful tone. "But I'm so terribly busy with all my royal duties. But if the Heir of the Obsidian Throne commands it, then I will have to comply."

"Then I do command it," Jaylyn said in a good-natured tone. "Come on Sosha. The Dwarf and Faerie were sent here to learn from us as much as I am to learn from them."

Evalee, Sosha, Yaroslav, Jaylyn, and Nickle had just stepped onto a massive vessel that dwarfed all those around it. They had seen it before docked in the Port of Marseille, but it looked so much bigger actually standing on the ship's deck. It appeared more like a floating island rather than a vessel of war. At the front of the ship, known as the bowsprit, was a massive bronze Eagle with sharp eyes and even sharper talons. As they talked, the ship began to depart from the port. All hands were busy running up and down the deck, securing rigging and opening sails. The large ship was slow-moving at first but picked up speed the further it went.

"Then so be it," Sosha finally said, her wings momentarily adjusting as she spoke. "This is the Ulanova, the finest vessel in the fleet of the Valkyrie. In case you were wondering, Dwarf, this is capable of taking on any ship in the Silver Army."

Nickle and Evalee could not help but stare in wonder. This craft was so much larger than any fighting vessel they had ever seen. It was more akin to the size of the large barges that were used at the Docker in EarthWorks.

"How does this ship work?" Nickle asked. "Dwarf Frigates all depend on Runes. Everything from their propulsion to the firing of the cannons to reinforcing the sides and bottom is done with Runes."

Sosha studied Nickle closely. "What is the biggest difference you can spot between a Dwarf Frigate and a Valkyrie vessel?"

"The sails," Evalee said. "Dwarf sails are so much smaller than those of your ships."

Sosha looked at Evalee appraisingly, studying the butterfly-like wings that sprouted from her back. "Yes, little Faerie, our sails are much bigger. We don't use Runes to drive our ship forward. We use the Wind."

"Just the wind?" Nickle said. "You couldn't match the speed of a Dwarf Frigate with just the wind."

Sosha shook her head. "No, Dwarf, you don't understand. You live among the Valkyrie, but you know so little about us. We don't depend on the Wind as much as we create it." She lifted her right hand, creating a spiraling jet of Wind from her palm, ruffling the hair on everyone's head in the group.

Nickle nodded, impressed by the sight. "Is your magic a form of Elemental magic?"

"All of you can do this?" Evalee said with excitement.

"Just the winged Valkyrie," Jaylyn answered. "Although, I'm not good at it."

"In order to master it," Sosha answered. "To use the Wind of the Valkyrie, you must be fearless. You must fight without doubt, so it is a type of Elemental magic."

"Let me show you the lower decks," Jaylyn said, eager to change the subject. She led the way down a thin stairwell and to a gundeck. The bodyguards went first, followed by all the others. Nickle was in awe as he stepped out onto the next level. There were a series of unique cannons against both sides of the vessel. The Dwarf approached one, studying it from a few angles. It was large but surprisingly simple, having only one tube, a release lever, a tank of some kind, and a track on which it slid back and forth. Dwarf cannons were just as big but considerably heavier.

"How do you fire these?" Nickle asked.

"You are a curious one, aren't you?" Sosha said, a slightly mocking tone in her voice.

"There are no Runes," he replied simply. "What propels the cannonball out?"

Sosha stepped forward, resting her hand on the base of the cannon. Using the same magic as before, she began to funnel Wind from her hand and into the tank beneath. Somehow the tank allowed air in but did not let it out.

Jaylyn joined Sasha's side. "The tank stores the Wind. The farther you want to shoot, the more magic you need to store." The young Valkyrie pointed at the lever in the back. "When you want to fire it, just pull this."

"Like an air compressor," Nickle said.

"An air…compressor?" Jaylyn and Evalee said at the same time.

"It's a Piddler thing," Nickle said quickly.

"You're Piddler born?" Sosha asked, now more curious of the Dwarf than ever.

"The first few years of my life are a little fuzzy," he replied. "But I spent a good chunk of my time on the surface."

"Interesting," Soshsa answered. "And to think you came so highly recommended from EarthWorks."

Nickle did not like the tone in the woman's voice. It was like she suspected him of doing something wrong.

"Pull the lever," Jaylyn said to Evalee.

"But…won't that fire the cannon?"

"It will, but it's empty," Jaylyn answered. "It will just release the stored air."

"Are you sure?" Evalee said, looking back to Sosha.

"Yes," the large warrior answered. "Don't question the Heir to the Obsidian Throne."

"Ok," Evalee said, her hand inching towards the lever. When she finally pulled the lever, the cannon made a loud sound as a white cloud of compressed air shot out.

"We load and shoot these cannons twice as fast as any Dwarf cannon," Sosha said, a wide smile on her lips. For a brief second, Nickle thought the woman was competing with him. Dwarves had staked their reputation on their skills as builders, and just by virtue of him being a Dwarf, she felt the need to impress him.

"But it's not as strong," Nickle answered, meeting eyes with the Valkyrie. "And I imagine it doesn't shoot as far."

"It is strong enough," the woman answered, her eyes now slits.

"But Dwarves reinforce their ships with thick, Rune-enhanced armor, protecting it even from Dwarf cannons."

"It *will* punch through a Dwarf Frigate," Sosha answered, all levity gone from her voice. "But our strength is not in our projectiles, it lies in our speed. While Dwarf Frigates flounder in the air, the Valkyrie can attack where their enemy is most vulnerable, along the deck, the mast, the rudder. Where you are the weakest, we will hit you the hardest."

Nickle nodded, thinking through the strategy. As he mulled it over in his head, he realized that the Valkyrie valued speed and agility in all aspects of their combat, from armor to ships to weaponry. It made sense, knowing they were gifted with wings and the force of the Wind.

They continued through the rest of the ship, visiting the kitchen, the barracks, the armory, and the munitions locker. As they walked, Nickle began to get the impression that the Valkyrie only took this much time to show them the entire ship because it was larger and grander than any Dwarf Frigate.

When they reached the bottom floor, Sosha gestured wide with her hands. "This is the most protected and vulnerable part of the ship."

Nickle nodded knowingly. This principle held true with Dwarf Warships as well. The Runes responsible for most of the momentum and maneuvering were all housed on the bottom level. For this reason, it was the second most heavily armored location, falling just behind the munitions locker.

"Why is this so important?" Evalee asked.

"This is how the ship is maneuvered, how speed is increased, how turns are made," Sosha answered. The Valkyrie Elite General walked over to several metal boxes, patting the side of one with a gloved hand. "Inside are counterbalances that have a Mystic spell placed on them. If the captain turns the wheel to the right, these counterbalances also turn to the right. Since they keep the same gravity, they pull the ship in that direction. The biggest box in the middle is the Eveation and is responsible for giving the ship its elevation. Inside are a series of massive weights controlled by a lever on the upper deck. By activating one, you turn a set of stones upside down, but since they keep their original gravity, they begin to pull the ship up. If you activate them all at once, you'll shoot into the sky. A true master of the ship can use their Eveation for all types of maneuvers, not just gaining height. Is this how a Dwarf Warship functions as well?"

Nickle nodded. "More or less. We just use Runes to activate the weights, but we pretty much use Mystic magic to offset the weight and steer." He whispered these words as if embarrassed by them. No Dwarf liked to admit that they needed Elf or Mystic magic to fly their ships.

"How do you communicate from ship to ship?" Nickle asked, eager to change the subject.

"We use the Wind to relay short communications," Sosha said. "But this form of communication has severe disadvantages, such as limited range and being unreliable. So, in combat, we typically default to using a complex series of flags, which are operated by a Flagonneer. The flags, once seen, are replicated on each ship, enabling other vessels to see them in the distance. Using our flags, we can communicate over two hundred formations and attack patterns."

"Not as effective as using a Rune Communicator," Nickle whispered.

"What was that?" Sosha asked.

"That's fascinating," Nickle supplied.

Sosha eyed the Dwarf carefully before taking a few more minutes to show them how to fly the ship. Once the tour was complete, she excused herself to attend to other matters.

Yaroslav yawned, clearly bored by the whole affair. This had likely not been his first flight on the massive vessel. "When is lunch served?"

"I imagine at lunchtime," Jaylyn answered smartly. "Don't be such a bore. At least put a smile on your face."

"If I could ever get around to stuffing that puma," Yaroslav answered. "Then I'd be smiling. The thing is massive. It took three people to carry it. Cost a small fortune, from what I hear."

Nickle sighed. Every time he helped Yaroslav stuff an animal, his fingers always smelled like mothballs for several days after. The Polix Saliva was just so hard to wash out of the skin. Still, he had to admit that Yaroslav had a natural talent for mixing the right potions to create the desired effect. Nickle had little doubt that Yaroslav could make serious gold dust if he did it full time. But for someone who had more money than he could ever spend in his lifetime, it did not really appeal to him.

The four of them slowly drifted up to the front of the ship. The sun was just starting to climb up in the east, casting a wonderful hue of reds and oranges. As they approached the Eagle in the front, Evalee closed her eyes, enjoying the air whipping through her hair and past her wings. A placid calm overcame her features, washing away the worry piling up over the last several weeks.

Then Jaylyn pushed her. Evalee's eyes snapped open, surprised by the shove.

"You're it," Jaylyn said quickly. She then spread her wings wide and leaped over the side of the ship. Two of her Valkyrie Elite bodyguards also followed the princess over the edge.

"You're it?" Evalee asked the others.

"It's called Touch and Run," Yaroslav replied. "Childish game, really. But one person is it, and they try and touch the other, but...."

With that, Evalee was gone, disappearing over the side with a broad smile, laughing as she did.

"Will they be able to keep up with the ship?" Nickle asked.

"If we were at full speed, it would be hard, but we're going only a quarter of that," Yaroslav answered.

The two peered over the edge of the vessel, occasionally catching glimpses of the ocean far below.

"How have you enjoyed Valenburg so far?" Yaroslav asked.

"It's amazing. So different than EarthWorks. Everything is orderly and well thought out. The Docker in EarthWorks has only half the ships coming in at any given time and is twice as confusing."

"Order," Yaroslav said, placing his hands behind his back. "Order is the most essential virtue a society can obtain.

"Well, in that case, your people are doing well."

"Not as good as when we served Kara'Kala," Yaroslav said, his voice low.

Nickle swallowed, not sure how to react.

He turned to the Dwarf, his face serious. "You know, the Demon Lord has a bad reputation, but I've never understood why?"

"Because he enslaved people," Nickle answered. "He wanted to structure society with him and his people on the top. He eliminated his opposition by assassination. Under his rule, no one had a voice. People either obeyed or were punished."

"It certainly sounds bad when you say it that way," Yaroslav said. "But you have to take the good with the bad. Did you know that during his reign, there was no poverty, no starvation, no riots, no protests, no blackouts. There was no trash in the streets, no near collisions with Taxi-Lators. Under Kara'Kala, EarthWorks was once like Valenburg, completely orderly and efficient."

"He seized land and possessions simply because he wanted them," Nickle said. "His Demon Brood became wealthy at the expense of the average worker."

"I would argue it was for the benefit of the average worker," Yaroslav said. "Are you telling me that someone is better off having more freedom than enough food? What's the point of being able to choose something if you can't feed your kids? Yes, he did strip people's freedoms, but it was all for the greater good. If we needed more people producing food, Kara'Kala simply assigned them to do it. If we needed more buildings built, Dwarves were ordered to get it done."

Nickle did not answer. In truth, sometimes it felt like there were so many opinions in EarthWorks that there was no direction. Almost every day, people were protesting one thing or another throughout the city, each of them demanding something different.

"And then you have the Elves," Yaroslav said. "They live like kings and let the scraps fall to us."

Nickle almost laughed at this. It was a little ironic hearing these words from a person who probably never cooked a meal in his life.

"Kara'Kala did want to restructure society," Yaroslav continued. "But the main reason he did was to put the Elves in their place. Tell me, how is it worse what Kara'Kala did than what the Elves are doing right now? The pointy ears use their vast wealth to control almost everything in EarthWorks. Do you call that freedom? Doesn't sound like it to me."

Nickle let out a long sigh, contemplating his response, but he did not have time to answer before Jaylyn appeared, sneaking up from behind and hitting Nickle in the back.

"You're it!" she screamed, laughing wildly.

The Dwarf turned around, a shallow smile on his lips.

"These games bore me," Yaroslav said. "I'm going to get something to eat."

"You're just mad because you can't fly," Jaylyn teased.

Yaroslav shrugged indifferently as he disappeared. "Sure."

"I can't fly either," Nickle replied. "I couldn't even reach you if I tried."

"Or maybe you're just not trying hard enough," Jaylyn said, taking a cautious step forward.

Nickle leaped towards her, but she was too fast, whipping back into the air, only inches from his grasp. She then dangled a foot within inches of the Dwarf. Again, the Dwarf lunged, but again she pulled back, cackling with laughter.

"You think you're funny, don't you?" Nickle asked.

"I'm just fast—"

Nickle Vicinerated, appearing by the Valkyrie's side. He poked Jaylyn in the side before disappearing. By the time she turned around, he had reappeared on the opposite side and jabbed her arm. She whirled around only to see him relaxing at the edge of the ship twenty yards in front of her.

"How did you that?" Jaylyn said, landing softly on the ground.

"I can show you," Nickle replied, a broad grin on his face. He stuck out his hand. She was hesitant at first but then took it, intrigued by a magic she had never seen a Dwarf use before.

Then Evalee appeared, her wings fluttering quickly. "There you are!" She landed hard on the deck, her expression changing, her eyes tracing up to Nickle and Jaylyn's interlocking hands.

Anger like she had never experienced burned through the High Faeries' body, sending chilling ice down her skin and into the deck below. Her eyes became slits as they narrowed around Jaylyn. Ice shards sprang up from the ground in a circle, reaching up to the one that created them.

Jaylyn let go of Nickle's hand and stepped back, momentarily terrified by the spectacle. The High Faerie looked so different now, filled with raw power. She was a beacon of ice and light.

The Valkyrie Elite swarmed in, landing between the High Faerie and Jaylyn, their weapons raised.

Nickle turned to the Valkyrie. "Don't worry. It's just Evie."

This seemed to calm Jaylyn ever so slightly. He turned back to the High Faerie, but she was gone. The only thing left behind was the layers of ice still on the deck in a perfect circle.

"Where'd she go?" Jaylyn asked.

"She just needs a…a break," Nickle said quickly. "Staying in a Human form for so long can be challenging for a High Faerie. She'll be fine."

"Are you all right, Heir to the Throne?" one of the Valkyrie Elite asked, her voice firm. "At your command, we will find the High Faerie."

"No, it's fine," Jaylyn answered. "It was just a game. She just startled me is all."

Nickle stepped closer. "It's ok. I'm sure she'll be fine by tomorrow."

"How did she disappear? How did you disappear, for that matter?"

"Vicineration," Nickle said. "All High Faeries can do it."

"But you're a Dwarf…."

"A thousand pardons, Heir to the Obsidian Throne," said a low, bellowing Valkyrie voice from behind. The two of them faced this newcomer, surprised at their silent approach.

The warrior continued. "The Queen requests to see you."

The Dwarf pointed at himself. "Me?"

The Valkyrie did not respond, an annoyed expression on her face.

"Ok," Nickle said. He bowed low to the Princess before heading off after the warrior. "I didn't know she was even on the ship. I guess she must have come on before…."

"Remember your protocols, Dwarf," the Valkyrie said, cutting him off.

Nickle nodded before falling silent. They went to the rear of the ship, a part that he had not seen before. This area was usually off-limits to anyone except the royal family and the Valkyrie Elite. The Dwarf brushed his hair with his hands, hoping that it did not look as messy as it usually did.

The Valkyrie pushed open a cabin door, allowing him to pass inside. The room was not big, but it was ornate. On the opposite side was a small throne that was lined with pillars. Queen Victra Petrov Godfrey sat upright on the throne, her palms down on the armrests. She was the picture of stoicism but looked even more terrifying in the low light of the room.

The Dwarf stepped forward, causing some unease among the guards.

"Let him pass," the Queen whispered. "I summoned him."

Nickle continued, this time a little more slowly. He could sense the presence of several more warriors just waiting in the shadows. He had no doubt that they would cut him down if he presented himself as a threat for even a moment. When he reached the center of the room, he bowed low, as was required.

"Rise," the Queen said. She stood as well, her hands going behind her back, much like her son had done only minutes before. "Tell me, what have you discovered so far?"

"Unfortunately, not much," Nickle answered. "We've found a few families who are adamant supporters of Kara'Kala; some of them are even stockpiling weapons."

The Queen quickly looked to one of her guards, giving a barely imperceptible nod.

"We also found that someone in the Palace is attempting to contact at least one former supporter of Kala'Kala," Nickle continued. "We believe that someone within the Palace is trying to contact multiple individuals with the claim that the Demon Brood has once again been reestablished."

"These rumors have been around for decades," the Queen said, her tone sharpening. "I need more than this. Who is responsible for the attacks on my people?"

Nickle swallowed. "One of our team members, a talented Thieftian, was able to examine the potions used in the attack on the Nest."

"And?"

"It appears consistent with what is used by the Assassins of the Midnight, but, of course, any talented potion maker could replicate it."

"And is that likely?"

"He doesn't think so."

The Queen paced around her throne. It was striking how similar she was to her son in mannerisms and tone. "Then it is likely the Nords hired an Assassin of the Midnight. First, they harbor Vampires on their island—a race that has long been our enemy—and now it appears they are using a trained Assassin. But you believe they had help from someone on the inside?"

"Yes, but I've been looking closely at your Palace staff, and no one sticks out."

"What could you possibly discover that I don't already know."

"I have…a unique ability."

"What is that?"

"I…can read mental impressions."

"A Dwarf Scathian? Impossible. You must be good to deceive Hawthorne, but I don't think so. Can you read my thoughts?"

"No," Nickle answered. "It appears that everyone in the royal family has been trained to guard their minds, and I wouldn't try even if you hadn't. Your Valkyrie Elite have also had some training in this, although it's not as thorough. I can still read general impressions of their mood or the occasional thought that bleeds through."

"Prove it."

Nickle cleared his throat. "Prove it?"

"Prove to me that Hawthorne has not deceived us both. Prove to me you are not an agent of the Assassins of the Midnight. Prove to me that I shouldn't kill you here and now."

Nickle raised his hands like he was under arrest. "Whoa, easy."

"Answer me. If I do not find it an adequate response, your next words could be your last. You will be cut down in this very room."

"Umm…ok…well…there are ten guards in this room, as opposed to the only two you have out in the open. Four carry spears, the rest have drawn their Falcata swords and carry circular shields. Sosha is one of them, which is odd. I don't know why you would hide her from me. If I took another step forward, two of them would come out and block my path. I can sense their tension, their desire to protect their Queen. But, I also can sense…hesitation.…"

The Queen did not move, her face emotionless as she looked to the shadows and nodded. A moment later, Sosha stepped out, her eyes falling upon Nickle. Behind her cold expression was a hint of disdain for the Dwarf, as if he was garbage that needed to be removed.

"The Queen…trusts you," Sosha said, her voice hesitant.

"But…you don't," Nickle said.

"If I had my way, you would not still be here," Sosha said through gritted teeth.

"Sosha," the Queen reprimanded.

The Valkyrie Elite General straightened up, remembering her duties. She touched the sidewall, using a Wind spell as she did. At first, nothing appeared to change, but then as the pressure built up, a table topped with a map began to emerge from the center of the room.

Nickle stepped back. It rose to his waist before the Queen nodded again, and Sosha stopped channeling Wind into the wall panel.

Nickle stepped up to the map, impressed by the detail. It was panned out enough so all the Isles of Balinbar could be seen. Sosha twisted her hand on the wall, adjusting the map's orientation, zooming in on the Balkinian Chain, the islands of the Nords.

Then the Dwarf realized that it was not a solid map, as it had first appeared, but one made by hundreds of small wind currents carrying different grains of sand in very particular patterns. The level of craftsmanship was exquisite, even though occasionally, one of the wind currents would falter, making an island or two disappear for a moment.

"It appears," Sosha said. "That the Nords and Cicurians are starting to elevate their military activities, each bringing ships to our borders."

"Why are they doing that?" Nickle asked.

"My husband, as noble as he is, can also be stubborn," Queen Victra said. "He now controls a small portion of our Valkyrie vessels. And under his command, they are conducting military operations near our borders."

"So the other islands are just responding to your aggression," Nickle said simply.

"Perhaps. But whatever the reason, a small conflict with any of these forces could lead to an all-out war. So we don't have weeks to figure this out. We might not even have days. It doesn't really matter which side fires first; the result will be the same."

"Do you think the other islands are all fighting together?" Nickle asked.

"No, but any conflict with any of them will likely pull in the Nords, who will act as if they are protecting themselves from Valkyrie aggression."

"Is there a chance the Nords could win?"

"If the Vampires didn't join the Nords, the answer would be a simple no," Sosha answered. "The Valkyrie have always had far superior military power, and that has helped maintain the peace among the Isles. But the Vampire's presence has shifted the power. Worse, we don't know how many Vampires have actually joined the Nords."

"How long do you think we have?"

The Queen looked at Sosha, who in turn faced Nickle. "If I'm being optimistic, I'd say we have only a week before all-out war breaks out."

The Queen returned to her chair, her face resuming its stoic expression. She stared at the Dwarf for several long, uncomfortable moments. "I need to have the truth—no matter where it leads. Hurry, Nickle, before this conflict escalates further and threatens the lives of my people."

Chapter 26

An Old Acquaintance

"We are running out of time," Nickle said to the group. "The Queen thinks we have days before border disputes become an all-out war. We need to come up with something quick before everything goes sideways."

He had just shared everything about his exchange with the Queen to his friends. They were in the basement of the shop. Besides Swiftrunner, they all looked exhausted. This seemed especially true for Sharlindrian. The only person absent was Evalee, who had not been seen by anyone after she had vanished from the ship.

Shemway sat up, nodding to the Dwarf. "So, any new leads? Anyone? Come on now."

"We've got leads," Nickle replied. "They just haven't taken us anywhere."

"Thornhead had some information, but that doesn't really apply to what we're doing here," Jason added. "Someone was trying to communicate with him, someone from inside the Palace. But if Thornhead was telling the truth, and honestly, why would he lie, then someone has reestablished the Demon Brood."

"And Sharlie found all of those Kara'Kala supporters among the nobles," Swiftrunner said.

"It does seem like several people here wouldn't mind if Kara'Kala returned, including the crown prince," Nickle said.

"What about the King and Queen?" Shemway asked.

"Oh, I don't think they'd ever support Kara'Kala," Nickle answered. "Even before the Demon Lord was imprisoned, the Valkyrie turned against him."

"But none of that makes sense," Sharlindrian said. "How does the Demon Brood being reestablished have anything to do with the coming conflict? We've been looking for clues for months, and we've found nothing that links the bombings to any of the other islands."

"Besides the specific types of potions used," Shemway added.

"Just because the Assassins of the Midnight are known for using Dragon Fire doesn't mean they had any connection to it," Sharlindrian said quickly. "A skilled Alchemist can create any sort of potion with the right training." She turned a critical eye to Jason. "What about the potion shop? Wasn't the shop supposed to draw out the potential spy? Or was that just a front to get money?"

"Hey," Jason said, his voice falling to a defensive tone. "Running a successful business draws more people in. The more people, the more likely we can find who we are looking for."

Sharlindrian folded her arms, a skeptical look on her face.

Shemway shrugged. "We've had a lot of leads, but nothing promising. We've placed Rune Trackers on all the people that have purchased ingredients that could be used to make Dragon Fire, but none of them have ever gone to the Palace or even appeared to have access to the Palace."

"Maybe it was a hand-off," Swiftrunner said. "Someone hired someone else to buy the items from the shop, and then they met in some random location."

"That is a real possibility," Shemway replied.

"Are we sure it's someone in the Palace?" Sharlindrian asked.

"After working there for a few weeks and seeing how tight security is, I'd say it would have to be," Nickle answered. "They knew where the vault was, and they knew the schedule for the royal Prince. Both attacks had intimate knowledge that is only held by a few."

"So we can assume," Shemway said as he placed his hands behind his back, "that whoever is behind this wants a war between the Valkyrie and the Nords. Who does that benefit? Why would someone be pushing for war?"

"The King seems like he wouldn't mind a war," Jason added.

"But why?" Shemway asked. "What does he gain?"

"Maybe he wants to take and keep the land for himself," Swiftrunner said.

"Or, maybe he wants to attack the Vampires before they get too strong," Jason suggested.

"Whoever did this might have well blown up their Lightning Reserves," Nickle replied. "If the Vault had not been reinforced only a few weeks prior, it would have destroyed at least a part of it. Even if the King does want a war, I doubt he would go that far to get it. Most likely, the saboteur has no connection to the royal family. If anything, it would be a disgruntled Valkyrie Elite who knew where the Lightning Vault was located."

"But would a Valkyrie Elite ever turn against their Queen?" Swiftrunner asked.

"I doubt it," Nickle replied dolefully. "It seems extremely unlikely, but I don't know who else it could be. I've read most of the servants' minds, and nothing has ever stood out to me. And if they were hiding a big secret like that, I think it would be pretty obvious."

"Can you just read the minds of the Valkyrie Elite?" Swiftrunner asked.

"No, they've been trained to defend their minds," Nickle replied. "Even if I could, I wouldn't do it without the Queen's permission. And I doubt she would give me that any time soon. She trusts her Valkyrie Elite far more than she trusts anyone else."

"So whoever the traitor is," Shemway answered. "They are very good."

"Both attacks were designed to deliver a crippling blow to the Valkyrie," Sharlindrian said. "If they would have lost their Lightning Reserves, it would have sent the economy in a tailspin or worse, destroyed a portion of the island. If they had lost the Eagle's Nest, it would have hampered their military."

"What are you saying?" Swiftrunner asked.

"That perhaps it's as simple as that," Sharlindrian replied. "Maybe the King is right and one of the Assassins of Midnight is behind the attacks. The Nords might be just as divided as the Valkyrie when it comes to war. Maybe a few Nords hired an Assassin of the Midnight to attack the Valkyrie so they could push the rest of the Nords to war while at the same time delivering a crippling blow to the Valkyrie."

"I guess there is no way of knowing," Nickle said.

"Not when we are here," Sharlindrian answered.

"What are you saying?" Jason asked.

"That we pay the Nords a visit."

"You're insane," Jason said. "I'm sure they'll be suspecting some Valkyrie spy to start poking around. Plus, who knows how many

Vampires they're housing. We'd be surrounded by enemies."

"What building are you thinking we should try and infiltrate?" Shemway asked.

"The Capital building," Sharlindrian answered. "Whatever they are planning on doing, or whatever they are doing, we will be able to find out there."

"That's got to be the most protected building on the whole island," Swiftrunner said.

"Impossible," Jason said. "We'd get caught before we deboarded a frigate onto the island."

Sharlindrian ignored the comment and looked to Shemway, her eyes glinting with excitement. "What do you say, Shemway, Master Thieftian?"

"Oh, please," Jason replied. "Don't inflate his ego."

"It is…impossible," Shemway said, "for the average Thieftian."

"Here we go," Jason said in a huff.

"But with disguises made by Evalee, we should be able to make it onto the island unnoticed," Shemway said. "Then we just need a few days to study the location and plan our entry and escape."

"We could just Vicinerate there," Swiftrunner suggested.

"Can't," Nickle answered simply. "I've never been there before, which makes it difficult."

"And we would also have no record of arriving," Shemway said. "I'm sure the security on the island has increased just as much as it has in Valenburg, and we will want to appear as normal and legitimate as possible—at least until we break in. We can travel there under the pretense of expanding our potion-making business."

"Is there enough time?" Nickle said.

"It will be tight," Shemway said. "Everyone is going to have to pitch in and pull their weight. But with my skills, we just might have a chance. Pack up. We leave tonight."

***

Nickle knocked softly at first but then louder as the door went unanswered. Finally, Evalee cracked open the door, allowing him inside.

He stepped forward, sparing a grin. Even though the room was dark, Nickle could see the tear trails beneath the High Faeries' eyes. "Have you been crying?"

"No, my eyes have just been leaking water when I think about sad things," Evalee answered.

"That's crying."

"Crying? How's that possible? I didn't even know a Faerie could do that. What's wrong with me?" She looked to her hands as if she could find the answer there. She tightened her fingers into fists and closed her eyes, forcing two tears to drip out.

Nickle stepped forward, pulling his friend into a hug. "You're going to be okay. Here, sit down." The Dwarf broke from the embrace and walked his friend over to the window and two chairs. Evalee sat in one, Nickle in the other.

They both spoke at once.

"What's wrong with me?" Evalle said.

"Do you want something to drink?" Nickle asked.

They both laughed.

The Dwarf nodded to the Faerie. "You go first."

"Seriously, I've been feeling so many weird emotions. I mean, I thought I knew what being sad or angry was, but it was nothing like this. Even when I Vicinerated back here, it didn't cheer me up. I didn't feel any different. That's never happened. Not in the two hundred years that I've been alive."

"Has the techniques I've shown you helped?"

"Yeah, they work most of the time."

"Then what happened on the ship today?"

Evalee's eyes became distant as she recalled the events from earlier in the day. "I dunno…when I saw…saw you holding hands with Jaylyn, something inside of me exploded. I actually wanted to punch something. It was anger. Real…deep anger. I thought I knew what that meant, but it went so far beyond what I thought it did. You must think I'm a monster."

"Not really. Among the Dwarves having the desire to punch something is actually pretty common."

"When I saw how Jaylyn looked at me, with fear in her eyes, I felt so horrible I Vicinerated out of there. What is going on with me?"

"You're feeling real emotions, ones that are felt by Humans, Elves, and Dwarves."

"Did Atlantia change me that much?"

Nickle nodded slowly. "Perhaps. But, that might not be all bad."

"Why would she curse me like that?"

"It's a bittersweet gift. Now that your emotions have a larger range, you are much more powerful. I can sense it in you—a raging storm full of raw potential, like a Human just discovering their power."

"I need to eliminate these emotions from my body," Evalee answered, new desperation creeping into her voice.

"I don't think you do. In fact, because you can feel them, you're a better person for it. As you now have the capacity for greater hate and anger, you'll appreciate friendships and love all the more. Now that you've felt true sadness, it opens up the possibility for greater happiness."

"How does that make any sense?"

Nickle sat back, contemplating his reply before finally speaking. "Imagine if you had never missed a meal in your life. Whenever your body was even close to being hungry, you were suddenly full. Then one day, you see a man starving—someone begging for food. It would hardly affect you because that is something you've never experienced—it is something you cannot even relate to. But then imagine, one day, you don't have food and your stomach cramps because it is empty. On that day, you feel your energy weaken, your limbs lose their strength, your mind losing focus. The hunger racks your body with a real, visceral pain as your flesh slowly begins to die. Next time you see that man who is starving, begging for food, you'll know at least in part what they are facing—since you have experienced it yourself."

"I think I see."

"The difference between you and a Human, however, is that this is a sudden change for you. Humans have a lifetime to learn how to control their impulses, while you've only had a few months. And in that time, you've done remarkably well. You are truly a remarkable and kind person."

Evalee shook her head. "I don't think you understand. A Faerie is born from a strong emotion—and if we don't stay true to ourselves, it can change us into something evil. Something dark and loathsome."

"Like what?"

"Like…the Witches of Stobbin."

"Witches? Well, I won't let that happen."

Evalee leaned closer. "You have to help me, Nickle."

"I'm here for you," Nickle said carefully. "And so are all of your friends. But despite your emotions, you will always have the choice on whether to act on them or not—and it's because of the good choices you make, the kindness that you show every day—that I know you will overcome this obstacle."

Evalee wiped at her cheeks. "Since when did you get so wise?"

Nickle laughed.

"Seriously. You've been so mysterious lately. What has been going on with you?"

Nickle let out a long sigh, unsure of how he should respond. But then he realized he could never lie to Evalee—not now, not ever. She had so much faith and trust in him, he just could not stomach trying to deceive her. So, instead, he pulled up his sleeves, revealing the black stripes on his forearms. There were nine of them, five on the left arm, four on the right.

"What are those?" Evalee asked.

"The Ten Stripes that are required by the Scathians."

"But you're one short."

"I'm still in the final trial," Nickle replied, pulling the sleeves back over his arms. "It's been challenging, to say the least."

"And when are you finding time to do all of this?" Evalee asked.

"At night."

"Night is for sleeping."

Nickle shrugged.

"Five minutes," Shemway shouted from downstairs. "Paddles up in five minutes."

"Five minutes?" Evalee repeated.

"Yeah, change of plans," Nickle said in a rush. "We're going to North City on the Island of the Nords."

Chapter 27

The City of North

There were no direct roots from Valenburg to the Island of the Nords. So they first had to travel to New Atlantis, where they took another ship to an Orc city called Firmunt. There Shemway picked up fake identification cards for each of them. After a few delays, they charted a vessel to North City on the Island of the Nords. The trip was long, but they enjoyed the break from their grueling schedules. Sharlindrian was the most relieved at the reprieve, and she spent most of her time sleeping on a mess of nets in the lower decks.

As they approached the island, Nickle felt like he was entering an old Viking city, complete with longboats and stretched wooden houses. The streets were orderly like Valenburg, but they were covered in a blanket of snow, despite it being summer. Each block consisted of an entire building. The lower floors contained various shops while the uppers consisted of housing.

Evalee did well on their disguises, changing their appearance ever so slightly so as not to draw attention. They wore the simple clothes of Storm Chasers—leather boots, baggy pants, loose shirts, and thick winter coats. As they began deboarding the boat, the High Faerie adjusted their appearances to better match the Nords' style. She could not help but give Jason a set of hairy ears during the process.

The Nords preferred fur collars, thick armor, and steel-toed boots. Most wore a mix of blue and green; others were dressed in white. It seemed colors such as orange and yellow did not exist among these people. There were other creatures living on the island, but not many.

As they walked over a plank from their vessel and onto the floating island, two large and very hairy individuals stepped in front of them, brandishing axes made from Ice.

"Papers," said a female with thick braids.

"Allow me," Shemway said, pushing past the others. He smiled broadly as he turned over a stack of identification cards.

"Your purpose here?" the other asked. This one had a thick chest and a wider stomach. The top of his paunch jutted out so much, it could be used as a cup holder.

"Business," Shemway answered.

"If you keep to one-word answers, we're goin' to be here all day," the first said. "What kind of business?"

"I am a potion's master, and these are my associates. We've been running several successful Alchemist shops in cities all over the surface. We decided to make a trip up here and see if we could expand our operations to the fine Nordic people."

"You a Thieftian?" the man said, his eyes full of new scrutiny.

"Thieftian?" Jason said with a laugh. "I'd rather dunk my head in boiling water than be associated with that filth."

"Quite right," Shemway added.

"As the old saying goes," Jason continued. "The only time a Thieftian isn't cheating someone out of their money is when they are asleep. And even then, they're dreaming about it."

"Aah, yes," Shemway said, his smile tight. "My young and…incredibly short associate speaks the truth."

"I've seen rats I'd rather keep company with than them," Jason said.

"No need to overdo it," Shemway hissed. "The man gets your point."

The Nord grinned, displaying a mix of missing teeth. "The boy is right. And it looks like your papers are in order. You've been granted three days. If you need to extend your time, return to the docks."

"Very kind of you," Shemway said, bowing low. They pushed passed the guards and into the North City. It was a mix of wood monoliths and timber structures lined with stones.

Evalee shivered as she looked around. "Why is it so much colder here?"

"They keep it cold all year in their cities," Sharlindrian answered. "Nords are masters of Elemental Ice and Snow, and they prove it by peppering the ground each day with snow flurries."

"Why?" Nickle asked.

"Almost all prefer the cold, and it allows them to use sleds year-round to transport their goods."

"What about summer?" Evalee asked.

"They still have it on the rest of the island, just not in the towns," Sharlindrian answered.

"Fall?"

"Nope."

"Not even spring?"

"They think different seasons make a people soft," Sharlindrian said.

"These are definitely the bad guys."

The Nords were large people, much larger than normal Humans but still shorter than most Giants. Many of them were sporting braided white hair and grey eyes. They all wore armor as if they were getting ready to charge into battle.

Sharlindrian and Evalee subconsciously pulled their coats tighter around their bodies. They were unsure if it was the cutting wind or hollow stares, but something was definitely sending a shiver down their spines. They did not walk too far before Shemway hailed a sled pulled by reindeer, which ferried them to the opposite side of the city, near the Capital Building.

Nickle closed his eyes, enjoying the wind against his features, the air whipping through his hair. When he opened his eyes again, the Capital Building was before him, looming like a massive mountain of stone with ornate wood columns. Two giant statues stood at the entrance, carved from an enormous set of trees. One was a woman, the other a man, each carrying axes. Their eyes were milky white as if they were overseeing the city caught in a massive blizzard. The Dwarf could not help himself. He swallowed.

"Don't worry," Jason said to his friend.

Nickle frowned. "Worried? Me? Nah."

Since arriving, Nickle had been prying into almost every mind that was not on guard. Despite their appearance, these people were different than Humans. Their minds were so singularly focused on their tasks that there was little room for anything else. When Humans or even Dwarves were doing mundane chores, their minds often wandered, but the Nords kept a singular focus that was inspiring. It was also annoying, as Nickle was not able to glean any useful information.

They finally deboarded the sled and checked into a hotel called the Frozen Cunuggets. Shemway did the talking and arranged for three rooms, one for the girls, one for the boys, and one for himself. Jason was about to protest, but Nickle shook his head. All eyes in the shabby hotel lobby were on them, and it seemed unwise to draw any more attention.

After dropping off their bags into their appropriate rooms, Shemway wordlessly ushered them into his own room.

Jason was about to speak, but Shemway raised a single finger, silencing the Dwarf. He then pulled a vial from a hidden pocket on his sleeve. He uncorked it, and a white gas drifted up and around the room. It first spread evenly but slowly, it seemed to concentrate around a small desk in the corner of the room. Shemway squatted next to the desk and glanced underneath, spotting something not long after. He placed the vial under the desk and then turned to the others.

"What was that?" Swiftrunner asked.

"A Detector and Decoy Potion," Shemway answered. "Our rooms have been bugged."

"Bugged?" Jason said.

"These were Ice Bugs," Shemway answered. "Nasty little creatures that consume and transmit sounds back to their icy home."

"Can they hear us now?" Sharlindrian asked.

"What a Detector and Decoy Potion does is look for listening bugs and then continues to transmit sounds to them so everything appears normal," Shemway said.

"Why don't we just smash them or something," Swiftrunner asked. "I'm not loving the idea of bugs being planted in my room."

"If we did, they would suspect something," Shemway answered.

"So what are they hearing in the room now?" Jason asked.

"I bottled some of the ambient noise from the potion shop in Valenburg. Just boring stuff, really, nothing with details of who we are and what we are doing. Mostly Jason accusing me of changing my name badge."

"Who would be listening to us?" Nickle added. "Do they suspect us of something already?"

"I'm sure it's standard procedures for the Nords," Shemway answered. "They are pretty untrusting of outsiders, and with the

Valkyrie doing routine patrols near their borders, I'm sure they are even more so now."

"So, what's the plan?" Nickle asked.

Shemway grinned. "Straight to the point, eh." The Thieftian went to the far window and opened it in dramatic fashion, a broad grin on his face. "That is our object, children. Take a good look. To my knowledge, no Thieftian has ever successfully penetrated the Nordic Capital Building. Take a good look."

"The window is facing the wrong way," Sharlindrian said. "Your room faces the market. Our room faces the Capital Building."

Shemway turned around, realizing this was true. His face flushed slightly red before he spoke. "Regardless, in just two short days, we are going to break into the Capital Building and find out what exactly is going on."

"What do you need us to do?" Evalee asked.

"Sharlindrian and Swiftrunner, I need you to sit in your rooms and observe the front gate," Shemway ordered. "Any movement needs to be documented and detailed. I need to know when the guards rotate, how many there are, and what they are wearing."

"Sounds dreadfully boring, but at least I'm not cleaning houses," Sharlindrian said flatly.

"That's the spirit," Shemway said. "Nickle, I need you to start Vicinerating back to Valenburg and transporting our gear here."

"Sure thing," Nickle nodded.

"Evalee and Jason," Shemway said with a grin. "You two get the fun part."

"Oh, great," Jason groaned.

"Evalee, I need you to disguise yourself and Jason as Nords and go mingle," Shemway said.

"Mingle?" Jason asked skeptically.

"We need you two to learn how to speak like a Nord," Shemway replied. "Evalee, can you adjust someone's voice with your illusion magic? Can you make Jason sound more like a Nord?"

"Yes."

"That's not so bad of a task," Jason said, his voice filled with relief. "I'm actually surprised. I'd thought you'd have me climbing through the sewer or something." He actually turned to the others, grinning as if he had just received a gold star from his least favorite teacher. The others all nodded in turn, offering their silent congratulations.

Finally, Shemway's voice broke the silence. "Well, what are you all standing around for? We've got a lot to do and little time to do it. Chop, chop."

Chapter 28

The Capital Building

"It's c-clear," Sharlindrian said through the Blue Tip Water Faerie balm, her teeth chattering. Given everyone's skill set, it had been quickly decided that she would prove the best at keeping an eye on the outside of the massive Capital Building to guard their escape. She had refused at first, but Shemway insisted, arguing that with her analytical talent and her decisive nature, she was best suited for the position. She was perched on a steeple just outside the capital building wall, her body bundled up against the cold. Despite wearing all the layers of clothing she had brought and a borrowed coat, she shook against the wind. It had been chilly during the day, but the night proved especially frigid.

It was a difficult time reaching the steeple. The snow made the roof tiles so slippery, that Exsiliogation was an impossibility. So she defaulted to manipulating the gravity of her body ever so slightly. She could not just make herself fly to the top, as Mystic magic was difficult to cast on oneself, but she could do enough to make the climb at least manageable. Evalee had asked her why Swiftrunner just did not make a set of wings with his magic so she could fly to the top. But Transformation magic did not work like that, as the Cennarian had explained. Just because something looked like something else did not mean it functioned like it.

The rest of the group had decided they would enter through the main entrance, as Shemway insisted that it would be the last place the guards would expect an intrusion. It was near a loud blacksmith shop that was still ringing with work. The noise, coupled with the bright lights of the shop, proved to be a good distraction.

The Capital Building was like an old hill fort, set up on a massive mound of dirt that made it taller than all the other buildings. Its architecture was far superior to every other structure in the city, built with fine stonework and metal. It was surrounded by thick walls that were patrolled by rigid guards who looked about as impassible as an iceberg.

"Looks like the guards are switching out," Sharlindrian said. "And just in case any of you are wondering, I'm freezing to death. So get in there and do what you're intending to do."

"All right," Nickle whispered. "Time to see if this disguise holds up. Are you ready, Evalee and Swiftrunner? I see the group of guards coming." He was just over four inches tall now, tucked away on the shoulders of Jason's armor. Evalee was next to him, her face set with concentration. They were all dressed in their armor, their weapons at the ready. Evalee did not need to take a Shrinking Rune, as Nickle had. Instead, she had reverted to her actual Faerie size and was just under five inches. It was usually much harder for her to concentrate in this form, but since receiving Atlantia's gift, it was easier for some reason.

"Let's do this," Swiftrunner said as his eyes narrowed. He pulsed out with his magic, changing Jason and his body with Transformation magic. They grew taller, their bodies and biceps becoming thinner. The Cennarian could not adjust their armor since it was infused with magic, so it looked pitifully small, as if they were wearing a set of bibs tied around their now lanky bodies. They became a much thinner version of themselves.

"I guess it's my turn to finish the disguise," Evalee said.

Jason and Swiftrunner's appearances began to change, their features becoming colder and sharper. Their hair turned long and white; their clothes shifted into a patchwork of blue and white.

"Now, the illusion will hold as long as I can concentrate, and you two stay close," Evalee said. "In this form, my range is not nearly as great. So, if you wander off, all those perfect little details will start to fade."

"Is it just me," Jason said. "Or do I look super ugly right now?"

"It's not just you," Swiftrunner said. "You look as mean as a bull bit by a bullet ant."

"That sounds pretty mean," Jason mumbled.

"Oh, I forgot to add the illusion to your weapons," Evalee said. The next moment, Jason's axe and Swiftrunner's bow turned to ice, as was the style of the Nords. They now looked like two guards who were supposed to be working at the Capital Building that night. The actual guards had been tucked away in a hotel room and given one of Shemway's sleeping potions. It would be an entire day before they woke up again, or so the Thieftian claimed.

"Here comes the group," Jason whispered.

They held their breath as twenty Nords walked past, their hands burdened with weapons and packs of food. Jason and Swiftrunner joined the rear of the procession, their stretched-out legs wobbling ever so slightly.

"This feels weird," Jason whispered. "Like I'm walking downhill."

"You'll get used to it," Swiftrunner answered.

It was a short walk to the front of the Capital Building, where they were greeted by a massive Nord with a crystal-clear clipboard. They stepped beyond the wall and into a small room. This new guard, whoever she was, appeared to be in charge. "Who do we have today? TorFirk and Lakenburn, take the west wall. Gofrin and Vlad...."

The giant warrior spoke on and on, doling out assignments to the waiting crowd. It seemed that this group of guards was specifically assigned to protect the exterior front entrance. Finally, Orwin and Tomikin, which were really Jason and Swiftrunner, were assigned the North Tall Tower.

Although they got turned around for a few moments, with Sharlindrian's guidance, they finally found their way up to their posts. Two guards were standing there, waiting to be relieved. They looked weary but still alert.

Jason grunted as they approached, something that he had noticed the Nords tended to do in abundance. The Nords turned around at the noise, their expressions placid.

"Anything exciting happen?" Jason asked in the slow cadence and tone of the Nords. In the little time he had to practice how the Nords spoke, he had grasped the general tone and cadence exceptionally well. He could even mimic the voice of the real Orwin, who he had spoken to briefly before he was given his sleeping potion. This was made all the easier with Evalee's magic, which altered his voice just enough so it perfectly matched.

One of the guards approached Jason, his jaw taut. He was massive, even for a Nord, a solid four inches taller than the other three. "You're a fool, aren't you? No one would dare raid the Capital Building.

Not even the winged Valkyrie. We are wasting our time. And you are wasting mine." The warrior pushed a thick finger into Jason's chest, pushing him out of the way.

"Hey," Jason said. "No need to mix blood with ice." He had heard this phrase used by other Nords a few times. He was pretty sure it meant, "chill out."

Whatever it really meant, it had the opposite effect Jason was hoping for. The Nord stopped in his tracks, turning around slowly. "You speak of blood and ice. When has your axe ever graced the battlefield? When have you fallen into a shield wall in defense of our people?"

"When the horn calls, I will answer," Jason said solemnly, touching his brow.

The other Nords mimicked the gesture, whispering the same phrase. Swiftrunner did too, but he was much more delayed. The taller Nord did not look amused. He frowned, his face a picture of hate. "You want to prove your mettle, then accept my challenge."

Jason swallowed. "Now?"

"Now."

"But…I must do my duty."

"I will ask for an exception to your duties. It will be granted. Face me, Orwin, and earn something you've never had before—my respect."

Jason frowned. He did not know Orwin that much, but from the brief conversation he had with him, he did not seem like that bad of a guy. Orwin did not deserve to be talked to like that.

"Easy, marshmallow," Jason replied. Admittedly, it was not his best insult, but it did get his opponent's attention. "If I fight you tonight, there will not be a big enough crowd to see you and your ego fall. Tomorrow, I will fight you when others have had the chance to hear your insults. And when they all gather around, I will put you in the dirt."

The other three Nords were shocked by this response, especially Swiftrunner, who kept glancing between the other two. Finally, the taller Nord laughed, a smile gracing his lips. "Then so be it, Orwin. Perhaps you are a warrior after all. Tomorrow our fists will meet."

With that, the other two Nords disappeared down the tower.

"You've been a Nord for only ten minutes," Swiftrunner said, "and you're already picking fights."

"He shouldn't be taking that tone with Orwin," Jason answered. "I was just sticking up for the guy."

"I don't think Orwin will be thanking you any time soon," Swiftrunner said.

"Are you in place?" Shemway said over the Faerie Lip Balm.

"Not yet," Nickle answered. "Jason, put me on the ground, and let's get the decoys up."

Jason complied, reaching back and placing Nickle on his palm before setting him on the ground. Then the Dwarf removed two seven-inch-high figurines from his belt buckle. In his hands, they looked more like Nordic dolls, each done with surprising detail. He placed each one on the ground a few feet apart.

Nickle grunted as he picked up the first one while at the same time ingesting a Restorative Rune. The next moment, he was full size, and so was the decoy. The Dwarf put it down, facing it towards the city in the distance. Then he looked at Jason and frowned. "Ugh, I hate taking Shrinking Runes back-to-back. This is gonna make me sick for sure."

"Just think," Jason answered. "Each one of those Shrinking Runes took me two hours to craft. You've literally spent four hours of my life's work in the last few minutes." While he spoke, he placed a few Sight Runes on the tower. He then spoke to Sharlindrian. "Runes are up. Are you getting visual?"

Sharlindrian frowned before adjusting a disc against her eye. The disc, in turn, pulled against her skin, creating a buildup of pressure. "Yes, I have visual. I really hate these things, but I have visual."

Nickle swallowed a Shrinking Rune and then ran to the other decoy, repeating the process as before. Within moments, the decoys were in place, staring off into the distance, each one standing just over seven feet tall. Nickle had swiped a little Polix Saliva from Yaroslav's potion set and now used it to spread on the decoys' chests, giving them the allusion they were breathing.

"Not bad," Swiftrunner said. "Wouldn't convince a cow that it's a calf, but it'd probably fool the bull."

"What is taking so long?" Shemway said through the Faerie Lip

Balm. "I'm freezing my butt off."

"Always the diva," Jason whispered.

"What's that?" Shemway asked.

"Decoys are set up," Jason answered. "We're just moving out now."

Nickle swallowed another Shrinking Rune and was placed back onto Jason's shoulder. Then they went down the stairs and headed to the front entrance. As they approached, the four guards at the main door looked up, their expressions filled with curiosity, no doubt wondering why Orwin and Tomikin had left their posts. But that soon changed as Nickle drew close enough to manipulate their minds. Two disappeared down a long hallway, responding to the call of their commander. The other two suddenly remembered that Orwin was not assigned to stand guard on the wall; he had been invited inside by one of the Nord nobles. In fact, now that they were thinking about it, Orwin was to be a distinguished guest at an important meeting tonight.

The Nords bowed low, one grabbing the door. But instead of just Orwin and Tomikin entering, Shemway also swung inside, appearing suddenly from thin air. The Nords did not notice, however, as their eyes were fixed on the ground.

As the door shut behind them, Shemway turned to the two Nords. "I got you this far, but that was the easy part, so don't get cocky."

"*You* got us this far," Jason said in protest.

"Yes, we've already established that," Shemway replied. "Do try to keep up, Dwarf. You four find the security office and take out any magical cameras and charms. It won't do any good for us to leave a trail of breadcrumbs behind. I'll go ahead and see what I can find." The Thieftian pulled a potion from his waist. He uncorked the small bottle and poured the contents down his throat.

"What's that do?" Swiftrunner asked.

"It will blur my image on the cameras, and if I can stick to the shadows, they won't see me at all," Shemway said, a tone of annoyance in his voice. "Now get going before someone sees us standing around. The security office should be on the first floor, close to the entrance."

"Don't forget to place Sight Runes as you go," Nickle added. "Sharlie can't help us if she can't see us."

The Thieftian nodded before he was gone, shooting his

Crossbow into the ceiling high above and disappearing into the shadows.

The entrance hall was grand and imposing, with large wooden pillars upholding an ornate ceiling. The room was decorated with paintings of Nords, all of them wielding Ice and Snow as they fought against the Valkyrie. It seemed that the rivalry between these two nations went back for centuries.

As Jason and Swiftrunner walked deeper into the Capital Building, Nickle placed additional Sight Runes on the wall, creating a network of magical links that Sharlindrian could scroll through. Since Nickle was still miniature, so were the Sight Runes, making them barely noticeable in the expansive space. They ducked into a room off to the left, finding nothing but a tall library and a cluster of desks. Unfortunately, the Nords did not seem fond of signs, and there was no indication where the security room was located. The next room they checked, however, held something much more valuable.

"What are you doing here?" a Nord in regal blue cried, his voice carrying the weight of his station. He had been hovering over a mess of papers and projects. "You are wall guards, are you not? Return to the wall."

Jason nodded, playing for time. "My Lord, we were sent here to provide additional security."

"Well, whoever gave you that order is a fool," the Nord replied. "The Arctic Guards secure the inside of the Capital. Return to your post."

"Umm...yes, my Lord," Jason grumbled. He continued to bend low, his eyes waiting for something to happen. Swiftrunner did the same. When nothing did happen, the air turned awkward.

"Nickle," Jason whispered. "Do your stuff."

"I can't," the Dwarf replied. "He started raising his mental defenses the moment we walked in. He's had training in blocking mental attacks."

"That's not good," Swiftrunner said.

"What did you say?" the Nord in blue bellowed. "What are you still doing here? Do I need to call for the Artic Guards? They will tie you to a block of ice if they find you've abandoned your post."

"Plan B," Jason whispered.

"Plan B? Swiftrunner repeated. "What's plan B."

"Get him," Jason yelled.

But the noble Nord was waiting for this, his arms raised high. Jason was struck hard and fast in the chest with an icicle. Had he not been wearing his armor, it would have gone clear through him. As it was, it pitched him backward and into a bookshelf. Swiftrunner fared little better. He was able to dodge the first attack, but a wave of ice froze his feet to the floor a second later.

Jason regrouped and went in again, this time raising his axe. But he was beaten back by a blast of cold. Swiftrunner managed to free his feet, but they were frozen against a table just as quickly. Whoever this lone Nord was, had some surprising skill with Elemental magic.

"Throw me," Nickle said.

"Throw you?" Jason asked. "At what?"

"At him," Nickle answered.

Jason obeyed, chucking the nearly five-inch-high Nickle a second later. In mid-air, Nickle swallowed a Restorative Rune, regaining his former size just before he collided with the Nord, knocking him flat on his back.

The old warrior was startled by the sudden apparition of a Dwarf flying straight at him. He would have called for help, but Nickle's beard got caught in the man's mouth, leaving him hacking for breath instead. The struggle ended a moment later as Nickle placed a finger against the man's temple, knocking him unconscious with a wave of mental energy.

Jason frowned. "That could have gone better."

"Well, I doubt it could have gone much worse," Swiftrunner said. "Who is that guy?"

"Somebody important," Nickle said. "I'm in his mind now. His name is...Ulgarian the Wise. He was just about to leave when we came in...there's a dinner event tonight...something important. All the members of the Nordic Council will be there. I know where the security room is located—it's not far, but we've been going in the wrong direction. But we better tuck this guy away before someone comes. There's no telling how much noise we made."

"That's why I'm here," Evalee said sweetly. "While you three were playing in the snow, I made sure no one outside could hear you."

"Quick thinking," Nickle said. "Swiftrunner, hide Ulgarian in a spot where no one will find him until morning. Evalee, can you change Jason so he now looks like Ulgarian? That should help us move more easily through the building."

"Yes," Evalee said, her voice trembling. "But, it's so much more tiring adjusting illusions in my tiny form. Give me a few seconds to breath."

"Sure," Nickle said. "I think all of us could use the break. Sharlie, is there any movement outside? Are the guards reacting at all?"

"N-no," Sharlindrian said, her teeth chattering over the Faerie Lip Balm. "N-n-nothing but hypothermia to worry about."

"Good deal," Nickle replied.

"Were you able to see if Ulgarian knew anything about the attacks on the Valkyrie?" Jason asked.

"He knows about them but has no idea who is behind them," Nickle answered. "Everyone ready to move out? We need to shut down the security room before Shemway lands himself in trouble."

Evalee sighed before finally nodding. During the conflict she had taken flight on her Faerie wings, but now she returned to Jason's shoulder. "All right, I'm ready. Let's move."

With this, the other three regrouped and moved out, following Jason out the door. Nickle had taken another Shrinking Rune and had returned to his spot on Jason's shoulder. Occasionally, he would relay directions of where they needed to go. The Capital Building was a maze of offices and conference rooms. With Nickle's new knowledge, however, they found it in short order. They reached a long, plain hallway that ended abruptly in a thick door. This part of the Capital Building lacked all the ornateness the rest of it contained.

"They've got this locked up tight," Swiftrunner said. "The door is solid steel."

"I got this," Jason said, his voice laced with new confidence. "I've been practicing for just this sort of thing."

"Are...y-you sure you know what your d-doing?" Sharlindrian asked through the Faerie Lip Balm.

Jason scoffed. "I'll have this door opened in seconds. And the best thing is, the lock will just have appeared defective." While he spoke, he pulled out two potions and a thin glass tube. He mixed them as carefully as he could before placing the glass tube on top of one of the bottles.

"What's that supposed to do?" Swiftrunner asked.

"If I just mixed it properly, I just created Faerie Fire," Jason said with a wink. "Stand back and watch the magic." He then inserted the glass tube into the lock, his grin persisting. But when the liquid did not slide out as expected, his smile faded. "Oh, crap."

"What's wrong?" Evalee asked.

Jason ignored the question and began talking to himself. "Did I...mix that right. I pour the Faerie Tears into the Cottonwood Sap, right? Or...is it the other way around. No...I did it right."

"Maybe we need to think of something else," Swiftrunner suggested. "What about using those Fire Runes on your axe to cut it open."

"That would leave a nasty burn behind," Nickle replied. "Not exactly subtle."

"I got this," Jason said. "It just needs to slide out of the bottle and into the lock." The Dwarf began to tap the back of the flask like it was a Heinz ketchup bottle. On the third tap, it suddenly all came out in a rush. But it did not pour into the lock like it was supposed to, but down the front of the door. The next second, the whole thing caught on fire, burning with a manic frenzy. Everywhere the Faerie Fire landed, it burned with a surreal intensity.

Everyone was so shocked, they just stood there watching the fire spread to the tops of the doorframe.

Then the security room door popped open, and a head peaked out. It was one of the Artic Guards—one of the Nord's elite warriors. He was so distracted by the flames, Jason and Swiftrunner were able to rush in and subdue him amidst all the confusion. Two more guards appeared a half-minute later, but they too were so distracted by the flames they were easy enough to deal with.

When the guards were all tied up, Jason looked up, a grin on his face. "I told you I could get us through that door in a matter of seconds."

Nickle could not help but laugh. "Yeah, I'm pretty sure that's not how Shemway taught you how to do that. You may want to put out that fire before it activates some alarm and everyone goes running out of the building."

"I can do that," Swiftrunner said, his voice full of confidence. He pulled a Water Rune from his pocket, releasing it with a whisper.

The flames were swept away under a torrent of water.

"See, you can hardly tell the door was burning," Jason said. "Besides a little tarnish, the steel was barely damaged. No one is going to notice a thing."

"Besides the fact that floor is now soaking wet," Evalee said.

"Besides that, no one will notice a thing," Jason said.

"Well, we better get to this," Nickle said, walking deeper inside the security room. There was a series of Ice Tablets against the wall, each broadcasting a different view inside the Capital Building. The system was expansive, showing dozens of different rooms.

"So…how do we take this apart?" Swiftrunner asked, looking to each of the others in turn.

"Can't we just…turn it off?" Evalee asked.

"I think they'd notice," Jason answered.

"D-d-didn't you r-read the material Hawthorne gave us?" Sharlindrian asked.

"Ugh," Jason answered. "It was a little dry in the middle…and at the end…and the beginning."

"None of y-you read it?" Sharlindrian said.

The other four exchanged looks, each one shrugging in turn.

"W-what am I doing out in the c-cold, when I'm the only one that r-read anything?" Sharlindrian asked. "Never mind. D-don't answer that. The Nord's magic is based on Ice."

Jason rubbed his chest where he had been struck by a magical Icicle. "I could have told you that."

Sharlindrian ignored the comment and continued her explanation. "The N-Nords magic is based on ice. Not only do they use it as w-w-weapons, they also use it to transmit images or conversations from one p-p-place to a-a-another. You should look for a b-block of i-ice that dumps into the back of the stone tablets."

It was not long before Nickle pointed it out. A six-inch wide trail of Ice traveled around the room before it disappeared into a wall. "I think I see it."

"What you need to d-do is break the ice at one p-p-oint, but then cover the break with a different kind of magical Ice," Sharlindrian said. "That should break the magical spell, severing the camera connections, b-but then also make it look like it's s-still functioning. Use an Ice Rune or something."

"Ice Runes aren't that precise," Jason said. "If we release a Rune in here, we're just as likely to cover the wall as the breach. I can try to use Elemental magic, but I'm much better with Fire than Ice."

"I can do it," Evalee said quickly.

"Do it," Jason said. "And let's get out of here." With this, he drew out his axe and fixed a HellFire Rune to the side. The blade glowed yellow as he activated the Rune and slowly slid it into the ice, instantly creating jets of steam that rose into the air. He then repeated the process a few inches down, removing a chunk of the ice.

Once this was gone, Evalee flew down, taking on her Human form. She stretched out her arms, focusing on the task at hand.

"Can you do this?" Nickle asked.

"I just need to…tap my newfound anger," Evalee said with half a smile. "Give me a second." She stretched out her fingers towards the breach—but nothing happened.

"*You* need to get angry?" Jason said. "Yeah, we're going to be here a while."

"How do you all get angry so easily?" Evalee asked. "You guys just seem to turn it on like a switch."

"Just think of something that makes you want to buck the hay," Swiftrunner said.

Still, Evalee struggled with the spell, attempting twice more but failing both times to even produce a snowflake.

"Or…," Nickle added. "Think of someone that makes you want to buck the hay—whatever that's supposed to mean."

Without any more prompting, a name flashed through her mind, and Ice shot out of the High Faeries' fingertips, covering the breach in ice. She was so shocked at the sudden explosion of magic, her aim was a little off, spraying some of the wall with flecks of sleet.

"Dang," Jason said. "I'm afraid to ask who the person was that you were thinking of."

"It's…no one," Evalee said quickly, her cheeks flushing red. "Did it work?"

"Yeah," Nickle said. "Good work." He then activated the Faerie Lip Balm and spoke to Shemway. "The Ice Cameras are down."

"It's about time," Shemway answered. "I was beginning to think you all got captured."

Swiftrunner nodded to the equipment on the wall. "Yeah, but

the Ice Tablets aren't displaying anything anymore. They've all been disconnected. Anyone who comes in here now will see that it's been sabotaged."

"You need to l-loop them to the saved archives," Sharlindrian said. "Adjust the video so it plays footage from a few days prior."

"How do we do that?" Jason asked.

Sharlindrian sighed. "Look for a s-storage device. Likely a big block of i-i-ice."

"Got it," Nickle said. "Just under the Ice Tablets. But how do we work it?"

"Elemental magic," Sharlindrian said. "Evalee, use your magic to m-manipulate the feeds. P-p-play something from a f-few days prior."

Evalee stepped forward, placing a hand on the ice, using her Elemental magic to peer within the frozen space. It felt odd, like trying to find a light switch in the dark. But the longer she persisted, the more it all made sense. Before too long, the Ice Tablets flicked on, broadcasting the events from a week ago at the same time.

"Did you see that?" Swiftrunner asked, pulling everyone's attention to the screens.

"What's that?" Jason asked.

"Evalee, can you turn this one back a few seconds?" Swiftrunner said while pointing to the largest of the Ice Tablets, his voice low.

"Sure," Evalee replied.

Everyone crowded closer around the screen, their eyes wide. It was brief, but for half a second, a large figure entered the screen, her body shrouded with armor.

"Ethilian?" Nickle asked. "In the Capital Building?"

"Looks like it," Jason answered.

"So, she really has teamed up with the Nords," Evalee said.

"Not only that, they're so open about their alliance, she's free to walk around the building unescorted," Nickle said. "Looks like they trust her as one of their own."

"Are you s-sure it's her?" Sharlindrian asked through the Faerie Lip Balm.

"Positive," Jason replied. "I'd recognize that bloodsucker anywhere."

"But that still doesn't tell us what they're up to," Swiftrunner said. "You can catch the milkmaid with a light bucket, but that doesn't mean she stole the cream."

"There's got to be a way to figure out exactly what she's doing here," Jason said.

"You know," Nickle said, inspiration suddenly hitting him. "I think…I might have a way." Nickle touched the Fairey Lip balm on his lip, ensuring it was still working. "Shemway, can you hear me? Change of plans."

***

Shemway moved as smooth as a breeze through the hall, using his stealth to slink into the shadows as Nords went about various tasks. During the day, this was the busiest part of the Capital Building, but at this late hour, it was mostly abandoned. Only a few Nords remained in their offices, working on some project or proposal.

He shot his Crossbow into the ceiling high above and pushed the retraction button, pulling himself up into a corner just as two Arctic Guards were walking past, their eyes scanning the area for trouble. They wore heavy armor, a mix of leather and Ice that was reinforced by magic. Once they continued on, he returned to the ground.

His senses had been enhanced by a potion he had taken an hour before, allowing his ears to pick up the slightest sound in the distance. Occasionally, he would place a Sight Rune at a critical junction, allowing Sharlindrian a greater view of the Capital Building.

Shemway pushed on, taking a flight of stairs to the upper levels where he hoped to find the offices of high-ranking officials. On the fourth level, he found what he was looking for—a series of ornate and large offices. Two of them even held the crest of the Nordic Council. But he had to be cautious, as the hallway was narrower and better lit by Ice spheres that flickered with an iridescent blue light.

Then he heard footfalls to his left; someone was twisting a door handle. Without hesitation, Shemway cracked a vial of Wind Rune enhanced Green Till in hand, instantly turning himself invisible. This had been another innovation that Jason had developed, much to Shemway's secret annoyance. Although they did not sell it in their shop, it proved extremely practical. In the past, Thieftians had to apply Green Till by pouring the cloud-like potion over their body. This took time, and since Green Till did not last long anyway, it greatly diminished the potion's application. But Jason's new concoction used a Wind Rune to disperse the potion instantly, surrounding the user's body with a blanket of invisibility.

An important-looking Nord official carrying a stack of papers walked out of the door, a look of exhaustion on her face. Shemway slipped inside before the door closed. A few other Nords were working at their desks, but they gave no notice to the invisible Thieftian. He pushed on, glancing at files piled on cabinets and placing Sight Runes all the while. He did not have much confidence in the Sight Runes capturing the information they were after. The building was just too big and the chance of seeing something valuable seemed so remote. If they were going to find something, he would have to be the one to do it. He looked over several documents—plans for new buildings, military training schedules, budget and balance sheets, and Lightning reserves quotas. It all seemed terribly boring.

So, he covered his eyelids with an Azure Bunsin cream and released a Tracker potion. It was a clear, odorless potion. If he did not make the potion himself, he would have sworn the vial was empty. It was only with Azure Bunsin cream on his eyelids could he see the blue traces of the potion. He released it into the air, tracking the air currents in the room. Buildings all had consistent patterns of airflow. The bigger the room in a building, the easier it was to spot the patterns. But Shemway was not interested in the pattern so much as the air that deviated from the pattern.

As he ventured into another room, venting the Tracking potion all the while, he spotted something curious. The air current predictably went down the room, but then it suddenly curved into a wall, flowing around the trim that ran up towards the ceiling. "Well, hello there secret passage. Funny running into you here."

He approached slowly, eyeing the airflow so he could better understand the size and scope of the entranceway. After a few moments of study, he was able to see the trigger to open the door—a barely visible button set into the trim. His hand hovered over the button, hesitating between two choices. It could be secured by charms that alerted the Nords as soon as he pushed it. But, seeing the wear on the walls, the secret doorway appeared to be regularly used. If that were the case, it would be unlikely to have been charmed as it would have to be reset every time someone used it. There were ways to try and detect the charms, but that would just take more time.

"Aah, what the heck," Shemway said as he pushed the button. "Jason's probably already caught the building on fire anyway." A small door swung open, revealing a long dark hallway.

"Shemway, can you hear me? Change of plans."

"Change of plans?" the Thieftian replied as he stepped into the hallway. "You get the Ice Cameras down?"

"Yeah," Nickle answered. "But I don't know how effective our original plan is. This building is huge. We could listen to a hundred different conversations for weeks and not find anything new. We don't have that kind of time."

Having already cleared several rooms, Shemway was starting to feel the same way, although he would never admit it. Initially, they had just planned on placing Sight Runes in as many rooms as possible, allowing them to spy on the Nords all the next day. But if the Nords were truly trying to sabotage the Valkyrie, it would not be something they would casually talk about in the offices of the Capital Building. If they had indeed hired an Assassin of the Midnight to attack the Valkyrie, it was likely very few of the Nords would actually know about it.

"What's your plan?" Shemway asked.

A spill of words flowed from Nickle's mouth. He explained how they had run into Ulgarian the Wise and how they were able to subdue him. The explanation was poor, to say the least, and left more questions than answers.

"So, what are you saying?" Shemway asked.

"We want to pop into the dinner party dressed as Ulgarian the Wise and an assistant," Nickle answered. "If we can direct the conversation, I think we have a much better chance of finding out what is going on."

Shemway mulled this idea over, considering the variables. This late at night, the dinner was likely just some sort of boring award ceremony. But, the room itself might later be used for discussing essential items of state. He did not like the idea, but they needed to do something different, or they would walk away empty-handed.

"Fine, but don't stick around. If you can get to the right spot, get there early, place Sight Runes, and get out. Sharlie can take it from there."

"Ok, we're en route," Jason said. "We'll let you know if we run into any trouble."

"I've also found a secret passage," Shemway said. "Likely leads to an escape route, but I'm going to check it out just to be sure. I'll be silent for a bit. I don't know exactly what I've discovered just yet."

"Good copy," Nickle answered.

Shemway pressed on, not waiting for a response. The hallway ended in a series of stairs. He slowly descended, occasionally pausing and listening before continuing. For some reason, alarm bells were ringing in his head. He went down five floors before the stairs ended at the appearance of a sturdy metal door.

Shemway retreated to the shadows, allowing his dark cloak to blend him seamlessly into the background. This gave him all the time he needed to study the lock and decide the best way through it. He finally settled on using a Ghost Key, an extremely complex potion that required different mixtures depending on the size, strength, and type of lock. He blended six different vials, each with an exact drop or two, before approaching the door. After shaking the final mixture, he uncorked the bottle, allowing a white cloud to drift into the lock. For only a brief second, the cloud turned solid, making the shape of a key. That was all the time the Thieftian needed to open the door and slip inside.

Instead of leading to an escape route, the room opened up to a massive training area. To his left was an elaborate obstacle course with everything from walls to scale, to windows to breach and doors to picklock. Another area had a series of wood targets, several of which had been skewered with metal stars. Directly in front of him was a large room that contained weights and exercise machines.

"What is this?" Shemway whispered. "This is no Nordic training grounds." Then his eyes fell on the sparring grounds, and a new understanding hit him like a Rinacon. The perimeter of the grounds was lined with curved blades and staffs, so different than the Ice axes carried by the Nords.

"These are weapons of assassins," Shemway whispered. "They didn't just hire an Assassin of the Midnight; they're allowing them to train on their island." Then with a gut-wrenching sound, the door behind him began to open. As quick as lightning, he fired his Crossbow, pulling him out of sight and into a dark corner of the room. When the door opened, thirty Assassins of the Midnight poured in, all wearing blood-red hoods and arrayed with the weapons of their deadly art.

Shemway swallowed. They were in real trouble. *He* was in real trouble. He barely dared to breathe. These psychos drank the same Sensory Potions Thieftians did, but unlike Thieftians, they drank it all the time, as if they were addicted to it. It was likely all of them had their senses heightened, their ears as sharp as a bat, their eyes as keen as an eagle. If Shemway made one false move, one deep breath, one wrong twitch of his muscles, they would know exactly where he was.

He had crossed paths with a few Assassins of the Midnight before, and it had always gone poorly. Thieftians and Assassins of the Midnight had a shared past and, consequently, they used similar potions and techniques, but the bloodthirsty killers had a completely different mentality. Collateral damage to them was just the cost of doing business—something that went completely against the ancient Thieftian Code.

Shemway remained motionless, barely daring to blink. Slowly, he activated a Sight Rune, placing it gently on the wall. As carefully as he could, he began to mime a person running away. It was not long before Sharlindrian caught on, watching the feed more closely.

"S-s-somethings...not right," Sharlindrian said over the Faerie Lip balm. "Shemway...is trying to s-sign something to me. I don't know why he just d-d-doesn't say something."

Once these words reached the Thieftians ears, he simply pointed at the thirty Assassins at the other part of the training room.

"Oh no," Sharlindrian said, her breath coming up short. "N-Nickle...Jason, get out of there. Abort the mission. Get out of there. The Nords didn't just hire an A-assassin of the Midnight, they're working with them."

Chapter 29

A Chilling Dinner Party

"Fine, but don't stick around," Shemway said. "If you can get to the right spot, get there early, place Sight Runes, and get out. Sharlie can take it from there."

"Ok, we're en route," Jason said. "We'll let you know if we run into any trouble."

"I've also found a secret passage," Shemway said. "Likely leads to an escape route, but I'm going to check it out just to be sure. I'll be silent for a bit. I don't know exactly what I've discovered just yet."

"Good copy," Nickle answered. He turned to his friends, letting out a long breath. "You guys cool with this? I mean, it's quite a bit different than the original plan."

Jason nodded. "I think we can manage it—although I wouldn't mind sticking around and seeing what they're actually serving. I was so nervous all day, I barely ate."

"Let's just get in, place the Sight Runes and get out," Nickle answered. "Every second we're in here, I feel like we're pushing our luck." He was once again on Jason's shoulders, reduced back down to four and a half inches.

Nickle had adjusted the memories of the Arctic Guards, who were still lying on the ground. When they awoke, which would be in the next five minutes, they'd believe they just nodded off for a bit. If they noticed the door, they would recall something their supervisor said a week ago about it being refinished.

"I agree," Evalee said. "Let's just get this done and head out. I don't know how much more I can keep these illusions up." She took a deep breath before changing Jason into Ulgarian and Swiftrunner into a regal Nord servant.

"Fine," Jason said. "But if I have to skip out on ice cream cake, you guys owe me."

"What time is this dinner going to start?" Swiftrunner asked.

"We have some time," Nickle said. "Maybe half an hour. That's the impression I got from Ulgarian the Wise."

They once again set off, heading out of the security room and down several stairs. Nickle knew the way, but the route was not a direct one. He was only able to see the path that Ulgarian was planning on taking, not the most direct route. For some reason, the Nord had taken a circuitous path to the upper levels before they ended up in the basement.

They walked through two security checkpoints but passed with ease, owing to Ulgarian's high position. The Artic Guards even held the door for the disguised Jason and Swiftrunner, as if they were honored guests. Within ten minutes, they stepped into a massive conference room decorated with a large table and dozens of place settings.

"This must be it," Evalee whispered from Jason's shoulder. "Let's just place the Sight Runes and get out of here. I'm starting to feel woozy."

A few Nords were already in the room, their eyes locked onto personal Ice Tablets as if they were reading important updates. Ten Artic Guards circled the perimeter, their uniforms sharp, the thick Ice Blades at their sides looking positively lethal. Swiftrunner stepped to the side, standing next to several other waiting attendants.

"We'll get it done in no time," Nickle said. "Jason, can you slowly walk around the room? Pretend like you're studying the pillars or something." While he spoke, he began throwing miniature Sight Runes along the wall, trying to catch all angles of the feast. Once they had walked to the other side of the long room, Nickle pulled closer to Jason's ear. "How about I put a few on the table—just so it's easier to pick up on the conversation."

"Great idea," Jason whispered. He approached the table, his eyes up high, studying the ceiling far above. But then someone slapped him on the back so hard that he almost doubled over. Unbeknownst to Jason, the impact sent Nickle flying off his shoulder and rolling across the table below.

"Ulgarian, you old polar bear, did you find the logistics meeting boring?" said a tall, toned Nord, his face set with a white beard that stretched down to his belt. "You've arrived early as if you had nothing better to do."

"Aah," Jason said, regaining the wind that was knocked out of him. "It's you, old friend." Then, strangely, the man's name suddenly popped into Jason's head. It was so surprising, he only whispered it at first, unsure of how it suddenly hit him. "BrackenBore...."

"You say my name as if you just learned it," BrackenBore replied, his tone low.

"You...just startled me," Jason answered. Then another thought hit him. BrakcenBore worked as the Minister of Agriculture. He was usually a severe man except after a few bottles of scotch.

As the information about the man continued to pour in, he realized that it was Nickle feeding him the impressions. "And, how are things going as the Minister of Agriculture?"

"Bleak," BrackenBore replied. "As you know, there is not enough land to grow sufficient crops. Our people are looking at another hard freeze. We must petition the surface cities for more food if we are to survive. But our Lightning does not trade as far with those cities. We need to trade with EarthWorks or Hurn or even the Dwarf outposts. Curse the Valkyrie for stealing all of those markets."

Jason nodded. "Yes, curse the Valkyrie. I hope they serve scotch tonight so we can drink to better times."

"As do I, my friend," BrackenBore said.

"Did someone mention scotch?" said a woman's voice from behind. Jason instantly knew that this woman was named Celda, her favorite food was pork chops, and she worked as the General Secretary.

"Celda," Jason said, a smile on his lips. "How did I not see you before?"

"Because you've ruined your eyes reading late at night," the burly woman answered.

The woman talked on, covering an array of meaningless topics. BrackenBore also added to the conversation, commenting on upgraded Ice Tablets, the recent snowfall on the mountain peaks, and the investigation of a new beetle in the pine trees on the Dark Mountain. It was all so dull Jason would have struggled to pay attention had he not been worried that a mistake now could cost him his life.

The participants during the conversation grew from three to four. Then four to seven. Soon, Jason was being peppered by questions about his research into why the Arctic Wolf was disappearing from their island. Luckily for Jason, Nickle continued to feed him mental impressions that provided just enough information for him to stay ahead of the conversation.

"Please, everyone, take your seats," said a voice at the front of the room. When Jason turned to the voice, he was surprised at all the people that now stood in the hall.

Then a mental impression hit Jason like a bullet. *"I'm not on your shoulder anymore. I'm on the table."*

"Table?" Jason whispered as he looked around, trying to understand the message he had just received.

Celda assumed he was talking to her. She laughed politely before adding. "Yes, Ulgarian, of course at the table. Are you so lost in your philosophy that you've forgotten how to have a proper dinner?"

Several others laughed, but Jason's face remained unchanged. He could just barely see his miniature friend hiding behind a saltshaker. Jason would have reached out to him, but that would most defiantly attract the wrong sort of attention. Then BrackenBore grabbed him around the shoulder and led him to his seat, a broad grin on his face.

"Even if they aren't serving scotch," the old man said. "You can share a little of my personal stock that I've brought in my flask."

Jason tried to break free, but someone again ordered them to sit down. The dinner party was beginning. He hesitated to sit, but then BrackenBore forced him into a chair. Jason kept track of his friend using his peripheral vision. More seats were taken, filling up the spaces around the table. Soon Nickle was trapped by a sea of people glancing around the table, each with severe expressions and sharp, cold eyes.

"T-t-this is bad," Sharlindrian said over the Faerie Lip Balm. "N-Nickle is on the table. C-can you get back to Jason?"

"Not without everyone thinking some rat-sized creature is running across the table," Nickle answered. "I need more cover. Evalee, can you put some sort of illusion on me?

"Not without passing out," Evalee said.

"Just w-wait for the food to arrive," Sharlindrian said. "Everyone will be much more distracted by then."

Evalee sighed. "I can't hold this illusion forever."

"Dang," Swiftrunner whispered from his spot on the edge of the room. He was standing between two hulking attendants, each with their arms at their sides as if standing at attention. "You need a distraction?"

"Not yet," Nickle said. "But think of something just in case."

Evalee grunted, a new anger pulsing through her veins. "You're killing me."

"S-s-somethings…not right," Sharlindrian said over the Faerie Lip balm. "Shemway…is trying to s-sign something to me. I don't know why he just d-d-doesn't say something."

There was a long pause as everyone thought of the implications of these words, the most dramatic scenarios playing through their minds.

"Is he all right?" Nickle asked through the Faerie Lip Balm.

"Oh no," Sharlindrian said, her breath coming up short. "N-Nickle…Jason, get out of there. Abort the mission. Get out of there. The Nords didn't just hire an A-assassin of the Midnight, they're working with them."

"What?" Jason whispered, his eyes widening at the news.

"G-get out of there," Sharlindrian repeated.

"Welcome honored guests and old friends," said a voice at the front.

After perusing a few of the closest minds, Nickle instantly knew who this individual was and transmitted it to the rest. "That's the Leader of the High Councilors, Lord Arkenslov."

"These are perilous times, and as such, I have called this secret meeting," the Lord continued, his voice filling the hall.

"Something's not right," Nickle said. "I'm sensing something…instructions from someone. His mind is blocked off from all others."

"We are an ancient people, born and bred on the Ice, away from the soft overworld. We are a people chiseled from the Icebergs of the poles and given life by Loki. We were not meant to be the footstool of the world but to be the axe that separates light from dark. Our people stand on the cusp of greatness; we just need someone to lead us to it."

These words sent a panic through several of the others seated at the table. A few of them exchanged worried looks, most turning a wary eye towards Ulgarian. Jason kept his mouth shut, however, prompting someone else to speak.

"We will not serve a dictator," a thin but muscular Nord said.

He stood as he spoke, straightening to an impressive height. "The Council has voted and cast down that proposal. If you want to debate it again, it should be before the Congress, not behind closed doors. Was this dinner nothing more than a ruse?"

"Waste of time...," another called out.

"Words are now at an end," the Lord said, his voice strengthening. "The Valkyrie muster their forces on the border of our air. Our spies report that even now, they goad their Queen to war. How long before the Queen gives in? How long before their Winged Armada comes down upon us from the skies."

"Bring out the food," another jeered. "At least let us eat while you bore us to death."

This brought a raucous amount of laughter, filling the hall. Only a third participated in the humor, the rest cast critical glares at those who did. The political divisions seemed perfectly clear now.

"If we go to war against the Valkyrie," a thin Nordic woman called out. "We go to our deaths. They more than double our ships and more than triple our warriors."

"I have brought new allies to our side," the Lord said. "We will not stand alone...."

"Sit down!" a white face Nord yelled.

"Let him finish," cried another.

The room devolved into shouts and jeers as battle lines formed. It seemed those against going to war were the minority, but they were certainly the more vocal. They began to skillfully shout down the others.

Then over three hundred pounds of lethal weight crashed into the table, sending plates and silverware flying through the air, silencing all those in the room. Luckily, Nickle was a few yards away from the impact; otherwise, he would have been crushed. The oak table underneath did not break, but it creaked in protest at the impact.

Ethilian stood from her spot on the table, her beautiful Vampire features being highlighted in the low light. "Have you no respect for your leader. He has been too soft with you, too merciful. Your people were once the spine of the forces that defeated Kara'Kala. Now you've become sniveling weaklings."

"What is this?" a Nordic woman cried. "First, you offer them sanctuary on our island, and then you allow their Queen to attend our meetings. She has no place among us."

"We should have turned those bloodsuckers over to the Tri'Ark," another cried. "They don't offer us protection. If anything, the Valkyrie are more likely to attack us now because we shelter them. And now EarthWorks and most of the surface cities won't trade with us because they inhabit our lands."

Ethilian began walking down the oak table, her hands gingerly resting on the hilts of her blades at her side.

Nickle swallowed as the tall woman approached, a foul memory returning to his mind. He could sense the power wafting from the woman. Apparently, Ethilian had been much weaker when they had fought her on the top of the Blood Spire. Now, she was nothing but raw power. Luckily, she stepped just to the right of Nickle's hiding place, barely missing him by inches.

"You are the most powerful leaders and families of the Nords," Ethilian said. "I am not here to protect you, so much as I am here to claim your allegiance. During the war against the Brood, I led your people to victory against the Demons. I have once again returned to this land to claim my throne."

These few words created an absolute uproar amongst the Nords, who began shouting their disapproval. But then Ethilian slowly slid out her two blades, enjoying how the light shimmered on the metal. This simple action again silenced the hall.

"Threats will not silence me," a Nord said, retrieving his axe from his side. Several others followed his lead, grabbing their own weapons and attacking in a fury. She ended this little rebellion in only seven seconds. Ethilian remained on the table, unscathed by their attacks. The Artic Guards would have moved in to help, but they were all laid low by Assassins of the Midnight, who had appeared from the shadows of the room and eliminated each one simultaneously.

Ethilian continued to walk down the table, acting as if she had not been interrupted. "True, when my people and I arrived upon your island, we were weak. We had been broken. We had suffered a defeat at the Blood Spire. But don't be a fool and think we stayed in that position. Our ranks have been flooded by Vampires, and we are stronger now than ever. I now command the Assassins of the Midnight and lead the Order of the DemonKillers, a group dedicated to eliminating every Demon and Kara'Kala supporter from here to

EarthWorks. And, among the Isles of Balinbar, one race consistently protects Kara'Kala supporters."

"The Valkyrie must be stopped," the Lord said, his voice rising in the room. "And the Vampire Queen is the only one who can do it."

This time, no one laughed when he spoke. No one moved to challenge his authority. Most looked down and away from Ethilian, electing to be silent. A few eyes turned towards Ulgarian, again expecting him to speak up. But Jason remained silent.

"Kneel before your queen and swear your allegiance," the Lord continued. He followed his own command, falling to his knees, his head bowed low. The room was slow to react, but it eventually did, each member bending a knee to their new Queen.

"If I may," a Nordic woman said, her voice much humbler than it was only minutes before.

"Yes," Ethilian growled.

"The Valkyrie are too strong. Even with your Vampire forces and the Assassins of the Midnight, we are no match for them."

Ethilian did not like these words, but she did not challenge the wisdom of them. Instead, she nodded to the Lord, allowing him to take over the conversation. "In her wisdom, the Queen has made new alliances, putting aside old hatreds to face a common enemy."

He nodded to several of his advisors, and they opened a side door. Four Cicurians entered the room, two with the heads of Jackals, one with that of an Eagle, and the final one with the features of a Lion. Behind these newcomers entered three Ynglings. One was an Orc, the other two were Humans.

"The Queen has done what could not be done for over one hundred years," the Lord continued. "She has united us with the Cicurians and the Ynglings. Never have we been thus united since we fought against the forces of Kara'Kala."

The Queen turned to those in the room, meeting eyes with all those who would dare look up at her. "My spies report that the Valkyrie have many people who openly support Kara'Kala; their Queen turns a blind eye to all of this. She allows this to happen."

The room filled with scattered shouts.

"As of late, the Valkyrie have claimed they are being attacked by saboteurs, by spies, by assassins. They blame the Nords and all those that work with them. But these are only a few lies amongst many that they have so recently spread. They seek war so as to bring our people under their thumb. To rule over our lands as they once did. They seek any excuse to wage war against our people. But...we will not wait for war. We will bring the war to them. In three days, our combined forces will take to the sky, and we will destroy Valenburg!"

The room filled with shouts.

"We will rip down the Queen from her Obsidian Throne and punish all those who still serve Kara'Kala, as the Tri'Ark should've done years ago."

Again, the room erupted with cheers.

Evalee was near collapse, her body drained by the strain of maintaining the illusion. "I can't keep this up...for much more."

Jason's face began to change, Evalee's spell breaking. His Dwarf features began to outshine Ulgarian's Nordic face. The Dwarf continued to clap along with all the other Nords, despite noticing his changing features.

"Oh great," Nickle said. "Jason, you're starting to look like a Dwarf."

Jason swallowed and clapped harder, as if this was a reasonable solution to the situation. "Anybody got a plan, now's the time."

Ethilian began to study Jason from her perch on the table, her keen eyes probing his features. She sent a mental wave forward, seeking answers to what was happening. Before she could discover anything, Nickle broke from his cover, running straight for Jason, shielding him from her mental attack.

"A rat!" one of the Nords screamed, pointing a finger at Nickle as he leaped over a tipped glass.

"If you've got a distraction, Swiftrunner," Nickle yelled through the Faerie Lip balm. "Now is the time."

"I'm on it," Swiftrunner said. Then, all three chandeliers high above snapped, the chains that supported their weight had been turned into thin vines. They crashed down one after another, creating a cacophony of noise.

Ethilian reached for her blades just as Jason's disguise completely evaporated. For half a second, the Dwarf and Vampire Queen just stared at each other.

Then Jason whispered, "Tarsin."

A vial of Liquid Darkness that he kept in his boot suddenly

exploded, turning the room pitch black. The next second, Ethilian's sword turned into a whip and was sent forward, skewering the chair upon which Jason had sat. Nickle took another Restorative Rune just before barreling into the Queen of the Vampires like a bull, knocking her off the table.

"Move," Nickle shouted as he pulled six HellFire Runes from his belt and threw them chaotically into the room. The next second they went off, sending explosions ripping through the room. Tables and silverware took to the air in dramatic fashion, creating an invaluable chaos.

Jason and Swiftrunner did not need any prompting. Guided by their memory, they headed for the far door. Evalee had gone unconscious, but luckily her body was tethered to Swiftrunner's shoulder guard, and she did not fall off completely. They all reached the door at the same time, pushing past two Vampires as they did.

"After them!" Ethilian shouted, her voice cutting through the chaos.

Once free of the room, Nickle, Swiftrunner, and Jason were able to see again. They broke into an all-out sprint, their bodies reverting to their normal size and shape as Swiftrunner released his Transformation spell on them. Waiting at the other end of the hall for them, however, were a dozen Vampires, each with swords drawn. But they had not expected to encounter a Cennarian and a couple of Dwarves, so they failed to react immediately.

"Get them!" Ethilian roared again. This took away all of their hesitation as they swooped in, several of them taking on the form of dozens of bats. Jason threw a Twister Rune into the ground, sending up a wind that tossed several creatures into the walls and ceiling.

"Anyone got a plan C?" Jason yelled. "Sharlie, how does our exit look."

"Blocked," Sharlindrian replied through the Fairey Lip Balm. "Vampires have sealed off the front and rear entrances to the capital."

"Tell us where to go," Nickle said as he sliced a Vampire in the leg.

Sharlindrian began to swipe through the Sight Runes, checking all routes for possible exits. She had kept a diagram of the Capital and where the Sight Runes were being placed, allowing her to have a much better idea of the building layout. But everything was happening so quickly, it made it difficult to know exactly where they needed to go.

"Left," Sharlindrian said.

"Left?" Swiftrunner said, releasing an arrow and notching another.

"Go left…through those doors," Sharlindrian said. These instructions took them into a narrow hallway that thankfully prevented the Vampires from swarming in from above. Jason laced the ground with Artic Runes, leaving a frozen wall behind. The Vampires crashed through it a second later.

"They are really mad," Jason replied.

"Now turn right," Sharlindrian said, her voice more confident now that she had picked an actual route. "Up the stairs!"

The other three did not argue, their feet hitting hard on the steps as they climbed. But the Vampires were so agile that it was difficult to keep ahead of them. More than once, Nickle successfully used his Scathian magic to confuse several Vampires, but still, they kept coming. The three continued on, passing the first, second, and third floors, Swiftrunner in the lead.

"Take that door to the fourth floor," Sharlindrian instructed.

As they passed through, Swiftrunner slammed the door shut, sealing it with a wave of Transformation magic. The metal around the door formed into one solid piece.

"Good thinking," Nickle said.

"Yeah, but it won't hold long," Swiftrunner answered.

"Go straight through that wall, and you'll find a balcony that heads off to the East," Sharlindrian interjected.

"Through the wall?" the other three said at once.

"Trust me," Sharlindrian answered.

Jason pulled out two HellFire Runes and attached them to either side of his axe. "I've never doubted you before—not about to start now." He began cutting with expert skill, slicing into the ice-coated wall. It did not open as quickly as he had hoped, as it had been reinforced with Nordic magic. But slowly he opened it, inch by inch, revealing the balcony behind.

Then the door burst open, allowing the Vampires in.

"Buy me some time," Jason said.

Swiftrunner raised his bow, releasing three arrows in two seconds. "You got it, little buddy." He reshaped the projectiles as they flew, adjusting them so they struck like a freight train.

The Vampires charged and Nickle met them with a fury, his axe raised. There were ten of them, but they were not ready for the Dwarf. He ducked and dodged, kicking one in the chest, sending her reeling backward. Nickle stepped into the middle of them, moving with uncharacteristic speed, barely dodging his opponents' weapons. His mind had been sharpened by the Scathian training and he was able to detect their attacks long before they were delivered. Every swing they took, Nickle made them pay, delivering wound after wound against his opponents. Between Swiftrunner's arrows and Nickle's skill, the Vampires were soon pulling back, leaving a few behind who were too wounded to walk.

Jason finished his work and turned to help his friends only to find that Nickle had cleared them all out. "How…in the world?"

"Move!" Sharlindrian yelled. "The Assassins of the Midnight are on your tail. Get to the balcony!"

"Right," Jason answered. "Where do we go from there?"

"Rendezvous at the dock," Sharlindrian said. "We'll have to steal a ship."

"It will be too heavily guarded," Shemway said, his voice sounding exhausted. "Time for plan D."

"D?" Sharlindrian asked.

"There's a small private dock on the far east side of the city," Shemway said. "You'll find a ship waiting."

"Why didn't you tell us this before?" Sharlindrian asked.

"I didn't want to have to use it," Shemway answered. "But I'll meet you there. Get to the dock. The ship leaves in ten minutes."

Chapter 30

Training Grounds

Shemway stared long and hard at the red garbed Assassins. They had been trained in stealth their whole lives, much like Shemway, but with one major exception. When they came across an obstacle, they tended to kill rather than evade. It was this subtle difference that drove their two people apart hundreds of years ago. Thieftians loved depriving those who had an abundance of wealth from their possessions. It gave them purpose, robbing from the wealthy and occasionally giving to the poor. But Assassins, especially from the Order of the Midnight, were ruthless and effective killers. Shemway might be able to take on a few, but he now stared at more than two dozen.

The Assassins began a series of training sequences, each one pairing with another and fighting in mock combat. They trained in disarming an opponent, first with one technique and then another. They had a brutal style of fighting that tended to inflict more pain than was required to accomplish the task.

Shemway's legs cramped as he kept himself upright, holding his place in the far corner of the room. His Crossbow held most of the weight, but he depended on his quads to keep him steady. Sweat beaded on his brow, sliding down his cheek and pooling on his chin. He could not stay in this position forever; already, his muscles were beginning to shake from the strain.

He tried to ignore the pain by paying closer attention to the conversation between Nickle and the others. But he found it more annoying than distracting.

Then a drop of sweat slipped from his face and struck the floor. In Shemway's enhanced ears, it sounded like a bucket of water was poured into a pool. Three of the Assassins turned in his direction, also picking up on the noise.

"So much for hiding," Shemway thought. *"Time to prove a Thieftian is better than an Assassin."* His hands slowly drifted to the bandolier of potions at his waist, pulling three of the vials out.

Two of the red-garbed Assassins approached, their hands drifting to the weapons at their sides. Shemway had at least one good thing going for him. The Assassins' eyes were drawn to the noise and not him, so they were looking in the wrong spot. But this did not last for long as one of the Assassins looked up, expecting to find a leaking pipe or something. Instead, he barely caught sight of Shemway's boot as it kicked him across the face.

The Thieftian unleased three potions at once, hoping to create chaos. One exploded into light, another into a cacophony of noise, the third covered everything in darkness. It did not work for more than a few seconds. Assassins now charged at the Thieftian, their blades raised. He was sliced across the leg and chest, but his armor absorbed the blows. He returned two of his own strikes, hitting the nerve clusters along the necks of several the Assassins, effectively making them little better than rag dolls for the next several minutes.

Shemway was hit across the cheek and kicked in the leg. He stepped back and attacked again, rendering an arm and leg of two more Assassins useless. Then a potion flew straight towards his chest and he flipped backwards, barely dodging the glass. Behind him, the wall exploded into flames.

Shemway growled, his face looking demonic in the light of the fire. He drew two short blades from his back and pointed them menacingly at his opponents. "I am a Thieftian of the Highest Order. I am not here for you, but if you stand in my way, I will shave you down as stray hairs on a witches' wart."

The Assassins drew their weapons and lined up, matching the Thieftian's intensity. Most of them carried Nunshun Sticks, a weapon that could be used offensively but also served a similar function to a Thieftian Crossbow.

Shemway frowned. "Oh boy."

They charged. Shemway ran, sprinting into one of the obstacle courses that the Assassins trained on. Instantly, he was assailed by massive swinging clubs that came at him from all different angles. He had to leap from elevation-changing platforms to avoid being crushed by the obstacles. Assassins followed behind, enjoying the sport of it.

As the first Assassin caught up to Shemway, however, his concentration shifted to catching the Thieftian rather than dodging the obstacles. The next obstacle swept this Assassin off his feet and pitched him to the side. He fell into a pit of murky water below.

Shemway proved his agility, ducking and dodging through the maze. He was so quick that neither the obstacles nor his pursuers could lay a finger on him. The obstacles increased in difficulty as he progressed, pushing him to the limit. Near the end of the course, Shemway grabbed a bar and swung up and around, landing deftly on the metal he had just been holding onto. From here, he began to pelt his pursuers with Electric Potions. He struck two of them, sending volts through their bodies and seizing up their muscles. They fell to the ground as their companion had before.

A cocky grin spread over the Thieftian's face. "I expected more from you lot." He could not help but laugh, enjoying the moment. But then a metal star hit him in the chest, releasing an explosion of flames onto his armor. He became a living ball of fire for a few seconds before crashing into the water below.

The Thieftian stood, wiping the filth from his eyes. It smelled worse than a latrine. "That's simply nasty. Why?"

But he did not have time to file a complaint before more metal stars flew in his direction, each infused with a different potion. He shot his Crossbow into the ceiling, barely dodging a metal star that turned a portion of the water into ice.

He was back on his feet, his legs pumping furiously, his eyes scanning for an exit. He ran past the training grounds, several bunks, a cafeteria, and a few small offices. There was no exit in sight. Despite his frantic movement, he could hear Sharlindrian's voice in his ear.

"Rendezvous at the dock," Sharlindrian said over the Fairy Lip Balm. Her comment was directed to Nickle, Jason, and Swiftrunner. "We'll have to steal a ship."

Shemway shook his head, considering the variables. On a floating island, the first thing anyone would do to prevent someone from escaping would be to shut down the docks. He narrowed his eyes as he considered other options. None of them would work. They had only one chance now—something that he would not even consider in any other situation. "It will be too heavily guarded," Shemway said, his voice sounding exhausted. "Time for plan D."

"D?" Sharlindrian asked.

"There's a small private dock on the far east side of the city," Shemway said. "You'll find a ship waiting."

"Why didn't you tell us this before?" Sharlindrian asked.

"I didn't want to have to use it," Shemway answered. "But I'll meet you there. Get to the dock. The ship leaves in ten minutes."

Then a fist slammed into his face, knocking him to his back. A commanding Assassin had just stepped out of her office and caught Shemway off guard, taking him to the ground. The Thieftian worked his jaw, a pulsing pain running through his head. When he looked up, he locked eyes with the biggest Assassin he had ever seen. The woman was tall, her eyes dark. On her chest, she wore the insignia of Three Stars, one of the highest ranks in their order.

"Did the little Thieftian slip and fall?" the woman said mockingly.

Shemway began to reach for a vial on his chest, but a sizeable red boot clamped his hand to the floor.

"Did you really think I wouldn't see that?" the woman asked.

Then Shemway winked at the woman, his cocky smile returning. "I was distracting you." His other hand reached his Crossbow and released the trigger, shooting the thin needle into a vent high above. Either by luck or skill, the needle shot clear through the grate and continued on, sticking into a vent high above.

Shemway then pressed the retraction button on the Crossbow and shot into the air. The large Assassin grabbed for his arm but missed. She tried again, this time latching on to the bottom of his pants. With a terrific noise, Shemway's pants ripped clean off his body as he continued on, heading straight for the metal grate above.

He quickly pulled a red vial from his bandolier and cuffed it in his free hand. As he impacted the grate, he broke the vial, sending out a wave of force, which blasted through the metal. Despite the showy exit, the Thieftian's hand broke on impact, and it now sent a wave of pain and nausea through his body. His Crossbow continued to pull him along until he reached a tunnel of vents far above.

"Come on," Shemway said to himself. "Focus." The pulsing pain in his free hand made his breathing irregular and short.

He shot his Crossbow down a long vent and then hit the retraction button, pulling himself into the dark beyond. While he went, he pulled out another vial, this one a faint aqua blue. He swallowed it in one gulp and discarded the glass. Not long after, the pain in his hand had disappeared, allowing his focus to return. He was able to lose his pursuers in the maze of vents, but alas, he too became lost.

He kicked open the next grate he ran into and dropped into a laundry room. Several Nords looked up, surprised by the half-naked man that stumbled out of a grate. He nodded once before shooting his Crossbow into the ceiling and swinging out a far window, which smashed into pieces as he sailed through and outside the Capital Building.

"He's getting away," cried a voice to his right. "Shoot him down."

Shemway did not have to look back to realize he was in real trouble. One of the wall guards turned an Ice Balista in his direction and began to unload a torrent of projectiles. The machine could fire two Icicles in just over a second, leaving nothing but devastation behind.

Shemway reshot his Crossbow, this time hitting a tower high above. The arc of his swing brought him close to the ground before bringing him back up so he could clear the wall. Just before he disappeared from sight, an Icicle slammed into his back, sending him tumbling forward. Luckily, his armor absorbed the blow, saving his life, but this soon turned against him as the ice began to spread and wrap him in a cocoon of sleet.

"Aah!" Shemway said, feeling a cold trickle run down his back. "It's so cold." He landed on the ground and rolled, glancing back only for a second to see if anyone was pursuing him. He counted six Assassins on his tail. His fingers found the quick release on his chest plate, and it fell to the ground. He left it all behind—his armor, his shirt, his bandolier of potions, his Crossbow, and his dignity.

He pushed all the speed he had left out of his body, making two turns before finally laying eyes on the ship. Nickle and his friends were already onboard, their eyes scanning the horizon for the Thieftian.

"Set sail!" Shemway said. "Go! Go!"

The Cap'n of the ship obeyed, having already been warned by Nickle of their situation. Without another word, she pushed off, her ship slowly gaining speed and pulling away from the dock. Shemway turned to his right, no longer heading for the ship but at a point where he hoped the ship would be in a few seconds.

"Come on," Shemway said to himself. "You can do this." He leaped off the island and into the air with all the strength he still possessed. For a few brief moments, he was sure he would make it—but then, as his mind considered the distance, he realized he was definitely not going to make it. He had tried to jump onto something that was over twenty feet away and getting more distant by the second. His head smacked into the bottom of the ship as it passed by, sending him flipping sideways and towards the Earth far below.

"You can still fix this," Shemway said to himself as he fell. His good hand searched for his potions, but they were not there. He then remembered that he was still wearing his boots. He always kept a couple of extra potions in his boots for emergencies. But one was Faerie Fire, good for melting metal but little use in stopping one from falling from the sky. The other was used for creating an explosion of noise, which would be funny once he landed and it broke, but again, it was useless now.

"I'm going to die," Shemway thought in mild amusement.

Then someone hugged him. He thought it was an angel coming to say goodbye. Shemway patted the strange angel on the head, acknowledging the tender moment.

"Truly," Shemway thought. *"The world is about to lose an artist of mischief that is ahead of his time."* The next second, he was on a ship, patting the head of someone next to him.

Nickle stepped back from the Thieftian. "I got you."

"He's alive!" Sharlindrian said with a grin.

"Dirt devils and dust demons, I can't believe you caught him!" Swiftrunner added.

This gave license for the others to step in and start exchanging hugs. Shemway was so confused for a moment that he did not know what to say.

Finally, Jason spoke. "You stink, Shemway. Did you have to climb through a sewer to get here?"

Sharlindrian plugged her nose and stepped back. "Eh, he's right. Glad you were able to escape but…at a heavy price indeed."

"How am I still alive?" Shemway asked.

"I Vicinerated down as you were falling," Nickle said.

"Grabbed you and then Vicinerated back to the ship."

"Agh," a feminine voice said with a hint of mischief. "If it isn't Shemmy, my baby brother. And here I thought you had completely refused my help for this operation. Now I find you were pursued by Assassins in nothing but your underwear. Truly, this is a tale worthy of our next family reunion."

It was Captain DeathDealer of the Argos, the older sister of Shemway. She was grinning so broadly you could see all of her teeth.

"Hello...sister," Shemway said. "And I am not your baby brother. We are twins."

"But," she cooed, "who came first?"

Shemway turned red, unwilling to answer.

"Come on," she persisted, her voice sounding sweet in the whipping wind.

"You did, but only by a minute," Shemway said quickly. "That does not mean you're older. We are literally the same age."

"Except, my baby brother, I'm one minute older," the Cap'n replied.

"Umm, Cap'n," a Rock Troll said. "You might want to come take a look at this."

This prompted everyone to run up the stairs to the upper deck and peer over the railing. The sight was so daunting at first, no one knew exactly what they were seeing. A black cloud was following them, one so dense it appeared unnatural. It looked more like a filthy lake than something that could be airborne.

"What sort of devil magic is that?" the Cap'n asked.

"Vampires," Nickle whispered back. "They've taken on their bat form and are now pursuing."

"Mr. Gribbling, raise all sails," the Cap'n said. "Batten all the hatches and full speed ahead. Let the Argos prove her reputation today!"

"Shannon," Shemway said. "It won't be enough."

"First of all, get some pants on," the Cap'n replied. "It's very hard to have a serious conversation with you right now without breaking into a fit of laughter. And second, this is the fastest ship on the Eight Winds. If it's not enough, then nothing will be."

"We need to lose weight," Shemway said. "Throw your cannons overboard."

"Then what are we supposed to use to defend ourselves?" the Cap'n asked. "Foul language?"

"If they reach your ship," Shemway said. "Your cannons won't help you much."

"I plan on using my cannons before they reach my ship."

"I have a better idea," Sharlindrian said. "Nickle can Vicinerate us back to Valenburg one at a time."

"And abandon my prize ship?" the Cap'n answered. "This is the Argos, the greatest craft in all the Isles of Balinbar. This ship was the first to beat the MoonBreaker in the Race of the Riptides. That suggestion makes Shemmy's idea sound perfectly reasonable by comparison."

"And besides," Nickle added. "It would be exhausting taking that many people back and forth. I don't think I could do more than a dozen trips without passing out. Plus, we're moving so quickly and with this cloud cover, it'd be hard to find my way back. I could very easily get lost along the way."

"See," the Cap'n said. "Even the Dwarf agrees."

"But Shemway is right," Jason said. "There has to be at least a few hundred Vampires on our tail. If they reach us, it won't end well."

"Throw the cannons overboard," Shemway insisted. "You don't get any gold dust if we don't survive."

"You're paying her?" Swiftrunner asked. "With what money?"

"He is going to split whatever the Valkyrie Queen was paying him," the Cap'n responded.

"You're getting paid twice to do this job?" Jason said incredulously. "Hawthorne was already paying you. Was that not enough?"

"Ahh, my boy," Shemway said, clapping an arm around Jason. "Rule number seventy-four of the Thieftian Code: 'Never do something for free when you can get paid to do it. And never do something risky unless two people are paying you to do it.'"

"You're sharing the Thieftian Code with this Dwarf?" the Cap'n asked ruthfully.

"Oh, don't act all high and mighty," Shemway answered. "You're the one pretending to be an Assassin so you can enhance your swashbuckling career."

The Cap'n stepped forward, whispering through tight lips.

"Easy, baby brother, I have a reputation to maintain with my crew. Don't you dare try to expose me in front of them."

"None of that matters right now," Sharlindrian said. "We need ideas. How can we get this ship moving faster? Anyone? If the Vampires arrive on our decks, you can be sure we will not be on the winning side."

"The same way the Valkyrie do it," Nickle said suddenly. "With the power of the Wind."

"Evalee might be able to conjure an Elemental Wind, but she's still out cold," Swiftrunner said.

"But we've got Wind Runes and Wind Potions," Nickle answered. "Jason and I both have dozens of Wind Runes on our belts. That will get this ship moving."

"Hmm," the Cap'n said, her hand rubbing her chin. "That could work—although I don't have many Wind Potions, and we don't have time to brew more. But, yes, it could work. It might damage the masts in the process, but if we reinforced them, it could work."

"Good," Nickle said. "I'll get set up."

"No," Sharlindrian said. "You need to Vicinerate to the Valkyrie. The Queen needs to know what she now faces."

"But they said the attack won't happen for three days," Jason answered. "We'll make it there long before they attack."

"Now that we know their plan, they will have to attack right away to preserve any chance of surprise they have," Sharlindrian answered. "The attack won't come in three days—it's coming right now."

"You're right," Nickle said. "But...what about the Wind Runes?"

"Just give them to Jason," Sharlindrian answered.

"What should I tell the Queen?"

"Tell her that the other three islands have been unified under the Vampire Queen and that they are coming to wipe them out."

Chapter 31

Tidings of War

Nickle appeared in front of the Palace still wearing his armor and carrying his axe. He was immediately spotted by Valkyrie Elite. Three of them swooped down from their perches high above, landing in loud successive thuds.

The Dwarf raised his hands, dropping his axe to the ground. "I need to speak to the Queen. You're all in grave danger."

"Where did you come from, Dwarf?" one of the Valkyrie asked. "How did you just appear before the Palace walls?"

"I can Vicinerate," Nickle said quickly. "But I don't have time to explain. I need to see the Queen."

"Who are you?"

"I'm an Attendant to the Princess, Heir to the Obsidian Throne," Nickle answered. "I know the Queen personally. I even know Sosha, your commanding officer. Although, she does not care for me much."

Two of the three Valkyrie exchanged a look. Finally, the leader nodded. "I do recognize this Dwarf. Yes, I believe he speaks the truth. I've seen him with the Prince and Princess on more than one occasion. But one does not simply request an audience with the Queen, even if they are an Attendant to the Prince—"

"—You're people are going to be attacked," Nickle said. "The Vampire Queen has united the other three Isles under her command and now leads their forces to Valenburg. They will be here in a matter of hours."

The three Valkyrie exchanged worried looks before the leader finally spoke. "If what you say is true, there is no time to waste. Follow me. We go to meet the Queen."

They set a quick pace towards the High Court. It was fast, but Nickle thought it was not nearly fast enough. Each second they wasted now was a second that could be spent in preparing the Valkyrie forces. Finally, they stepped into the High Court, which appeared to be in session. The King stood off to the left, the Queen sitting upon her black throne. Sosha stood to the right of the Queen, regaled in her shiny armor, and Jaylyn and Yaroslav sat on smaller thrones just behind her. The Valkyrie Elite stirred, brandishing their weapons defensively as the others approached.

The leading Valkyrie raised her voice, getting the attention of the High Court. "Queen of the Obsidian Throne, please excuse this interruption, but this Dwarf brings news that you must hear immediately."

The Queen looked first angry but then curious as she met eyes with Nickle. He took two steps forward before bowing low, his eyes to the floor.

"Your people are in grave danger, my Queen."

"Rise and report," Queen Victra said. "What is it that you speak of?"

"The Vampire Queen has united the other three Isles of Balinbar and has amassed a great army. Even now, they are coming against you with the combined forces of the Vampires, Ciciruians, Ynglings, Nords, and Assassins of the Midnight. They will be here within hours, my Queen."

These few words caused a stir among the High Court.

"Silence," the Queen yelled. "This High Court is one of order, not whispers and confusion. What proof do you have of this?"

"I don't have any proof," Nickle said. "But in a few hours, I won't need any as they will be here. The Vampire Queen has become a powerful force, even greater than when I faced her on the Blood Spire."

"Did you set them on this path?" Sosha asked, her voice unforgiving. "Did you set them on the path of war!"

"No," Nickle answered. "They planned on attacking three days from now, but soon after we found out, they found us out. So they've moved up their timetable. My friends risked their lives to find out this information. They are currently being pursued by hundreds of Vampires on the ship known as the Argos. They could use all the help you can offer. Please, Queen of the Valkyrie, you have to believe me."

"I'm sure he speaks the truth," King Boris said, his deep voice filling the hall. "The Nords have long since sought our lands, and with the support of the Vampires, they finally have their chance to take it. With your leave, my Queen, I will take our fastest forces and help the Dwarf's friends fight off the Vampires."

The Queen let out a long sigh, processing the information behind dark, cold eyes. She turned to Sosha, wordlessly asking her opinion.

"I don't care for the Dwarf," Sosha said. "But he is no fool. War is upon us, my Queen, whether we sought it out or not."

Victra remained silent for several moments longer before standing, her voice becoming law as she spoke. "Gather all our strength and prepare for war. The Nords have set us on this course, and I reluctantly must turn to it. But they shall pay as no generation has ever before, for they will face the full might of the Valkyrie!"

With this, the hall exploded with applause. When the cheers died down, the Queen turned to her husband. "But you, my love, must transport our Lightning Reserves to EarthWorks. We cannot allow our greatest strength to become our weakness. I would trust no one else with the task."

The King stirred, his face becoming hard. "My Queen, there is no time. The battle calls my name, and I must answer. Nickle's friends are in danger. I must lead our forces into battle."

"I will take the Lightning," Yaroslav said, his voice sounding a little higher pitched than normal. The Queen and King turned to their son. Somehow, in the light of the room, he looked older, more wise, as if he was finally finding his role in all of this.

The Queen did not answer right away. She did not want to question his courage, as that would offend the High Court, but she also thought the task was too risky. Nickle could not read her thoughts directly, but he could pick out the Queen's hesitancy. She did not believe her son was up to the task. At that moment, Nickle felt bad for Yaroslav, a weird kid that was always overshadowed by his sister.

"I will go with your son, my Queen, if your husband is allowed to aid my friends," Nickle said. "I will protect Yaroslav with my life if needs be."

"Then go," the Queen said, turning to her son. "Take our two largest Cargo vessels and three Hawks as your escorts. You have command of the vessels, Yaroslav. Unload the Lightning Reserves onto the Tube in New York and make sure it is safely away."

Yaroslav bowed low. "With your leave, my Queen."

"Go, my son."

"I will go with you," Jaylyn said quickly.

"No, Heir to the Obsidian Throne," the Queen answered fiercely. "You are our future—you will remain in the Palace."

Jaylyn opened her mouth to protest, but she shut it again a moment later. She knew her mother better than anyone, and in this situation, it was best not to question her. So she bowed her head low, accepting her mother's will.

With this, Yaroslav gestured to Nickle, and the two headed out a side door.

***

Although moving the entire Lightning Reserves was a tedious process, the Valkyrie were experts at the task, utilizing a series of cranes powered by Wind to complete it in record time. They were a pragmatic people, a people always prepared for war. So this task, as daunting as it first seemed, was completed quickly. In the last one hundred years, they had to move their Lightning Reserves on five different occasions as they prepared for war. The last time was just over twenty years ago during a conflict with the Cicurians.

Within thirty minutes, a large Valkyrie man approached Yaroslav, bowing low. "My prince, it is done."

"Then set sail," Yaroslav said, his upbeat tone not matching the situation. He wore a broad smile, no doubt thrilled by the chance of being given command.

He selected to ride aboard the YarenNaut, the biggest cargo vessel ever constructed. The entire side of the ship could be opened up to accept cargo, making it extremely efficient to be loaded and unloaded, something the Valkyrie had specifically designed for moving their Lightning Reserves in times of war.

The ship was slow in gaining speed, despite its numerous sails and the Wind that was shot into them. As they left the docks, they gained momentum, shooting straight down for a time before leveling out and setting a course for New York City.

"This is quite the adventure," Yaroslav said. "I've never been given command before."

"Why aren't we on one of the fighting vessels?" Nickle asked. "Doesn't it make more sense for the commander to be aboard one of them?"

"Oh no," Yaroslav said. "This is the safest place we can be. This ship has walls three times as thick as the strongest war vessel. It's light on cannons, but it can take a beating and still keep on moving."

"Oh," Nickle said. He had asked the question because he thought it would be better for the commander of their little group to be on the vessel where he could do the most good, not where it was safest. But, he wisely did not push the issue.

Nickle felt nervous standing next to Yaroslav. The boy seemed to think this was all just an exciting adventure, one that would eventually become just a good story to tell in the future. The young Prince had never seen conflict, never faced off with an actual enemy. Despite his education, he was naïve. He had read about war, but he had never faced it. Never faced the harsh realities of living in it.

The Prince talked on and on, filling Nickle's ears with the most mundane details. The Dwarf barely paid attention, instead keeping his eyes on the skyline behind them. Occasionally he would Vicinerate off into the distance, ensuring they were not being followed. If the Vampire Queen had planned on attacking their Lightning Reserves while it was being shipped to EarthWorks, the plan could have easily been thwarted by their quick departure.

After several hours of traveling, New York came into view.

"Alas, our journey ends so soon," Yaroslav said. "What a great story this will make one day."

"How can we fly over the city and not attract attention from the Piddlers?" Nickle asked.

"Air currents," Yaroslav answered knowingly. "The ships use Elemental Wind to circulate along the bottom and sides of the ship, creating the illusion of clouds. They'll think they are odd-looking clouds, but clouds nonetheless."

The closer they drew to the Chrysler building, the more Nickle's heart pounded in his chest. He just knew something bad was going to happen—one of their ships was going to explode, the

Lightning was going to become unstable, a swarm of Vampires was going to descend upon them. But it was not long before the side of the YarenNaut opened up, and the Valkyrie began to unload the Lightning onto the waiting Tube.

The Tube conductors were at first confused with what was going on, as it had never happened to them before, but Yaroslav explained to them in a calm tone what was happening and why. They relayed the request to Tri'Ark officials, and the request was quickly approved. Hawthorne herself spoke to the conductors through a magical link and assuaged their concerns. All passengers on the Tube were instructed to deboard as this was a public emergency. The Tube then magically transformed, its insides stretching out to impressive widths and heights even though the outside dimensions remained the same.

It took twice as long to unload the Lightning as it did to load it, something that sent panic up Nickle's spine each time he thought about how long the process took. Within an hour, the Tube was full with the entire Lightning Reserves of the Valkyrie.

"Wow," Yaroslav said. "This is exciting. But, now the task is done. Time to return in glory."

"Done?" Nickle said, hardly believing the word. He still looked around in the sky, waiting for something ominous to happen. "It's finished?"

"The Tube is setting off now," Yaroslav said with a friendly smile. "I'm grateful my father did not spend his time on this trip, as he would have thought it terribly boring. Well, now for the return journey."

"I really thought...," Nickle turned around, his eyes scanning the distance.

"What?" Yaroslav asked. "What's wrong?"

"Usually, when I say something like that...I'm interrupted by something bad happening," the Dwarf replied. "It's just...nothing went wrong. We did it."

"Why do things always have to go wrong?"

"It just seems to go that way usually."

"Interesting," Yaroslav answered, turning to the ship's captain. "Take us home."

"Yes, sir," answered a well-built Valkyrie woman.

They rode and talked on for hours as they returned to the city. The longer it took, the more nervous Nickle seemed to become. His instincts were screaming that something was wrong—he just did not know what.

Finally, Nickle could not stand the tension anymore. "Let me Vicinerate you back to your city. Just to be sure you make it there alive."

"Alive?" Yaroslav said with a smile. "My goodness, you're a bit paranoid, aren't you?"

"This is war, Yaroslav," Nickle said. "Capturing or killing the Prince of the Valkyrie would be a great victory for the enemy."

"Can you Vicinerate that far? Is it safe?"

"It will be a little tiring, but I can manage it. I promised to protect you, and honestly, I think that's the best way I can."

Yaroslav shrugged. "If you think it's wise, sure." He turned to the captain. "Who is second in command?"

"Captain Yosofut," the woman replied. "He's on the Yadmr."

"Thank you," Yaroslav said. "Can you kindly tell him that he is now in charge? I'm going to take a quicker route home."

"Yes, sir."

"All right, Nickle," Yaroslav said. "Take us home."

Chapter 32

Rule Number One

Jason's hands were red from use. He had used more Wind Runes in the last ten minutes than he ever used in his entire life. The ploy worked, pushing their ship just out of reach of the hundreds of Vampires in the air. Over the next hour, the cloud of bats had diminished in size and color, as fewer Vampires could maintain the rigorous pace. But it still proved an ominous threat, one that was drawing ever closer.

"I'm down to our last two WindBlast Runes," Jason said. He crushed them in his hands, sending a gale of wind into the ship's sails. The mast creaked but did not break as the vessel lurched forward with a burst of energy.

"Shemmy," the Cap'n said, turning to her brother. "If my ship gets damaged in all of this, I'll be going after your little shop in Valenburg to pay for the damages."

Shemway had showered and changed into new Thieftian garb. His sister had even furnished him with a set of armor, a couple of swords, and a few potions—for a steep price.

"Nonsense," Shemway answered. "You knew what you were getting into. You weighed the profit versus the risk and decided it was worth it. You know rule number one of the ancient Thieftian Code: Life is not Fair—so try not to cry when it doesn't go your way."

"Oh, that is so rich coming from you," the Cap'n answered.

As the effects of the last Rune dissipated, the bats drew ever closer. It would only be a matter of seconds before they could reach the ship.

"We've got incoming!" Sharlindrian said, her hands raised.

The first wave of bats swooped in, their shrieks piercing the air. They had already tried firing cannons at the little creatures, but it proved next to pointless. Even when they were lucky enough to strike a bat, it did nothing to slow them down.

Then the bats dove against the deck, forming into a dozen fierce Vampires. Both sides yelled as they charged each other. Jason attacked two of them at once, slicing one in the back and the other in a leg. One beast turned and roared, swinging a powerful backhand at Jason's head. The Dwarf ducked, rolled, and kicked the creature over the edge of the ship. The creature separated into bats before reforming behind Jason, a sword in hand.

Sharlindrian shot out a series of Light Lances, hitting the creature several times in the arms and chest, pushing it back and away and sparing Jason from being stabbed in the back. She then shifted the Vampire's gravity and threw him against another Vampire that was squaring off with Swiftrunner.

"They're trying to burn the ship," the Cap'n cried. She was locked in a fierce battle of blades with a massive Vampire, but out of the corner of her eye, she saw a burst of flames spread across the deck. "Put out that fire!" She then head-butted the Vampire, sending him reeling back. The Vampire turned his sword into a whip, cutting the Cap'n's leg and sending her pitching to the side.

Despite a few crew members' frantic attempts, the fire persisted, spreading to much of the railing and one of the thinner masts. Two Vampires seemed especially apt at Elemetal magic and were attempting to burn the whole ship down.

"Focus on putting out the fire," the Cap'n said through gritted teeth. "Save the ship, or ya'll have to find another vessel to crew!"

Jason used his Thieftian Crossbow and shot it into the thickest mast. Placing his axe on his back, he then swung through the air. It was an awesome move in his own mind, one that would likely be on the cover of a book if he ever wrote one. But then he swung into a mast that sent him twisting in circles and crashing into a Vampire, knocking her over the edge. He pulled out a Flood Rune with his free hand and released it, partially putting out the fire on the deck. He then released the Crossbow and landed on charred wood, smiling broadly from his success. But the wood he now stood on had been severely weakened by the intense flames and broke a second later, sending the Dwarf falling to a lower level.

Jason landed hard on his back, the wind knocked out of him.

"It's too early for Human studies," Evalee said in a sleepy voice from a hammock across the room. "Let me sleep for five more minutes."

Jason looked over at the High Faerie, confused by the comment. But he did not have time to consider it long before a Vampire jumped down on top of him, his sword raised. The Dwarf rolled to the side just before the dark blade skewered him to the floor.

Jason shoved a boot in the Vampire's chest and activated a Wind Rune, sending the Vampire back out the hole and off the ship. When he climbed out a few seconds later, the Vampires had withdrawn, reverting back into their bat forms. They still pursued the ship, but now they were keeping their distance.

"Why'd they pull back?" Swiftrunner asked. The Cennarian had his bow in hand, a small cut just above his right eye.

"That's why," Sharlindrian said, pointing to the sails above. Only one sail was left untouched. The rest were shredded to ribbons by the claws and fangs of bats that had been swarming all around them. "They don't need to stop us, just slow us down so the rest of their Vamp friends can catch up. While we were dealing with the Vampires on the deck, several of them had concentrated on taking down our sails."

"My ship," the Cap'n said. "My beautiful ship." Within a minute, the ship had been completely torn up by the battle. Chunks of the railing were missing, there was a massive hole that led to the lower deck, and the intense fire the Vampires used had severely weakened several other parts of the ship, including the mainmast, which now creaked as they moved.

Shemway shrugged, his voice turning a little higher pitched than normal. "It's fine. Replace a few boards, add a new stain, and it will be as good as new."

"You said this would be a simple smash and grab," the Cap'n answered. "You said that you weren't even likely to need my ship, but it was just a precaution."

"Well, I'm sure glad you were there," Shemway said. "And isn't that the important thing to focus on? Family supporting family."

"They're coming in again!" said a peg-legged Satyr.

This time, over twenty Vampires appeared, reforming from their bat visages onto the deck of the Argos. Both sides rushed each other, and the clamor of battle rang in the air. Jason began throwing

HellFire Runes at the enemy before him. Now that the ship was already damaged, he figured a little more would not hurt. They successfully broke up the formation of the Vampires allowing the crew to take the initiative. At first, it seemed like an even conflict, but slowly the defenders began to push back the Vampires, who were becoming both more exhausted and wounded by the second.

As the attackers became too wounded to continue, they would pull back, reforming into bats and retreating the way they had come. For a few precious moments, Jason allowed himself to think they were winning. But that's when a much larger and fresher group of bats reached their now very slow vessel.

The deck thudded in quick succession as Vampires began to appear, their wicked teeth flashing in pure ecstasy. Their numbers grew to thirty as the seconds passed and then thirty-five.

"Fall back," the Cap'n answered. "Form a line on me."

A lead Vampire stood before the rest, his massive frame dwarfing all those around him. Jason recognized the warrior—it was Clive—better known as the Wall—Ethilian's second in command. He held a massive sword that was more for butchering than simply cutting.

The Wall pointed a blade straight at Jason's head. "Drain their bodies of their blood and refuel your energy. After this, we destroy the Valkyrie!" The Vampires cheered but not with as much enthusiasm as he had expected. Most of them had their eyes on the horizon, looking at something in the distance.

Shemway turned around. "What are they all looking at?"

In answer to his question, several dozen cannons went off, raining down on them from two different Valkyrie vessels. The projectiles were all aimed at the Vampires. They exploded into their ranks, pitching several of them up and over the ship's edge. More firepower rained down, scattering the vile creatures with each volley. Soon the Vampires were driven back, disappearing as they reverted to their bat forms. With this brutal barrage, the Vampires finally broke off their pursuit, the survivors heading back towards the Nordic ships in the distance.

The crew of the Argos cheered as a Valkyrie ship sailed slowly by, barely dodging their main mast. The King of the Valkyrie grinned at them from above, his smile a welcome sight to all those who looked up at him.

The only one that did not was the Cap'n. Her eyes remained fixed on the rear of the ship, which was now a pile of rubble. The entire upper deck and the captain's quarters had disappeared in an instant. All of her possessions were now whipping in the wind like they were at a yard sale. A black contrail of smoke followed behind them, no doubt from some magical failure or fire down below.

She finally turned to Shemway, her eyes narrowed. "You did this on purpose!"

Shemway shook his head. "Be happy, my equal-in-age sister. We were just saved. Let's try to focus on the positive."

The Valkyrie ship turned around and pulled up next to them, matching their speed. The King of the Valkyrie's grin persisted as a plank extended between the two ships. "Hello, friends of Nickle. I see the Dwarf's word was true."

"Aah, King Boris," Shemway said. "It's a unique experience to be rescued by a King."

"Well, hop on board," the King replied. "We'll make sure you make it back to Valenburg in one piece."

The crew roared their approval, grabbing what items they could as they headed off the ship. Jason picked up Evalee, who was surprisingly still asleep. At some point during the battle, she had reverted to her Human form. Swiftrunner and Sharlindrian followed closely behind, joining all the others on the Valkyrie ship.

"Are you coming?" Shemway asked, turning to the Cap'n.

"And abandon my ship?" the Cap'n said. "I'd rather drink a gallon of saltwater."

"There's...not much left to abandon," Shemway said delicately.

"We've got to get moving," the King said, all levity from before gone. "We need to drop you off before we form our battle lines."

"Just go," the Cap'n replied. "I'll bring my ship safely to dock."

Shemway glanced between Boris and his sister, his mind at war with itself. Finally, he let out a long dramatic sigh before standing next to Shannon. "Fine, then I'll stay with you, equal-in-age sister. We'll bring her around...together." He turned back to the Valkyrie and waved them off. "We'll take her back. She looks worse than she really is."

The King's face set in a deep frown, his expression showing his doubt that the ship could be salvaged. But he did not have time to debate it. They withdrew the gangplank and were off, heading back to Valenburg.

"The first thing we need to do…is find a way to steer," the Cap'n said, her eyes scanning the debris below.

Shemway looked around at the floating woodpile and then back to the Valkyrie ship that was sailing away. "And, now I'm full of regret."

"We just need to dig down to the Eveation," the Cap'n replied. "It's still intact; otherwise, we'd be falling through the sky."

"Thank goodness for that," Shemway said grumpily.

"Help me dig through this debris."

The two Thieftians began to dig with all their strength, but Shemway was never one for physical labor. Twice he accidentally stuck his hands in a plate of moldy food and he shut down completely, overcome by a wave of nausea. The entrance to the lowest deck was blocked, so they had to cut their way in using a set of axes. By the time they made it through, the Cap'n was sweaty and Shemway was ready to take a nap.

"Now we need more control," the Cap'n said. "Find something to make a sail and tie it to the mainmast."

Shemway's shoulders fell, he had thought the hard part was already over. He began poking and prodding through the debris, picking up random pieces of cloth as he went.

"Get going, little brother," the Cap'n said from down in the ship's lower deck. "If we don't have enough speed, we won't be able to control the ship." She did not need to observe Shemway to know he was taking his time, as he always did when they were kids and chores needed to be done.

Shemway let out a long sigh, but as he discovered another piece of clothing, he began to smile. Soon, he was hard at work. When the Cap'n popped her head above deck, she was surprised by what she saw. A new sail now billowed in the wind. She at first smiled, a general relief in her features, but then she realized it was entirely made out of her underwear.

"We're really moving now, my equal-in-age sister," Shemway said. "I can see Valenburg in the distance."

The Cap'n sniffed—the smell of burned oil hitting her nose. She turned around to see that the rear part of the ship was now burning like a bonfire. "When did that happen!"

Shemway turned around, trying to see what she was referring to. "Aah! The ship's on fire…again."

"No time to deal with that now," the Cap'n said. "We've got to set her down first. You control the Eveation; I'll be your set of eyes."

"No way," Shemway answered. "I don't know how to steer the ship."

"That's why I'm up here," the Cap'n answered. "Just do what I say, and we'll get through this, little brother."

Shemway grumbled, but he did not protest further. He slipped down the two levels until he was next to the Eveation. His sister had rigged a few sticks together to make an impromptu steering wheel.

"Five degrees starboard."

Shemway turned the stick to his left.

"What are you doing," the Cap'n said. "That is the exact opposite of what I told you to do. Starboard is to your right."

"Why don't you just say right then," Shemway yelled back.

"We're so going to die," the Cap'n whispered to herself. She let out a long sigh before she provided more instructions. "Right six more degrees." Already, her back began to sweat from the heat of the fire. The broken wood pieces proved to be excellent kindling and it was now spreading rapidly.

Through the holes in the lower deck, Shemway could just barely see buildings coming into view. They were coming in too fast—they were going to crash.

"Four degrees to the left!" the Cap'n yelled.

Shemway obeyed but not quickly enough, as the side of their ship scraped against a bell tower.

"React quicker," the Cap'n said.

"React quicker," Shemway said in a mocking tone.

"I heard that."

Shemway continued to obey the instructions as the Cap'n continued to give them. Their ship was losing altitude, however, and Shemway could see the ground blurring past just ten yards below them.

"Now, pull the Eveation back!" the Cap'n said. "Full stop!"

Shemway obeyed, operating a different lever than the steering, but then the wood snapped in half. "It broke!"

"Hard right! Hard right! Now left. Left!"

Shemway obeyed, twisting the steering wheel first one way and then another.

"Brace for impact!"

The next second, with a horrendous noise, they crashed into a building, both of them being thrown forward. The hull screeched as it was dragged across the cobblestone. It went ten yards before the vessel stopped completely.

Shemway sat up, patting himself gingerly. He did not feel any blood. He was still alive. "Hah! We did it!" He climbed out of the lower deck, a smile spread across his face. "We did it! We're still alive."

By the time he reached the deck, the Cap'n had already found her feet. Besides a few bumps and bruises, she looked like she had survived as well.

"You're brilliant, my sister of exact equal age," Shemway said. "Well done." The Thieftian took a deep breath, enjoying the life that still flowed through him. That is when he noticed a street sign not far from their location, Dunbar. His shop was located on Dunbar. This was at first a big relief. If his shop was not too far, he could run over and take another quick shower and change. But then more details began to stick out in his head.

"That shop across the road…that looks exactly like the one right across from my shop," Shemway said slowly. "And…the building next door sells cross stitch supplies…just like the one next to my shop. Wait a minute…did you just land your broken down and beat up vessel on top of my shop!"

The Cap'n smiled and winked. "Well, at least we're still alive—try to focus on the positive little brother."

"You did that on purpose."

"Technically, you did it. But, it's times like these I like to reflect on rule number one of the ancient Thieftian Code: Life is not Fair—so try not to cry when it doesn't go your way.'"

Chapter 33

Glorious Combat

There was very little ceremony as they were hurried off the ship and onto the expansive Docks of Valenburg. Both Jason and Swiftrunner begged to stay, telling the King how much help they could be. All the King would say in return was that they had done enough.

The docks were a mess. People pushing and shoving, fighting their way to move cargo off and passengers on to ships in an attempt to escape the city. It did not take long of watching the struggle before realizing that there were far too many people trying to board far too few ships. Many of the ships' captains had decided to stay and fight, dropping their cargo and heading off to join the ranks of the Valkyrie fleet.

Jason carried Evalee in his arms. The High Faerie was so light, he barely noticed her weight. Behind him was Sharlindrian and then Swiftrunner. Once the crew of the Argos deboarded, the Valkyrie ship departed in a rush, heading back into the sky.

"Let me take Evalee," Sharlindrian said.

"Where are you going to take her?" Swiftrunner asked.

"Somewhere out of the way," Sharlindrian said, pulling her from Jason's grasp. She took a step back, struggling with the new weight, surprised by how light Jason made Evalee appear.

"Are you sure?" Jason asked.

"You two should lay low," Sharlindrian said. "This is not your war."

"First ship we find, we're hopping on board," Jason said. "We've got to help out."

"We can't just sit back and let the Vampire Queen take over," Swiftrunner added.

"Just be safe," Sharlindrian answered, directing her words mainly towards Jason.

Then she was gone, Exsiliogating through the city. She suddenly stopped as she arrived at her destination, her eyes looking up at the large house in front of her. It was the estate of the Kinnunens, a wealthy family that just happened to be out of town for the week. She and Ginger had been assigned to do a deep cleaning of the place, that is, before Sharlindrian took off to spy on the Nords.

She struggled to keep Evalee from falling. "*Why is Jason so strong?*" She then used her Mystic magic to shift the High Faeries' weight, so she weighed only a third of what she had before.

Sharlindrian kicked the door open with her foot. "Ginger! Are you here? Ginger?"

It was not long before the red-headed girl appeared, her apron covered in black soot. "Sharlie, you're back from vacation already? Who are you carrying there? Is she all right?"

"A friend," Sharlindrian said.

"Come in," Ginger said quickly, opening the door wider. "Let me just grab a blanket to throw over the couch, and you can lay her down there."

The Elf placed Evalee down on the couch and sat on an ornate chair.

"No offense, darling," Ginger said. "But let me grab a cover for that chair as well. You're filthy, smell like wood smoke, and are bleeding. What happened to you? You're wearing armor? What is going on?"

Sharlindrian took in a deep breath, relieved to be taking a small break. "Can you get me a drink of water?"

"Sure," Ginger said. She retrieved a cup from the kitchen a minute later, her eyes wide with curiosity. She wanted to ask again about what was going on but did not want to come across as being annoying. So she waited.

Sharlindrian finished the cup and wiped her mouth with the back of her hand. She was surprised by a trail of blood smeared on her wrist.

"Let me help you with that," Ginger said, raising her Mystic bracelet. Over the last few weeks, she had been steadily improving in the Mystic Arts. It was only moments before the cut and pain completely disappeared, something that Sharlindrian would have been unable to do any quicker. Truly, the girl had a natural talent for healing.

"The Vampire Queen united the other Isles and assembled a massive army," Sharlindrian said finally. "They are heading this way to attack Valenburg."

Ginger was surprised by so many of the words she was hearing that she did not know which to respond to first. Finally, she squeaked out. "We're being attacked?"

"Many of the citizens are fleeing the city, but there aren't enough boats.

"And who is this?" Ginger asked, nodding to Evalee. "I'm not sensing any major wounds, although it looks like she did pick up as many cuts as you did. Mind if I heal her too?"

"I would appreciate it if you did. I was going to but I'm still a little winded."

Ginger set to work, healing a cut first along Evalee's arm, then one on the side of her neck. The healing sensation drew the attention of the High Faerie, and by the time Ginger finished, Evalee was awake.

She sat up, looking at the opulence around her. "Am I in heaven? No, it can't be. There'd be more Slurpees if I were. Are we still in North City on the Island of the Nords?"

"You were in North City?" Ginger asked.

"You were out for quite a while," Sharlindrian said to Evalee.

"What's happened?" Evalee asked, her eyes widening in panic. "Is everyone ok? How's Nickle?"

"Everyone is alive and well…for the moment, but the Vampire Queen is leading a massive army this way. I don't know how many warriors she convinced to follow her, but I don't think this will turn out good for the Valkyrie."

"Where do we need to go?" Evalee asked.

"Just rest for a bit," Sharlindrian answered. "You once again pushed yourself way beyond your capabilities. You have to be careful with that, or you could really hurt yourself."

"Are you a High Faerie?" Ginger asked, nodding to the girl's wings.

Evalee smiled. "Yes, of course."

"I've never met a Faerie before," Ginger said.

"And I've never met a Human so good at healing," Evalee answered.

Ginger blushed before turning away, suddenly eager to find a way to change the subject. "So, what should we do?"

Sharlindrian let out a long sigh, looking at the two women in turn. She finally spoke. "We get ready to fight for our lives."

***

Jason was turned away from two boats that were taking on warriors to fight the Vampires. It seemed that if one was not a Valkyrie, they had no chance of finding a ride to the battle lines.

Then Jason literally ran into Major Q, the commanding officer of the forces that had been sent to aid the Valkyrie.

"One side, little man, one side," Major Q said in his trademark superior-sounding voice. At his side was his faithful second in command, Lieutenant Joey.

"You?" Jason said.

"Quarter?"

"What are you doing here?"

"I'm off to claim glory, my boy," Major Q said in a rush. "The Vampires are coming."

"That's right," Jason said with excitement. "You have a ship."

"No…I have three ships, all part of New Atlantis' growing fleet."

"Well, take us with you," Jason said, pointing to himself and Swiftrunner. "We can help out."

"You haven't trained with us, nor do you know our tactics," Major Q answered. "You'd likely put all our lives at risk."

"Sir," Joey said from behind. "If I may speak."

"Fine, Joey, but make it quick, as the first notes of our epic ballad are just about to be penned into history."

"I've seen this Dwarf and Cennarian fight, and if anything, they'd greatly improve our chances of keeping you alive," Joey said simply.

"Keeping me alive?" Major Q said, startled that there was even the possibility that he might die.

"I heard that this Dwarf picked up a statue and cracked it over the head of the Vampire Queen," Joey continued.

"Is that true?" Major Q asked.

"More or less," Jason admitted.

Swiftrunner nodded earnestly. "He smacked her over the head and sent her flying like a cobweb in a windstorm."

Major Q looked the two over again, this time paying attention to their armor and weaponry. "Fine. You two can tag along. Follow me."

"Sir," Joey said quickly. "We actually docked on the southern side. We need to go the opposite direction."

"Of course, Joey," Major Q said. "Lead on."

The four pushed through the crowd making little progress. Once they drew closer to the south side docks, however, the crowd began to thin. Jason struggled to cross the gangplank as always, but not as much as the Major, who had to have a rope tied around his waist before he would even make the trek.

Then they were off, the three blue sailed ships taking to the sky, heading away from the comfort and safety of Valenburg and towards the battle lines of the Valkyrie.

"Straight backs and eyes up," Major Q said. "If we are going to war, we're going to look our best."

"I think he's got the wrong priorities," Swiftrunner said to Jason.

"Just to let you know," Jason said, his voice taking on a rare serious tone. "I've got your back."

"Hopefully, this just blows over," Swiftrunner answered.

"I don't know. The Vampire Queen seems pretty committed."

The Atlantean ship was not large, but it was well made. The sides were twice as thick as a Valkyrie ship would be at that size. These vessels had been made to withstand the rough ocean waves long before they ever took flight. Both sides of the vessel had a complement of fifteen cannons, with six at the aft and rear, all charged with the azure light of Atlantean magic. It was reassuring to be in such a strong vessel.

Nickle and Jason wandered up to the upper deck, where they could get a better vantage of the ships ahead. The Valkyrie vessels were not far off, each one separated by a few dozen yards. They were lined up in three rows, one row on top of the next, waiting for the battle to begin. It had been one thing to talk about the Valkyrie's forces, it was another thing entirely seeing them lined up and ready for war.

Opposite them was the enemy, setting up their formations. Even though the other three Isles of Balinbar were fighting on the same side, they seemed to all have different strategies—something that would undoubtedly give the Valkyrie a significant advantage. But the enemy appeared to have double the ships.

Major Q positioned his ship in the middle, right where the fiercest fighting was likely to be. He was glaring over the railing of the upper deck, staring at the far-off enemy.

"Sir, make sure you put on your Descender," Joey said, placing a small backpack on the commander's shoulders.

Jason had noticed that all the Atlantean soldiers were wearing them. "What is that?"

"Just in case you get pitched overboard," Joey said. "It won't enable you to fly, but it will slow your descent enough where you won't break your legs."

Jason and Swiftrunner exchanged a quick look. Then they both stepped forward, speaking at the same time.

"You've got an extra one?"

"Sure," Joey answered, handing each of them one of the small backpacks. "Just make sure they're good and tight, and they will do the rest."

Swiftrunner and Jason quickly pulled them on.

As they did, Major Q approached the upper deck, overlooking his soldiers below. "Gather round, my warriors, and hear my words before we head into glorious battle…." Then a cannon on the lower deck fired. All eyes looked around, trying to spot who was responsible for the interruption; by the time they looked back, it was just in time to see Major Q tumbling over the side of the ship.

Joey grumbled. "Aah, crap. That's going to be a bunch of paperwork explaining that. Who fired that cannon?"

A woman's head popped up from the lower deck. "I'm sorry, sir. I haven't gotten used to how sensitive the new triggers are on the forward cannons."

"Sir, you want me to set a course to retrieve Major Q from the surface," the helmsmen asked.

Joey contemplated it for a second before his eyes caught sight of the enemy ships as they began to charge forward.

"No time," Joey answered. "Besides, he's safer where he is now.

I'll assume command of our three ships. Batton the hatches and get to your guns. It's time we show these air-lovers just what an Atlantean can do."

Chapter 34

Among the Atlanteans

"Charge!" Joey said, his voice filling the air like flotsam on the sea. "Attack formation Willow. This is what we trained for!"

He had received the orders directly from one of the Valkyrie Command ships. The instructions to attack had been transmitted through the Wind.

"I guess peace is off the table," Jason said to Swiftrunner.

Swiftrunner swallowed, his eye set on the oncoming ships. The Valkyrie all moved in a line, perfectly synchronized, advancing towards the enemy at a steady pace. Soon they were just a mile away and closing quickly.

"Jason and Swiftrunner," Joey said. "Stay close to me and do what I tell you when I tell you."

"Yes, sir," they both replied.

"Stay on the upper deck unless it's on fire," Joey said. "And if I tell you to abandon ship, make sure you do."

"Yes, sir."

When they were less than half-mile away, several long-range cannons on the opposing side opened fire, making ominous echoes of the battle to come. These shots rarely hit their targets but proved effective when they did.

"Steady lads and lasses," Joey said, his eyes trained on six ships that were making a beeline for his vessel. "Hold your fire until you see their limbs trembling with fear. Helmsman, prepare to change Eveation by forty-five degrees sunward," Joey said, his voice now as course as steel. "Relay my orders to our other two ships."

A young Comms Specialist did just that, directing the other two ships via an Atlantean communicator.

"Won't that prevent us from using our forward cannons at the oncoming enemy?" an Atlantean named Marian asked, her voice trembling with fear. "We have the best cannons of any up here, and we lose our advantage if we tilt up." From the insignia on her shoulders, she appeared to be the third in command.

"Yes," Joey answered. "But we don't fight alone, as it were. We've trained with the Valkyrie, and now we're going to fight with them."

The tension grew so thick one could almost choke on it. The two sides drew closer and closer. Soon they were in range of cannon fire, and the air erupted with smoke and noise.

"Now!" Joey yelled.

The ship tipped back hard, responding to the helmsman's movement, sending them shooting into the sky. Despite the change in direction, Mystic magic enabled them to keep their original orientation. As they went up, so did all the Valkyrie ships in their same row. Likewise, all the Valkyrie ships on the upmost level pitched their ship down. From afar, the movement made it look like a massive set of jaws were being opened up.

"Aim the forward cannons at the top of the enemy's line!" Joey said.

"Yes, sir," the Atlantean weapon's master said. "Fire?"

"Hold," Joey replied, his voice low, his eyes narrowed in concentration.

Several seconds later, the master of arms repeated her questions. "Now?"

"Steady," Joey said. "Steady."

They were getting so close now, Jason was able to pick out the details on the bottom of the vessels they were approaching. For a brief moment, he half thought Joey was going to ram them.

"Now!" the forward cannons rang out in quick succession, two of them striking their intended targets. The other two Atlantean ships had similar success, setting one of the vessels ablaze. Chaos erupted on all sides as the two forces began to pass each other in the air.

"Fire side cannons!" Joey yelled over the noise. This order was repeated and quickly obeyed. Explosions erupted from the Atlantean vessels in a constant wave, spraying the enemy ships with glowing blue projectiles.

Jason quickly realized how brilliant the Valkyrie maneuver had been. By changing elevation, the enemy had no clear idea who they should fire at—their original target or the enemy that now swarmed in all around them. The enemy ships took a beating as the Valkyrie and Atlanteans passed by, sending chunks of wood and debris flipping through the air. Three Nord vessels appeared to be disabled, a fourth had their mast completely ripped free. All along the battle lines, despite their smaller numbers, the Valkyrie fared much better.

A raucous cheer went up among the Atlanteans.

"Helmsmen, bring her back around!" Joey said. "It's not over yet. Reload the cannons."

The careful battle lines broke down as both sides pursued and evaded their opponents. Joey ordered them to dive quickly to aid a Valkyrie ship that was being chased by two Circurian vessels. They peppered the enemy's decks with a barrage of azure-infused cannonballs, leaving a trail of destruction behind. This allowed the fleeing Valkyrie ship to break away from their pursuers

"We've got a tail!" Marian said as she pointed directly above them. Four Nordic ships had pitched their vessel ninety degrees and were now stabbing through the clouds like a dagger, their decks blazing with cannon fire. It was an effective, albeit dangerous move. Their slim profile enabled them to avoid being spotted while allowing them to shoot at all enemy ships they passed.

Then one of the Nord's vessels crashed headlong into a Valkyrie ship in a terrific explosion of wood and metal. The two ships only saw each other at the last moment and had no chance to react. Still, the other three Nordic vessels continued their insane dive, punishing the Valkyrie at every possible chance.

"Order the other two Atlantean ships to break off the formation," Joey said quickly. "And bring us around to our starboard side. They might have speed, but as soon as we turn, we will have the cannons."

"Aye, Captain!" the helmsmen roared.

The maneuver seemed insane. As the enemy approached their position, they were simply turning away, like a wounded walrus stuck in a pool of piranha. The maneuver seemed so slow as it was carried out. It was not long before the Nords above began to fire their frozen projectiles at the ships below.

The Atlanteans were struck three times in quick succession, sending a few of the crew pitching over the side. From where the projectiles hit, Ice spread like a growing fungus, making seven of the fifteen cannons on the port side temporarily inoperable. Their ship was still turning at an agonizingly slow pace.

"We need to free up those cannons!" Jason yelled, slipping his axe on his back and pulling out two Hellfire Runes.

"Stay on the upper deck," Joey said, his voice taking on a rough tone. "Don't make me regret taking yah aboard."

"You need all the cannons you can get," Jason said. "Otherwise, even if we manage to turn this around in time, we won't have anything to shoot at them."

Joey only took a few seconds to make a decision, but it seemed like an eternity.

"Why are we here if not to help?" Swiftrunner asked.

"Go, but be quick about it," Joey said, turning his back to the two friends.

Jason and Swiftrunner jumped through the air as another bombardment of Ice projectiles rained down on them, encapsulating the main mast in a layer of sleet. The ship rocked to one side as they reached the stairs, sending them stumbling the rest of the way down. More projectiles hit their ship, cutting the side to ribbons, opening more holes than a block of Swiss cheese.

The lower deck was pure chaos as Atlanteans struggled to help up the wounded and cut free the blocks of ice. Several of them were using swords infused with azure light, but the weapons only sliced off a few inches at a time. At this rate, it would be another five minutes before they could even free one gun.

Jason turned to his friend. "Here, take some of my HellFire Runes."

"I've got a set of my own," Swiftrunner said while pulling several out from this Cennarian Shoulder Satchel.

"Then let's get this done," Jason said. He released several Hellfire Runes into the Ice, driving their warmth into the middle of the Elemental magic, trying to find the source of the spell. The Ice resisted his magic and still pulsed out a new wave of cold energy, refusing to be removed so quickly.

Jason's hands were soon soaked in water as the Ice gave way. He had to activate another set of Hellfire Runes before he found what he was looking for—a ball of Ice so smooth it could be used as a bowling ball. With a tremendous grunt, he pitched it out one of the holes in the wall. The effect was immediate as the Elemental spell broke, freeing two cannons at once.

"Good work," said the master of arms through the noise. "We'll get these guns back into action."

Nickle and Swiftrunner continued working at a frantic pace as more projectiles rained down on them. From up above, Joey gritted his teeth, knowing how much abuse his ship was taking by the second. "Fire port cannons!"

Only ten of the weapons were able to obey, sending spirals of blue light up and around their massive barrels as they did. Most of them missed, but two struck with so much fury that it shredded one of the Nordic vessels from bow to stern, forcing it to break off the assault as a trail of smoke billowed somewhere down below.

Just as the final two Nordic vessels were closing the distance to finish them, the other two Atlantean ships that had disengaged earlier now circled back around, pulling up deftly next to the Nordic vessels. Blue cannon fire erupted the next second, damaging the opponent's ships so much they were sent spiraling towards the ground below.

"It's about time they showed up," Joey said.

Jason and Swiftrunner returned to the upper deck, their clothing soaked clear through.

"When did you find time to take a shower?" Joey asked, only partially joking.

"Got your cannons working again," Swiftrunner reported. "That Ice is something nasty, like thistles among dandelions."

The conflict with the four Nord ships had pushed their vessel towards the edge of the battle, giving them a slight reprieve. Jason looked up, seeing the massive Ulanova ship far in the distance. It was on fire at several places, but it was standing firm, obliterating every ship that dared approach. Circling its decks were hundreds of flying Valkyrie, their wings pumping furiously as they dove at the enemy, distracting them as the Ulanova's cannons ripped their opponent's ships apart.

"King Boris is on that ship," Joey said in a whisper. "I pity the man or woman they send to face him. That Valkyrie has got more fight in one fist than most ships have among their entire crew."

"We're winning," Swiftrunner said in a whisper. "They can't

take down the Ulanova while the flying Valkyrie are defending her. The longer that ship stays in the air, the more devastation it causes among the enemy."

"They can take her down with those," Marian said, pointing at ten small and fast-moving cargo ships that appeared out of a thick cloud. The vessels were on the edge of the conflict, so far removed from the battle that they had not taken any damage as of yet.

"They don't even have any cannons," Swiftrunner said. "I doubt they could do anything to the Ulanova."

"They're rigged with some sort of explosive magic, I'm sure," Marian said.

Joey stepped up to the railing, squinting his eyes in the distance. He could not see nearly as well as the others. "No cannons. Are you sure?"

"Yeah," Jason concurred. "They just look like cargo vessels."

"This is bad," Joey said. "Those are Sapper ships, and they've got enough firepower aboard to rip any vessel to pieces. If even one of them can ram the Ulanova, it will explode on impact, opening her up like a gutted fish. Flagoneer, start signaling to the Valkyrie of the danger."

"Yes, sir, but we're really far," the Flagoneer replied. "They won't see us from here—that is, even if they're looking in our direction. We need to get closer."

"Those Sappers are moving too quickly," Marian said. "There's no way we could get close enough in time."

"Curses," Joey said. "Well, we'll have to try. Helmsman, full speed to the Ulanova."

The order was obeyed, but it seemed like a hollow gesture. Their sails had already taken enough damage where they were much slower. The Sapper ships, however, were untouched and worse, it seemed that none of the Valkyrie had even noticed them.

"I just had a crazy thought," Jason said.

"Don't do it," Swiftrunner replied.

"How did you know what I was going to do?" Jason asked.

"When someone says they just had a crazy thought, it means they are about to do something crazy."

"I've got to," Jason said. "If the Ulanova goes down, our chances of winning go with it. That ship is the only thing that balances out the battle."

"What's your plan?" Swiftrunner asked.

"Taxi-Lator running," Jason answered. "I've always wanted to try it again, and now I have the right tool to do it."

It took a while before the Cennarian realized what his friend was talking about. But as he studied the battlefield, spotting the scattered ships in the area, he realized Jason was thinking of leaping from ship to ship like Thieftians did on Taxi-Lators in EarthWorks.

"Just think about this for a second," Swiftrunner said.

"If I did," Jason answered with a grimace, "I probably wouldn't end up doing it." With these few words, he ran towards the front of the ship.

"Where's he going?" Joey asked.

Before the question was answered, Jason dove off the front of the vessel. Before he had fallen a few feet, he shot his Crossbow at the bottom of an Atlantean ship and swung forward in a terrifying arc of speed. Once he reached the peak of the swing, he detached the Crossbow and fired again, this time hitting the bottom of a wounded Cicurian ship that had contrails of smoke pouring from its lower decks.

The closer Jason drew to the Ulanova, the more ships he was able to see and anchor to. The air was a mess of battle with cannons ringing out, soldiers yelling, and magic being used. But the Dwarf simply swung through the midst of battle, never staying attached to any one ship for long.

"Keep the momentum," Jason whispered to himself. "That… and don't look down."

Then he heard a loud whistle as a cannonball sailed right passed him. He doubted someone was actually aiming at him, but it sent a new spike of adrenaline through his body. Slowly, he began to gain on the Sapper ships, which still held a tight formation as they headed to the Valkyrie center. Since the ships were not firing at other vessels, they did not attract much attention. They were also not marked with flags of any of the Isles of Balinbar, making them appear as merchant vessels that had accidentally wandered into the battlefield.

The Dwarf landed on the front of a Nord ship and sprinted towards the back, unloading PyroBlast Runes as he did. The enemy was so confused that no one had any time to respond before Jason was once again sailing in the air, leaping from ship to ship—sometimes swinging from the masts, other times running across the decks.

It took another couple of minutes before he reached the last Sapper ship in the precession. His lungs were burning for air, his endurance all but used up. He regained his feet and stood, steadying himself on the deck of the fast-moving vessel.

"Get him!" cried a voice from behind.

Jason glanced back just in time to see Icicles being shot towards him, tracing closer with each passing second. He tucked away his exhaustion and continued on, pushing through the cramp that was developing at his side. He was able to reach the next ship, but now that the Nords were aware of him, he was under constant fire.

He was hit once in the shoulder with Nordic magic, but his armor protected him from taking any damage. He finally anchored his Crossbow on the mast of the leading Sapper ship and pulled himself on board, drawing out his axe as he did. He knocked out two Arctic Guards as they rushed him.

"Now to set this match on fire," Jason said, reaching for the Obliteration Runes on his belt. These were the strongest Fire Runes he had, and they were his best chance of starting an explosive chain reaction that took out all the Sapper ships. But then his stomach tightened as he realized he had used his last Obliteration Rune on the way over to the Sapper ships.

He checked his belt for other Fire Runes—he only had two Hellion Runes and one PyroBlast Rune. These were certainly potent but probably not strong enough to do the job.

"Crap," Jason said. "After coming all this way, I've got no way of stopping them." He looked ahead, spotting the Ulanova. He was closer to it now than he ever had been during the entire battle. So close, in fact, he could just barely make out the faces of the Valkyrie that ran along its decks. He only had seconds to do what he came to do.

"But how?" Jason asked, looking over his gear. He had exhausted almost every Rune he carried. Then an Icicle hit him in the tricep, stabbing clean through his arm. He grunted against the pain and ducked behind a hatch, which protected him from more oncoming fire.

Then his eyes fell upon his Crossbow—the one that he had "improved upon." According to his calculations, his Crossbow could easily hold over ten-thousands pounds. But that was all in theory. He still had not tested it yet.

"Well," Jason said, his voice falling low. "Now is just as good as any time to give it a test. This is going to suck." Then he shot the Crossbow at the Sapper ship that was running parallel to his own ship, hitting the front of the vessel, just behind the point of the ship that would act as a trigger once it rammed into something else. Still, he hesitated to enact his plan—the memory of excruciating pain giving him pause. It was not until he saw how close he was to the Ulanova that he finally gave in, activating the Rune of Power on his chest.

Instantly, his body was infused with incredible strength. All pain and fear disappeared as he was encircled by a glow. He stood up, anchoring his right foot on a kicking strap, and began to pull the cord on his Crossbow towards him, which in turn changed the direction of the Sapper ships.

It was slow at first, but the more he pulled, the more the two ships turned to face each other. Within seconds, Jason had changed the ship's course so its explosive trigger was headed straight for his own.

"It worked!" Jason said, his mind alight with joy. He had successfully rerouted the neighboring ship. It was now headed straight for him.

"It worked," Jason repeated, this time his tone was completely different as he realized what he had just done. He only had seconds to escape. With all the strength he still possessed, he leaped into the air and away from the ship just before the two collided, triggering the magical explosives deep inside the Sapper ships.

The explosion of the first ship ignited the second, which then spread to the third and fourth. Soon, the entire precession of Sapper ships was being consumed by a massive magical wave of flames. Despite the distance Jason had put between him and the explosion, he could still feel the intensity of the heat on his face.

"It worked," Jason said for a third time as he fell through the air, the Atlantean Descender on his back slowing his fall. Jason's actions had effectively removed him from the battle, as there were no ships close enough to shoot his Crossbow at. But he took comfort in knowing that, at least for now, he had protected the Ulanova.

"You haven't won yet, Vampire Queen," Jason said with a smile. But his smile soon faded. These thoughts did the opposite of giving him comfort. Something in the back of his mind felt wrong—something he should have noticed before but was now just realizing.

"Where are all the Vampires?" Jason asked. "I haven't seen a single one the entire battle."

Then a horrible, shrill sound filled the skies, sending adrenaline shooting through his body. Hundreds of thousands of bats suddenly appeared from the decks of dozen ships that were on the edge of the battle closest to the city of Valenburg. The vessels were largely unharmed, their decks absent the fierce exchange of cannon fire.

Then Jason suddenly realized what was happening. "They knew they didn't have a chance to win against the tactics of the Valkyrie, so they didn't even try. They weren't trying to win; they were drawing away the Valkyrie forces from the city of Valenburg." Jason swallowed, his mind resting on one final depressing thought. "That swarm of bats there—that's the real invasion. They're heading straight for the Palace."

At that moment Jason's Rune of Power ran out, and all of his thoughts disappeared with an explosion of crippling pain.

Chapter 35

In the Throne Room

"What is that?" Ginger asked, her eyes wide.

Sharlindrian stood and walked to a window, staring off into the distance. She could see a black cloud approaching Valenburg. The piercing shrieks continued, vibrating the windows with their rhythmic sound.

"What is that?" Ginger repeated.

"Vampires," Sharlindrian said. A knot of dread tightened in her chest as she said the word.

Evalee stood and peered out the window, her voice weak but clear. "Where are they headed?"

"To the Palace," Sharlindrian answered. "They're coming for the Queen."

"The Valkyrie Elite will stop them," Ginger said quickly. "They are the best warriors in all of Balinbar."

"As true as that might be," Sharlindrian answered. "There can't be more than a hundred Valkyrie Elite still at the Palace. The Vampires will have hundreds of warriors—perhaps more. And worse, they are undoubtedly led by the Vampire Queen herself."

"But the Valkyrie armies will come back as soon as they realize the danger," Ginger supplied.

"No," Sharlindrian answered. "Even if they could break off from the battle, which would result in mass casualties as they retreated, they would not get there in time. The Queen is in real trouble."

"Well," Evalee said with a smile. "We better get over there and help out."

"Help out?" Ginger said. "What can three girls do against that?"

"You'd be surprised," Evalee answered.

"But we need your help," Sharlindrian said.

"Me?" Ginger replied. "I'm no warrior."

"But you're a Healer," Sharlindrian answered. "That is your gift to the world. You were never meant to clean the houses of rich people, nor put up with worms like Lady Fiurda. Your skills are just as important as ours, and right now, they are very much needed. If we are to save the Queen from being captured, we will need all the advantages we can get. Are you with us?"

Ginger's eyes drifted up towards the approaching black cloud. She had never been brave. She had never stood up for herself, let alone anyone else. She had simply thought that was the way she needed to be to survive. But Sharlindrian had shown her a different path, one that was rooted in strength and confidence, one that she did not think she could choose until now.

"Yes," she said simply.

"Then hang on," Evalee said with a smile, clapping both women on the shoulders.

The world blurred for a second before stopping suddenly. They were now outside the Palace, just before the massive iron doors of the servant's entrance.

"What just happened?" Ginger said in a high-pitched voice.

Evalee slumped to the ground, the little energy she had recovered now seemed depleted.

"Why didn't you let me Exsiliogate?" Sharlindrian said. "I could have brought us here."

"You need...all...of your strength...to face the Vampire Queen," Evalee answered simply. "I'll follow...when I can...but you need to get in there...and protect the royal family. If they can capture Queen Victra, the Valkyrie will fall."

Sharlindrian gritted her teeth before looking up at the approaching cloud. Already, the cloud of bats looked much closer than it had been before. She turned back to the High Faerie, rubbing her brow with a gentle hand. "Find a place and lay low. We might need you to Vicinerate all of us to safety. So save your strength. Can you do that?"

Evalee nodded sleepily.

"Good," Sharlindrian said, turning to Ginger. "Come on. On this day, you will have the chance to meet two different Queens." With this, she set off towards the Palace at a run, Ginger close behind. No

Valkyrie guards stopped them as they entered and headed down the hall. Sharlindrian had never been in the Palace, but Ginger had, and she quickly took the lead, guiding them towards the High Court.

They passed through a few rooms before they ran into fifty of the Valkyrie Elite, all of whom were proceeding into the Throne Room. All eyes turned towards them as they entered.

"Who are you?" a tall woman asked.

"We're friends of Nickle," Sharlindrian said quickly. "Is he here?"

"He was," the Valkyrie replied. "But he was assigned a different task."

"We've come to warn you."

"We know about the Vampires," the Valkyrie replied dismissively. "Now run along before this room is turned into a battlefield."

Sharlindrian ignored the advice and drew the sword at her side. It was a curved Elven blade, the only thing that she still possessed that had been given to her by her family. Her father had given it to her uncle a few hours before she was disowned by her people.

The Valkyrie first studied the blade and then the black armor, coming to a new conclusion. "You are no Human."

"I'm a Dark Elf," Sharlindrian answered. These words surprised all those in the room, but none so much as the person that spoke them. It was not something she had just whispered as if it were sin. She had said it with pride as if it was something she had achieved. And at that moment, the Valkyrie who had heard this simple proclamation bowed their heads in respect.

"My name is Sosha," the Valkyrie said. "Your people are great warriors. It will be an honor to die alongside you." This simple proclamation caused a shout to ring through the voices of the other warriors. At that moment, Sharlindrian was not only accepted, she was also respected.

"My sisters, enter the High Court and secure every entrance and window," Sosha ordered. "Nothing goes in or out except by leave of the Queen."

Sharlindrian and Ginger stepped inside the opulent room, spotting the Queen of the Valkyrie, who was armed for war. Standing near the Queen was Jaylyn, her body protected by a set of gilded armor, a spear in hand, although she did not look anxious to use it.

The High Court rang with noise as Valkyrie locked the doors and stacked the furniture by all the entrances. When they finished, Sosha turned to her warriors, her chin raised high. "In minutes, the Vampires will be here, flooding our Palace with their stench and blood lust. But we are the Valkyrie Elite, we may fall, but we will never yield!"

The Valkyrie Elite roared their approval.

"Now lock shields, my sisters," Sosha said. "For as long as one of us breathes, those vile creatures will not lay a finger on the Queen!"

The Valkyrie formed a protective circle around the Queen and Jaylyn. Sharlindrian found herself in the middle next to Sosha, right between the main entrance and the Queen. The first row of warriors held shields and spears. The ones behind them were armed with swords and bows.

The Elf turned to Ginger, her voice low. "Stand next to the Queen and be prepared to heal as quickly as you can. Despite the quality of your Mystic Relic, it will drain quickly from so much use. It will recharge, but it will take at least an hour—maybe longer. But once it is depleted, you will need to take the Princess and hide. Do you understand?"

Ginger nodded and began to turn around but then stopped short before she took a step. "Be careful, Sharlie."

Sharlindrian nodded, trying to sound more brave than she felt. "You too."

Then they waited, standing in silence, their shields raised. The door handle shook. Once. Twice. Something pounded against the thick wood. A horrible shriek pierced the air, unnerving even the most stalwart of Valkyrie. It was a scream edged with pain and sorrow.

Then...nothing. A minute went by, and the silence continued. It was almost as if the Vampires had moved on.

The main door suddenly exploded inward, flying dozens of yards through the air before crumbling to a stop. Ethilian stood in the gaping entrance, her bloody swords in hand. At her back were a dozen of her best Vampire warriors. She let out a piercing shriek, and all the windows above suddenly ruptured as hundreds of bats poured in, each hitting the ground and forming into bloodthirsty warriors.

There were no words exchanged, no threats uttered, no surrender offered. Sharlindrian shot forward a hail of Light Lances, striking several of the leading Vampires down to the ground. A storm of air-infused Valkyrie arrows followed, piercing the enemy with precision. The first row of Vampires collapsed, but then the second wave collided with the golden shields of the Valkyrie. Screams from both sides echoed the hall as deadly wounds were inflicted. The Valkyrie used elemental Wind to great effect, enhancing the speed of their weapons and movements. Several of them took to the air, swooping down on their enemies with tremendous momentum. Against a weaker opponent, this would have shattered their ranks, but it was only moments before Ethilian adjusted to their tactics, commanding several of her warriors to take on their bat forms. Soon, the Valkyrie were forced to land, their wings cut to pieces.

Sharlindrian shifted her focus from fighting to healing, taking a step back and allowing the others to work together. The Valkyrie were a momentous force, fighting with unmatched ferocity. Despite their numbers, the battle was even, neither side could gain an advantage over the other. But the Valkyrie were too few to hold for long. Slowly, despite Sharlindrian's best efforts, the Valkyrie warriors began to succumb to their wounds. Still, they made the Vampires pay a high cost, taking out the best of their warriors.

Sosha gritted her teeth, a wound on her arm making it feel sluggish. There was only one way to end this conflict—only one way to end the battle. She used her agility and wings to take to the air and dive towards Ethilian, her spear raised. Just before the weapon found its mark, the Vampire Queen dodged.

Sosha recovered and twisted around, lunging forward in a desperate attack. Ethilian dodged and ducked, using her swords to skewer the Valkyrie's shield. Sosha abandoned her shield and leaped, using all the Wind she could summon to add weight to the edge of her blade. But Ethilian raised a hand, breaking the magic with a Mystic spell. She then changed the gravity of the General and sent her flipping towards a far wall.

It would have been a fatal blow, but she was stopped by some unseen force. Ethilian released Sosha, allowing her to fall to the ground, and turned a deadly eye around the room, looking for the person who had dared interfere with her magic. Sharlindrian stood tall, an Elven blade in hand. She had been cut across the cheek, flushing her face red.

"You are impressive," Ethilian said. "But not without equal."

"I'm full of tricks," Sharlindrian said, using her Shadow Stride ability. She then ran forward, attacking in a fury.

Ethilian blocked each swing before returning her own, slicing Sharlindrian across the leg. The Vampire Queen was hit in the back by a large rock that had its gravity manipulated by a spell. The Queen realized the whole thing had been a ruse to distract her.

"You are a clever girl," Ethilian said. "Pity, you were raised by your father. If you were raised in my house, you would be a warrior without peer. A blade without equal. Your talent was wasted among the MeithDwins."

"I am not a MeithDwin," Sharlindrian said fiercely. "You do not know me."

"I did not raise you, but I do know you, child," Ethilian said. "I was the one that named you, as is the tradition of our people."

"What are you saying?" Sharlindrian said.

"Decades before you were born, I became the blade that broke the back of the Demon Brood. I did what few others were willing to do—take upon the ancient Vampire form of power. And their reward for me was to blot out my name from the history books. They did not publicly shun me, as I was their secret weapon, but they would not condone my actions. So, they simply made it so I no longer existed. Not to them, not to my husband—not to you. They took you from me."

"I'm not who you think I am," Sharlindrian accused.

"They shunned you, burned out your face in your portrait, and ripped the Drink for Elvenduur from your veins. You thought you were alone in this, but you are not. They turned their back on me long before they ever did anything to you. Sharlindrian, you are my only child. Born to me, but then ripped from my arms as I slept."

"That's a lie."

"You know it's true. But you don't have to walk this path alone—for there are others like us. And we are growing in power."

"I don't want any part of what you do."

"Then stand aside, child. For I must deal with the Queen of the Valkyrie."

"Why?"

"Because they still serve Kara'Kala!"

Sharlindrian sent forth a flurry of Light Lances, but Ethilian blocked each one with her own spells, sending them exploding off to the side. She then used her Mystic power to force Sharlindrian to the ground, first doubling and then tripling her weight. She fought against the magic with her own, but she was already too exhausted. She had pushed herself too hard healing the Valkyrie, and now she was powerless before her mother's magic. Soon the weight knocked her unconscious, her sword discarded at her side.

The remaining Valkyrie were too injured to continue to fight, leaving the path open to the Queen and her daughter. The Valkyrie Queen herself had been horribly wounded in the side and along one leg. Despite the wound, she still kept her feet, her sword raised. Ginger and Jaylyn stood behind her, a spear in each of their hands.

"Stop!" Nickle cried, his voice filling the hall. The Dwarf stepped forward, his axe in hand. Behind him was Yaroslav, who was amazed at the sight of the battle.

As the young prince looked around, he spotted the Valkyrie Queen. "Mother!" He ran to her, stepping over the wounded. Ethilian let him pass unhindered—she did not even consider him a threat.

Ethilian looked at the Dwarf, her jaw set. "Grab Sharlindrian, and take her somewhere safe. You can do nothing for the Valkyrie now. I have won."

Without a word, Nickle began to slowly walk forward, his mind slipping into absolute concentration, taking in all of his surroundings. A Vampire to his left lunged forward, but he returned his own attack that leveled the warrior. Another swooped in from the right, but with three quick strikes, the woman was unconscious. Then the blades of Ethilian and Nickle met in a terrific arc of sparks. The Queen and Nickle's minds slipped into the familiar SogoroKu, the great game played by the Order of the Scathians.

She was immediately put on the defensive, taking two quick steps back to avoid being overwhelmed. The Dwarf pulled Runes from his belt, activating them with a word and sending them forth in a chain of spells. This proved little more than a distraction as the Vampire Queen easily avoided such predictable attacks.

Ethilian reverted to using her Mystic magic, pulling dozens of weapons from the floor and lancing them towards her opponent. The Dwarf sliced a spear in two before kicking a dagger to the side. As a shield came for his face, he reversed the spell and sent it right back towards Ethilian, knocking her in the chest. More weapons came for him, but Nickle sensed them all, destroying them with ease. His movements were so precise, Ethilian stepped back, her confidence waning.

"Is Locke your new teacher?" Ethilian hissed, her voice full of scorn. "Is he that desperate he has elected to teach a Dwarf the ancient Scathian art?"

The Vampire Queen changed her blades into whips and sent them forward, catching the Dwarf off guard, sweeping him to the floor. But then he grabbed the Vampire's blade and forced it into the ground, holding it in place with his thick armor. She finally pulled it free a second later, but the weapon no longer functioned correctly. Nickle had used Alteration magic to snap the magical core in the weapon, preventing it from changing forms.

Nickle regained his feet, slowly stepping forward.

"You will never pass the Ten Trials," Ethilian said. "A Dwarf would never be able to become a Scathian."

Then three Vampires attacked Nickle, but they were subdued almost as quickly. The Dwarf continued his steady pace towards the Vampire Queen.

Nickle's voice rang out as steady as his gait. "For the first Five Trials, I took no food or drink, relying solely on my mind to ration my body's strength. In my First Trial, I climbed the Lonely Spire amidst a blizzard, better known by the Scathians as the Frozen Stairs. Only through sheer force of will was I able to survive the cold. We began the trek with two hundred Initiates, but by morning there were only forty-five."

"Liar," Ethilian accused. "No Scathian Order has taken on new Disciples in the past year. You did not reach the Lonely Spire."

"In my Second Trial, I descended the mountain's peak, as a Disciple, my body cut by the razor wind. Two of the Disciples fell. When I placed my foot on the ground, another Disciple broke their Oath and drank from the Forbidden River."

The Vampire Queen pushed forward, using her last blade in a tremendous frenzy. She held nothing back, using her Mystic magic to add weight to her weapon. Axe and sword met in a horrific exchange of metal. Their movements blurred as Nickle pushed on, driving the larger woman back several more steps.

Nickle's voice grew in strength as he continued. "My Third Trial, I was given The Serpent's Kiss, a poison so potent it is said it can kill a hundred people with a single drop. I was left to die on the Rocks of Gal Deed. There I sat retching, my body shaking in pain for hours. Only through my mind was I able to contain and eventually expel the poison."

"The Rocks of Gal Deed has broken even the best," Ethilian roared. "If you had taken the Serpent Kiss, you would have died."

Nickle attacked quickly, sending a wave of mental energy forward, momentarily confusing Ethilian. His actions were so forceful she tripped over a spear and fell backward.

"In my Fourth Trial," Nickle said, his pace steady. "I lifted the Boulder of Bawdier so that I might enter into the Spiraling Cavern, where I met my Fifth Trial, Hitilanda the Horrible, a Valkyrie who I defeated in hand-to-hand combat."

"Now I know for a surety you speak falsehood," Ethilian said. "The Fifth Trial is always when one faces a fellow Scathian."

Then ten Vampires attacked the Dwarf using a mix of lethal speed and power. Nickle busted the hand of one, cracked the breastplate of another. Their attacks were so predictable, it was like it was in slow motion. It was not long before Nickle put all the rest on the ground.

"In my Sixth Trial, I faced my fears reborn in the Tunnel of Nun. In the Seventh Trial, while caught in the Eye, I suffered pains like no other, my mind racked with the torments of this world. Few suffer as I have suffered."

"Do not speak of sacred things," Ethilian said. "Cease your tongue before I cut it out." She went in again, giving the best she had to offer, calling upon all of the training she ever had endured. For over two hundred years, this Elf turned Vampire had forged herself into a weapon. Since becoming a Vampire, she used her newfound powers to absorb the energy of every magical object she encountered. Her mind was expansive, her power immense. She shot forth a series of Light Lances that filled the room with blinding power, but the Dwarf cut through some and completely deflected others, leaving him unscathed.

"In the Eighth Trial," Nickle said, his voice so low it was barely audible. "I faced the loss of all that mattered, as it was ripped from me by the Three Fates of Time. Bitter tears left my eyes until I had none left to give. In the Ninth Trial, I endured the Flames within the Flesh before the Alter of Lord Scalimon of the Scathians."

"Then you still have one trial left to face," Ethilian said through clenched teeth. She pushed with all her power, but she was not enough. Soon she was cut across the leg, another time across the arm and back. A fourth cut sent her twisting to the floor.

"Impossible," Ethilian yelled. "You are but a Dwarf."

Nickle exchanged a mad series of blows with the Vampire Queen before ducking down low and kicking her in the chest. She flew back into a pillar, her form slinking against the floor, her sword discarded.

The Dwarf slowly removed the bracer from his right arm, revealing his skin. There were four black marks burned into the flesh. Then a final mark began to appear, sizzling as if by an unseen brand.

"For my Tenth Trial, I defeated the Vampire Queen of Nordum," Nickle said reverently.

Ethilian gasped for air before lowering her head. Her body was beaten and broken. She had lost.

The Queen of the Valkyrie limped closer to Ethilian, Yaroslav, Ginger, and Jaylyn at her side. "Why would you break the peace that has unified our people for over a hundred years?"

Ethilian spat blood. "Because many of your people still serve the Demon Lord."

"Surrender, Queen of the Vampires," Victra said. "Or your life is forfeit."

"I will die before I yield. Even if I fall, our forces will overrun your island. Those who serve Kara'Kala will be purged."

"I doubt that," Yaroslav said with a youthful grin. "You're lucky Nickle was the one to defeat you. You'll simply be imprisoned now instead of having to face the Demon Lord yourself. He would show you no mercy."

"I would relish the chance to face him once again," Ethilian said.

"What do you mean face the Demon Lord?" Nickle asked. "He's imprisoned behind the FireWall."

"Yaroslav can say random things at times," Jaylyn defended.

"What do you mean, Yaroslav?" Nickle repeated, a biting tone in the Dwarf's throat.

"Well, it's done now, so I guess I can talk about it. The Demon Lord is no longer behind the FireWall," Yaroslav said. "I freed him."

"What nonsense is this?" the Valkyrie Queen asked.

"I'm truly sorry, mother," Yaroslav said. "But it had to be done. This day will be remembered as the day I saved the world."

"Speak sense, boy," Victra said. There was a sharpness to her tone that only a mother could wield.

Yaroslav suddenly looked down. "I'm sorry mother. I was the one that attacked the Vault, but I had to."

"You?" Jaylyn said.

"The Nords had nothing to do with it?" Queen Victra persisted. "What about the Nest?"

"That as well," Yaroslav said. "You know how I like my potions. So I used my talents to impersonate an Assassin of the Midnight."

The Queen was so shocked by this, she did not know how to respond.

Nickle's voice cut through the silence. "Why would you want your people to go to war?"

"I didn't want to start a war," Yaroslav replied simply, as if this was obvious. "I just needed our Lightning Reserves to be shipped to EarthWorks through the Tube. It was the only way to make sure it was done properly."

"Why would you need that?" Jaylyn asked.

Ethilian began laughing, her voice sending an ominous echo down the hall. The other three turned to her, not understanding the joke.

"What is so funny?" Queen Victra asked.

"Your son just freed Kara'Kala," Ethilian said in amusement. "Many great men and women have tried to do what he has done and failed. And, now your little child has done what no other could do."

"How?" Queen Victra asked.

"The Lightning Reserves," Nickle said in a low breath. "During times of war, your people ship them through the Tube to EarthWorks so they can be quickly hidden away. But the Tube travels directly through the FireWall."

"And with a clever concoction of potions," Yaroslav said, "I was able to create a mixture that would rupture the Lightning and turn it into a massive explosion, eliminating the FireWall."

The Queen of the Valkyrie put a hand on her chest, her breath suddenly leaving her. "What have you done?"

"I've just saved the world, mother," Yaroslav said. "You must see that. Everything is falling apart. The Blight is spreading, the tensions between all magical races are increasing. EarthWorks is just about to rip itself apart. If we weren't going to war with the other Isles of Balinbar over this conflict, it would have been over something else."

"Could you have made a mistake with the potion, Yaroslav?" Nickle asked. "Perhaps, you miscalculated when the Tube would be passing through the FireWall."

"I don't think so," Yaroslav said. "I am very precise with my potions, as you well know."

Ethilian pushed against the pillar, grimacing with pain. After righting herself, she looked to the Queen of the Valkyrie, her face drained of all blood. "Now that he is free, will you serve him as your people did before? Will you bend a knee to the Demon Brood and the monster that leads them?"

"Never," Queen Victra answered. "My grandfather errored when he sided with Kara'Kala. I will not make the same mistake. The Demon Lord brought us nothing but war and pain."

Ethilian studied the Valkyrie Queen for a second, an unheard conversation passing between the two of them. Finally, she nodded. "Then we are no longer enemies—we are allies. Call back your forces, and I will do the same with mine." With this, Ethilian disappeared into a flurry of bats. Like Ethilian, the creatures were injured and slow, but they were able to gain enough altitude to exit out one of the broken windows high above. The rest of the wounded Vampires took on their bat form as well and followed their Queen.

As the last one disappeared, Nickle turned and bolted for the door.

"We have much to talk about. Yaroslav, must be mistaken," Queen Victra said, her voice taking on a commanding tone.

The Dwarf ignored the Queen and ran on, pumping his legs harder towards the exit. Only one thought pulsed through his brain, pushing out everything else. *"It's not true. It can't be."* His feet skid across the floor at the next turn. When he reached a long hallway, he activated the Air Runes in his boots to propel himself forward through the servant doors. He exited with so much force, one of the doors was almost ripped off its hinges.

Surprisingly, he ran into Evalee outside, who was walking towards him. "Nickle?"

"Evalee, something has happened."

"I know the Vampires are retreating," she chirped.

"No, something bad," Nickle replied. "Stay right here. I need to see it for myself."

"What are you talking about? We won. We protected Valenburg."

"Please, Evalee," Nickle said, a surprising desperation in his voice. "Please stay right here. I'll be back soon."

Chapter 36

The Face of a Demon

Nickle opened his eyes, slightly drained from the considerable distance he had just Vicinerated. He now stood in a dark tunnel, the tracks of the Tube running beneath his feet. The metal track twisted like gnarled roots passing in and out of the ground until it disappeared over the edge of a cliff.

Nickle swallowed as he stepped closer to the edge, his hands trembling. He recognized this spot as being the beginning of where the FireWall had once been. A feeling of dread made his feet move slowly across the rough ground. As he stepped up to the ledge, his lungs tightened.

A large portion of the FireWall had simply disappeared, along with a massive section of the track from the Tube. Lava lightning bolts no longer fell from the sky. Demons below no longer moved with a lethargic pace. The red creatures looked much larger than the Demons Nickle had seen before, their power much more intense. These creatures were all warriors, tried and tested on the field of battle. They were the elite warriors and leaders of the Demon Brood, the very best at what they did.

Now they moved with purpose, rallying their forces. Several of them were already attacking the separate cell that held Kara'Kala. This structure still burned with fire, but it was much more diminished than it ever was before. As Demons were burned from the process, they began rotating in and out of the task. More red warriors joined the effort, scrambling over the cell like a flurry of ants. Despite the sheer size, the Demons cut into it with unbelievable strength. It would only be minutes before the Demon Lord would be freed.

"Form ranks!" cried a Dwarf far below.

Nickle had not noticed them before, but as he looked down, he could see a Cohort of Dwarves.

"Lock shields," the Centurion said, his voice echoing over the crimson land.

Nickle first looked at the hundred Dwarf defenders and then at the thousands of Demons in the distance, comparing the two forces. The Dwarf Cohort was armed and armored with the finest of Tines, while the Demons only had their claws and their magic. But in a moment, Nickle knew the Dwarf Cohort did not stand a chance.

Nickle Vicinerated down to the commander's side. "Pull your warriors back."

"Where did you come from?" the Centurion asked, his voice high pitched.

"They will roll right over you. The only reason they haven't yet is they're still freeing the Demon Lord."

"I figured as much," the Commander replied. "What happened? That explosion took out more than half of our forces and our Dwarf Warships. Comms are down. We have no idea what is going on."

"The Tube exploded," Nickle supplied. "You need to get your warriors out of here."

"The Demons cannot be allowed to escape," the Dwarf Centurion said. "We'll have to hold them back until reinforcements arrive."

"From EarthWorks?" Nickle said. "Even if the Tube was not just destroyed, that would take at least an hour. And like you said, the Comms are down. They have no idea what is going on up here."

"We'll have to hold on until reinforcements arrive," the Centurion said, now adding more emphasis to his words. It was then that Nickle realized that the Centurion already knew all of this. His soldiers already knew this. And yet they stayed—they would not abandon their post.

The Centurion let out a long sigh, his voice low. "Tell them...we fought with Honor and Glory."

Nickle did not know how to respond for a few moments, a raw panic rippling through his body. Then he drew his axe and flipped it around in his hands. "Tell them yourself. I'll buy some time. You get your Cohort to safety."

Then Nickle disappeared. When he reappeared again, he was in the middle of the red land, among dozens of Demons. They first stared at him as if he was a mirage. Then the Dwarf attacked, cutting deep into a Demon to his right and slicing another to his left. He Vicinerated back just as an Elemental spell ripped into the space where he once was.

He attached Hellion Runes onto the backs of several of the creatures, creating a series of explosions. These effectively injured the beasts, but they did not stop them. The more Nickle fought, the more attention he began to receive from other Demons. Soon, he had the eye of every creature within a hundred yards. He moved with a speed and strength that defined his small stature.

Then something hit him in the head, sending him spilling to the side. He fell back, his blade getting caught under a red boulder. Three spells hit him in the chest, another in his thigh. He skid across the ground, his helmet rolling free. He fought on, defaulting to using his magic, pushing several Demons down to the ground with a powerful wave of Mystic magic while skewering several others with Light Lances. When they closed the distance, he transitioned to using his fists to knock several of them to the ground.

But the creatures kept coming, their power increasing as their hatred of the Dwarf grew. He was hit twice in the chest, a third time in the leg. He made the attackers pay with a series of Fire and Water Runes, creating jets of steam that sent them flying back. He was dodging so many attacks he had no reprieve. He recovered his axe and sent a wave of Inferno Runes forward. But the Demons simply growled from the pain.

A massive Demon pushed passed the others. Its lower body was like that of a Rhino, its upper body that of a giant. It bellowed as it charged, knocking Nickle back several dozen yards. A name suddenly popped in the Dwarf's head. "Belial—the Demon of Destruction."

The creature came in again, but this time Nickle was ready, unleashing a torrent of Runes. But it did little to Belial, who knocked Nickle in the other direction. The Dwarf pushed himself up on all fours and vomited, overwhelmed by a sudden wave of nausea.

The Demons laughed as if this was all a game. This gave Nickle a last surge of energy. He charged in, delivering strike after strike against Belial. The creature bellowed as it began swinging its limbs in a fruitless effort to catch Nickle off guard. Then Nickle was struck hard against the side, a powerful spell that sent him flipping across the ground. A piece of his shoulder guards broke free and rolled among the rocks. He was hit again and then again, more of his armor flaked off each time.

He Vicinerated to the side and fought on, but it was in vain. Two more epic Elemental spells lanced him in the chest and sent him to his knees.

"Hold this one," said a Demon with a booming voice. "The Master will want to see him."

Nickle was spent, his lungs ragged. His face was bloody, his lips split. His armor now appeared like it had been polished with a cheese grater. He looked over at the Dwarf Cohort that was a hundred yards to his left. He had at least hoped that his sacrifice would have enabled them to escape. But true to Dwarf stubbornness, the fools were still there, cheering him on as if he was their champion.

Two Demons grabbed an arm each, pulling the Dwarf to his feet. He felt the urge to vomit again, but it soon passed.

Then a cry arose among the Demons, one that filled the space and echoed for miles in the distance. The noise persisted, threatening to rupture Nickle's eardrums.

Then he saw him, the Demon Lord. The creatures parted for him as if he were royalty. On his head were two curved horns that ended in dagger points. He was large, his body muscled and rippled with scars and black tattoos. Over his eyes, he wore a bandana, covering the old wound from his last battle. Despite his lack of sight, he walked without stumbling, passing through the crowd without hesitation, relying on some unknown sense to guide his steps.

Then he stopped, his body holding as still as a mountain. The cheering ended as well. The Demon Lord breathed deeper, turning his chest a darker shade of red. He turned directly towards Nickle, a slight smile on his lips. He began to walk towards the Dwarf at a steady gait. A power unlike anything Nickle had ever sensed wafted from the creature in waves. It was a mix of new and ancient magic coupled with an underlying current of raw charisma.

Nickle's lungs tightened as the beast approached. A fear he had never known filled him. Even when he had visions of Kara'Kala before, they were not like this. Nothing was like this. He wanted to scream and turn away. But fear kept him captive, not even allowing him to blink.

The Demon Lord bent closer to the Dwarf, his dagger-like teeth in a wicked smile. "Vicinerate away, little Nickle, for I have a message for you to deliver to the Tri'Ark that you serve. Run away and tell the world that their Lord has returned."

Chapter 37

Back in Valenburg

Nickle suddenly appeared in Valenburg, only inches away from where he left. The Dwarf's energy had completely left him, and he began to fall. Evalee grabbed him, but he was too heavy to catch completely. She first looked at the state of his armor and then his wounded features. Her lips pursed in worry the more she examined his wounds. But all that faded from her concern as she saw two trails of tears running down his face.

"Nickle, what's wrong?" Evalee asked.

The Dwarf did not respond until the High Faire repeated the question.

"The Demon Lord has returned."

Evalee did not challenge these words but instead pulled Nickle into an embrace. This sudden empathy released some pent-up emotion in the Dwarf. He found more tears silently slipping down his cheeks, pooling on his chin.

After several long minutes, Nickle spoke, his words so faint only she could hear. "I'm not ready, Evalee. He's something so far beyond anything I've encountered. I'm not ready."

"The Tri'Ark will sort all of this out," Evalee answered. "Don't worry. It will all work out."

He appreciated the sentiment, but he knew it was a lie. He did not have to be a Scathian to realize that not even she believed her own words.

Epilogue

An Old Acquaintance

"By the hammer of Freyr and the Belt of Hurn, I swear all the words I share are true," Nickle said, his voice low. At a gesture from the Purveyor, Nickle took the stand in the middle of the room. He looked around at the Tri'Ark Counsel, taking in the four Dwarf Lords and the Holders of the Five Seats. Finally, his eyes rested on Elishna—The High Elven Goddess, and her two advisors each one glistening with blinding light. Behind them were four elite Arcons, armed with long and threatening blade staffs. Their Elf armor was magnificently crafted, trimmed with olive green, silver, and gold.

    Nickle knew he had never been in this room—he was sure of it. But a strange feeling of déjà vu overcame him as he looked around. It was an ornate space. Marble pillars crowned with gold circled the chambers. It was built with the goal of showing the power and strength of the Tri'Ark, but now it reeked of fear. The Dwarf could sense the sickening emotion wafting around him in waves. The audience seating above was packed with other races, from Goblins, Orcs, and Trolls to Cennarians, Hamadryads, High Faeries, and Satyrs. These were the most important leaders of their respective people, now crammed together with little thought of comfort. They all had undoubtedly heard the rumor, but they had come here to find out if it was true.

    Nickle wasted no time. "The Demon Lord has returned."

    These few words filled the room with a chorus of whispers and hisses.

    "You will not speak unless you are asked a direct question," Elishna said, her voice commanding. She was possibly the most beautiful woman Nickle had ever seen—her dark skin complemented by her ornate armor. Her eyes burned with a violent rage. She rarely spoke during these meetings, but when she did, her voice was law. No one person in the world ever held as much power as Elishna, the High

Elven Goddess.

Nickle was annoyed by the interruption, but he did not speak further. From a nod from Elishna, the Purveyor began to question Nickle about the recent events. With every question, the Dwarf felt more annoyed, as often times his answers were cut short.

His audience was held captive by the story. He told about their mission to prevent the war between the Valkyrie and the Nords. He relayed the encounter with the Vampire Queen, the battle for Valenburg, and the conflict in the High Court. The whole thing took nearly an hour, but finally he arrived at the part where he Vicinerated down to the FireWall.

Everyone was so entranced by the tale, no one seemed to question that Nickle even could Vicinerate. He detailed his fight with the Demons and the freeing of Kara'Kala from his cell. Finally, he arrived at the part where the Demon Lord approached Nickle.

"And did he say anything to you?" the Purveyor asked.

"Yes," Nickle said. For the first time since the questioning had began, he was hesitant to add more to his answer.

"What did you say?" the Purveyor insisted.

The Dwarf looked up, meeting eyes with Elishna. "He told me to, 'Run away and tell the world that their Lord has returned.'"

The room erupted with noise. Several of the leaders began shouting to withdraw the Tri'Ark forces to EarthWorks while others called on their armies to pursue the Demons as they fled. The room devolved into chaos and disorder. Fear gave way to panic as individuals in the crowd stood. Several Cennarians began accusing the Orcs of being sympathizers of Kara'Kala. They began to push against each other as accusations filled the room.

"The Dwarf is a liar!" a Human accused.

"The Silver Army is more than ready to deal with any threat," said Gimli, one of the four Dwarf Lords.

"The Calameer can rid us of the few Demons that escaped," shouted Brutus.

More screams were added to the mix, making regular conversation impossible.

Then Elishna's body erupted into a blinding light that filled the room. All eyes turned away, shielding their faces with raised hands. Silence fell as the light faded until it disappeared. Elishna looked more powerful and terrible than ever before. She now was standing—something that she had not done during a Tri'Ark Council meeting for over two hundred years.

"We will not descend into disfunction," Elishna said. "We are a house of order, a house of discipline. As such, I am ordering the immediate arrest of Jane Hawthorne for engaging in unsanctioned military actions."

All eyes turned to the slender woman. Hawthorne stood, her eyes narrowed. She had saved thousands of lives, first in the conflict between the Orcs and Atlanteans, and then again between the Valkyrie and the Nords. She could not stop the conflict completely, but her actions had certainly prevented a much greater loss of life.

The Holder of the One of the Five Seats did not utter a word of decent as Praetorian guards flanked and cuffed her in Byzantine shackles. There would be a time to plead her case, but that was not now—not when the High Elven Goddess felt so threatened. The Elf warriors escorted Hawthorne out of the room.

"We must first verify what the Dwarf has reported before we act," Elishna said. "Fear and panic of a pending threat often creates more damage than the threat itself. Speak nothing of this to your people as we continue to investigate this matter." With this, the Elf disappeared, flanked by her two advisors.

This released all the chaos that she had held back. Nickle was stunned—first by the arrest of Hawthorne, and second by the fact his words were even up for debate. It would be a simple matter to verify his words—it would only take a few hours at most. The FireWall was not far from EarthWorks—especially in a fast-moving ship.

The Dwarf did not wait to be dismissed. There was no point anymore. The meeting was now more akin to a riot. Nickle stepped off the stand and walked out the room, pushing past the guards with ease, his eyes set on the exit. A crushing claustrophobia tightened in his chest as he shoved through, making it difficult to breath. He had to push past a mob of individuals just outside the door. Once free of the crowd, he took a deep breath and let it out slowly. The anxiety he felt persisted until he was able to Vicinerate back to Valenburg.

His friends were all waiting for him—Swiftrunner, Sharlindrian, Evalee, Jason, and even Shemway and Shannon.

"How'd it go?" Jason asked.

Nickle shook his head, unsure of how to answer.

***

The next seven days were a blur for the five friends. The Queen of the Valkyrie had allowed them to stay in the palace, since the shop had been destroyed. They spent a considerable amount of time meeting with Queen Victra, who was very much interested in the steps the Tri'Ark was taking to apprehend the Demon Lord. When Nickle told her how the meeting went, she doubled down her efforts of forging a new alliance with all the Isles of Balinbar. This seemed odd—especially since only days prior she was bitter enemies with the Vampire Queen. Now she talked like it was the most logical solution for them to pull their resources together.

They finally returned to the shop and began picking through the wreckage. The Queen had graciously sent several of the palace staff to help out and the debris was cleaned up rather quickly.

To Jason's horror, his large book on blacksmithing had survived unscathed. The Dwarf dusted it off as he picked it up, shaking his head as he did. "Dang, of all the things of mine that had to survive." He then looked at the shattered vials and spilled potion ingredients that marbled the floor. "We really had a good thing going here."

Nickle came up behind his friend, placing a hand on his shoulder. "Doesn't mean you can't open another shop."

"I doubt that is going to happen anytime soon."

Sharlindrian dusted her hands and placed them on her hips. She had proven her skill at cleaning and did far more than the rest combined with her use of Mystic magic. She joined the two Dwarves' side. "Well, at least we're all still alive."

"True enough," Swiftrunner said. He was smiling broadly, his optimism and energy never depleting.

"Is that your friend over there?" Evalee asked Sharlindrian.

The Elf turned a careful eye towards a redheaded figure standing nearby. It was Ginger, a tentative smile on her lips. Sharlindrian walked over to her friend and took her in a warm embrace.

"How you feeling?" Ginger asked, casting a careful eye over the devastation.

"I'm fine," Sharlindrian said.

"Is it true what they're saying?" Ginger asked.

Sharlindrian nodded slowly. "Yes, it is. The Demon Lord is back."

"I just can't believe it. Did you hear that Mr. Kinnunen and Mrs. Kinnunen were placed under arrest. It turns out that they were big supports of Kara'Kala."

Sharlindrian nodded. She actually knew very well about the arrests since she was the one that provided the information to the Queen regarding the family's support of the Demon Lord.

"The world is changing so fast," Ginger said, her voice breaking mid-sentence. "I guess I've got to change too."

"What do you mean?"

"I've given up on becoming a Healer."

Sharlindrian grabbed Ginger by the shoulders. "No, you can't do that. Not now. Not when someone so talented as yourself is going to be so desperately needed. Without you healing the Valkyrie Elite as much as you did, they would have broken through their ranks in a matter of minutes.

"You did more than I ever could," Ginger answered.

"Don't...don't give up on your dreams."

Ginger looked up, a small tear appearing in the corner of one of her eyes. "Why does it matter."

"It just does."

"I can't...."

"Why not?" Sharlindrian replied. "If you could put up with Lady Fiurda, you can deal with anything."

Ginger laughed. "It's not the same."

"Why?"

"I don't know...I just can't afford it. It seems so selfish for me to chase my dreams while the world is in such chaos."

"Here," Sharlindrian said, handing Ginger a piece of parchment.

"What this?"

"It's the transfer of ownership of a Gold Account into your name. It contains one hundred and seventy-three kilos of gold dust—

enough to fund your entire education."

Ginger's eyes widened for a second, not quite comprehending what her friend was saying. "I...I can't...."

"It's already done," Sharlindrian said. "Just promise me that you will study hard and be the best Healer you can be."

The tears Ginger held back before now began to flow. "How in the world do you have this much dust saved?"

"Promise me," Sharlindrian said, her face taking on a new intensity.

"I promise," Ginger said as more tears flowed. "Thank you, Sharlie. Thank you so much. You don't...you don't know...."

"I might not know exactly," Sharlindrian replied. "But I think I have a pretty good idea. It can change everything to have someone that believes in you."

Ginger took Sharlindrian into another embrace. It was not long before she broke the embrace, tears sparkling on her cheeks. "I've got to get working. The Academy applications are due in a just a few days."

Sharlindrian smiled as Ginger stepped away, her mind preoccupied with all the things she suddenly had to do. She turned to go before stopping suddenly, "Thank you, Sharlie. I won't forget this. I won't ever forget this."

The Elf only smiled in reply. And with that, Ginger was gone. Very slowly, Sharlindrian returned to her friends, a new happiness in her chest.

"Everything ok?" Jason asked.

"It's perfect," Sharlindrian said, locking eyes with Jason, who smiled back.

"So, what are we going to do now?" Swiftrunner said.

"We need to help Hawthorne get out of jail," Sharlindrian said. "If it wasn't for her, EarthWorks would be a lot worse off. She might have bent a few rules, but she's no criminal."

"We can break her out tonight," Jason said.

"Not that way," Sharlindrian answered, her voice taking on a scolding tone. "We need to help her get out the right way—the legal way."

"Looks like we got more visitors—these ones appear to be of the royal type," Swiftrunner said, nodding towards a Pigeon pulled cart.

Nickle and Evalee exchanged a quick glance. Ever since the

battle in the High Court, they had not seen or heard from Jaylyn. Now she appeared in her splendor, wearing an elegant dress that was far more suited for her mother than her. Despite her serious expression, she appeared uncomfortable in the garb.

Nickle and Evalee approached, bowing low. A dozen Valkyrie Elite surrounded them, their weapons held at the ready. Despite the recent peace talks among all the Isles of Balinbar, the Queen had become very protective of her heir.

Jaylyn looked at her two friends for a second, trying to maintain the dignity of her position. But it did not last long. She stepped forward, taking both Nickle and Evalee in a desperate embrace.

"Oh, how I've missed you two," Jaylyn said, her voice low.

"We've missed you just as much," Evalee answered, tears springing to her eyes. "And now I'm crying. My goodness my emotions are just running amuck."

Jaylyn broke the embrace and grabbed a hand from each of them. She then first looked to Evalee and then Nickle. "Everything is going to change now, isn't it?"

Nickle nodded. "Yes, I believe it is."

"Well, as long as…," Jaylyn said, choking back her emotion. "As long as it doesn't change you."

Evalee nodded. "Oh, Jaylyn, you're such a wonderful person. And I haven't been the best to you."

"Whatever do you mean?" Jaylyn asked, genuinely confused at the statement.

Evalee did not know how to explain, so she did not even try. Instead, she just gave the Heir to the Obsidian Throne another hug—something that was a serious breach of protocol. The Valkyrie Elite were going to step in but Jaylyn waved them away.

"Promise me," the Princess said. "That we will stay friends forever."

"Of course," Evalee said.

"How's your brother doing?" Nickle asked.

"He's still in prison," Jaylyn answered. "But he is doing as well as can be expected. I keep trying to convince him how horrible Kara'Kala is. He doesn't believe me yet, but he still listens—so that is something."

"Well," Nickle said. "He's a good person—just misguided."

"I'm surprised to hear you say that," Jaylyn said. "From what I've been told, you've taken it particularly hard that the Demon Lord has escaped."

Nickle did not know how to respond.

In the silence, Jaylyn stepped closer to Nickle, her eyes first low and then being raised to meet his. "Be careful. I don't know what it is that wears you down, but don't let it destroy you."

Then she stepped forward, kissing him on the cheek. Both Nickle and Jaylyn were so surprised by the show of affection that neither one could find words. Finally, the Princess blushed red before cracking a quick smile and retreating to her carriage.

As Evalee watched the quick exchange, she felt a raw anger spread throughout her body. She did not let her emotions overtake her, but it took all of her concentration to prevent icicles from forming on the ground. She liked Jaylyn, she really did. But she did not care for the strange emotion she felt every time Jaylyn afforded Nickle such affection.

The High Faerie took a deep breath, focusing on the calming techniques Nickle had shown her. *"I'm better than that,"* Evalee thought. *"I will have to be better than that."*

The High Faerie and Dwarf watched as the carriage sped off, disappearing around a far street corner. They returned to their friends, a somber mood falling over them.

Jason opened his mouth to speak but he was interrupted before he could say another word. A tall, handsome Satyr with curling horns spoke. "Jason Burntworth? Nickle Brickle'Bee?"

The two Dwarfs turned to the messenger just in time to be handed each a letter. It was a brown envelope penned in golden ink. They had each received a letter like this before, but it was uncommon to receive one now. Despite this, they both knew instantly what it meant.

Jason opened his letter and scanned the paper.

"What's wrong?" Sharlindrian asked, new concern in her eyes.

Jason continued to read for a few moments longer before looking up and reading in a loud voice.

"Son of Hurn,

As of now, you likely have heard the rumor that the Demon Lord has escaped. The Cogs of Hurn, in conjunction with Tri'Ark officials have conducted a detailed investigation and can now confirm the Demon Lord is at large. This message may shock you, it may frighten you. But remember who you are, Son of Hurn, and remember what you have been called to do.

Kara'Kala once subjected the world to his will, and likely he will seek to do so again. But he will not succeed, as the Silver Army will stand in his way.

You have answered the call of your people once before, but now your strength is needed more than ever. Even though you will only be starting your fourth year of study, you are to report to Tortugan to receive your final training. It is time for all honorable Dwarves of a noble heart to prepare for war."

A Note from the Author

Sterling enjoys hearing from his readers. If you have any comments, thoughts, critiques, questions, and/or just want to say hello, please email him at isbnwriter@gmail.com. It may take some time for a response, but he tries to answer each email personally. Or, you can visit his website at stelringnixon.com to learn about additional details of upcoming releases or pending projects.

If you enjoyed this novel and want to see more written by Sterling, please take the time to leave a review on Amazon. Your comments and support help out tremendously.

Other Books Written by Sterling Nixon

Historical Fiction:
Gladiators of the Naumachia

Dystopia Fiction:
Acadia
Titan
Charron

Young Adult Fiction:

Nickle Brickle'Bee: In the Heart of EarthWorks
Nickle Brickle'Bee: In the Halls of Harbordeen
Nickle Brickle'Bee: In the Home of Atlantia
Nickle Brickle'Bee: In the Floating Isles of Balinbar
Nickle Brickle'Bee: In the Throne Room of StormHaven

Made in the USA
Middletown, DE
18 April 2023